Fate and Lightning

Sweet Briar Series Book 2

April Gaisford

Book Cover by Lee Taylor at Coffin Print Designs

Triggers and Content

This series contains sexual assault, abortion, infertility, violence, kinks and use of a safe word, homophobia, and death of a family member. This list is not all inclusive.

Your mental health matters. Please read at your own discretion.

Contents

Prologue

Dahlia

Nine Years Ago

I hate to leave her like this. I know she is right; if her mother catches me with her now... I don't even want to finish that thought. I do not want to sneak through the hallways to escape her wing of the castle. Jasmin was in the middle of the floor, sobbing, bleeding, and doubled over in pain. Walking away from her is easily the hardest thing I have ever done. The months I spent apart from her when her mother caught us the last time were nothing compared to the overwhelming need to stay with her now.

The halls are quiet and cool, with the winter wind blowing outside. Cold air streams through the drafty hallways that are mostly unused. Jasmin showed me these paths when I first befriended her. She is so much more to me than a friend. From the beginning, Jas has been my whole world. She is my everything. It's still improper for women to be in a relationship with other women, especially a young princess with no heirs. But she is mine. She may be forced to marry someone else, but I will always be there with her.

I grind my teeth at the thought of what her mother has allowed. That bitch of a queen let some piece of shit man abuse Jasmin for months. I refuse to let her suffer through a marriage or a child with that fucking ass from Arkaley. He has tormented her for months. The Queen has turned a blind eye to his actions in the name of continuing her bloodline. I won't turn a blind eye, though. Once Jasmin makes it through this, I will deal with Jackson. She doesn't want me to, but he can't get away with what he has done to her. I won't tolerate it.

Once through the castle, I return to my family's living quarters. When the King purchased Vesper as a gift for Jasmin, my father was sold along with him. My father was compliant, believing we would receive better conditions when we arrived in Sweet Briar. What a fucking joke. We now live in the back of the stables, in two rooms with just enough warmth that we don't freeze. It's easier to stay busy working than trying to relax or do anything else in our "home." Jasmin is the only good thing about this kingdom, and they are trying to fuck her over now. I clench my fist, anger coursing through my body. I grind my teeth, press my nails into my palm, anything to relieve some of the tension inside me.

"Dahlia," Mama coos as she wraps her arms around me. She always knows when I need a soothing touch. I sigh, relaxing in her arms.

"It's started, Mama," I whisper against her shoulder. Her arms tighten around me, but she doesn't say anything else. Saying anything else about what I have done is too dangerous. I didn't actually tell Mama, but she knew. Mama always knows. I stay in her embrace for several moments. Her warmth soothes some of my anger. Mama is good at consoling me when I'm upset. People say I am similar to her. We're both tall, dark, with long locs. Most people don't know I also have her passion and desire for justice. Mine is always visible; my words are angry, my voice loud. I don't hide my opinion. Mama is more careful with her thoughts. She is better at being cunning and conspicuous. Those aren't skills I inherited from her. I prefer to take what I want, damn all consequences.

She releases me but speaks softly before walking away. "Keep your eyes open, girl. If the Queen suspects anything, you will be her first target."

"I know, Mama."

She returns to our small stove, where she prepares supper for us. We aren't allowed to eat in the castle with the other servants. Some get that privilege, but not us. The single window in our space looks up toward the princess's wing. It was my only reprieve for months when I was isolated. Jasmin doesn't realize I can see her quarters. I can't see into the rooms; the windows aren't angled to allow that. I can see shadows, though. People are scurrying around her room. I hope Emmeline is with her, offering comfort. I don't spend much time with her, but Jasmin loves her. That is good enough for me.

I can't stand sitting right now. Jasmin is in pain; I should be with her. I gave her the tea to end her situation with Jackson. I scoured all the texts I could find when she told me. The concoction I made wasn't listed; it was a mix of multiple teas for her situation. Better safe than sorry. She will not suffer through childbirth with that shit stain of a man. I wanted to stay with her to watch for adverse side effects, but neither wanted to risk her mother's wrath.

"I'm going for a walk," I announce, rising to leave again.

"Take a cloak, Dahlia. It's cold." Mama doesn't turn from her pot, just speaking over her shoulder at me. I don't respond but grab my cloak anyway.

"Be safe, Dahlia." Her voice is quiet, cautious. She won't try to stop me, though.

I don't say anything as I walk outside. I tighten my clothes as a gust of wind blows. A storm is coming. Dark clouds litter the sky above. I'll walk for a little while and come back in time for dinner; that will help calm my nerves. I walk my favorite path toward the west of the castle. It leads to Arkaley but is impassable now due to snow and ice. I've never gone to Arkaley, and despite Jackson being from there, it has always interested me. Something about the village feels right like a voice is calling me there.

As I reach the trees, I glance back at the castle. I can't see Jasmin's room anymore. A few servants are preparing animals for the incoming storm. Glancing at the skies tells me I only have a short time before it arrives at the castle. I huff out a breath, trudging along the path. The trail is quiet and calm. No animals are out, all hunkered down for the storm. There is a bridge just ahead. I stop here, looking out at the undisturbed ground ahead. Animal tracks are left in the snow like blankets with tiny prints and scuff marks. I inhale the crisp air, blowing steam as my body settles. Jasmin will be fine. She is strong, stronger than she knows. I'll deal with Jackson later. Her mother will find another man for her. We will convince him that I am the important one in her life. Things will work out. I repeat this to myself several times, hoping one of these times I believe it.

Just before I turn back, hands wrap around my eyes. A folded cloth covers my nose. I am pulled against a large man's body. I struggle, grabbing his arms, hands, and anything I can to free myself. He tightens his grip on my head. This cloth has a strange smell. I don't recognize it but know I shouldn't breathe. I twist and turn, trying to get away. More hands grab mine, restraining me. I try to scream; my body is tense. I have to get away. I have to breathe. This isn't my ending. The world is fading away. Jasmin needs me. I can't leave her...

Part One

LIGHTNING

Chapter 1

CLEM

"Dahlia."

Jasmin is transfixed on this woman. Could it really be Dahlia? The girl Jasmin was in love with as a teenager. The one whom this curse starts with. They said she died; is it possible she didn't? Questions race through my mind, everything else frozen while the woman I am marrying stares at this woman who is intruding. Jasmin takes another step toward her. It's a small step, but enough that her hands are pulling away from my own.

She can't step away from me now. The entire kingdom is watching. My mind changes from frantic questions to sheer panic. My eyes begin darting around the room. Everyone is watching Jasmin and Dahlia. People are starting to whisper. Sunette has tears in her eyes but isn't moving. Zander and Sabeko stare at this dark-skinned woman, assessing every inch of her. We need to get away from the crowd. We need privacy to deal with this situation. An idea strikes me suddenly, and without even considering it, I move.

I relax my body as much as I can as I drop backward. My hands rip from Jasmin's, then I crash against the floor. She screams as I hit the floor behind me; my head stings with the impact. Others are yelling and running. Guards shout to control the crowd as Jasmin lands on my chest, rubbing her hands against me. Pain rips through me, both physical and emotional, when I see her. Tears streak her face, ruining the powder and kohl on her eyes. My ears must be ringing because I can't hear what she is saying. I whisper her name, raising my hand to her head. She leans in close, my lips against her ear.

"I'm fine, Jas. Clear out the hall. Send Emmeline to get Dahlia. We'll deal with this and finish the ceremony later."

Her head drops against my chest as she sobs. I lace my fingers through her hair, trying to comfort her. I can't imagine how she feels if I am overwhelmed by this situation. She rises from me, speaking with Kian. Guards crowd in, along with Emmeline and one of the healers. I lie still, letting them think I am ill. Jasmin whispers to Emmeline, who rushes off. Kian announces that everyone should adjourn to the courtyard to enjoy the feast prepared. Jasmin returns to my side, holding my hand. She is biting her lip, unable to control her emotions.

As people filter out, I let Erik and Kian pull me to standing. Some in the crowd cheer as we slowly exit the room through the side door. Jasmin shuts the door behind us, and I step away from Erik and Kian, letting them know I am fine. They release me hesitantly, but Jasmin steps in, swatting me with her hands. I raise mine, trying to protect myself against her anger.

"What the fuck is wrong with you?" She demands, still trying to hit me. I grab her body, pulling her close and wrapping my arms around her tightly. She heaves a sob against my chest but stops fighting, settling in my grip.

"You were about to walk away from me at the altar," I say calmly. Jas lifts her head, a look that she will argue with me, but I raise my eyebrows. We both know she was ready to go to the other woman. Her arms wrap around my waist, not saying anything else.

"We need time and privacy to figure out what just happened. I gave you that."

She huffs a breath against my chest. "You're so dramatic, Clem." I chuckle but lean down to offer her a small kiss. I press my lips against hers gently. My head aches at the change in position, and I flinch against her. She jerks back, staring at me with concern in her eyes. I rub the back of my head, where a bump is forming.

"Maybe I landed a little too hard."

She looks defeated, so small in my arms. Kian steps up, saying we should get back to her room. Erik looks nervous and tense, unsure what to do about this situation. I feel terrible for him; we've put him through many difficult situations since he accepted an official position on the guard. As much as I would like to offer him peace, I don't think it's coming soon. Jasmin's hand slips into mine as we walk back to her room. We are all silent, lost in our own thoughts. The only sound is the swish of the material of Jasmin's dress. Our shoes tap against the floor as we walk. For the first time since the ceremony started, my mind is quiet. I savor the silence, knowing it won't last.

We reach her room, the four of us entering together. Erik stays next to the door, guarding from inside. Jasmin ambles toward her vanity while Kian and I sit on the couch in the sitting area.

"It may not be ideal, but it is a good thing Clem bought you time." Kian starts slowly, looking over at Jasmin. She doesn't move, staring at the mirror in front of her. "Was that really Dahlia?" His voice is quiet, timid, meeting her eyes in the mirror. A tear rolls down her cheek, slowly dripping over the scars. Her face is streaked with makeup. She removes the crown and necklace, placing both gently on the vanity. She closes her eyes, taking a deep staggered breath. Her hands reach behind her back, pulling wildly at the laces in the dress. Her sobs become louder, more distraught.

"Get me out of this dress," she begs between breaths. "I can't breathe."

Kian and I jump up, rushing over to her. The door opens and closes as Erik steps out of the room. She collapses in my arms as Kian begins working with the laces. He quickly loosens it, then pulls the strings of the skirt. Her legs start kicking, trying to step out of the material. I support her chest, only releasing her so she can pull the sleeves and collar away. It takes a couple of minutes, but soon the dress is on the floor, and she is only in a shift in my arms. I lift her, carrying her back to the couch and pulling her into my lap as I sit. Kian brings a blanket over, covering her more.

"How is she here?" Jasmin whispers against my chest. I stroke her arms, unsure of what else to do now. I did what I could to get us away from the crowd, but now that we are here, I'm lost on what to do next. Kian returns with a small mug of water and a wet cloth. Jasmin takes the cup while I grab the cloth. After she drinks it, I rub her face gently, removing the ruined makeup. My intention is to offer her comfort. Cradling her in my arms, surprise fills me at how small she feels. Her breathing settles against my chest. So many questions need to be answered, but at least I can provide warmth.

The door opens as Erik leans in, announcing Emmeline is here. She enters, Erik closing the door behind her from the hallway. Jasmin sits up, looking over to Emmeline. We all stare at each other momentarily, unsure what to say. Finally, Emmeline speaks up.

"She's waiting in the nursery."

Jasmin nods but doesn't shift away from me. I want her to get answers. I want to go with her, to meet Dahlia, to hear what is going on. However, Jasmin needs time with her on her own. I can't help her in this situation. They need to be together to reconnect after all this time. I sigh, resigning to let her go alone. I adjust in my seat, not forcing her up but making it easier for her to get up. Her eyes meet mine as a small smile spreads across my face. She is still the most beautiful woman I have ever seen, even wholly distraught. I kiss her forehead, holding her tight against my chest.

"I'll be waiting here for you."

She stares at me for a minute, not moving at all. She finally rises, nervousness showing in her shaky stance. I stand, pulling the blanket tighter around her. She glides to the door slowly as if hollow. She enters the hallway, closing the door behind her. I watch the woman I love leave the room, on our wedding day, to reconnect with her lost lover. I collapse on the couch as that realization sets in. Emmeline sits with Kian and me.

"Where has she been?" Kian asks. Emmeline shrugs, her fingers fidgeting in her lap.

"She didn't say anything to me. Sunette didn't want her to go. I'm not used to seeing Sunette so frayed, but she knew Dahlia wouldn't stay with her. Sabeko and Zander were just staring at her, unable to speak through their shock. It's so much worse than a ghost because she's real. A ghost would make sense, but to see her alive and well...." Emmeline shakes her head, dropping it to look at her lap. I look at Kian, who is lost in his thoughts.

"Could she have been cursed too?" I question, tearing Kian from his own thoughts. He nods slowly.

"It's entirely possible."

"But why now? Why is she just showing up at this point?" Fear and confusion wreak havoc within me.

Kian shrugs, leaning back in the chair he is sitting in. "You two are close to breaking the curse. You were on the cusp of it when she entered the room. You heard the thunder and saw the shimmers. The magic probably wore off early, allowing her to enter at that moment."

"Did you see how the flower was glowing in her hands?" Emmeline asks, looking between Kian and me. The flower that holds the curse was glowing bright orange in Dahlia's hands when she was staring at Jasmin.

"I've never heard of an object glowing when the spell ends, but the curse is old magic. I don't know how it functions." He pauses for a moment, considering some thought. "We should ask my grandmother to observe the flower. She would have a better understanding of what it means. She has more experience with older magic. That magic is before her time, but she is better versed in it than I am."

I glance back at the door, wondering how long Jasmin will be with Dahlia. I don't plan to rush her, but there is no telling how long she will need or even want. They could be in there for a long time. The thought of sending Kian to fetch his grandmother crosses my mind, then I remember all the other people in the courtyard.

"Shit, what do we tell the kingdom?" Kian, Emmeline, and I look at each other, unsure what to do now. Emmeline chews on her lips. If Jasmin is done quickly, we could finish the ceremony tonight. Since she is already out of the room, it's too late to ask her if she wants that. Doubt courses through as I realize she was about to walk away from me at the altar. I have been so sure of my position in her life I haven't considered what the return of Dahlia means for me. She needs me to break the curse, but then what? Will she want to be with Dahlia instead of me? She can't have children to carry on her line anyway, so what's to stop her from being with Dahlia instead?

I can feel Kian's eyes on me as he speaks up. "I'll inform everyone the ceremony has been postponed due to your sudden illness. That will afford us some time to sort through this. I will set up a meeting with Matron Maud for tomorrow morning." He stands, offering a hand to Emmeline as well. "I'll check in tonight, then again in the morning." His eyes rake over Emmeline as she stands next to him. He holds her hand a moment longer than necessary before releasing it. "Why don't you come with me to fetch some wine to bring back to Clem? Then you can assure him Jasmin won't just abandon him that easily. That could be a long task." He grins, winking at me, eliciting a scowl. Emmeline giggles but has the decency to try to hide it. "She's not going to leave you, Clem." My scowl deepens.

"What are you talking about?"

Kian smirks. "Your every thought is written on your face. Which reminds me," he raises his eyebrows and nods slightly, "Nice work with the fainting earlier. Very believable." Emmeline turns her face, pressing her cheek against Kian's shoulder as her body shakes with quiet laughter. I sneer at him, trying to cover my own laughter. My thoughts and feelings are always visible, and I have never been able to hide anything on my face.

He clasps my shoulder as he and Emmeline walk to the door. "We'll be back shortly." I nod at them as they leave the room. My mind wanders back to this situation. Part of me knows Jasmin won't leave me. After everything we have been through, even without the curse or being true loves, we have built a good relationship. She means everything to me. I can't let her go. We will find a way to deal with this situation. Things will work out in the end. I repeat this to myself, waiting for the moment I believe it.

Emmeline returns before my thoughts have time to devolve into total ruin. She has a basket with several bottles of wine, bread, cheese, and fruits. I'm glad she had the forethought to bring food. I don't know how tonight will go, but I don't think we will leave the room. Emmeline sets everything up on one of the tables, then brings me a goblet of wine. I sip on it, not wanting to get drunk but needing relief and something to do with my hands.

"She won't just give you up," Emmeline says softly, sitting across from me with her goblet.

"Tell me what they were like, before the curse," I ask softly. I want to know what I am facing. Jasmin doesn't talk much about Dahlia, even after everything she told me. Seeing them when Kian examined the flower didn't paint a complete picture of their relationship. Emmeline stares at her goblet, tracing her fingers along the intricate designs on the side. She huffs a small laugh before she starts talking.

"They were inseparable. Always together, always mischievous. The Lords hated them. They never cared for Sabeko's family anyway. He was meant to be a servant." She looks, meeting my gaze, with a sad expression. "So when his daughter befriended the princess, they tried so hard to end it. But Jasmin had none of it." She shakes her head, looking back down at the goblet. She sighs, looking back at me with uncertainty.

"Tell me. I want to hear it."

Emmeline nods, speaking softly. "Jasmin would light up when Dahlia entered the room, similar to how she is with you now." This statement is both comforting and upsetting. I didn't realize she would light up when I entered a room. To hear that she did for Dahlia first doesn't bring the same peace. What if that isn't something she wants to give up?

"They were good at displaying a friendly facade in public, but in private, they weren't so conspicuous. We had many evenings that began platonic but ended with me leaving early due to certain activities." Emmeline shakes her head, still fidgeting, not meeting my eyes. "Similar to the two of you now." I shouldn't have asked this question. It isn't making me feel better about this situation. The wine settles heavily in my stomach.

"What if she wants that with her again?" I ask meekly, somewhat embarrassed by my own doubts. Emmeline finally meets my eyes, and her face shows pity and uncertainty.

"She won't abandon you, Clem. But I can't say how she will react to Dahlia being here. They went through so much together. Same as you and her. Jasmin has not had an easy life. Give her time, Clem. Things will work out the way they are supposed to."

That doesn't bring me any comfort at all. Doubt plagues me as time passes. Uncertainty swirls through the air. I could drown in this apprehension. How will things work out? What are they supposed to be?

Chapter 2

DAHLIA

I pace around the rug in the nursery. When Emmeline said Jasmin wanted to meet me, this was the first place that came to mind. What better place to reconnect than the last place I saw her. She was so beautiful in her wedding gown. She looked divine with her crown and the matching necklace. The scars on her face struck me. I don't know what they are from, but I'll kill whoever damaged her beautiful skin like that. I never dared dream that I could marry her myself, but I knew she would marry one day. She is more perfect than I had ever imagined. Seeing her like that made me realize I would give anything to stand opposite her.

Instead, a man was there, with his long blonde hair, broad shoulders, and tall stance. I've never been attracted to a man like him, but I can see why Jasmin likes him. He is handsome, and he is marrying her. Clem may be at the altar now, but he will not stand in my way. She is still and always will be mine. I'll find a way to break the curse, then keep her to myself. I'm sure we can find some job to send Clem out on, keep him out of the way. Maybe give her a few children and occasionally appear with her. But I'll be the one warming her bed every night.

The door clicks, opening slowly. I freeze, turning my attention to Jasmin. She is wrapped in a blanket, her face clean and soft. It feels like no time has changed at all. Her appearance has changed slightly, but I can still see the woman I love so deeply. My chest burns with the intensity of my feelings for her. I know time has passed since I saw her last, but nothing has changed for me. From my perspective, I was in this room with her yesterday, giving her the tea.

Fear dances in her eyes, a fair reaction given the situation. Behind her stands the guard that escorted her from the ceremony. She whispers something to him, and he nods, then shuts the door once she steps inside. She pulls the blanket tighter around her shoulders, not moving toward me. I expect her to run into my arms, crying with relief that I am here. Her distance hurts, despite the logic of it.

"Jas," I say softly, stepping closer to her. She watches me for a moment, then walks to me. She steps cautiously at first, then rushes to crash into my chest. I hold her tightly as she inhales deeply, releasing several sobs and shaking her whole body. Relief fills my veins over her reaction.

"Jasmin, my love. My life." I whisper, peppering kisses across her head. Her arms wrap around me, dropping the blanket from her shoulders. She grabs the shift on my back, pulling the material. Her grip is tight, as if she will never let me go. My hands caress her back, feeling her smooth skin under her gown. She takes a deep breath, trying to return to a regular breathing pattern. She rests her cheek against my chest, just above my breast, listening to my heartbeat. I hold her in my arms for a long time, soaking up every moment I can get with her. I have missed nearly a decade of her being in my arms. I'm not passing up any chance to keep her where she belongs.

A chill passes over her body. The weather is temperate on this spring day, but the nursery is cool without a fire burning. I release her to grab the blanket, pulling it back over her shoulders. The shift she is wearing does little to cover her body. The outline of her breasts, with budded nipples, tests my ability to restrain from sucking them. In the past, I wouldn't have restrained from that action. I realize I need to maintain some decorum at this moment. I am only human, though. My hands caress her shoulder, down her arms. My fingers wrap around her elbow, allowing my thumbs to stroke her breasts. She doesn't react.

"How are you here?" She whispers in a hoarse voice. "They said you were dead."

"I wasn't dead. I've been under a spell for the past nine years." I guide her over to the rocking chair in the corner. She doesn't need to hear this story while standing up, in the state she is already in. I drop into the chair, pulling her into my lap like I have many times before. She gasps my name, trying to pull away. I tighten my arms around her.

"No, Jas. Stay with me." She settles but doesn't really relax. I want more from her, but I can't ask that yet. It has been nine years, so I start talking instead.

"I was taken the night I gave you the tea." Her head drops on my shoulder, unable to hold herself upright any longer. "I don't know who did it. They ensured I never saw them. A man took me, but that's all I know." I sigh, pulling her against me. It feels so good to have her weight on me again. She fits against my body perfectly; this is where she belongs.

"I awoke this morning alone and locked in the tower above your suite. I made my way down, finding your room empty. The dahlia I gave you was on your mantle, and I was drawn to it. When I grabbed it, I saw everything that had happened in the past nine years. You being cursed, the chaos, the loneliness. And most recently, all the men... and your betrothed." I whisper the last few words. I won't give him that title willingly. That is what I want to be to her; I don't care what the magic or current culture says.

I stroke my fingers through her hair. It's not as long as it was when I saw her last. I enjoyed her long hair, but I also like the shorter waves she has now. She is beautiful with short or long hair; nothing could make her less gorgeous. Images of her sitting in front of her vanity, sighing over her short hair, flash in my mind from the magical flower I held earlier. She thought the scars and hair changed her beauty, but they didn't. She is always perfect.

She doesn't say anything as she rests against my body. I don't need her to speak now. Her fingers trace small circles against my arm. I tighten mine around her, wanting to hold her as long as possible. Desire to kiss her finally takes over. I can't avoid her lips forever; I'm no god. I kiss her forehead, then each cheek. Just before I reach her lips, she jumps from my lap. The blanket drops to the floor as she stands in front of me.

"Dahlia! I can't. I love him. I love Clem." Her words cut through my chest, his name a serrated knife in my heart. Before I can respond, I spot the bite marks on her shoulder. I stand, stepping toward her. She takes a step back, but I reach out to her shoulder, tugging the collar of the shift aside roughly.

"What the fuck is this? Who hurt you, Jas?" I demand, anger coursing through my veins at what could have caused this. How could that magical flower have left this part out of the images? I don't know who did this to her, but I will fucking end them.

"It's...I..." She's nervous. Her hands rub together. She won't look me in the eyes. She has never been nervous with me before. I don't understand what is happening now.

"You better tell me before I find out on my own." My breathing is harsh and staggered as anger turns to rage over who would hurt my girl.

"It was Clem, but it isn't what you think." She meets my gaze, her eyes begging me to understand. "I...we get...rough. During sex." She stutters through her statement. It takes a minute to process what she means. A smirk spreads across my face as she tries to hide from me. We were never gentle when we fucked, but I never left her with marks like this, either. I step to her, grab her hips, and pull her tightly against my own.

"Of course, you like it rough, my sweet girl. You always did." I lean in to kiss her again, unable to help myself. She turns her head away from me before I catch her lips. It frustrates me that she won't return my affection. "I love you, Jas. That hasn't changed. I don't care what he is to you. You are mine. I was yours first, and he won't take that away from me."

She looks at me, hurt and longing showing on her face. "It's not as simple as that, Dahlia." She steps back from me, wrapping her arms around her body again. Her skin is pebbled with chills. Conceding slightly to her, I grab the blanket and offer it again. Even if she doesn't let me warm her, I won't let her stay cold. She drapes it over her shoulders, turning to the shelf in the room. There are three burned candles with a journal in front of them. She reaches up, touching the cover, not opening it.

"Father told me you died in the winter storm, eaten by animals. The curse started less than a week later. On the same night, I learned my parents died." She turns back to me, tears in her eyes. Heartache slashes through my chest at the emotions she is expressing. "I was barely recovered from the pregnancy. You were gone. My parents were gone. I was left alone to rule a cursed kingdom." She sniffles, pulling the blanket tighter. Hearing her words is much more impactful than seeing them in the cursed flower. The flower just showed images. Jasmin is showing me her feelings. The hurt, abandonment, loneliness, fear.

"I was a ghost for years, Dahlia. Years. He..." A sob shudders through her body. Her hands cover her face, rubbing away more tears. My girl has cried more in her lifetime than anyone ever should. I hate that so many of those tears are at my expense. She finally looks up, eyes red, tears streaming down her face, but determination showing through. She was always stronger than she gave herself credit for.

"Clem helped bring me back to normal. He gave me life again." I take a deep breath, letting her words settle in my body. "I won't do anything to hurt him." She pauses, assessing me with the cutting gaze she has always had. However, this is the first time she has used it on me.

"I love you, Dahlia. I always will. But we can no longer have what we had before." My breath hitches, hearing her words. I can't accept that. I refuse to. She is mine. She has always been mine.

"Jas..." She holds her hand up to stop me from moving closer to her.

"I need time to process what this all means."

She steps to me, wrapping her arms and the blanket around my waist. I drape my arms over her shoulders, resting my cheek against the top of her head, trying to hold in the emotions wanting to burst free. I'm not going to cry and scream now. Not this time. Her hair smells like before, with a slight floral scent. I close my eyes, breathing her in deeply. My world is imploding as I hold her. This won't be the last time. I'll find a way to win her over. Her arms tighten around my waist, squeezing me tightly. She steps back, letting the blanket hang loosely on her shoulders.

"This isn't the end, Dahlia. Before I return to Clem, I must tell you one more thing. It won't be easy for you to hear." What could possibly be worse than hearing she is leaving me for him? My heart is already shattered. I spent nine years cursed in her tower, unable to be with her, only to return and be shunned for a man with long blonde hair. She takes a deep breath, pulling strength into her body. My own tenses at what she thinks could be worse than refusing me.

The blanket drops from her shoulders, falling to the floor around her feet. Her fingers slowly pull the shift up, rising above her knees, then thighs. As her sex is exposed to me, confusion rings through, but the shift continues to draw up. The massive bruise on her abdomen is exposed. The angry skin stretches from one hip to the other. Red marks course through. My eyebrows furrow in anger and confusion. If he did this to her, I don't care if it was during sex; I will end him. I step near her, reaching my fingers out to trace the edges. She doesn't stop me, just watches as I take in the damaged skin.

"This is from the pregnancy, Dahlia." My eyes jerk up to hers. "I am infertile because of the tea. The blend you mixed is used to end pregnancies permanently." My eyes go wide as I snap back from her. I did this to her. Not Clem. Not someone else. Me. She can never have children because of me. She drops her shift as my hands fall. "I don't care about having children. I've found peace with it. Clem is also accepting of this situation." Her fingers caress the damaged skin beneath her shift. I am stunned into silence.

She inches closer to me, her hand reaching to caress my cheek. My head tilts into her touch, comfort, and longing coursing through my aching body. "I want you in my life, but we need time to figure out what this means before we redefine our relationship." She leans up, pressing her lips softly against mine. Tears threaten to spill from my eyes.

"Please," I whisper as she pulls away, unsure what I want. I just don't want her to leave.

"Go to Sunette. She needs you, too. I'll find you tomorrow." Her thumb strokes my cheek before she pulls her hand away. She grabs the blanket, turning back to face me. "I'm so glad you're back, Dahlia. I really do love you very much."

With that, she turns and leaves. The door closing echoes through the room like a canon firing. I drop to my knees, unable to support my body any longer. I permanently hurt her. My body shudders with tears now that she is gone. She left me for him. My mind races through everything that just happened. She still fits in my arms perfectly. How can he be better for her than I am? She was meant to be mine, true love or not. I can't give her up. I won't. I will fight to stay in her life. My body is so heavy now. I take several deep breaths, calming myself. I can't win her back if I am overcome with my emotions. I will win her back.

Chapter 3

Jasmin

Walking across the hall to my room feels like an eternity and the briefest of moments. It's really Dahlia. She's still alive. I was in her arms again. I listened to her heartbeat, the one that was my lifeline before the curse. I still feel so complete in her arms. The magic has decided Clem is my true love, but Dahlia is something else entirely. However, I can't risk what I have with Clem for her. He treats me so well; he knows me so well. He's so important to me and the kingdom. He also gets so jealous; trying to find her new role in my life won't be easy.

Inside the room, Emmeline is clearly trying to comfort Clem. He looks nervous, as he probably should be. I offer him a soft smile, knowing what he is scared of and how wrong he is. I ask Emmeline to escort Dahlia back and send Finn in later tonight. Clem stands, waiting for me to say something as Emmeline leaves, and I don't hesitate to find my way into his arms. He releases a deep sigh as his arms wrap around me tightly.

"It's really her," I mumble with a giggle. The laughter grows until setting into total hysterics. Clem holds me tightly as my body tries to process everything that has happened this afternoon. Tears stream down my face from the laughter. I let him go, reaching up to wipe them away. He smiles at me with concern in his eyes.

"I'm sorry. This is just so unbelievable." I chuckle again as I rest my head on his chest. I listen to his heartbeat, letting the steady thumps calm me. His sounds similar to Dahlia's but different at the same time. His fingers stroke through my hair, similar to but different from Dahlia's touch. I look up at him, needing to see his face. I rise to kiss him gently, wanting more intimacy from him at this moment. I would have taken more from her if I weren't scared of hurting Clem. A strong pull, a deep desire has me tethered to Dahlia.

A quick knock on the door draws our attention away. Kian walks in, offering thanks to Erik, who is still in the hallway. I call him in, waving them both over for a glass of wine. Erik hesitates, causing me to realize I am still in the shift I had under my wedding dress. Kian and Clem have seen me in far more compromising positions, but Erik hasn't. I instruct Clem to pour wine for everyone while I change.

After I slip on some leggings and a thicker sweater, I return to the sitting area. All three men are sitting on the chairs in various states of discomfort. Kian looks somewhat relaxed with an arm over the back of his chair, but his body is still more tense than usual. Clem still looks nervous. I haven't actually said anything to relieve his fears. Erik looks entirely uncomfortable, with his arms crossed over his large chest, sitting upright in his chair. He's officially been in the guard for only a few months and has dealt with more strange situations than most guards have in the past nine years.

I sit between Erik and Clem on the couch, leaning into Clem's side. I don't care about formalities at this point. This day has gone to shit, and we don't need to be proper now.

"The witches received word of an incident in their territory and need to return immediately," Kian announces.

"What?! What happened?"

"There weren't any details provided," Kian responds, shaking his head. "They are packing to leave now and should be gone within the hour."

"Why so soon? Is it safe for them to travel at night?" I question, worried about such a large group making that journey.

"With so many people here, the roads will be less busy tonight. They can make it to the base of the mountains faster and rest before finishing the journey tomorrow." I nod, accepting his answer. I don't know enough about the witches and their habits to try to argue. I have several other issues to deal with. I don't need to argue if they are confident they want to leave.

"Send my regards and be sure they have everything they need." He nods, leaning forward to rest his elbows on his knees.

"Which brings me to my next point of concern." He pauses, looking between Clem and me. I sip from my wine, waiting to hear what other catastrophe needs to be dealt with. "What do you want to do about the wedding?"

"Oh, shit!" I exclaim, sitting up to face Clem. "I've ruined our wedding. Oh, my gods. I am so sorry. We..." I look to Kian, then Erik. "We can still have it now?" Kian holds his hands out to stop me.

"I think we should postpone it," Kian supplies.

"That would be easier on the guards right now, too," Erik offers.

I turn to Clem, devastated over this realization. My chest tightens as the full impact of Dahlia's return in the middle of the ceremony really sinks in. I take his hand in mine, worried he is upset. He smiles, bringing my hand to his lips. He presses a gentle kiss against my knuckles, keeping his eyes on mine. Despite everything, butterflies begin to flutter in my stomach. A slight blush spreads across my cheeks.

"I don't care when we get married, Jas. You're already mine."

Why does that make me want to giggle like a little schoolgirl? My emotions are wreaking havoc on my body right now. I settle back into his side, turning back toward Kian.

"Okay, then. We'll postpone it for now." I rest against Clem's shoulder, basking in the warmth of his touch. My mind is purely focused on Clem at the moment. Dahlia is still dancing around the periphery of my thoughts, and nothing else seems to matter.

"Has anyone inspected the border at all?" Kian asks Erik.

Fuck.

"We have dispatched a few people to search the closest location. We've also sent riders to the other villages to search their borders. We should have reports from them within a week." I listen to Erik speak, but I have a hard time comprehending everything he says. I look at Clem, realizing he is consuming all of my thoughts. I want him to, but I need to be Queen now, at least for a few minutes. I stand and walk away from him, needing some distance so my body will stop focusing solely on his.

"Let's set up a meeting with the Lords in the morning. I will update them on everything, and would like to hear from the guards, too." Kian and Erik nod at my request. "We will send everyone home tomorrow and plan another ceremony later in the summer when we know what is happening with the curse." Clem is watching me with a blank face. It's such an unusual experience to see him without expressions.

"Kian, I hate to keep leaning on you so heavily for information about the magic," he cuts me off before I can say anything else.

"I already have several texts pulled to research. I hoped my grandmother could help, but that won't be possible now. If I am unsuccessful, she should be our next course of action.

"Thank you, Kian. I appreciate all of your efforts." I turn around to face Erik. "And yours too, Erik. Your diligence to our safety has not gone unnoticed."

"Thank you, Your Majesty." I scoff, waving my hand at him.

"Shut up." We all chuckle over my response. A quiet pause settles in the room as the three men watch me patiently. I am trying to think of anything else that needs to be added to this discussion that I might have overlooked. Their gazes are expectant while I scour my mind for anything else we should discuss.

"Where has she been?" Clem finally breaks the silence. Oh! Obviously, they want to know about Dahlia.

"She was in the tower above my suite," I point to where the tower rises. "I never cared for my tower, preferring the one in the castle's center instead. So I haven't been up there in years, even before the curse." I shake my head as the reality settles that she was above me for years. Kian contemplates this new bit of information.

Clem's face flickers through a range of emotions, a mix of fear, confusion, and anger. Erik is watching the three of us, not showing any reaction. Kian finally nods, turning toward me.

"I'm going to read more about these complex curses. We can chat more tomorrow. I would like to talk with her soon." I nod in response, hoping she'll be cooperative. She tends to do what she wants, which isn't always what needs to be done.

Kian and Erik rise, ready to leave us alone. I'm ready for that too. I give them hugs before they go. Clem stays seated on the couch, offering a wave as they exit. A sense of relief and belonging washes over me as I realize I am building my own group of trusted advisors. I have relied on my father's advisors this entire time. These are men I have chosen, that I trust, that I know hold my desires at hand before their own. I can do this; I can rule this kingdom the way it should be governed. I can be the Queen I need to be.

After they leave, I turn back to Clem, who is still sitting on the couch. His eyes are on mine; his face is back to being mysteriously blank. I don't like not knowing what he is thinking. It's an unusual feeling for me. He is always so expressive. I walk to stand in front of him, bending at the waist to press my lips against his. He is tentative at first but settles in quickly. His fingers wrap around my head, pulling me against him harder. I part my lips, allowing him in. Our tongues swirl together, desire pooling in the depths of my core. My hands land on his thighs, caressing, slowly moving toward his cock. I palm him through his pants, causing him to groan against my mouth. He hardens quickly under my ministrations, exactly how I want him. I drop to my knees in front of him, breaking our kiss.

"Fuck me, Clem," I beg. "Claim me as yours again." I open my mouth, holding my tongue out to show my intentions. He hasn't fucked my throat since the first time. Despite the painful repercussions, this is something I want from him now. I need to feel that pain; I want to feel him taking me the way he desires.

Clem groans, sliding to the edge of the couch. He grabs a fistful of my hair, jerking my head back. I grunt at his sudden forcefulness. He drags his nose along my neck, sending chills through my body.

"Does my little flower need some pain after her eventful day?"

"Yes," I mumble as he tightens his grip on my hair.

His lips press against my neck, kissing over the bite marks he left yesterday during our last tryst before the wedding. He told me then I had to be in charge of our wedding night, but since we aren't technically married, he doesn't seem to be holding me to that. His hand closes over my breast, crushing it between his fingers. I moan at the pressure, loving every bit of his intense touch.

All at once, he releases everything, my hair, my breast, and he pulls away from my neck. He stands, forcing me to lean back, his crotch taking the place where my face was. He stares down at me maliciously, clearly excited about what I have asked for.

"Take off your clothes. Wait for me here."

He walks into my closet while I do what I'm told. I may not always follow the rules, but at this moment, for him, I will do anything he asks. I remove my leggings and sweater, tossing them on the chair, then resume my position on my knees. I scoot away from the couch, unsure where he would prefer to be. I wait, focusing on breathing, clearing my mind of everything that happened in the past day. My eyes close, allowing my body to settle into a quiet, submissive mind. My pussy throbs as cool air brushes against it. My nipples pebble over with anticipation. My entire body is electrified, waiting for him to return.

He saunters behind me, dragging his fingertips over my shoulders. My skin tingles under his touch. His trousers brush against my back. One hand caresses down my chest, gripping my breast between his fingers. He twists the hard bud between his index finger and thumb tightly. I lean back against his legs, wanting more touch. Just as I find his touch, he moves away, leaving me empty and longing.

"You're such a little slut, thinking you can take what I haven't offered you."

I open my eyes, watching as he steps in front of me. His shirt is gone, leaving his chest exposed. His muscles are well-defined from a life of working farmland. His shoulders are losing their sun-kissed glow since he hasn't been in the fields this season. My eyes trace every line, every indent across his chest, his abs, leading to the v of his muscles at his waist. The strings of his pants hang loose, but that does nothing to hide his throbbing erection. His cock jerks as my eyes finally reach it. I bite my lip, wanting to taste him. I need him in my mouth.

His fingers clamp around my jaw, forcing my eyes up to his. The forcefulness of his grip causes my core to clench around nothing, dripping with anticipation.

"Like what you see, my little whore?"

His words send another surge through my body, making it hard to breathe with the desire coursing through my veins.

"Of course you do." His foot wedges between my knees, spreading them apart. I shift my knees, spreading them wide as he demands. "I'm going to fuck your face, but you'll come for me too. Because you do as I say. You are mine." His words are laced with venom. A tiny thread of unease spreads over the choice of his words, but not out of fear for my safety. He is going to hurt me in the best way possible.

"Give me your hand."

I hold my hand out for him, face still in his tight grip. He drops an object in my hand, just outside of my vision. Before I can figure out what it is, he taps it, and it vibrates. My core tingles as wetness pools deep inside. I moan as a wide grin spreads across Clem's face. It's the most magnificent thing I have ever seen, and I want to do anything to keep it there.

"Use it," he demands. I don't hesitate, dropping the object to my clit. I moan again the instant it touches the sensitive spot, pressing into his fingers on my chin. My eyes close as arousal courses through my body. His fingers squeeze my cheeks, forcing my jaw open.

"Eyes open."

My eyes spring wide, staring at him as my body convulses from the intense waves of pleasure coursing through my body. My breath quickens, so close to climax. Clem has a sinister gleam in his eyes as he watches my body twitch and jerk beneath his.

"Come for me, Queen, on your knees like the slut you are."

His words send me over the edge. My body tenses with pleasure, hips jerking with release as moisture drips from my empty, throbbing pussy. His fingers cling to my cheeks, forcing my mouth to remain open. I do my best to keep my eyes open, but my vision is clouded with explosions and pleasure. I remove the magic fun ball from my clit as my body calms, deep breaths bringing me back to reality.

"I didn't say you could stop."

My eyes widen, realizing he wants me to keep the vibrating item against my sensitive clit again. I slowly return it, jerking as it makes contact. My body tenses, feeling waves spread through my body again. Clem uses his free hand to shift his pants, springing his erect dick free. My mouth begins to water, ready for a taste of him. His fingers loosen on my face while he slowly strokes his cock from tip to hilt.

"Stick your tongue out. Don't take the magic fun ball away from your clit."

I do as instructed, trying to hold off the impending orgasm. I want to feel Clem down my throat without being overwhelmed by my pleasure. He places the head of his cock against my tongue. My eyes are still on his. As I swirl my tongue against the backside of his cock, his eyes roll in his head. I want to give him more of that feeling. I wrap my lips around his cock, sucking him in, swirling my tongue around him as I slide back. He groans, lacing his fingers in my hair. My pussy spasms from his noises. I'm so close to my own release again. I pull the vibrating toy away, not wanting to reach the climax so soon again. His eyes are closed. He won't know the difference.

I suck him down again, closing my eyes as I enjoy giving pleasure to him. My tongue caresses his hard cock in my mouth. I slide down, but he withdraws wholly and quickly just before he hits the back of my throat. My eyes dart up, finding him glaring down at me. I realize my mistake. My hands are on his thighs now, and I reached out to touch him without thinking about it. My hands jerk back to my own thighs, biting my lip.

"Did I, or did I not, tell you to keep that item on your clit?" he smolders, stepping back from me.

"No," I whine, making a show of returning the magical cylinder to my clit. Fire courses through my body, already so close to orgasm. I watch as he bends down, intentionally not touching me. His fingers grab the vibrating cylinder from my hand. He taps it again, increasing the speed, then presses it hard against my clit. I writhe under his touch, so close to climax. He grabs the back of my head, slamming his mouth against mine. His tongue surges into my mouth, scouring mine as my orgasm rips through my body. The sensation borders on pain as pleasure and intense pressure course through my body. His kiss is devouring, but he refuses to remove the vibrating item.

"Keep it there this time, slut."

My breathing is hard and fast as my body struggles to decipher pain from pleasure. My sensitive clit is tingling but still sending pulses of pleasure through my body. His hands grip the side of my head as he presses his cock against my lips. I open my mouth, ready to take him deep inside me. His dick glides into my mouth smoothly until my lips reach the base, forehead pressed against his stomach. I shut my eyes tight, my cunt clenching with another round of sensitive pleasure.

"This is how I like my little flower. On her knees with my cock buried in her throat."

He pulls out, slamming back in. He sets a brutal pace of thrusting deep in my throat. Tears build in my eyes with the impact, but he brushes them away. His fingers squeeze the back of my head, holding me in place as he fucks my mouth. I shift the magic fun ball, hitting a different spot. My body lights up with another orgasm, stronger and more intense than the previous one. I focus what little consciousness I have left on keeping my mouth loose as he pounds against my throat. I gag when he hits a particular area in the back, causing him to relentlessly lash that area. The gagging sends him over the edge again, his warm release dripping down my throat. Another sudden orgasm crashes through my own body. I lean into him, overwhelmed with sensation. He holds my head tight until his orgasm is finished, no longer expelling the salty semen down my throat.

I keep the item pressed against my clit, unsure when he wants me to stop. He hasn't said to, and I don't know what he would do if I stopped again. It is painful now, though. He removes his limp member from my mouth, but I grab onto his thigh, rubbing my face against him. Tears are still streaming down my face.

"Please." It's a hoarse whisper, but he hears me. His hand caresses the back of my head. He tugs my hair, forcing my face up to his.

"Is my Queen done?" I try to nod against his leg, but his grip on my hair is too tight. The cylinder sends waves of pain through my core, and my hips are shifting to get away, anything to relieve the ache. He smirks at me, releasing my hair to stroke it instead.

"You can drop it, Jas."

I do, relaxing against his leg entirely. I sigh, relishing the calm washing over me. He slowly kneels, taking my weight off his leg. He lifts me into his arms and carries me over to the bed. Clem sits me down gently, finding a wet cloth to wipe my face and then cunt. He brings a mug of water and crawls into the bed beside me, wrapping the blanket around us. He holds me against his chest for several moments, caressing my back as I return to normal.

As much as I love the orgasms, I cherish these moments with him. The calm, quiet bliss that can only be found after intense orgasms. As I drift off, I feel Finn climb into the bed with us. Clem argues with my oversized furry beast to keep him from wedging between us. Finn concedes, but not without much whining about not getting the middle spot. Finn curls up against my back for now, but we all know he'll be in the middle before the morning. I fall asleep with a slight smile, temporarily distracted from all my other problems.

Chapter 4

CLEM

Finn made his way between Jasmin and me at some point during the night. I'm doing well if I get an hour without him wedging between us. This dog is so spoiled. Jasmin is snuggled against him while his back is pressed against my side. I reach over, pushing a strand of hair from Jasmin's face. She's so lovely. My fingers trace the scar on her cheek. This whole situation is exhausting. If we had finished the ceremony, would the curse be broken now? What would we face then?

Jasmin's fingers wrap around mine, holding my hand close. I smile, savoring the touch. Her eyes are still closed, pretending she can sleep longer. We both know we must get up and attend meetings, deal with people, and do things we don't want to do. My fingers trail down her neck, over her shoulder, across her arm. I want her next to me, not Finn. I shove his side, trying to get him to move, but he gives a lazy snarl. I keep pushing, but he whines louder. Jasmin just giggles, not helping me at all.

"Go on, you big oaf. I want to cuddle with her now." I shove him harder, but he just yips, annoyed at me. The fact that he weighs more than Jasmin prevents me from trying to actually pick him up. Jasmin lifts the covers off her body, stepping over Finn onto my side. I shift over, letting her slide under the covers. For a brief moment, her bare pussy is right near my face. An idea strikes, but before it comes to fruition, she is under the covers. I'll think about that later because any idea involving her delicious cunt is one I want to explore wholeheartedly.

Her petite body settles against mine, warmth spreading across our touching skin. My lips find hers as my fingers skim across her back. Her breasts press against my chest, her nipples poking into my skin. She wiggles her ass, eliciting another whine from Finn. He saunters off the bed toward the hallway, where someone will let him out. I chuckle, but Jasmin moves. One leg slides over my waist, then she lifts her upper body until she straddles me. I smile at her, pushing her hair back over her shoulders. It falls in front of her face, but I want to see her now. She matches my smile, leaning down slowly to kiss me again. My dick is already hard and waiting for her. I graze her sides, landing under her breasts to cup them, dragging my thumbs across the buds. She moans at the touch, pressing her ass back against my throbbing cock. It fits so perfectly between her cheeks.

Jasmin shifts her hips, rubbing her wet pussy against my length. I take a quick breath, squeezing her breasts tightly in my hands. She presses my dick back, lining it up with her entry. Then she slowly drops down until she is sitting on me. She pauses, sitting up straight, watching my reaction.

"Good morning." Her voice is rough and hoarse from last night's activities, causing me to smirk at her. I open my mouth to say something, but she lifts up, dropping down quickly. I place my hands on her hips, wanting to hold on to her. She sets a quick pace, bouncing up as soon as she comes down. At this rate, I'll only last a few more minutes. My thumb finds her clit, rubbing small circles around it.

"Yes, Clem. Fuck, don't stop," Jasmin mumbles. I can't help the chuckle that escapes at the sound of her broken voice. She gives me an evil glare, but it fades quickly as her pleasure takes over. I feel the familiar tingle in my spine. My balls tighten just before my release erupts deep inside her. I press her clit harder, driving her over the edge with me. She shudders before collapsing on my chest. I tug the quilt over us as we both breathe heavily.

After a moment, she clenches her muscles around my soft cock. I look down at her, unsure of what she is doing. Then my cock is pushed out of her, dropping with a funny sensation. I jerk at the sudden change. She giggles, leading me to laugh too. I love that I never know what to expect from her. She can be so ridiculous sometimes.

"I'm going to see Ma before breakfast and the meeting with the Lords." She lifts her head, resting her chin on her hand against my chest. She doesn't say anything but looks enamored. "What?" I question why she is looking at me like I am something special. She shrugs.

"I love you, is all," she says softly. She kisses my cheek then climbs off me, rushing to the washroom. We both clean up and dress quickly. She says she will visit the dining hall with whoever is still here and will see me at the meeting. We leave together but separate before the dining hall. Ma is staying in my old room again, but Claire is in there with her this time because of all the other guests. Bea got her own room, but the three of them tend to take breakfast in Ma's room instead of joining everyone else. I don't blame them. Starting the day with so many people can be overwhelming when you aren't used to it.

I knock on the door; once they answer, I walk in, but Ma rushes to my side. She begins fretting, asking questions about what happened.

"They told me you were fine, but no one would say what happened. I even sent Bea to find Erik, but she couldn't find him. Lord David just said you were okay. What is wrong? Are you hurt or ill?" She is rambling, clearly upset. I feel terrible that I didn't think to send a message to her, but there were other issues at the forefront of my mind.

"I'm fine, Ma. I wasn't sick. I'm sorry I didn't get a message to you." I glance at Claire, realizing she will likely repeat anything I say. "Hey, Claire, I hear they have jam-filled pastries downstairs. Do you want to get some? Jasmin is in the dining hall." Her eyes light up. The pastries might have failed to work, but Claire loves Jasmin as much as I do. She looks to our mother, who just nods. Claire takes off without even saying goodbye. I shake my head at her but notice Ma with concern on her face.

"Who was that woman, Clem?" Bea walks around the room to sit in the chair in front of the window. I don't know what to say about this, and I really should have asked Jasmin what she doesn't mind sharing.

"It was her best friend." That seems innocent enough. "We believe she was cursed, too, and the ceremony lifted her magic enough to free her."

"Are you still marrying Jasmin? Why did you fall?"

"Yes, we're still getting married, but we'll have to postpone it until the covens can return. Something came up, and they needed to leave." Ma looks sad over the delay. I am too, but I know things aren't over between us. We just need time to figure out what the hell is going on. "I fell yesterday to buy us some time. I didn't want Jasmin to walk away from me at the altar." Ma looks stunned while confusion spreads on Bea's face.

"She would leave you at the altar? Clem…" Ma's shock has changed to pity.

"No, Ma. I worded that poorly." Bea huffs a laugh from the corner, but I ignore her. She's more accustomed to my poor choice of words than Ma is.

"She wouldn't leave me, but she was going to. Well, not like that." I should have saved this conversation for the afternoon. Or maybe ask Jasmin to have it. She's better spoken than I am.

"She… okay. Jasmin believed Dahlia was dead. That was what they told her before the curse. When Jasmin saw her standing in front of us, she wanted to go to her. I realized how that would look in front of the kingdom. So I faked being ill to buy us some time." Ma crosses her arms over her chest, unimpressed with my response. I don't have anything else to add at this point. Bea shrugs at me, staring out the window.

"I'm sorry you were worried, Ma. I didn't even think to send a message. I was so consumed with why Dahlia is back; I didn't think about anything else." Ma sighs, pulling me into a hug.

"Oh, you're right, Clem. You didn't need to send a message. For gods' sake, you're a grown man, about to be King." She squeezes me tightly, then motions toward their food tray. "Can you stay for breakfast?"

"I can't. We have a meeting with the Lords to discuss everything. But I want you to come to dinner tonight." She nods as I lean in and kiss her cheek. "You, too, Bea. I'm sure Erik will be there." She jumps out of the chair, rushing toward me. I bolt out the door into the hallway laughing hysterically. Ma just sighs, frustrated with our silly games in a profound moment. She steps out to yell goodbye before I get too far away. Thankfully, Bea doesn't follow me. My eye is still bruised from my last comments about her and Erik. Jasmin threw a fit over the previous punch. She would probably find a way to curse me if I got another.

I enter the meeting room where Kian, Erik, Henry, the Head of Guards, and the Lords are already waiting. Jasmin has yet to arrive, so I walk over to chat with Erik and Kian. The other men are much older than the three of us. We've grown close in the last few months. Despite not being Jasmin's true love, I commend them for staying at the castle. I probably wouldn't have remained if it had been someone else. I couldn't watch her love another man and be content to go about my day. We make idle chat until the guards announce Jasmin's entrance. I make my way toward her, bowing quickly. She pulls me up, allowing me to escort her to her seat after a quick kiss. She has a mug of steaming tea in her hand, so I throw her a sly wink before we sit. Before she can even say anything, Lord Gustavo from Tilrade speaks up.

"What is she doing here? We were told she was dead." There is too much anger behind his words for his intent to be innocent. The Lords never liked Dahlia and Jasmin's relationship, but to be this angry nearly a decade later feels excessive.

"Apparently," Jasmin speaks with equal amounts of malice, "she was also cursed, locked above my tower for nine years. We believe the magic of her curse weakened, allowing her to break free before anything else. This brings me to my first point. Erik, Henry, have we heard anything about the borders?"

Erik looks at Henry, but Henry waves his hand, allowing Erik to speak. Erik nods, acknowledging the respect that has just been shown to him by a higher-ranking member. "The border is still in place but does seem to be weakening. It was reported as being softer and more malleable. It will be another week before we have any further information."

Jasmin asks Kian, "What should we make of this information?"

"The curse is undoubtedly shifting. I would like to spend time with Dahlia and see where she was to determine her involvement in the curse."

"Are you saying she's the one who placed the curse?" Lord Alwyn asked. With all of the covens located within his territory, he is surprisingly unsupportive of them.

"Absolutely not," Jasmin exclaimed, slamming her hands down on the table. Kian speaks at the same time as her.

"No, but she was also cursed. The magic that contained her may also contain keys to what will break Queen Jasmin's curse." It rings odd to hear him refer to her with her title. I'm more accustomed to him being informal.

Lord Alwyn shakes his head, eyebrows knit in disappointment. "We just need to go on with the ceremony for these two and be done with all this nonsense."

"Forgive me if this has been explained before, Lord Alwyn," Kian speaks respectfully, but I have a feeling he doesn't mean any respect toward the old man. "This curse is ancient magic. With Dahlia's return, there probably is more to the curse than just a marriage between the two. After all, their love hasn't broken the curse. I've personally heard them make commitments to each other in private. What's a legal document or ceremony in the face of old magic and true love?" I bite my tongue, grabbing my goblet to hide my discontent. Jasmin doesn't look at me, but she does take my hand. I squeeze hers in return as the room sits quietly for a moment. Kian just dropped a heavy thought that none of us have really considered. Why hasn't the curse already broken if she just needs to find her true love?

Jasmin finally speaks, breaking the awkward, heavy silence. "Lord Alwyn, what is the reason for the covens' quick departure?" His lips purse together as he shifts in his chair.

"I do not know. Those hags do not speak to me." Jasmin's hand tightens in mine. Kian has a fire in his eyes that I don't think I have ever seen in him. Erik shifts his position, ready to jump into action should either react poorly or, rather, appropriately. While I would love to see Jasmin and Kian take on Lord Alwyn, I don't think either will do anything dramatic. Alwyn notices their demeanors and has the decency to look scared.

"I mean, the witches." His correction is weak. Jasmin rises from her seat after another bloated silence, walking to the corner of the room. Everyone is watching her, waiting for her response anxiously.

"Lord Alwyn, last summer, when the true love edict was presented to me, I asked if we had spoken to the witches about the curse. Do you remember that?" She reaches a bookshelf in the corner, scanning the titles. She doesn't actually give Alwyn a chance to answer the question. "I was informed we had exhausted all possibilities, and allowing men into the castle was the only option left." She pulls a book from the shelf, turning to walk back to the table. "Now, I will concede the edict did what it was supposed to, as Clem is here." She waves her hand at me, then slams the book on the table, causing several men to jump. She flips through the pages, stopping on one as she scans it. Her finger drags across the written words, stopping near the bottom.

"Kian, how many covens would you say there are?" Kian thinks, tapping his chin as he considers.

"Probably around 30 in total. They have different numbers ranging from about 15 members to over 400 in the largest." Jasmin taps the page, glaring at Lord Alwyn.

"And what is the youngest coven, Kian?"

"The youngest has probably been established for 50 years now." Everyone in the room is silent, watching the reaction of their Queen to this bit of information. No one is quite brave enough to interact on Alwyn's behalf. He sits up straight, meeting her gaze, but the fear in his eyes is unmistakable. Her fingers continue tapping the page. It is the census for Greynon, last performed five years ago. The numbers are significantly smaller than what Kian just shared. In fact, the number of witches hasn't changed in the past several censuses. The numbers have just been copied from the previous report. She turns the book, sliding it across the table. It stops directly before Alwyn, but he doesn't break his gaze with her.

The two stare at each other for several minutes. Others start to squirm, not wanting to be the one to break the silence but also not wanting to be so uncomfortable anymore. Lord David leans over, looking at the information in front of Alwyn.

"Gods," he mutters. "Queen Jasmin, we will rectify this."

"Immediately," she demands.

"Yes. Immediately."

"Communication between a Lord and *all* of his people is essential. Do better with the witches," Jasmin seethes.

Lord David asks for Kian's help updating the census numbers until Alwyn can return to his village for an accurate count. Kian agrees, as long as it doesn't interfere with his pursuit of the curse. Several other topics are discussed in the meeting, including my desire to meet with the head of gardens from each location. I ask each Lord to send a message requesting their presence if they aren't already on the grounds. Plans are made to assist families in returning to their homes, and we schedule the next meeting for later in the week when we can hear back from the guards checking the borders.

After the meeting is dismissed, Jasmin and I walk through the grounds, greeting people still around, chatting with others, and just spending time outside in the nice weather. Claire and Finn join us soon. Claire tells us about all the trouble they have been causing. The afternoon is enjoyable, even though Jasmin is still tense over the meeting. I sneak kisses and playful touches, trying to lift her mood. Before we head to dinner with everyone, she seems much happier, smiling and returning my playfulness. The past few days have been stressful for everyone. I plan to do what I can to help her forget about that, even if just for a few minutes.

Chapter 5

DAHLIA

This couch in Mama's living quarters is better than anything she has ever owned. She told me Jasmin gave it to her when they first moved into the space, and I was surprised to learn it was that old. It's so soft and plush. I have spent most of my time lounging on this couch. Jasmin was at breakfast this morning without Clem, which would have been the perfect opportunity for me to spend time with her. However, she was greeting people from the kingdom and updating them on his condition.

Ugh, I just want to go one day without hearing about Clem. I roll my eyes, despite being the only person in the room. I don't get what the big deal is. Surely, there isn't anything he can offer her that I can't. I can definitely pleasure her well.

Zander walks in, distracting me from my thoughts, returning from his time helping Baba in the stables. He always loved the horses. I'm not surprised Zander's following in Baba's footsteps. He steps over to me, picks up my feet, and sits on the seat they were just in. My feet drop to the floor, grunting at the forced change. I haven't spent much time with Zander since I was released from the curse. He has been busy helping people ready their horses, and I've been preoccupied with Jasmin, like always.

"I can't believe you're really here." His voice is soft, shrouded in disbelief.

"I am." I shrug, getting a good look at him. He looks so much like Baba, both average height and stocky. Their skin is so dark it's almost black, with hair so tight and coiled it seems more like a cap of dark fuzz. Zander's accent has faded most of all of us. Mine is more noticeable when I am angry. Baba's is thick, but he tries to lessen it when he speaks with local men. I find it insulting that he needs to do it. Mama also tends to lessen her lilting accent around new people but doesn't hold back around Jasmin. Our accents are one of the few remaining pieces of us from our homeland. I'd love to return to our home one day, but I need to help Jasmin break the curse before any of us can go anywhere.

"So, tell me, little brother, what have you been up to these past nine years?"

He shrugs, turning away from me. I am struck by how grown he looks. I know he is now 22, but he was only 13 when I was taken. I have missed so much with him and Mama and Baba. I take a deep breath, not letting the emotions overwhelm me.

"I work with Baba most days. Usually, have dinner with Jasmin and her people, and then spend time with Tomas." He shrugs casually, but I get the distinct feeling Tomas is anything but casual.

"Who is Tomas?" I wiggle my eyebrows at him. He rolls his eyes at me, shaking his head before fiddling with some invisible fuzz on the couch.

"Tomas is one of the bachelors that came for Jasmin's, er, the Queen's, True Love Edict. He's a natural with the sword and loves being around horses. Queen Jasmin created a position within the guard for him to be a liaison with the stables. He's been accommodating in prepping for all the changes happening."

"It's so weird hearing her called Queen." He nods quietly. She was always meant to be Queen; I just thought I would be along for the process. Sadness creeps through my body at all the time we have lost.

"It's actually about time to head to the dining hall. Want to go with us? Mama and Baba usually eat here by themselves. There are always a lot of people in the dining hall." As much as I would love to spend more time with my parents, I'm not passing up any opportunity to get closer to Jasmin. She just needs to remember how good things were with me. I jump off the couch, rushing toward the door.

"Yes! Let's go."

I tear the door open, not waiting for Zander. Who needs him when my girl is on her way to dinner?

"D!" Zander calls behind me. "You need shoes!" Oh, right.

I race back, grabbing my shoes. I walk with my brother, looping my arm through his. He tells me about something that happened in the stables today. I listen absentmindedly, observing the art in the hallways. It's a vast difference from our quarters before the curse. Before, the castle walls were dark, with giant portraits of old, fat men or dark curtains. Sometimes a tiny sconce would be lit, but cobwebs were more common. Now there are bright, colorful paintings of flowers and landscapes. Windows have been uncovered, letting natural light in. The halls feel warm in the sunlight. Jasmin has done a lot to improve my family's quality of life. I make a note to thank her, preferably while we're naked, but I won't push that. Yet.

In the dining hall, people are crowding all around. There is a long table near the center where the guard and witch sit, chatting animatedly. An older boy with tanned skin and brown hair sits beside them, listening but not joining the discussion. Dozens of people are crowding into other seats. I spot Jasmin walking away from the food, heading toward the table with the three men. Clem is still at the food table with an older woman and a young girl that looks to be his family. I grab a half loaf of bread and fruit and rush toward the table to sit beside Jasmin. Emmeline is moving like she will sit next to her, but I walk faster, sliding into the seat before she gets there.

"Oh, Dahlia! I didn't see you in here." Emmeline sits next to me, giving a quick, shy smile to the witch across from me. It's a fascinating, not entirely innocent, look that I will definitely raise questions about later. Before I can do that, Jasmin sits down next to me.

"Hi, Dahlia! I didn't know you were joining us. I thought you'd be with Sunette." Her beaming smile is so enchanting it takes my breath away. Forcing air into my lungs again, I manage to reply to her.

"And miss time with my favorite girl? Never." I wink at her, nudging her shoulder playfully. Clem walks over, setting his food down to take the spot on the other side of Jasmin. Before he does, the young girl standing with him barges in and sits beside Jasmin. She squeals Jasmin's name, throwing her arms around her. Jasmin returns the hug, asking the girl how she has been. The girl starts rambling as Clem sighs, sitting beside the girl. The older woman, who must be his mother, sits on his other side. Another woman closer to our age takes the seat on the side of the guard. Finally, Zander walks over, sitting suspiciously close to the older boy beside the witch. He leans in and whispers something to him. The moment is so intimate shock freezes my entire body. Who are all these people? I don't recognize any of them.

"Oh, Dahl. You don't know anyone." Jasmin manages to pull my attention back from my brother and this child sitting beside him. She always knows exactly what I am thinking. We are meant to be together.

"You remember Emmeline," she points to my side, where Emmeline sits. I nod, tearing my eyes away to offer her a small smile. "And that's Bea, Clem's sister." I can see some resemblance, but I probably wouldn't have pegged them as siblings. Now that I look at her, I can see how she is a slightly more feminine version of Clem, with a softer jaw and shorter hair.

"This is Erik, Kian, and Tomas." So this is the boy that has my brother enamored? Before I can think on that, Jasmin continues rattling names I don't have much interest in knowing. "Then Mrs. Byrne, Clem's mother. And this is Claire, Clem's other sister. And I can't remember," she turns to face me fully, "have you been introduced to Clem?"

I do everything in my power not to grit my teeth, not wanting to meet him. He is the reason Jas isn't already in my arms. I don't need to officially meet him. She leans back enough that I have a clear view of him. "This is Clem. Clem, this is Dahlia." Jasmin has a hopeful look as she looks between the two of us. Clem turns, wiping his mouth with a cloth napkin before holding his hand to mine. I plaster on a fake smile and take his hand. As I grab his hand, a strange emotion rolls through my body. It's not something I have ever experienced before. Desire like I haven't felt in years floods my body. I strain to hide this feeling from my face, not wanting to give anything away.

Obviously, there is a reason Jasmin is in love with him. Fated or not, she wouldn't willingly tolerate anyone that didn't treat her well. Is there something more to Clem that I have missed? Or just not even considered? I have been so focused on Jasmin; I barely gave a second thought to him. Not that I need to. I just need him out of the way. That is all that matters. Not whatever this feeling is. I pull my hand away, saying it's a pleasure to meet him. As I turn back to my seat, I notice the witch staring at the space around our heads as if he is watching a bug flutter by.

"Did you see that?" He asks, turning his attention to everyone else at the table. Jasmin meets his gaze but doesn't say anything. Everyone else says they didn't see anything. There must be a fly or something in the dining hall. It wouldn't be unheard of. I scan the table, spotting Zander, whose entire side is pressed against Tomas. I misinterpreted their relationship when he first mentioned his friend. I also misjudged his age greatly.

"Wait, Tomas was here as a bachelor for Jasmin?" I give a confused look, and Jasmin gives an exasperated nod.

"Yes. He was the youngest, but not by much." My eyebrows shoot up in surprise.

"How old are you, boy?" If I didn't know better, I would swear my mother just asked that question. Jasmin chuckles beside me, hearing the same thing I did. She smacks my thigh with her hand as Tomas tells me he is 18 now.

"Calm down, Sunette," Jasmin teases. "Tomas is a wonderful man who is very skilled and very close to your brother." Tomas's cheeks stain a bright red at her words. Even Zander's cheeks have a red tint beneath his dark skin.

"Thank you, Your Majesty," he mumbles. Jasmin rips a piece of bread, throwing it at him.

"We are not about to start that shit again, Tomas," she scolds but laughs as he shields himself from the bread. "Kian and Erik were also part of the bachelors. Most returned home after the winter solstice. Oh, one is still in the dungeon." She sips her wine so relaxed that I am angered by how she could be so cavalier. "How is he doing, Erik?"

Erik offers a slight shrug before responding. "About the same. He eats about once a day, rarely bathes. He's entirely miserable. He has started telling anyone near him that he was framed." This statement leads nearly everyone at the table to fall into laughter. Clem's family and I are the only ones not reacting with humor. I'm angry that a man sent to marry Jasmin is in the dungeon, and no one will tell me why. Is it Jackson? Would she laugh like that if it was him? Has she changed that much?

"Who is it? What the fuck did he do?" Erik and Bea flinch at my tone, but everyone stops laughing. Jasmin turns to me, her face stoic.

"Do you remember the Morrin's from Tilrade?" I shake my head. I don't remember the Lords' names from the villages. Why would I remember some shitty family? "It was their son. His name is Oscar. He is in the dungeon now because he attacked Tomas." Tomas lifts his shirt sleeve, showing me a thick scar across his bicep. It's healed but still red, indicating it is recent.

"He tried to cut my arm off." An air of melancholy settles around the group. Some people sip wine while others nibble on their food. Tomas lowers his sleeve as Zander stares at him with worry and fear in his eyes. This was an impactful event for them all. Clem is the one to break the silence.

"Erik planned a sparring contest. He trained many of the bachelors as an activity to spend time with Jasmin." Out of all the activities planned for that True Love Edict, I know, without a doubt, Jasmin was the one that forced that event. A knowing smile spreads across my face as I look at her. She is still focused on her food, either reliving the events or trying not to. Clem continues the story. "Erik and Tomas were in the second to last battle. Oscar would face off with the winner for a chance to have a private dinner with Jasmin. Tomas was very close to winning when Oscar attacked him with a sword. Luck was the only reason Oscar made it as far as he did in the competition. He nearly maimed Tomas." Clem pauses, shaking his head. Tomas rubs his arm as Zander strokes his back. It will take some time to get used to whatever their relationship is.

"The best part, though," Clem continues, "is Oscar wouldn't drop the sword. So Jasmin grabbed a mace and smashed his hand to bits. I think they got it back together, but he'll never use that hand again." He chuckles after he stops speaking. Erik nods in agreement, having been in contact with the prisoner more recently. I imagine Jasmin with a mace beating some guy with a sword. She always loved the mace more than the sword. While the blade is effective, there is nothing quite as satisfying as hearing the crunch. Not that I would know that.

I drape my arm over her shoulders, laughing against her skin as I picture her in the training ring. "Oh my gods, Jas. I love that you did that." She pats my arm gently with her hand as she laughs weakly with me. I take a deep breath, breathing in her scent, the floral smell of her hair, the scent of her skin. I lean away from her, not wanting to raise suspicions in front of this many people, especially so many that are close to Clem.

We sit back, returning to our food. Dinner passes quickly. I press my thigh against Jasmin's, making contact with her. She pulls away at first but slowly returns her leg to touch mine. The touch isn't enough, but knowing she wants it too is comforting. After I finish the measly food I grabbed for my dinner, I drop my hand on my thigh, letting my fingers rest against Jasmin's thigh. Again, she doesn't react; I'm taking that as a win. The group gets along well, chatting and laughing about various topics.

After a while, Clem's mother takes his younger sister, and they retire to their bedroom. Everyone else remains at the table. Zander and Tomas are huddled together, whispering gods only know what. Erik and Bea also chat quietly, but not quite as intimately as my brother and his "friend." Clem shifts closer to Jasmin, causing her to pull away from me just enough that I am not in contact with her anymore. She leans against his shoulder as jealousy burns through my body.

"Clem, no one has told me how you managed to be the oldest bachelor. Why aren't you already married?" Erik visibly flinches at the question. Clem only looks at me, unimpressed with my question.

"The same reason Jasmin isn't." He kisses the top of her head as she pats his leg. I dig my fingernails into my thigh, needing the pain to distract me from the anger.

"Oh, you were cursed and had to find your true love to break it?" He will not get the upper hand on me.

"No, though that would be a better answer. No one ever made me feel the way she does and I didn't want to be married to someone just because it was what we were told to do." Jasmin looks up at him with these eyes that basically have hearts and kisses flowing out of them. Eros would be disgusted with her look too. But dammit, if his answer wasn't a good one. He bends, kissing her sweetly. I have to look away, taking a large gulp of wine. I realize this was actually Jasmin's goblet, not mine.

"Well, she is easy to love. I'm going to get more wine." I walk toward the table with the food, looking for a decanter, trying to forget his lips against hers. Zander walks up beside me, grabs a decanter from the back, and passes it to me.

"You should give him a chance, D. He is good for her." He shrugs as I snatch the decanter, filling it from the cask of wine.

"Fuck off, little brother." He just laughs at me, walking away. He grabs Tomas, bidding farewell to everyone before they leave the room, hand in hand. When I return, I place the decanter in the middle, refilling mine and Jasmin's goblets. Emmeline switched to the other side of the table beside Kian, and Erik and Bea slid closer to them. Now they are directly across from me, creating a smaller group of friends. It strikes me how Jasmin now has a group of people she can call her own. This is something she never had before. It is one of the reasons I was so important to her. She needed her own people that her parents didn't choose for her. Even though I don't want to admit that, they seem like good people with her best interests, including Clem.

Erik and Kian debate a scenario about a warrior and a witch in battle. The way the others groan when they start the discussion informs me this isn't a new conversation for them. I listen apathetically, uninvested in the outcome of this conversation. Soon, a great white beast comes barreling into the dining hall, headed straight toward us. I yell, trying to scare it away and throw my arms out to prevent it from getting to Jasmin. The great animal dives under the bench at the last minute, circumventing my position. Next to me, Jasmin is laughing as she reaches under the table, rubbing the enormous head. I stare in confused outrage.

"Dahlia," she says between chuckles, "this is Finn. He's my dog."

"That is not a dog."

"Tell me about it," Clem replies. I give him a wary look, glancing back at the "dog" under the table. The animal is easily as large as Jasmin. What in heavens is she doing with such a giant beast?

"Does he protect you?" I question why he is in here now.

"No," Clem responds sardonically.

"Yes, he does! He took you out when you first waltzed into the castle."

"Okay, but he was after food, not attacking."

"That's not relevant. Finn still put you on your ass." Jasmin looks down at the dog and speaks childishly to him. "Yes, you did, didn't you? You protected me from him, huh? Do you need some food?" As Jasmin grabs bread from the table, Kian and Emmeline jerk their feet away from the dog's wagging tail. I am still unsure about this beast, but if he took out Clem, he is a friend of mine now. I grab another loaf of bread from the table, tearing off bites to give him. Clem sighs loudly, looking between Jasmin, Finn, and me.

"He already weighs too much. Stop feeding him." He snatches the bread from Jasmin, tossing it on the table. She huffs at him, crossing her arms in false outrage. So I drop my half loaf on the floor, letting Finn claim the whole thing. "Oops," I shrug as the dog inhales the bread. The others laugh over the interaction. Jasmin gives me a genuine smile, and my insides warm. Her smile is one of the best things about her, followed closely by her amazing cunt and tits. I'll get those soon enough.

Chapter 6

JASMIN

I relax into the deep tub, closing my eyes, letting the warmth consume me. Clem and I have been in and out of meetings all week. Despite our irregular schedule, Dahlia always seems to show up at the right moment to steal some time with me. Even after all the time apart and everything that has happened, I still have strong feelings for her. I can't deny that forever. She must be aware of that, too. I have tried, gods, how I have tried to keep her away. I don't want to hurt Clem, but he certainly will be if he realizes what she is up to. Either he is oblivious or doesn't actually care. I don't believe it is that last part. He was too jealous of Kian. Hell, he's even jealous of Finn at times.

Dahlia, though. She is everything I remember her being. She is strong and brash and beautiful. Oh, she's so beautiful. Her skin is the smoothest brown, still as delicately soft as I remember. Her warmth is encompassing, different than Clem's, but so welcome. This leads me to wonder if other things are the same. She always knew exactly where to touch me to light my body up. Her fingers would caress my clit, glide over my slit, and I'd be soaked, similar to this moment. I drag my fingers in the same manner, disappointed by the difference in feeling. I should have brought the magic fun ball. I've been aroused nonstop since she returned. That's unfair to Clem; I'm always ready for action lately.

Honestly, I would give anything to have both of them taking my pleasure, demanding more, touching more, claiming more. My deepest, most secret desire comes to mind as my body fills with heat not caused by the warm bath. I slowly circle my clit as I imagine Dahlia's fingers touching me. She would massage my clit, dipping one finger, then two deep inside me. Stroking that rough spot that causes lightning to flash in my eyes. My fingers find it, but I don't have the same effect as her. While it feels good, there is no lightning now. While Dahlia tends to my cunt, Clem would fuck my throat, making me gag around his hard length. I bite my tongue, unable to mimic that feeling alone but still wanting some oral pain. I shut my eyes tight, envisioning them forcing me to submit to their desires. Dahlia's tongue stroking across my opening as my eyes water at the forcefulness of the cock in my mouth.

I would graze my hands through Dahlia's long hair, twisting curls around my fingers as her expert tongue brings me closer. My fingers increase their speed inside me, massaging my clit harder. I would grab Clem's thigh, feeling his course hair in my fingers, different and thinner than Dahlia's in my other hand but offering the same comfort.

"Open your mouth." I jerk up, screaming a long string of obscenities.

Clem stands over me, stroking his cock as he looks down at me. As my heartbeat thunders in my chest, I take a couple of deep breaths.

"What the fuck, Clem?"

"I said, 'open your mouth.'" He doesn't stop stroking himself as he lowers his body until his cock is in front of my face. I look between his cock and his eyes as my irregular heartbeat changes from fear to arousal.

"What were you thinking about?"

"This." The half-lie is easy to tell. I open my mouth, letting my tongue drop down against my chin. He gets a crooked smirk as he slaps the head of his cock against my outstretched tongue. He slides his dick in, gliding effortlessly into my mouth. I wrap my lips around him, swirling over the sides. I let my eyes close as my fingers find my clit again. I pretend it is still Dahlia touching instead of me. He may be in my mouth but doesn't know what I envision.

He slowly fucks my face, not the rough brutal pace I am used to. Despite his change to my imagined pace, I still groan with pleasure as my orgasm draws close. My free hand is on his thigh, scraping my nails across his skin. He grunts, pushing deeper into the back of my throat but still going slow. When he pushes back in, I gag, my orgasm tearing through me. My back arches, sending me soaring toward him. I swallow him further down as my body convulses. He explodes simultaneously, his warm release hitting the back of my throat. I moan, wanting to suck him but unable to control my body now.

"Lick it clean." His voice is caught somewhere between his demanding voice and his regular voice. I meet his eyes, bringing my hand from his thigh to his cock. I hold it still while I lick around the head, removing all fluids. He groans, eyes rolling back in his head. I kiss his cock as he shudders, sinking into the bath beside me. His lips find mine in a tender but deep kiss. He breaks the kiss to pull me against his body, holding me close. I love the feeling of being in his arms.

"Were you really thinking about me fucking your throat earlier?" he questions.

"Yes." I press a small kiss on his jaw. His fingers stroke up and down my arm.

"You looked so intense." He grabs the soap, washing my arms. "What do you have to do today?"

"I'm planning to help Kian with some of the research for the curse," I tell him. "What are you doing?"

"Lord David wants me to get more court training in. He's taking full advantage of our delay to the wedding." He rolls his eyes, a movement he has picked up from me. I smile, realizing the effect I have on him. He slowly washes my back, caressing my skin gently. Clem is wonderful to me, even if he has picked up some of my less-than-royal mannerisms.

"Hopefully, Kian will find some answers today, and we can set the date again," I offer. I take the soap from him, turning to wash his body. One hand with the soap caresses his skin as the other follows smoothly behind it. I want to set a date for our wedding, but I don't want to get his hopes up or put too much pressure on Kian. I will always love Clem, and no ceremony will ever change that.

"Ma is planning to leave tomorrow." His words are laced with sadness. His family means a lot to him, and he is still adjusting to not having them here constantly. He misses his mother and Claire a lot, and I'm sure he doesn't want to miss Claire growing up. We've asked Ada to stay, but she always says she would rather be at home. It's understandable, but I wish we could change her mind. We've offered her housing, schooling for Claire, and even jobs, but she won't take any of it.

"I want to offer Bea a position in the barn. She is so good with animals. Plus, Erik is very fond of her," I say casually, despite my doubts. I have been thinking about that for a while, just haven't officially offered her the job. He chuckles as I return the soap, relaxing against him to enjoy the last few minutes we have together like this. "Will she stay without your mother?" He shrugs, wrapping his arms around me.

"I don't know. She clearly has feelings for Erik, but I don't know if that's enough to keep her here." He is lost in thought, considering what it would take to keep his eldest sister close.

"Do you think she would stay if you asked?" I question, an idea I have been toying with recently.

"I can talk to her. It might be helpful if you ask, though." I nod, telling him to let me know what will be best. Emmeline bangs on the door, demanding we get out without any funny business. I get up, but Clem tugs me back, whispering. "Speaking of people with hidden feelings. I'm pretty sure she and Kian have something going on." I gasp, spinning to look at him. He can't be serious about that, can he? He raises his eyebrows in a slight nod but shrugs his shoulders again. He climbs out, grabbing two towels for us, leaving me questioning everything I know about my best friend. Surely she would say something if she were dating my favorite advisor. Would she keep it a secret out of fear of my reaction? She knows me better than that, I hope.

He dries off, wrapping the towel around his waist. The contrast of his muscles against the fluffy softness of the towel sends an ache through my stomach. He genuinely is such a beautiful man. Clem exits the bathroom as Emmeline sneaks in, trying not to look at him. I snicker at her modesty. She's seen all of Clem at this point, and there is no need to hide that fact. But Emmeline still shields her eyes when he walks around in partial dress.

"Are you planning to help Kian today?" I question, watching her reaction to his name. I don't notice any change in her body, but it's probably too subtle.

"I wasn't planning on it, but I can if you think it will help."

"Do you think it will help?"

"What?" She turns her head, giving me a curious look.

"What?" I retort, unsure what to actually say. Can I ask her if something is going on? Of course, I can. I am Queen; after all, that has some privileges attached to the position. I don't want to do that to her, though. I can watch her with Kian. Yes, that is a better course of action. "I do think it will help." I don't think I have ever said anything more awkward in my life. That sentence sounded so forced that it's painful now. There is literally an ache in my chest over how terrible that sounded. Thankfully, Emmeline laughs, bringing my clothes over to help me dress.

Clem has already left to attend his meetings. I wish we had more time together. We steal quick moments throughout the day and have the evenings together. After spending weeks in our room, followed by all the time on the road, I've become accustomed to being with him all day. Emmeline and I pad to the library, where Kian awaits us. Unsurprisingly, Dahlia is waiting outside the hallway to my room, and I invite her to help us. I don't know what Kian has discovered, but surely more people will be helpful.

In the library, Kian already has several texts pulled out. He is intensely focused on one when we walk in. Emmeline walks through the shelves, looking at other titles. I sit at the table, with Dahlia sitting beside me. Her chair scrapes as she sits down, drawing Kian's attention from his texts.

"I brought extra help," I offer, motioning to Dahlia and Emmeline behind him. He smiles at Emmeline briefly, then turns back to Dahlia. His expression changes faster than I can process what his looks mean. I can't tell if his smile was anything other than kind toward Emmeline.

"Oh, good. I want to ask Dahlia a few questions. And I want to see the room where she was kept soon." I cringe at his choice of words. He means well, but it's still an awkward situation. He asks her questions to determine if her curse is different from mine. From the sounds of it, she was cursed separately, but my curse definitely impacted hers. They chat for several minutes while I flip through one of the books Kian has on the table. I don't know what I am looking for, but nothing catches my eye. After several more questions, he walks back through the shelves near Emmeline. They are out of our view, just between some of the rows.

"I was hoping to get a moment alone with you," Dahlia whispers in my ear as her fingers caress my arm. My eyes close, savoring her words, her touch, her closeness. I need to let it go. Clem is my true love. Dahlia will always have a place in my heart, but she can't continue taking up as much of my space as she has been.

"Dahlia," I turn toward her, but her lips catch my cheek. Her warm lips press against my skin. My closed eyes tighten as I bite my lip, fighting the urge to turn the rest of the way to kiss her. I place my hand on hers, finally finding the will to pull away from her. "We can't have moments alone," I whisper sadly to her. She doesn't pull away, just stays where she is. Emmeline and Kian's voices grow louder as they return to the table. Dahlia leans away, and I focus my efforts on Emmeline. She seems comfortable, but not in an unusual way.

"I think Dahlia wasn't included in your curse," Kian starts, placing a thick book on the table before us. "This is good and bad news, though." I give him a curious look, waiting for him to elaborate. He flips through the book, searching for a particular page. "Due to the depth and detail of this curse, the witch has to be one of the most powerful. That's the bad part," he says, looking up from the text he is pointing at. I see a list of witches with a ranking next to them. "There are only two witches in our kingdom that possibly could have pulled this off, but there is no motive, and they have suffered from the effects. Why would anyone curse their own kingdom and remain in it? Whoever cursed you likely left before the border set in. So it's a witch we don't know." I nod, understanding what he is trying to say. I've spent the past nine years trying to figure out who would hate me enough to put this curse in place.

"And what is the good news in Dahlia having her own curse?"

"If it's the same kind of magic, which I think it might be, it could be the same person who cursed you both. It's not much, but it may help narrow down who would want to do this."

"Your mother," Dahlia snorts, answering a question that hasn't been asked.

"Yes, but she died before my curse." I snap back at her. I've made my peace with my mother being dead, but that doesn't mean there aren't still sore feelings concerning her. Dahlia has the decency to look regretful over her comment.

"Could it have been a man?" She asks, turning the attention away from the sore subject. Kian shrugs. There has been a lot of shrugging happening lately, and I wish there were more solid answers to all of these questions. Even if some questions were easier to answer, that would be great.

"We don't have any records of men being that powerful, but I suppose it could happen."

"Possibly a prominent family? Someone stuck up your mother's ass. There were plenty of them around." I nod absentmindedly. I hate trying to think of who it could be, and it always means focusing on people that hate me and want me to suffer. That isn't something I want to spend my time considering.

"I've been searching for similar spells but can't find anything even remotely as detailed as this curse. With the true love and now Dahlia, I can't even comprehend what this curse was meant to do anymore." Kian rubs his forehead, trying to piece together a puzzle.

"It was all just to hurt me," I speak dismally. "I would find my true love only to have Dahlia return, my first love. Its only purpose is my pain. I need to just marry Clem and break the curse." I stand, feeling a deep ache, unsatisfied with this conversation.

"I don't think it's as simple as that. If it were, why would she be freed before the curse ends?" He raises a good point. He holds a finger up, indicating he has an idea. He requests Emmeline's help, and they disappear from the shelves again, moving further away than last time based on the sounds of their voices. Dahlia walks over, hugging me tightly against her.

"I'm not just here to hurt you, Jas." Part of me knows that, but a voice tells me the curse's only purpose is to hurt me. It's hard to silence those words. "You are mine, no matter what fate has decided. Some part of fate released me before you married Clem. I'm here for you now." Her lips find my cheek again. This time I welcome her comforting touch. I close my eyes, settling into her embrace. I love being in Dahlia's arms. The way she holds me shows me she will always be with me. She will always do her best to keep me safe, but most importantly, she will always love me.

"You see this, right?" My eyes shoot open as Kian and Emmeline walk to stand in front of us. Tiny bursts of lightning are popping across the space around Dahlia and me. It looks similar to what happened at the wedding but smaller and more isolated. During the ceremony, lightning burst throughout the entire throne room. Here, they only occur within a few inches of Dahlia and me. She lets me go as the lightning stops. Before anyone can say anything, Zander walks into the library.

"Um, Queen, ma'am?" He calls out in a very awkward manner. I chuckle, pulling away from Dahlia to walk over to the railing around the upper level.

"It's just us, Zander. What do you need?"

"Mama is looking for Dahlia. Wants her to come back to our home." Dahlia sighs, walking over to kiss my cheek. "She's always sticking her nose into something. I'll see you later, Jas." She squeezes my arm as she walks down the stairs and out of the library with Zander. The longing for her to return strikes me. It's similar to finding my room empty when Clem left this morning. This time last year, I wanted nothing more than to be alone. Now I'm sad when my people leave the room. What is happening to me?

Kian is sitting at the table, reading over some text. Emmeline has disappeared between shelves again, looking for gods only know what. I sit across from him, trying to read the text. It was handwritten and hard to read upside down. I give up, settling back in my chair, waiting for something to happen.

"Here it is," Kian points to the page as he reads. "Certain incantations have been known to have a visual and auditory effect upon completion. These incantations are usually accompanied by an offering to the gods, thus eliciting their magic." He pauses, thinking for a moment before pressing on. "These spells are often hard to break and are harder to properly execute. Though, very powerful and effective when done correctly. The wording of these incantations is particularly important as many words have double meanings that can be interpreted in many different ways." He looks up at me. "Is the curse the hag recited written anywhere?" I shake my head. I could never remember the whole thing. As far as I know, neither could anyone else. "Can I borrow the flower to listen to the curse again?" I nod, torn between focusing on or ignoring the memory of the old hag that night she burst into the castle.

"The lightning, is that part of the incantation?" I question as he scratches his head, gazing over the text again.

"If it is, that means Dahlia is involved in breaking the curse. We've assumed the thunder was due to Clem being your true love. Maybe there is more to Dahlia's return than we realize." I sigh, exhausted already. "I would like to see her room soon. And," he pauses, meeting my tired gaze. He lowers his voice just above a whisper, "You need to talk to Clem." My eyebrows furrow in confusion. Kian gives me a pointed look, then glances toward the door Dahlia just recently passed through. Frustrated over this situation, I blow a hard breath out of my lips. He is right; Clem deserves to know what Dahlia is up to. It's obvious she is trying to win me over again. I won't give up on Clem, but I'm not strong enough to always say no.

"You're right. I will, Kian. Just give me time." He nods, not pushing me any further. That is one of the reasons I like to keep him around. He knows how to urge me to do the right thing without pushing too far. He is easily one of my favorite advisors. I need to be sure he stays with me. Emmeline passes behind him, going from one aisle to the next. A woman might be an extra incentive to keep him around.

"Emmeline is pretty helpful, hm?" I'm changing my title to Queen of Awkwardness today. Kian just hums and nods, not looking up at me. "Okay, well." I stand, preparing to leave. "I'm going to the wine cellar to drink today away.

Tomorrow is our meeting about the border with the Lords. Let's plan to go to the tower sometime next week. Come get that flower whenever you want it. Keep Emmeline as long as you need her." I give a half-hearted wave as I walk down the stairs to the library's main level.

I want answers about this curse. I want to know why Dahlia is here and how to break down the border, and how to just be fucking happy. I also need time to recover and process everything that has happened. I was so withdrawn after the curse began. I could not process my feelings and emotions around everything that it affected. Years of my life were wasted, drowning in a sea of despair and self-deprecation. I cannot risk doing that to myself again. I need more time to understand things, to feel my feelings. Waiting until next week to visit her room will allow me to reconcile that she was trapped above me for nine years, and I never looked there. Facing that reality is no simple task.

Finn and Clem are in their favorite alcove. Clem is reading while Finn is napping on the floor. I step over, pressing a kiss to his forehead, but whisper I'll see him later, not wanting to disturb his reading. He shakes his head, pocketing his book before signing it on the ledger. Together with Finn by our side, we make our way to raid the wine cellar. The rest of the night is spent drinking our body weight in wine, laughing, relaxing, and naturally, fucking.

Chapter 7

CLEM

The weight of everything happening is taking a toll on Jasmin. She has been tired and more removed than usual. We spent half the night drinking wine then she did a very sloppy job of sucking my dick before passing out. I am surprised to learn that I enjoy said sloppy sucking. I would certainly not say no to that next time. She is still sleeping, sprawled out on the bed. Finn slept on the floor last night because of Jasmin's fitful slumber. It's undoubtedly bad if Finn won't even stay in bed.

Emmeline strolls in, walking toward the window to pull the curtains open to let the bright morning sun tear through the room. I lunge to stop her, catching her before the light hits the bed. She squeals at my sudden movement, causing Jasmin to groan from her spot on the bed. My attempt to prevent the light from waking her was undone by Emmeline's squeal. Jasmin gags, rolling over. I bring her a bowl and a cool, wet cloth. She mumbles about how much she drank last night as Emmeline clears the bottles. I shift to get dressed when she leaves the room, not wanting to upset her again. I wonder at what point she will stop being concerned by my nakedness.

Jasmin slowly begins moving around the room. She walks to one chair and plops down, moaning, then shuffles to another, doing the same thing again. I chuckle at her hung-over antics, knowing she brought it on herself. Emmeline finally returns with some bread and tea, helping Jasmin get dressed. Finn and I saunter down for a walk, giving them time to prepare. Erik is heading toward the dining hall, and I call out to him. I catch up with him, but he looks upset. I inquire about his mood, but he just waves me off. He asks if I'm eating, but I tell him I just came to let Finn out and will head back to Jasmin before the meeting. He just nods sullenly and walks into the dining hall. Erik is rarely upset. Is something going around the castle, or is everyone under untold amounts of stress?

I spot Bea in a small alcove with her back to me. I walk up, patting her back as I greet her. She doesn't turn toward me, and I realize her hands cover her face. She sniffles behind her hands, and I hug her. She shudders under my arms. Bea has never been one to cry. I can count on one hand the number of times I have seen her cry, the most recent being when our father died nine years ago.

"Bea, what's wrong?"

"I'm going home today." Oh, now Erik's sullen attitude makes sense, too.

"Why?" She has a job here. She has me and Erik, and Finn. I'm sure she could make other friends too. What more could she possibly need?

"Ma needs help. I promised Ferd. And Erik…" She inhales a deep stuttering breath, trying to return to normal. I'm going to kill him if he told her to leave.

"What the fuck did Erik say?" She pushes away from me, wiping her eyes on her sleeves. I grab a handkerchief from my pocket, always carrying one now for all these crazy situations I seem to end up in with someone crying. She takes it, wiping her cheeks.

"He didn't say anything. Just wished me well." I shake my head, gritting my teeth in anger. Why wouldn't he tell her he wants her to stay? It's clearly true that they both want to be together.

"He's an idiot. I'll talk to him. I assure you he wants you here as much as I do. You can't leave, Bea." My voice changes from anger toward Erik to pleading to keep her. "Ma doesn't need you. She took care of all three of us. She can manage Claire on her own. Besides, if you're here, that's more reason for Ma to stay here too. And Ferd will be fine without you. Please stay, Bea."

"Ferd's already lost you. He can't afford to lose me too."

"Yes, he can, Bea." I shake my head, walking away from her. "I'm going to talk to Erik and Jasmin. You're staying here!" I yell the last bit as I near the doorway. If I honestly thought Bea didn't want to stay, I wouldn't fight so hard, but I know she does. She loves the animals here, Finn, and all the others that are solely in her charge. Plus, I'm here, and I'm a pretty spectacular brother. I guess Erik is a good reason for her to stay too. I spot him at the table, sitting quietly with Kian and Emmeline. Seriously, why is everyone being so morose?

I plop down next to Emmeline, across from Kian and Erik. He looks up at me with skepticism in his eyes. Before he can talk, I speak up.

"You need to tell my sister you want to fucking keep her here." His eyes go wide as I realize how my words came across. Kian snickers next to Erik while Emmeline blushes at my side. Erik looks embarrassed, as he always does when we discuss my sister. "She's leaving because you just wished her well. Go fight for her, mate. Don't let her leave. We all know you two are up to something. Don't let that go." Erik doesn't seem convinced but doesn't argue with me either. Maybe there is still hope. Emmeline asks if I will check on Jasmin or if she needs to. I tell her I will, but she has to convince Erik to make Bea stay with him. She just chuckles as I rise to leave.

Bea is walking in as I am heading out the door. She holds the handkerchief out for me to take back. I smack her shoulder, telling her she doesn't need to worry about packing. She just stares at me as I leave the large room behind me. Erik can deal with her now. They are both being ridiculous, and I know a thing or two about being ridiculous in the face of love. I'm kind of an expert in that area. I try to suppress all the awkward memories of my and Jasmin's relationship trying to make their way to the forefront of my brain.

I finally reach our room, where she is moaning on the couch. I laugh at her, shaking my head. We spend several minutes sitting and cuddling while I try to force more bread into her. This meeting will be challenging; she needs to be alert, not sick and tired. She finishes the tea and bread before we go to the meeting room.

Once everyone is seated, I request the butler bring two mugs of tea for us, realizing I forgot to eat and drink myself in all the activity. Jasmin begins by asking for updates from the villages. No one has any, which would typically be a good response, but Jasmin is staring daggers at Alwyn. We still haven't heard any update on why the covens left as quickly as they did. She inhales deeply, gathering herself for whatever response she has been preparing. We knew it would come to this.

"Kian, how are the covens?"

"They are recovering. There was some structural damage, though no one was seriously injured. They are working to rebuild now."

"Thank you. Alwyn, after this meeting, you are to ride straight to the coven grounds. Assess the damage, offer financial support to cover repairs, support affected people, and provide anything else they may need."

"Your Majesty, will you be sending royal coin?"

"No, I will not. The funds will come from Greynon. All village budgets include allocations for such events. The covens are part of your village." Alwyn grumbles but has the mind to not argue with her any further. That is a wise decision today. I don't think he would last the rest of the meeting if he tried to argue.

"Henry, what is the update on the border?" She sighs, sipping her tea while resting her hands on the table. This informal position isn't one we see from her in these meetings frequently. She tends to stay true to the court protocol. It's a testament to her state of mind that she does not want to be here at all.

Henry goes into detail about the borders. Spots along Arkaley and those closest to the castle are waning, showing signs that they will open sooner rather than later. I watch Jasmin remain stoic, listening intently but not visibly reacting to this information. I reach out, taking her hand in mine, squeezing gently. She turns to me as Henry explains there will be constant patrols around our border, with an increasing number in the coming weeks, depending on several weakening spots. I bring her hand to my lips, kissing her gently. We are breaking the curse. It's closer than it has been in years. There could be holes within a week or so. I can't help the smile that spreads across my face, realizing what this means for us. I didn't need more confirmation that she is mine, but I won't deny it either. Before I can devolve into elated giggles, she turns back to Henry.

"Thank you. I want updates on any holes forming. I don't want this information to leave this room for now. We don't need more people going to the border and wreaking havoc." She squeezes my hand, referencing when I went to the border with friends when it first fell into place. Unlike some other groups that went, we didn't wreak havoc. One kid in a different group died because of how volatile and unpredictable the border was in the early days of the curse.

The meeting wraps up with a few more boring points. Once adjourned, Erik rushes out of the room, followed by the Lords. They don't stick around as long as they used to anymore. They got away with whatever they wanted before the True Love Edict. Jasmin isn't tolerating as much bullshit, and they aren't happy. The room clears out, but Jasmin is still standing at her spot. I step up, wrapping my arm around her shoulders. I pull her in, kissing her forehead.

"We're doing it, Jas. You're ending the curse."

She wraps her arms around my back, lifting her head so her chin is propped on my chest. I kiss her nose delicately, feeling so much joy now. She doesn't seem to have the same feelings as I do, but I'm sure she's just stressed by this situation.

"Hey, let's go outside. We'll have a picnic, play with Finn, and enjoy the warm weather. We haven't done that in a while." A small smile creeps across her face as she nods, pulling away from me to leave the room. I snort at her, tightening my arm around her shoulders. "Not that quick, ma'am." I tease, planting a passionate kiss on her lips before she can respond. She melts into the kiss, moaning gently as I engulf her completely in my arms. I trace my tongue across her lips, requesting permission to taste her. Just as her lips part, my stomach grumbles loudly. She breaks the kiss, pulling away. My stomach tightens with hunger, but I'd rather keep kissing her.

"Clem, did you eat today?" I shrug, shaking my head.

"I may have forgotten between you and Bea and the border." She smacks my chest, pushing away from me. I wrap my arm around her as I walk by her side. I don't want to give up kissing her, but my stomach loudly demands food. Near the kitchen, I spot Dahlia, who now has braids in her hair instead of the natural style she has worn for the past few days. I call out to her, motioning her over. Jasmin watches stoically, not indicating how she feels about seeing her friend. I invite her to lunch with us, and she excitedly agrees. I also invite Erik, Bea, and Claire, finding them all in the dining hall. We work together to gather enough food for all of us to eat. Jasmin wanders off, searching for a large blanket, while Claire fetches Finn and some of his favorite toys.

Soon, we all meet under the trees that overlook the castle. Claire is already chasing Finn around the grassy area, wearing him out before we settle in to eat. Jasmin spreads out two large blankets, so we have plenty of room. The weather is warm and sunny, perfect for a mid-spring picnic. Erik and Bea are still tense near each other, but they are clearly trying not to let that interfere with our picnic. I had hoped Bea would change her mind, but it doesn't appear she has.

We pile on the blankets, sharing bread, dried meats, and fruits. Finn soon collapses on the edge of the blanket, dozing like the lazy dog he is. Bea fiddles with fuzz between her and Erik, not acknowledging him but staying close. I rest against the tree while Claire sits beside me, resting against my arm. I'm going to miss seeing her every day. I wrap my arm around my younger sister, enjoying the contact while I still can. Jasmin lays down by my side, her hand resting on my knee while her other hand tucks behind her head. Dahlia lays beside her, oddly close, but it doesn't really phase me.

Ma steps out of the castle, calling for Claire and Bea. They have to finish packing before they leave, and there isn't much time until they do. As Bea leaves, Erik looks like he will follow her but doesn't. I tell him to go after her, if for no reason other than to enjoy the last bit of time. I offer to clean everything up as he finally rises, chasing after my older sister. It's odd to see him literally chasing her and encouraging it, but they are so good together. They deserve each other.

Jasmin rolls onto her side, cuddling against my leg. Her arms grip my leg tightly, leaving Dahlia at her back. Neither woman says anything. There is some weird tension between the two, but this lunch has been friendly, and I want to avoid dragging up their awkward problems. My hand rests on Jasmin's head, stroking her hair.

"Tomorrow, I have my meeting with the heads of gardens from the villages," I speak softly, not wanting to break the calm trance. "Why don't you two go to the pond then? You can reconnect and relax together." Dahlia looks excited at my suggestion, propping up on her side to look at Jasmin. She still holds against my leg, lost in her own thoughts.

"Is it still there? Wait, how do you know about it?" Dahlia looks suspicious now.

"Jasmin took me there when we first met. We think it has something to do with true love." Dahlia sits up, deep in her thoughts, as she processes this information.

"It's possible the language I used to protect it would include you. I don't remember." She shrugs, tapping Jasmin's hip playfully. "Let's do it, Jas. Let's go to the pond tomorrow." Hearing Dahlia call her 'Jas' sends a pang of jealousy through me. Jasmin told me that was what she called her, but she also said I was the only that did it currently. I am used to that being my nickname for her. I suppose it was Dahlia's nickname first, and I don't have any right to be upset about it. It still stings, though.

Jasmin finally nods. "Yes, we can go. That will be nice." I continue stroking my fingers through Jasmin's hair as Dahlia lays back closer to her. She keeps her hand on Jasmin's hip. This also strikes me as odd, but I don't fully process why it would be. We stay silent on the blanket, Finn snoring softly at our feet. After several moments, a cart is pulled to the front of the castle, ready to take my family home. I sigh, brushing hair back from Jasmin's neck. She slowly turns her face up to me, offering a small but sad turn of her lips.

"We should go say goodbye to my family." She nods in response as we rise, gathering everything we brought out. Once packed, Dahlia offers to take everything back inside, allowing us to go straight to my family. I thank her as we head off to meet up with them. They are already in the foyer, loading their bags into the carriage. Erik walks away as we come in, heading back toward the wing where his room is, appearing forlorn and dejected. My shoulders drop, accepting what his demeanor means. I find Ma and walk over to her.

"You can stay, you know? You don't need to leave. There is enough for you to do here."

"Hush now, Clem. We aren't going to interfere with your life." She sighs heavily, "Besides, I can't give up your father's home." I pull her into a hug, knowing my words won't change her mind at this point.

"But, why Bea? She should stay with Erik." Ma nods, looking frustrated as she watches Bea load her bags onto the carriage.

"I know, but she won't listen. Maybe she'll change her mind in a few days." I huff a laugh, hoping that is the case but not believing it. Bea can be incredibly stubborn when she wants to be.

"I'll just issue a decree that she has to return." Ma chuckles, turning to look at me. Her gaze is searching mine, content with what she sees.

"I'm so happy for you, Clem. You look so happy here. I hope this life suits you after the curse is broken." I nod, looking down at her. I have fears and concerns about what happens after the curse is lifted. I still need to improve at most of the court protocols. I hate sitting through the meetings and would much rather be working with my hands somewhere. I am hopeful for tomorrow's meeting, but who knows how well that will go for me.

Claire walks up, inquiring after Finn. "I think he's still out in the grass sleeping. That dog won't wake for hours now that you have run out all of his energy." We laugh as I scoop her into a hug, swinging her around a time or two. I put her back down, leaning to whisper in her ear. "When you get back, go see Ingrid. I may have requested a special piece for a certain sister of mine." Her eyes light up, and she literally bounces with glee. I asked Ingrid to make her a small tiara to wear around since they won't stay at the castle. It's a small consolation for Claire. Bea walks over, giving a quick hug. I start to say something, but she stops me, asking me not to say it. I let it go. She knows what I want to say; there isn't a need to continually repeat the same thing.

Jasmin walks over, tucking into my side as my family climbs into the carriage. The driver guides the horse down the trail, returning them to our home. Their home, now, not mine anymore. I would prefer that they stay longer, but I can understand why they don't. Even when they are here, I rarely get to spend as much time with them as I want. It is easier to feel less guilty about spending all my time with Jasmin when they aren't here anyway. I kiss her, waving to the carriage once more before turning inside. I'll see them again soon. Now that we know I am her true love, I have more freedom to travel through the villages if I choose, not that I have. It's nice to know that I can if I want to.

Chapter 8

Dahlia

She turned away from me yesterday.

The hurt from her actions still burns in my chest today. She turned away from me. I was stroking my fingers over her ribs as we lay on the blankets. Then she rolled over and wrapped herself around Clem's legs. And it fucking hurts.

"You need to let her be, Dahlia." Mama reminds me again, for the umpteenth time. She braided my hair the other day, twisting it into a protective style. She spent half the time telling me I shouldn't be pursuing Jasmin. Then she spent the other half of the time talking about how much Jasmin missed me but is happy with Clem. What am I supposed to do with that information? I roll my eyes at Mama's words. I'm not going to let her be. She is mine. I may change my plan, though. Instead of showering her with my affections, I can take a more subtle approach. Let her see I can be accommodating. Then she will want to be with me again.

Mama walks through the royal gardens, pruning flowers as she sees fit. These gardens are more beautiful than before the curse, and I don't think it is just because Mama is curating them. There is more life and meaning behind every plant and flower and bench. Mama and Jasmin have put effort and love into these gardens, which is evident to anyone who walks through. The pebble path crunches beneath our feet as we pad along. She wants to show me the greenhouse, which I haven't seen since my curse broke.

She pauses, taking a deep breath at the door. I watch with curiosity, wondering what could have my strong mother so flustered. She is never this hesitant about anything. She opens the door, and the smell is overwhelming before I even pass through the threshold. A sweet sensual, but also musky aroma consumes the greenhouse. As I step in, I see jasmine growing around the entire room. The flower has flourished and is taking over nearly every inch of the building. A surprised laugh escapes from me as I look at the different plants. The two original plants that I planted climb on the trellises I built. At least a dozen other plants are scattered, wrapping around garden tools, benches, and door frames. One flower on the plant I started is nearly the size of my palm, which is unbelievable since they don't typically grow that large.

"That plant has been producing the largest flowers of all. That one," Mama points to the bloom cradled in my hands, "is the largest one I have ever seen on any of them." I stroke my thumb over one of the petals, astounded by how pure and white this blossom is. "Two years ago, I had four plants. Your two and two more that I managed to propagate. Now I have all of this." Mama spins, waving her hand at the numerous plants around the room. A joyous laugh sounds from my chest, unable to contain that reaction.

"She is mine, Mama."

I walk around the plants, smelling some, touching others, enthralled by the plants filling the space. If the gods ever wanted to send a sign that I belong with her, it would be this. Allowing my plants to flourish, to thrive, to eclipse all other plants in the garden is all the approval we need. Mama sighs.

"No, baby girl. This is a sign. You have already lost so much by letting her consume your very spirit. Don't let that happen again. I can't lose you a second time." Mama sniffles, the action striking me in the gut. It's so rare to see her upset. I hug her tightly, whispering that I am still here and not leaving.

Jasmin hasn't consumed me, and she wouldn't do anything to hurt me. Not in a life-threatening way. She may hesitate to show me affection because of Clem, but that won't last long. She will see how things should be soon. She walks through the door as if on cue, smiling at my mother and me.

"Have you seen these?" I ask excitedly, waving at all the flowers. She smiles, nodding to me.

"Yes. Your mother has done a phenomenal job growing them." Jasmin gives a soft smile to Mama, then motions back toward the door, indicating we should leave. I kiss Mama's cheek before following Jasmin through the gardens to the road that leads to the pond. Finn is waiting at the edge of the gardens and walks between Jasmin and me.

"I like the braids you have," Jasmin compliments softly. I grin at her.

"Mama insisted they would be better for the upcoming summer." We walk quietly, side by side. The weather is gorgeous today. It is warm with a soft breeze. Bright green leaves rustle in the wind as wildflowers of varying colors shift gently on the ground. A few clouds glide through the sky, covering and uncovering the sun at random intervals. Spring has always been my favorite season. Life, renewal, and return after the hard months all symbolize a fresh start.

We turn at the bright red flower growing along the path, making our way toward the secluded pond. "You should really thank Clem, you know." Jasmin is still speaking softly, which is odd for her. She is ordinarily confident in her words. "He convinced Erik to tag along and allow me out of his sight while we are here. No other guard would be that trusting." I huff a laugh at her.

"Sounds like I should thank Erik then."

"Or both." She retorts testily, causing a huge grin to spread across my face.

"Or just Erik." I tease her, hoping she will play along. I love seeing her feisty side but have not seen it much since I returned. I fully intend to blame Clem for that change but unwillingly admit that maybe it's stress that causes her to be so severe. I peek behind us and notice Erik pacing on the trail we just left. I'm glad he is willing to allow her this space with me, even if Clem is the one who convinced him of it.

Once we reach the clearing, Finn runs off, crashes through the plants, and soars into the pond. The loud splash of water sends Jasmin and me into giggles. She drops the bag on her shoulder, sitting on the large rock we like to lounge on. She removes her shoes and dips her feet in the water. I am mesmerized by how comfortable she is here. I spelled this place to be a safe place for us to get away. It's obvious she has been using this space all this time, and that warms my heart. I want her to have a safe area to hide away when she needs a break. I want her to have everything she could dream of. I would do anything to make her happy.

I sit beside her, remove my shoes, and drop my feet into the water. The water is cool but not too cold, thanks to the magic around it. Finn exits the opposite side of the pond, shaking his fur out. Thankfully, we don't get sprayed with his wet coat. We sit quietly for several minutes, not speaking. I know what I want to say to her, but I don't want to spoil our time together so early. Jasmin is lost in her thoughts. Her brown hair is down, falling softly over her shoulders. The soft sunlight sneaking through the tree branches casts an ethereal glow over her skin. I wish I could see more of her skin. An idea strikes me; I can see more.

I stand, pull my dress off and toss it on the ground. I wore nothing under the dress, knowing I would get in the water eventually. I wrap a long cloth around my braids to keep them out of the water. My breasts are taut with my arms above my head. Jasmin watches with reserved but hungry eyes. I wade into the magically warm water, sinking to a squat position when the water is deep enough. I turn back to face Jasmin. She is still fully clothed but watching me intently. I splash water at her, raising my eyebrows with a smirk.

"Come join me." Somewhere in the distance, Finn barks at something he is chasing. Jasmin glances at him and then turns back to me. She stands, pulling off her shirt. Her breasts are exposed, causing my breath to hitch. She has perfectly round breasts, her soft nipples pebbling at the cool air caressing them now. She bends, sliding her trousers off. My mouth waters as her hands glide the pants over her thighs, down her calves, then her feet pull out, leaving her as naked as I am. My eyes skim her body again but catch on the bruised skin on her abdomen. My first thought is anger, but then I remember I caused that. I am the one who permanently marked her body. Shame washes through me as she glides toward me in the water.

She spreads out, swimming on her stomach as she nears me. I wait, watching her body slice through the water as smoothly as a fish. She is graceful in everything she does. I swallow hard, trying to focus on anything but my deep arousal for her.

"How, um, how often do you come out here?"

Jasmin rolls on her back, closing her eyes as she floats in the water. The sun caresses her face, creating a shimmering effect on her skin. Gods, she is beautiful, breathtaking, stunning. I breathe deeply, needing more oxygen in my body.

"I visited near monthly after the curse. It's been less frequent in the last few years. I've only been once since we signed the True Love Edict." Her hands tread through the water, helping her stay afloat. "Well, twice, but Kian was with us the second time, and we couldn't get in. I didn't realize you limited who could come in here." I nod to her, trying to muster my voice from wherever it hides.

"I didn't want just anyone to get in here. This is your space." She smiles, offering a small thank you. Finn walks over, flopping down on the rock we were sitting on.

"Finn, you better not be on my clothes," Jasmin shouts without even opening her eyes. The dog whines from his spot while Jasmin gives another warning. Finn slinks off the rock and, surprisingly, off Jasmin's clothes. I laugh at how familiar she is with the dog. I ask her about him, and she recounts finding him while riding Vesper. She tells me about all the havoc he creates around the castle, all the locations he is banned from, and how he has even prevented Clem from working. We laugh over how much trouble a single dog can cause, nostalgia coursing through our afternoon.

She continues to float on her back, basking in the warm sun. I am still squatting in the water, watching her. The bruise is more obvious at this angle against the bright blue water and her creamy skin. I glide over smoothly, lifting my fingers slowly. Water drips off my skin, dropping into the pond. Jasmin turns her head, watching me with her stoic expression. I meet her eyes briefly, turning back to look at the scar. "Are you mad at me?" I whisper softly, finally allowing my fingers to touch her skin. It's as soft as it was before. There aren't any scars or any raised attributes of the damaged skin. I trace across the length of the bruise, touching her gingerly. The touch isn't sexual or meant to arouse. My fingers just feel her.

"No, I've come to terms with the consequences. I may never have children, but I don't need them."

"I just didn't want you to have his." My voice is barely above a whisper as pain sears through my chest. I never wanted to take away her ability to have children. Her predicament was unacceptable, but she didn't deserve such a devastating consequence. I would do anything to take that back. Jasmin drops her legs, shifting to an upright position, then turning to face me. A soft, sad smile spreads across her full lips.

"He's dead now." She speaks simply, knowing I will understand what she means. She tells me how Jackson tried to take her on her coronation tour. Clem broke his nose while Erik cut his arm off. Now, I need to thank the two of them for multiple reasons. I try to hide my scowl over owing them gratitude. As much as I hate to admit it, Clem does treat Jasmin well and deserves some praise for that. Not that I will ever admit that out loud.

Jasmin changes her position to stand in front of me. Finn softly snores in the background. Leaves rustle as the wind blows gently through our secluded area. Jasmin's fingers rise to caress my cheek. I close my eyes briefly, savoring the warmth of her touch. I open my eyes slowly to meet her gaze, filled with longing and desire.

"I've missed you so much, Dahl," she whispers, voice hitching on my nickname. Her fingers draw circles around my cheek. She presses just hard enough to make her intentions known. She pulls me closer to her, her eyes focused on my lips. As she nears me, she closes her eyes, but I keep mine open, wanting to see everything. She leans in so close I can feel her breath on my lips. I slide my fingers through the water, finding her hand by her side. I wrap my fingers around her wrist, hoping to encourage her to move the final inch and kiss me.

She is so close; her breasts bump against mine as she breathes. In and out, caress and emptiness. I don't know why she is hesitating. Why hasn't she kissed me? My breathing increases with anticipation. Her eyes are still closed as her eyebrows knit together. She's not going to kiss me. She's going to pull away. Just one kiss. That's all I need right now. I won't ask for more. Just the one kiss.

"Please."

My voice is so soft it's barely audible. Jas opens her eyes, pulling away from me. Tears brim her reddened eyes as she moves toward the rock with her clothes. My heart drops as she climbs out of the pond, water dripping down her body. I take a deep, stuttering breath, feeling every bit as empty as the pond is in her absence. She pulls a large cloth from her bag, drying her body. She puts her shirt on, holding the towel out for me. I approach her, climbing out of the water to dry off. My heart hurts, and I couldn't care less about being dry or clothes. She pulls on her trousers, handing me the thin dress I wore. She sits on the rock, pulling out food from her back. She has sausages, fruits, and cheese. It looks delicious, but I have no appetite now. This isn't what I want. All that I want sits in front of me quietly.

"Do you not want me here?" I hate my voice's desperation, but I can't hide these feelings from her.

"Of course, I want you here, Dahlia. I've wanted nothing more for the past nine years."

"Then what is the problem, Jas? I'm here. Let me love you."

"Dahlia," she scolds, turning to look away. "It's not simple anymore. I can't just be with you. I have a duty. To the kingdom. To Clem." Her voice fades as she tears off a piece of the sausage, throwing it to Finn. He shifts his large head to grab the bite, not rising from the ground. I would laugh if my heart weren't shattering into a million pieces.

"You can be with me. You're Queen. You can do whatever you want. Tell Clem to go work somewhere, and I'll take care of you while he's gone." She rolls her eyes, shaking her head at my statement.

"I'm not doing that. Clem is so good to me." She waves her hands around as if to show what he's done. Anger sears through me because I made this pond. It's quickly followed by the understanding that he helped set up this situation so that she and I could be together. "He deserves someone that will love him with everything. I can't give him half and you half. That isn't fair to anyone."

"But Jas. You deserve to be happy too. If you want to be with me, you deserve that. After everything we have been through," I don't finish my statement. She knows what I mean. She knows my heart like her own, just like I know hers. We are meant to be together; she will see that one day.

"Can we just enjoy our time together as friends?" She asks sadly. I nod, not trusting my voice any longer. I don't want to be friends with her. I want more, but I'll take what she is offering for now. She pulls out a wineskin, takes a long drink then passes it to me. The warm sweetness slides down my throat, warming my stomach. It settles something, but not everything.

"Will you allow me to touch you?" She looks startled, but I quickly add, "In a platonic way?" She nods, giving a soft chuckle. She squeezes my shoulder, taking the wineskin back and taking another drink. She passes it back to me while I watch her. My mind is railing against the desire to claim her and not wanting to force her to do something she doesn't want. I try to reason that there is still hope, but I also understand that I shouldn't feed that hope. "Will you lay with me for a little while?" I ask sheepishly, leaning back against the rock.

We spent many afternoons swimming then napping in each other's arms. There were usually orgasms and kisses involved, but if those aren't possible, I will at least take the other events. Jas soon nods, relaxing against my side, resting her head against my chest. I wrap my arms around her, unable to avoid the closeness. She sighs, relaxing against me. We doze in the warm afternoon sun, leaving most of the food untouched.

She eventually wakes, stating we need to return. We gather all of our things, walking back toward the path. Finn walks ahead of us, heading out of the clearing. Just before we reach the edge of the secluded area, I stop her, pulling her into a hug. I kiss her cheek softly, then whisper in her ear.

"I will always love you. You will always be mine, even if that means only as a friend." She squeezes me back tightly, burying her face in my neck. When she pulls away, she kisses my cheek, continuing on the path. She calls out to Erik, who visibly relaxes. He must have been tense from not being able to see her. I would probably be tense in that situation too. I thank him for being patient and accepting of this unique situation. He simply nods, turning to walk back to the castle. We chat about our afternoon and the nice weather we are having. While it isn't how I wanted the afternoon to go, I am glad I had time alone with Jasmin.

Chapter 9

CLEM

The meeting with the heads of gardens was amazing. I can't believe how well it went. I'm on cloud nine now that it is over. I am trying to return to the room quickly to tell Jasmin. I hope she also had a great day with Dahlia, but I just can't contain my excitement.

In the room, I only find Emmeline and Finn. Emmeline is doing some cleaning, so I dismiss her. On second thought, I ask her to take Finn until after dinner. We can go find him then, but I fully intend to celebrate this victory, no matter how small it is. I wait anxiously for Jasmin to return to our room. I sit on the bed, then move to the chair. I walk to the window, looking out for her. I don't see her, but it's possible she came a different way into the castle. I reorganize my drawers, not that Emmeline will appreciate it, but I need something to do with my hands.

Jasmin walks in by herself. She still looks exhausted but more settled. I don't stop to consider it before my excitement takes over.

"My meeting went amazing." I beam at her, scooping her up in my arms. She drops her bag, draping her arms across my shoulders. I press several quick kisses to her cheek, then sit her down as I pace the room. "I told them what I knew about gardening and my experience. Mikhail backed me up, but I don't think he needed to. I think the others respected the plan I brought to them. Oh, and the best part,"

I turn back to find her sitting on the couch, pouring herself a glass of water. "I gave them ideas to improve their efficiency this season. With being limited by the curse, they have continued farming with little change. I suggested changing the layout, and they agreed my plan is solid. They are all going to implement the changes when they return." I kneel in front of her. She gives a kind, but small smile, placing her hand on my shoulders.

"That's amazing, Clem. I knew you could do it." She has believed in me more than I ever realized. I lean in, pressing my lips against hers. She wraps her hands around my neck, tangling her fingers in the hair tied back at the nape of my neck. It needs to be brushed, but I didn't have enough time before my meeting. I was nervous and focused on other things. I pull back from the kiss. Jasmin finally looks happy, maybe not as ecstatic as I am, but still content.

"How was your time with Dahlia?" I sit beside her, pulling her legs into my lap.

"Good. It was nice to relax with her like we did before. Everything has been so crazy lately. It was nice to have an afternoon of nostalgia." I stroke my hand over her leg in a gentle manner. She rests her cheek against my shoulder. One of her hands wraps around my back, holding me close to her. I love these intimate moments between us, but I still have a ton of excited energy coursing through my body. I stretch my fingers out, caressing her thigh, pressing deeper into her skin. I wrap my thumb around the inside, stroking right up to the bend of her hip, then pulling back. I do this several times before she moans, arching her back to look up at me.

"Are you trying to tease me?" She wiggles her eyebrows at me, slowly dragging her hand up my chest. Her fingers trace over my neck as my thumb continues its pursuit along her thigh. I make another pass across her thigh, bumping her clit this time. Her fingers grab onto my cheeks, dragging my face toward her. It's a move I've done to her many times, but this is the first time she's done it to me. My cock goes from half-mast to full-blown erection before her lips touch mine. Her domineering grab sends shockwaves through my body. I shove my hand against her pussy, rubbing her clit through her trousers. She moans, grinding against my hand. I pull my hand away, scooping her legs and carrying her over to the bed.

I drop her on her back, tugging at the hem of the pants, wanting them gone now. She sits up, removing her clothes as I quickly shed mine, throwing them across the room. I stroke my cock a time or two, needing to touch it so I don't burst instantly. She scoots back, her legs open, exposing her perfect cunt to me. I lick my lips but stop before diving in. The memory of her climbing onto my side of the bed strikes me. Having her bare pussy near my face while I'm on my back is a thought that has consumed so much of my brain power lately. Instead of diving in, I stroke my finger through her slit, unable to avoid touching it. She groans at the slight touch.

"I want to try something different." She turns her head to the side, sitting up to see better. I fall back on the bed, stroking my cock slowly. My free hand waves at her. "Come up here." She turns over, scooting closer to me, but not in the position I want her in. How do I explain what I am thinking?

"I want to lay here," I motion to the bed behind me, "while I devour your cunt." She looks up and down, at my face, down her body, and around the bed.

"How will that work?" At least she hasn't shot down the idea entirely. I shrug, tucking my arm behind my head. "Crawl over here to me, and let's see." She shifts her position, crawling over my chest. As she gets closer, I realize I need to put my arms down. It's awkward to get my arms beneath her legs when neither of us knows what we are doing here. We both giggle, trying to move our bodies into better positions. I slide my body down further, then she sits on my chest, just below where I need her to be. I nod my head up, trying to motion for her.

"Put your hands on the headboard and lift your hips up." She does as instructed, so obedient. I scoot down until I am finally under her. I stretch my tongue out, lifting my head to reach her properly. My tongue licks from the back of her slit to her clit, eliciting a moan. She shifts her hips, lifting away from me. I grunt at her, wrapping my arms around her hips to pull her back down. My fingers dig into her hips, forcing her to be still. I resume my ministrations with my tongue, tasting her as she hovers above my face. She wiggles as I lick her, causing me to tighten my hands around her waist. She rises up from my face.

"Stay down!" My voice is deep and scratchy, desperate to keep her cunt in my mouth.

"But I don't want to hurt you or suffocate you."

"I want you to." I snatch her hips, tugging her down forcefully on my face. She whimpers, but I drag my tongue through her soaking pussy. I swirl my tongue around her clit, holding her tightly against my face. She is sitting firmly against me. Her cunt is my life right now. Her scent, her taste, her warmth, it's all consuming me and call me greedy, but I want more. I drop one of my fingers to her clit as I thrust my tongue in and out of her pussy. She moans loudly, wiggling her cunt against my face to get more friction where she wants it. This is what I wanted. I wanted her to fuck herself on my face. I am in heaven right now. I debate moving one of my hands to stroke my dick, but I don't want to let her go just yet. I'm so engrossed in all of Jasmin that I don't actually want to think about my own cock. Just her.

"Fuck, I'm going to come, Clem."

I growl against her slit before sucking her clit into my mouth, sucking hard between my lips. She screams, collapsing on my face. Her pussy is clenching, releasing fluids. I remove my mouth from her clit, moving to tongue her and lap her wet cunt. She finally pulls away, laying on my side with her feet near my head. I can't wipe the grin off as I watch her flushed skin and heavy breathing return to normal. She looks over at me, laughing and trying to hide her face.

"You are doing that again."

"Yes, ma'am."

She swats my leg as I turn to see her better. My cock is still hard, but I don't have a plan now that I have tried what I wanted. She licks her lips, shifting onto her side also. She adjusts her position so her head is directly in front of my crotch, but she is still upside down. She swirls her tongue around my cock before slipping the whole thing in her mouth. My eyes flutter as the sensation differs from when she is on her knees. The tip of my dick is hitting a different spot in the back of her throat, and her tongue is against the top side, covering it in the luxurious warmth and wetness. I groan loudly, unable to stop the noises she is wrenching from me.

She shifts her hips to get a better angle on my dick. My eyes roll in my head again, but I realize how close her cunt is to my mouth again. I'm not far from my orgasm, but I am optimistic I can bring her to another before I am spent. I grab her ass, jerking her closer to my face. Her legs part for me, but she holds her leg awkwardly, unsure where to put it. I can feel hesitation in her mouth, sliding slower over my cock. I grab her ankle, pushing it down to the bed. This gives me better access and makes her more comfortable as she swallows me deeply. I groan before I latch my lips over her cunt. She takes my cock in her deep mouth, her nose hitting my thigh. She moans around my dick, sending a wave of vibrations that causes me to thrust my hips into her face. She gags, and it takes what little willpower I have not to fuck her face.

I wrap my arm around her hips, sliding my fingers over her ass to the back side of her pussy. My tongue still works against her clit as my fingers tease her opening. She moans again around my cock, causing me to jerk several times. I wrap my arms around her waist, then roll onto my back. I drag her with me, leading her to squeal at the sudden change. I chuckle against her pussy, but with this new position, I have better access to her. She continues working my dick expertly. She holds her fingers around the base, keeping it steady as her mouth works up and down the top.

I slide two fingers into her wet slit, teasing her lightly. My other hand is wrapped around her ass, and I tease her back hole, pressing and circling the entrance. She groans, pushing back against me as I take her clit between my lips. With her fingers still wrapped around the base of my cock, she slides her fingers and palm down to caress my balls. I moan against her, flicking my tongue out against her clit. Her tongue continues to stroke the top side of my member, sending intense waves of pleasure through my entire body. My balls clench as my orgasm nears. With my mouth around her clit, I can't warn her that I am about to release in her mouth. Instead, I suck harder, ensuring she comes with me. I press my finger knuckle deep in her ass as my other two relentlessly pound her pussy. She sucks hard on my cock, as if trying to suck my orgasm out. She is successful. I explode deep in her throat with her lips sealed tight around my cock. Her orgasm crashes through, sending fluids squirting and landing on my forehead. I pound into her, drawing out more fluids as she sucks every bit from my dick.

We're in competition to see who can last the longest. It's a game where we both win, and we both lose. One of us has to cry mercy before our bodies turn to pure pain. I refuse to lose, though. She wiggles against me, trying to pry her clit away from my lips, but it doesn't work. Her teeth scrape against the underside of my cock, causing me to jerk and cry out in pain. Probably not the best action since she still has her mouth around me. She releases me, laughing as she turns around to lie with her head on my chest.

We are both breathing heavily, giggling, savoring the orgasmic ecstasy. I wrap my arms around her, pressing a kiss to her forehead. She reaches to run her fingers through my hair but looks confused when she finds it wet. Then realization dawns on her face. She turns a deep red color, trying to hide her face behind her hands. I laugh at her, trying to pull her hands away.

"Oh gods, Clem. I don't know what happened!" She is torn somewhere between embarrassment and humor over this situation. "I didn't know it would go all over you like that." I grab her chin, pulling her face up to mine, pressing my lips against hers. She kisses me gently, then pulls back to look at me. Her face is still bright red, causing the three scars along her face to stand out more than usual.

"I don't know what possessed you to do that," she waves her hand down our bodies, "but I fucking loved it." I chuckle at her words, wrapping my arms around her shoulders.

"Good, because I am absolutely going to be doing that again."

Chapter 10

JASMIN

Holy gods, Clem is everything when it comes to orgasms. His talents are unparalleled. He is well endowed, and his tongue is a whole other entity. I won't even get started on his mind. He's not just horny; he's creative, resourceful, and curious. He's also very understanding. I have never had orgasms with so much fluid before him. Sex is always messy, but I've never soaked someone's hair like that. Despite my morbid embarrassment, he was so calm about it, maybe even a little excited. He worships me and my body in ways I have never experienced.

We walk toward the dining hall, planning to have dinner with our friends before we find Finn and retire for the evening. I watch his face as we walk, so consumed with my thoughts, I don't realize he is looking at me. By the time I notice he is watching me, too, we have slowed down, staring at each other.

"What?" I ask, nudging him, turning my gaze back down the hallway. He grabs my waist, spinning me around him. I crash against the wall, and he is pressed against my front, his lips against my neck. I gasp at the sudden change and the impact. The wetness pooling in my core feels excessive at this moment, but I can't deny its presence.

"Someone loves me." He croons out in a sing-song voice. I playfully smack his arm.

"Well, it's not me." He presses his teeth against my neck, sending another wave of moisture to my leggings before pulling back.

"Oh. My mistake then." He jerks away from me quickly, walking toward the dining hall, leaving me hot and bothered against the wall. "I don't like to fuck someone that doesn't love me. Guess I'll have to find someone that does." Before I can respond to him, Tomas and Zander walk up from a different hallway. Clem playfully calls out to them, shoving his way between them both. They look confused and a bit uncomfortable with his close contact. He's not typically one to be so friendly. He looks back at me to wink before disappearing into the dining hall with the two younger men. I hear him loudly exclaim to love someone inside the hall and just shake my head as a smile spreads across my face. He has been in a delightful mood lately, and I love his carefreeness. It's such a stark contrast to his demeanor after the autumn equinox. Even the week he was here before everyone else, he wasn't quite as giddy as he had been the past few days. My chest swells with love and happiness for him.

Dahlia walks up next to me, looping her arm through mine to pull me into the dining hall. My mind does a full circle of emotions. I'm thrilled to see her, then crushed knowing I can't give her what she wants because it would destroy Clem, then realize I can use her to my advantage to get back at Clem for teasing me. If he pretends to love someone else, I can too. Even if it isn't entirely an act. As we walk in, I explain to Dahlia what I want her to do, knowing she will do anything for me. Her eyes go wide and bright at my request. Her whole face lights up with excitement. I wish I could make her feel that way all the time.

We walk into the dining hall, whispering to each other. Then we explode in loud, raucous laughter. She leans in so her lips are against my neck. My eyes lock with Clem's. He is sitting between a nervous Tomas and Zander with an exasperated expression. Clem's face darkens when he sees me. Fear of taking this too far creeps in, but I refuse to give in. Instead, I plaster on my best courtly smile and give him a wink. My eyebrows wiggle a time or two before I guide Dahlia to the food tables. We are grabbing our food when two arms wrap around my waist.

I yelp at the sudden intrusion but quickly recognize Clem's warm embrace. He rests his chin on my shoulder while I settle my free arm over his around my middle.

"Are you sure you don't love me?" He turns his head so his lips are right against my ear. His words are so soft that even Dahlia, mere inches away, can't hear what he is saying. "It sure would be a shame if I didn't get to eat your pussy for breakfast in the morning."

"CLEM!" I scold. That is not appropriate talk for the dining hall, not that it has ever stopped any of us before. We both fall into a fit of giggles. Dahlia scoffs at us, walking away to take her seat at the table. She sits across from Zander and Tomas. After Clem and I grab food and sit at the table, Dahlia gets up immediately to go back for tea. Tea does sound like a good idea. Apparently, I say this out loud because Clem offers to get it for me. I kiss his cheek quickly to show appreciation before he walks away.

Kian walks over, sitting next to me. We start to chat about his research when Dahlia returns. My attention is on Kian, and I don't notice where Dahlia sits. Kian is telling me about a different book he found in the library when I hear Clem speak.

"Oh, Dahlia, that is my seat." I look over, realizing she is next to me and has pushed Clem's food to the other side of the table.

"No. Your food is over there."

"Dahlia," I rebuke. She shrugs her shoulders carelessly, then dives into her food. Everyone at our table is silent, watching the awkward interaction. Kian stands next to me.

"Here, Clem. Take this spot."

"No, Kian. You were already in that seat. We don't have to give up our seats because he wants to sit by Jasmin. He's not the only one who deserves to sit beside her." I stare in astonishment at Dahlia's words. I thought we had come to an agreement; I don't understand why she is acting like this. Kian pauses, considering her words. Clem looks stunned but begins to walk to the other side of the table.

"Clem," Kian and I speak simultaneously, but my tone is filled with more sadness.

"No, she's right," Clem says as he reaches the other side of the table. "I don't have to sit next to you every day." He winks at me then hands the mug with tea over. He sits across from Kian, not even in front of me. A wave of displeasure rolls through me. I understand his point, but that doesn't change my feelings. I still want him next to me. The table is quiet for another moment while everyone slowly rises out of the awkward cloud, settling around our table. It's never been this uncomfortable before. There have been embarrassing moments, like the first time Clem throat fucked me. He ran off awkwardly, but it didn't linger like this moment.

"Kian, what did you find in the book?" I ask in a feeble attempt to return to normal conversation.

"I think I found some clues to help with the curse. Are you free tomorrow? I would like to see Dahlia's room. And her with the flower if she is free, too." We glance over at her. She looks aloof as she eats her food. I know she heard what Kian said. There is a slight curl to her mouth. She only does that when she is trying to be coy. Most people never notice it, but it's there, plain as day for me to see.

"Dahlia, are you free tomorrow?" My tone is stern and unrelenting, though not entirely angry.

"I can be." She winks at me, and I swear I can hear Clem's scowl. This is going to be a long dinner. At least the food is good. The cook prepared roasted duck and the last of the winter vegetables in butter and rosemary.

"I can attend, too. I would like to be there," Clem adds; I can't be sure whether it's genuine or he doesn't want me alone with Dahlia.

"That won't be necessary, Clematis. We can handle it without you." Dahlia retorts, despite no one asking her. His scowl deepens. He doesn't particularly like being called by his full name, especially not so casually.

"That would be helpful, Clem," Kian explained. "Having all three of you there may offer more answers than I can get individually." Now Dahlia scowls while Clem just nods. This whole dinner is a shit show. I am ready to go to bed and have today over with. I don't know what has gotten into Dahlia. She was so wonderful at the pond, now she is being rude and condescending. Maybe she doesn't realize how much it hurts me when she acts like that toward Clem. I will tell her next time we are alone. I want to avoid dragging that conversation out in front of everyone.

Dinner finally ends with only a few more awkward moments. It is still easily one of the more uncomfortable dinners I have had in the past five years. Clem and I hunt down Finn, discussing Erik's absence from dinner tonight. As far as I know, he wasn't scheduled for guard duty. I'll check in on him soon. Once we find Finn, we head straight back to our room, much more subdued than our walk down. I hold Clem's hand as we walk, but it's not enough to bring him out of the stupor.

"What the fuck was that?" He practically yells once we are in the room. I wince at him, staying close to the door. Angry yelling has always been a sensitive area for me. He notices my reaction and apologizes quickly, walking over to wrap his arms around me. I settle into his warm body, wanting his touch so desperately.

"I don't know. She was out of line."

He helps me get ready for bed silently, brushes my hair, and helps me dress. Neither of us brings up Dahlia. I do the same for him, then we crawl into bed. Finn is already in bed, so Clem pulls me over to his side. I squeeze between him and Finn, who whines quietly at the intrusion. Before falling asleep, we chat about dinner, Dahlia, and the curse. Sometimes I wonder what our lives will be like when we aren't ruled by the curse. What will we talk about? Where will we go? What will we do? I suppose all those questions will be answered eventually. Hopefully. Possibly.

The bloated silence in the room is unbearable. Dahlia showed up a few minutes ago, and now we are waiting for Kian to arrive. She sits casually on the couch as if this is her personal space. Clem is hovering near the dying fire. With the weather warming, there hasn't been any need for it. Last night was unseasonably chilly, but we likely won't need a fire again. I am sitting in the chair situated between them, uncomfortable and ready for Kian to arrive.

A quick rap at the door lets us know he is finally here. I practically jump out of my chair, rushing to the door. After awkward pleasantries, Dahlia leads the way to the room she was kept in. I hold Clem's hand, both needing his comfort and wanting to offer some to him. We enter the hallway, turning toward the end, where the door to the tower is. Just before we get to the end, Emmeline calls out to Clem.

"Henry is looking for you!"

"Now? Why? Why me?"

"He's worried about Erik and thinks it has to do with Bea. Erik didn't show up for his shift this morning."

I curse, looking at everyone in the group. We need Clem to go with us, but we also need Erik to be well. Is this really about Bea? He has been more absent since she left.

"What if Clem and I went in a few minutes after Kian searches the room?" I offer a possible compromise to this situation. Emmeline just shrugs, though. "Henry just asked for Clem. I think he has seen Erik but couldn't help him. I don't know his reasons for wanting Clem."

Clem scoffs, "Because I am an amazing brother and friend, obviously." Emmeline smiles, nodding exaggeratedly.

"Yes, yes. That must be the reason." I turn to hide my giggle, but not before Clem notices. He rolls his eyes, shaking his head.

"Just go, Clem. I'm positive Kian and I are smart enough to figure this out. We'll see you later." With her last words, Dahlia turns and walks through the door leading to the tower. I just sigh. Her actions toward Clem are so frustrating. I really wish she weren't so rude to him. A discussion needs to happen with her again. Fuck, I don't want to do that, though.

"We'll figure it out," I repeat, wrapping my arms around Clem's waist. He wraps an arm around my shoulder, kissing the top of my head. If Henry thinks Erik needs him, he should go. We can always revisit this room later. It will always be there. Kian repeats my sentiments as Clem pulls away from me. His eyes express his sadness and worry but also anger and hurt. Such a stark contrast to what I saw yesterday afternoon.

Clem walks in the opposite direction with Emmeline while Kian, and I turn toward the door. We walk up the stairs quietly. The silence is heavy with things unspoken. Kian obviously has an opinion about Dahlia, but he won't share it with me without knowing whether she can hear us. The need to get him alone to discuss this whole situation is thrumming in my mind. I need to find an excuse to send Dahlia away or keep Kian longer. I'll come up with something.

As we walk through the winding staircase, a sense of dread and worry fills me. I wrap my arms around myself, trying to protect myself from the impending doom. My mind goes on high alert as I search for any threat. Kian is walking behind me, also looking around for some unnamed danger.

"Do you feel that too?" I ask him, slowing my steps, scared of what is around the corner. He nods slowly, glancing at me before scanning the area again.

"How far are we from the room?" I glance up the stairwell considering his question, unsure how many are left.

"Maybe eight or ten steps?"

"The magic is surprisingly strong to have released her already."

Fear strikes differently, deeper. Did it suck her back in? My new fear takes over as I rush up the stairs. I just got her back. Even if she acts like an envious cad, I won't let her disappear for another near-decade. I rush up the stairwell, taking two at a time. Kian increases his speed behind me, trying to keep up. I slam through the door to find her standing over the window, looking at the ground below. The morning sun shines through the room, casting a golden glare around her dark skin. She looks so exquisite in her pink dress. Her locs brush against her shoulder blades, the beads clacking together as she turns to look at me. Then she smiles. Every fear, every worry, every concern, anxiety, and lousy thought dissolves. The only thing in my mind is how absolutely stunning she looks.

I'm broken from my trance by Kian clearing his throat behind me. I blush over how it must look, me staring at her like a love-struck schoolgirl. I need to chat with Kian about what I should do about Dahlia and Clem. I love them both so much. I hope Kian has an answer and isn't uncomfortable or angry with me for leaning on him so much. He is paid well above his position within the kingdom. His title is officially Coven Advisor, but he should be my Court Advisor. He is so much more than just a liaison between the covens at this point.

The room is bare, with only a tiny bed, barely large enough for Dahlia to fit on. There are no curtains, no paintings, and no chairs. A small, thin blanket is crumpled on the end of the bed. Dahlia always hated making her bed. Sunette would always complain about that particular habit, but it never changed. I don't remember this room being so empty. I never used it much, but there was still some furniture.

Kian takes in the room, walking around, touching the walls. He doesn't say anything. I move to the bed to sit, feeling overwhelmed by everything. She was in this room for nine years, granted she was asleep the whole time. She was so close to me, and I never knew it. Hands settle on my shoulders, rubbing softly. My eyes close, relaxing into Dahlia's comforting touch. I rest my head against her arm, wanting more contact with her. I really shouldn't, not with how she has been acting lately, but I can't stop my feelings.

I open my eyes as I hear the small crackles again. The lightning is flashing around us. We watch as the light bursts through the room. It's frustrating that this keeps happening. What does it mean? Why is it occurring? Kian takes the flower from Dahlia, holding it between his hands. His eyes dart back and forth like the first time he touched the flower. Is he seeing something new now? His face remains neutral while Dahlia's fingers continue to work on the tension in my shoulders. His eyes stop moving, and he focuses his sight on me.

"There wasn't anything new, but parts are more amplified. This flower won't give us the answer, but Dahlia is involved in breaking the curse." Her hands tighten on my shoulder as I sigh.

"What does that mean, though?" My voice is tight, laced with emotions.

"I'm not sure," he admits quietly. "It's clear that being with her is important. You see these flashes." His hands wave at the lightning, still flickering. "What does Clem think about her?" I wince at his question. Dahlia's fingers tighten as I try to turn away from the question. I wrap mine around hers, looking up at her. My favorite angle was always looking up at her. Something about her cheekbones makes her even more gorgeous in this position. Or maybe it's because I spent so much time between her legs, seeking pleasure for both of us.

"Dahlia, can you give me some time alone with Kian?" I ask softly, not wanting to upset her but needing time to process everything. Before she can answer, I add, "I'll come find you later." She purses her lips but nods, leaving the room. Once the door latches behind her, I turn back to Kian, trying not to look as desolate as I feel. His sympathetic gaze tells me I am unsuccessful this time. Kian knows me too well, and it brings me both comfort and concern for my ability to hide things if I need to.

"Clem isn't Dahlia's biggest fan right now. Her behavior lately has upset him." Kian nods, understanding. "Is the curse not broken because I still love her and don't love Clem enough?" The words come out as a whisper as doubt fills every inch of my being. He steps over to sit beside me, pulling me into his arms. His soft assurances that my love for her isn't interfering with the curse are appreciated but do little to curb my doubts. He squeezes me tighter as I cry quietly.

"I don't think that's the case. Maybe the opposite, actually." I sniffle, leaning back to give him a confused look. "I think her role in the curse may be more important than we give her credit for." I sniffle again, pulling away to see him better. I need to gauge whether he is trying to coddle me or not.

"What do you mean?"

"She was released before your curse broke. What kept her here is still intact but is overpowered by the magic of your curse. She would still be under this spell if she wasn't vital to you." His hand motions to the small bed we are both sitting on. The meaning behind her release has been a constant puzzle.

"Okay, so now what?"

"That I don't know," he sighs. "I've made some interesting discoveries, but nothing that will help us here." I rest my head against him, exhausted from this afternoon's emotional turmoil. "I think it's time we visit Greynon."

Chapter 11

CLEM

Erik's room is surprisingly messy. I always assumed he would be an organized tenant, having a specific location for everything. I've not been in his room before, but even this mess shows signs of some organization. Some of his uniforms are hung neatly; other clothes are tossed on the floor carelessly. There is a neat stack of paper on his desk and several crumpled near the wastebasket on the floor. Blankets are thrown everywhere. A bouquet of flowers is in shreds on the floor. I pick up the stems, a few papers, and some of the petals, dropping them in the waste basket.

Erik is lying on his bed, turned away from me. I told him I was coming in, asked what was wrong, even checked to make sure he's still alive. He is; he nearly gave me another black eye. My vision is thankful he missed. I can't afford a third black eye at this point. He didn't feel feverish when I checked to see if he's alive, but I'm no healer. I sit in his chair, unsure of what to do now. I don't know why Henry thought I would be able to help.

Although, I also didn't know why Jasmin thought I could be the Master of Gardens. I turned out to be better at that than I expected. I also managed to get Jasmin to fall in love with me. I must be good at something more than just orgasms. I take a deep breath, convincing myself I can do something here. The only thing I can think of is to tell him something about Bea. He is wallowing over her. I know a thing or two about wallowing over a woman, especially a strong, steadfast one.

"When Bea was 10, I was 9, and Ma and Da were going to the market without us. They said Bea was in charge, but I was 9. I didn't need her to watch me like I was some baby. After they left, I decided to go chase our chickens. It was the best activity we had at the time. Bea decided she didn't want me to do that. She insisted I stay inside. We started arguing, and I ran out the door anyway." Erik rolls over, looking at me as I talk. His eyes are red and swollen, but his face is dry. I continue with my story, not wanting him to change his mind about listening. "Bea tried to grab me but wasn't entirely successful. She essentially tackled me, but since I was so close to the door, I fell, hitting my head on the doorframe. The gash was huge, and blood was oozing everywhere. We both started screaming." I huff a slight chuckle, looking down at my fingers as if I can still see the blood before continuing. "She had the mind to get a cloth to press on it. Bea spent the next quarter of an hour convincing me to tell them I just fell. Ma and Da finally arrived, and the first thing out of my mouth was that she pushed me." Erik's lips curve slightly, not a full smile, but an improvement.

"That was the first time she injured me." I push the hair back from the side of my face, where a small scar is barely visible. "It's still there too." This comment sends Erik into a fit of laughter. I laugh with him, glad I could help. He stands from his bed, walks over to his table, and opens the top drawer. I watch with a smile on my face as my laughter dies down. He is still laughing, though it sounds more forced than natural now. He pulls something out then closes the drawer. He turns to me, fiddling with the item in his hand. He abruptly tosses it to me, giving me barely enough time to register the thing flying at my head. I catch the small wooden box, glancing back at him. This looks to be a ring box. He can't be about to tell me he wants to marry my sister.

"I offered that to her the day before she was supposed to leave." A single tear rolls down his cheek. He doesn't move to wipe it away. The powerful image of a man with a tear on his face strikes me in the gut. Erik is a large man with broad shoulders, short hair, and a robust build. He is built to be a guard, a protector, a warrior. His expression of emotion is endearing to me; he trusts me enough to show me his feelings. I take solitude in his trust in me.

"She told me she already has a family to care for."

I look down at the box, opening it to reveal the ring beneath. A wide gold band is engraved with swirls and waves and several small rubies embedded in the gold. The ring is likely more than Bea could ever afford on her own. She turned him down because of how much this ring cost. I know her well enough to know she was frightened by how much he made and worried she wouldn't be allowed to work if he provided for her. I toss the ring back to him.

"You idiot." He looks stunned, catching the ring with his eyes focused on me. "She didn't turn you down because of the family, though that is an easy excuse. No. She turned you down because of how much that ring cost." Confused, he looks at the ring, knitting his eyebrows together. "If you make money, she won't be able to work anymore. At least, that is how she sees it." It's a stupid idea. Plenty of women hold jobs, despite what their husbands do. Hell, by her logic, I shouldn't be allowed to work. Jasmin is obviously the one bringing the monetary value to our relationship. I wonder if that thought occurred to Bea, especially since she would be working for Jasmin.

"Go to Arkaley. Tell Bea to quit being stupid and come back with you. Tell her she will be the animal keeper for the castle, whether she likes it or not. In fact," I walk over to his desk, shoving him to the side. I start to write, but not only is my writing terrible, she will know it's my writing. I hand the pen over to Erik. "Write out this for me," I explain what he needs to write. After my schooling, I didn't have much need to write anymore. So I haven't since then, and it shows in my penmanship. I need to practice writing. It will probably be important in the coming years if I am to be king.

After he finishes my dictation, I sign it and hand it back to him. I instruct him to leave now and get there by sundown. He can take as long as he wants, and I will deal with whatever needs to be done around here to assist with his departure.

He's packing and in better spirits when I finally leave his room. In the hallway, Henry is walking around frantically, looking for someone.

"Have you seen Queen Jasmin, sir?" It's going to take a long time to get used to these honorifics.

"No, but I am on my way to find her."

"Good, yes. There is a situation, and we need her in the meeting room immediately."

I nod and rush off to find her. I hope she had time to finish whatever Kian needed to do in the tower room. I am still upset over Dahlia's comments. She has been rude and out of line lately, especially given my position over her. Her actions upset Jasmin too, but I don't think she realizes that.

Jasmin is in the room, resting on the couch. She looks comfortable, and I hate to bother her when she is like this. Henry's frantic reaction leads me to wake her, though. I press my lips against her forehead, stepping back to offer a soft smile to lessen the blow of the news I need to give her.

"Henry needs you in the meeting room immediately."

"Fuck."

She sits up and adjusts her hair before we leave the room together. On the way, I recount my time with Erik, explaining why he will be gone for several days. She tells me the visit to the tower room was helpful, but we reach the meeting room before she elaborates. I walk in before her, leading us to our seats. Henry and Erik are already at the table, along with Lord David and Gustavo.

"What is happening?" Jasmin's question is blunt, but it is nearing dinner. I wonder if her afternoon didn't go as well as planned or if she is just hungry.

Lord David is the one to speak. "There has been an issue at the border, Queen. A young boy from Arkaley was playing when he managed to press his arm through. The border was weakened only long enough for his arm to go through, then it closed, removing the boy's arm."

Jasmin places her hand across her mouth and cheek, showing no other signs of a reaction but clearly in deep thought. She finally speaks up, "Has the boy been to a healer? How is he doing?"

"He is with several now. I don't have any further information on his condition."

"Very well. Keep me updated. Let's issue a decree that no one is to go near the border. I want signs posted where people are likely to be. How often are the guards patrolling? It doesn't matter. Decrease their range so they can be more visible. Erik," Jasmin turns to him, offering a soft smile. Henry must have brought him in while I was fetching Jasmin. "While you are in Arkaley, I want you to check in on the family and the guards working the border. Before you return, I want you to visit Greynon to ensure the guards work with the covens. Your wife can return before you if she does not want to travel." Henry and I audibly gasp while Erik just looks stunned. Jasmin looks between the three of us as if confused by our reactions. "Are we not sending him to Arkaley to get married?"

I start to respond, then stop, then start again. I scratch my face. Jasmin isn't entirely wrong, but no one specifically said marriage. I assumed they would be together for a while before getting married, but there isn't anything stopping them from getting married. He has already proposed marriage to her. If they marry in Arkaley, my mother could attend. I finally find my voice. "Well, yes. I suppose."

"Okay then." She turns back to Erik, who is frozen in stunned silence. "While you are gone, we will prepare a suite for you. Once you are back, you may take several days to celebrate with Bea. Congratulations." She shifts to face the Lords, who are bewildered by this interaction. "Signs, increased guards; Erik is checking in; keep me posted on the boy. Send his family my regards and the same allotment other families received for damages." She pauses, waiting for anyone to acknowledge her recap. After a moment, we all nod. "Anything else?" Everyone shakes their heads, still somewhat shocked. "Good, safe travels, Erik." She leaves the room before anyone has time to react, forcing the rest of us to jump awkwardly to bow. I chase after her, eager to find out if she is okay.

"I need rest." She spouts out as we round a corner leading to her hallway. Once I am next to her, I keep pace with her easily. In the room, she doesn't even dismiss Emmeline or Finn; she just topples on the bed, fully dressed. I inform Emmeline of everything that just happened, asking for privacy for Jasmin for a while. Finn and I walk outside together, chasing each other for a few moments before heading back inside. We both snuggle into the bed with Jasmin, napping together before dinner.

At dinner, Jasmin and I sit with Kian and Emmeline. Zander, Tomas, and Dahlia are with her family. Erik has already left to go to Arkaley. It would have been nice to go with him, to see my family, especially if he does marry Bea. I want to be there with her, but I understand the circumstances. I have other duties to attend to here. We are planning the trip to Greynon in a few days.

The excitement over revisiting the area is building quickly. I had grown stagnant in Arkaley, letting the curse be my excuse for staying home and not venturing out. The four of us plan to travel together with several guards. We want Dahlia to remain at the castle so Matron Maud can assess Jasmin and me without interference. Jasmin also has some court business to attend to while we are there.

"Can we please not talk about the curse?" Jasmin interrupts our current conversation with her outburst. "I'm sorry. I just really need to not think about it. For a little while, at least." I shrug, not really caring what we talk about. I'm just happy to be friends with people that aren't terrible. My friends from Arkaley weren't all awful, but they weren't that great either. Kian and Emmeline are great. Both together and separately.

"What do you want to talk about, Jas?" I ask, popping a piece of dried fruit into my mouth.

"I don't know. What about summer solstice?" The solstice is about a month and a half away. We still have a little way to go, but it is close. I'm sure Emmeline has plans. As that thought crosses my mind, Emmeline starts listing her plans. She wants to do a masquerade ball this time. They have hosted them in the past, but not in several years. The plan is to invite people from the villages to the ball. It sounds like a wonderful idea. We spend the rest of the night discussing decorations, gowns, masks, music, food, every little detail. I always thought it would be boring to discuss, but I find it entertaining to think about.

Dinner passes quickly and pleasantly, a welcome change to the past few awkward nights. After we leave, I invite Jasmin to walk with me before bed. She agrees, and I lead her to the gardens, walking through the blooms and shrubs. We walk quietly, her hand draped over my elbow. The stars are shining bright in the sky. The moon is half full tonight, appearing as a perfect half circle. Our feet crunch softly on the gravel path as we weave through the green shrubs basking in the moonlight.

I pull her over to sit on her favorite bench, settling between the blooming peonies she loves. There is still another week or two before they fully bloom, but a few blooms are starting early. Jasmin leans over to rest her head against my shoulder, sighing contentedly. I'm glad to offer her some peace after the last few weeks. She deserves peace and happiness, and quiet, at least sometimes. I press a small kiss to her forehead, comfortable with the silence.

She looks so beautiful in the moonlight. Her dark, soft curls illuminate the cream color of her skin. The scars on her face are hidden by the shadow of her hair, hiding her dark secrets with them. She looks like an angel in the night, like she came straight down from the heavens. And she is mine. She is with me. She even chose me before we knew we were fated. Unable to resist any longer, I lean down, pressing my lips against hers. The kiss starts gently but soon turns more passionate, more desperate. I need more of her now.

She wore a dress tonight, and I'm suddenly very thankful she did. I don't want to go back to our room. I want her now; I need to claim her. I wrap one hand around her neck as I force my tongue into her mouth. She groans against me as my other hand falls to her knee. My fingers tug the soft, loose material of the dress until I reach the hem. I graze the tips of my fingers against the inside of her knee. She tries to pull away from the kiss, but I tighten my fingers around her neck, holding her in place. I'll stop this kiss when I am ready.

My tongue swirls against hers while I trail the inside of her thigh agonizingly slow. The first time I saw her on this bench after the autumn equinox, I knew I wanted to claim her here. In the light of everything else, I forgot that particular desire, but now I will be the one that makes her come on this bench. I break the kiss, but my fingers remain tight around her neck, not letting her move. She grunts at the pressure on her neck. I graze the slit between her legs, feeling the evidence of her own arousal.

"Oh, my little slut," I whisper against her neck, rubbing my thumb along my chin. "You want to get fucked on this bench? Ha," I huff out a spurious laugh. "Of course you do."

I jerk her head back, licking the front of her neck. She shivers under my touch as I press the tip of my middle finger inside. "You're so wet. How long have you been aroused, slut?" A second finger teases her entrance. Her legs spread apart, giving me better access. Her chest rises and falls quickly as her body reacts to me. "Is this what you want?" I slam my fingers deep inside her. She arches back against my hand, opening her mouth to cry out. Before she makes a noise, my mouth closes around hers, kissing her intensely, trying to swallow her sounds.

I stand, hovering over her. I slide my hand from the back of her neck to the front, holding her tightly, but not enough to cut off her breath. I brutally thrust my fingers in and out of her as I lean over her body.

"Yes, take my fingers in the gardens like the little whore you are. Just waiting for someone to fuck you well." I curl my fingers inside her, stroking the spot that always sets her body on fire. She arches again, forcing her neck harder against my hand. Her eyes widen at the new pressure while her pussy clenches around my fingers. I growl at the feeling. "My dirty girl. Take your tits out for me." Without hesitation, she unties the band holding her dress up. My mouth closes over one nipple as soon as it's free. I suck the hardening bud into my mouth, letting it pop free before doing the same to the other. I muster all of my self-control, pulling my fingers from her body and bringing them to my mouth. I savor her taste on my fingers, licking every bit I can. I shove my fingers in her mouth, releasing her neck. I ensure her dress is out of the way for me.

"You don't come until I say you can, understand?" She shakes her head in understanding.

I drop to my knees, realizing the small rocks uncomfortable. I quickly rip off my shirt, fold it, and place it under my knees to protect me from the rough terrain.

Grabbing Jasmin's knees, I tug her closer and press them onto my shoulders. Once her hips are on the edge, I dive into her wet cunt. I lick my tongue across her slit, making a quick circle around her opening. I focus on her entrance, tonguing it thoroughly. She moans loudly, and I shove my fingers back in her mouth. I slip my other hand on her breast, circling her clit with my tongue again.

Her moans are still loud, despite my attempts to silence her. I don't really care at this point. Everyone knows what we do, and I'm pretty sure most people in the castle have heard us at it before. We are in a public space now, though. I would rather she didn't make too much noise. I feel her clenching, that telltale sign she is about to orgasm. I debate whether I should stop so she doesn't come without my permission. She knows to snap when she is gagged. She isn't doing that. Does she think I won't notice her orgasm? I suck her clit into my mouth. Her body arches as both hands land in my hair, pushing me tight against her pussy. So I remove my hand from her mouth, shoving my damp fingers straight into her pulsing cunt. She erupts, body arching, chest heaving, eyes closing, as she spasms around my fingers. My little slut didn't follow the directions.

I continue pounding her as her body calms down. I remove my fingers from her, sucking the taste off again. Gods, I love her taste. I rock back on my heels, giving her a devious grin. Her hands drop to my shoulders, caressing my bare skin. When her eyes finally meet mine, fear strikes her.

"You didn't follow my one rule, you naughty girl." I stand, grabbing my shirt off the ground. "Up." My cock is achingly hard, pressing against my pants. I toss the shirt on the bench, letting the fire shine through my gaze at her. I grab one nipple between my thumb and forefinger, pinching tightly. She tries to hide the wince at the pain.

"I was going to be kind and let you use my shirt. But I don't think I will." I look down at my protruding cock. "On your knees." She lowers herself slowly, wincing at the pebbles against her knees. It's uncomfortable, but it won't cause lasting damage. "Suck me." She unties my pants, wrapping her delicate fingers around my cock. Her warm lips wrap around the head as her tongue swirls around. She begins to bob up and down, causing my eyes to shut. I open them again, watching her as she swallows my dick. She watches me, waiting for me to take over and fuck her. That's not my plan for tonight, though. She is going to suck me off.

I tangle her hair between my fingers, pressing a curl between my thumb, index, and middle finger. It's so soft and smooth. She realizes I won't be fucking her and increases her ministrations. Her mouth is magical, as comforting as her cunt, but with different pressure points. I could die happily like this. My release is building, so close to the edge. Her fingers lightly graze my balls, causing my stomach to tighten. I push her back from me before I explode down her throat. "Open." It's the only word I can manage at this point.

I begin stroking my own dick as she kneels back. Her mouth is wide with her tongue pressed out. Her breasts are still exposed, full and heaving. My balls tighten, seeing the back of her throat exposed for me. She knows what I want without me needing to say it. I grab one of her breasts in my hand and grit my teeth. My orgasm crashes over me as it spills out on her face. I shift my cock, sending the white fluid flying all over her face and chest. Once I am spent, I place my cock on her lips, letting her clean me up. She stays on her knees as I dress again. I lean next to her face, breathing deeply.

"Mm, you smell like me, whore, because you belong to me." I kiss her forehead in a spot that doesn't have my release on her. "Put your fucking breasts away." I help her stand once she secures her dress over her coated tits. I stare for a moment, committing her to my memory. My orgasm glows against her skin in the moonlight. I would keep her like this all the time if I could. Instead, I pull a handkerchief from my pocket, offering it to her.

I bite her ear, then whisper, "You're lucky I have a handkerchief, or you'd be walking through your castle with my release all over you. Break my rules again, and that will be your punishment." Her eyes widen at my threat, and her body shivers under my words, but she cleans up and hands the handkerchief back to me. I shake my head.

"No, you can carry it, my little slut." I kiss her forehead and smack her ass before leading her back to our rooms to clean up properly and get some sleep. I hold her close as we walk together. Usually, I would linger and cuddle, reaffirming how much I love her, especially after such harsh treatment. Since we are outside, I'll give her extra comfort in the bath. I kiss her forehead again, one of my favorite affirmations of love, catching another whiff of my cum on her. A smile at the perversion spreads across my face. She really is the perfect woman for me.

Chapter 12

DAHLIA

Mama wanted us to have dinner as a family tonight. It is her and Baba's anniversary, and she has always liked celebrating as a family with a special meal. She says we are the reason our whole family exists and should all celebrate together. I don't care either way, but I am here, pleasing her. I asked about bringing Jasmin, and Mama said she didn't mind; then, I learned Jasmin was in meetings and couldn't come. Some emergency came up last minute, and she needed to deal with it. Now, I am having dinner without her.

Zander brought Tomas to the family dinner. I'm surprised to learn Tomas is considered part of the family now. Mama has accepted him; even Baba seems like he doesn't hate the boy. I haven't been around the two of them outside of dinner here and there to see how they really act together. They are working together now to set the table. Tomas has brought in the dishes, while Zander is bringing the silverware. They work well as a unit, smiling and moving in sync. Jealousy courses through my body. Jasmin and I used to be the same way. She would have dinner with us about once a week before her mother intervened.

Mama is making her favorite meal from our home, sweet potato stew. The suite smells fantastic. The spices and fragrances fill the entire area with nostalgia and love. The recipe is different from the one I grew up with. She can't find all the ingredients within this kingdom but has found suitable substitutes. She has always done her best to remember our first home. She says our old culture is just as important as the new one, and we mustn't ignore either.

During dinner, Zander and Tomas talk about the horses and the things they are doing within the stables while Baba just nods along. It sounds both interesting and boring. Mama sits happily, eating her food. It's all reasonably dull, but at least the food is delicious. I drag a piece of bread Mama made through the stew, grabbing chunks and bringing them to my mouth. It is warm and spicy and my favorite meal Mama makes. She has always been an excellent cook. Since I was locked in a sleeping curse for the past nine years, I didn't get to enjoy any foods, let alone Mama's. I savor each and every bite, then help myself to a second bowl. This food is really the best.

After dinner, we all retire to the living room. In past years, Baba would read a story or two. They said he stopped that with the curse, though. I thought he might do it tonight since I am back, but it doesn't seem like he will. I decide to take the conversation into my own hands.

"Zander, what is this here?' I wave my hand between the two of them. "What's going on?"

"Dahlia," Baba scolds. His voice is weak and raspy. This is one of the first times I've heard him talk since I returned. "Do not ask questions that do not have safe answers." I scoff at his response.

"Safe answers," I huff a breath, angry at his response. "So Zander and Tomas are fine to be together, despite the threat of death or imprisonment, but Jasmin and me? That's the line. Explain it, Baba. Why?"

"Usana." Mama speaks firmly, in our native tongue, *"Baby."* It's strange to hear her talk in our home language. We typically use the local language, even trying to mimic their accents and inflections. Though Mama has never been good at dropping her own accent. She continues to speak to me in our native tongue. *"Your brother has been promised safety by the woman you claim to love. I know she loves you too, but has she offered you the same? Does she want you the way she wants Clem? You are here fighting for something you can't have, Dahlia. It isn't healthy."*

I open my mouth to respond, only to realize I have forgotten many words of my home language. It's been nearly 13 years since I last used it. The language spoken here is one we also used back home. It wasn't as common, so there was an adjustment period. Mama and Baba insisted we speak in the local tongue to improve our communication skills. I try to respond, but my words are lost. Instead, I huff and stomp to the other room. As soon as I reach that room, my language crashes back into me. I'll be damned if she'll get the last word now. I storm into the room, shouting in our native tongue.

"She may not have offered me safety, but you and I both know she would. That is a ridiculous thing to say."

"Dahlia," my father warns with a croaking voice. I glance at him but continue on.

"Of course she wants me! Clem is the only thing stopping her! Him and this fucking curse!"

"Don't you use that word around me, Dahlia," Mama is stern without yelling. I would like to have that same ability, but my anger comes out loudly. *"She needs him to break the curse and free us all. Let her do that, then you can do what you want."* Mama is practically begging at this point. It strikes me as odd. Why should I be the one to cave? Who's to say I'm not the one who will help her break the curse. I'm convinced I am her true love, regardless of Clem and what others think.

"Maybe I'm her true love. Have you considered that? You'll let Zander be with Tomas, but not me with Jasmin? What kind of logic is that? And why do you care so much about breaking the curse? You seem to be doing well now."

This time my father stands. The motion is intended to be fast but is labored instead. I watch, torn between anger, confusion, and fear of his condition. He was always able to shoot up from his position. His voice is so broken when he speaks to me.

"Stop being so insolent." He speaks in the local language instead of arguing like Mama and I. "My days are numbered. With the freedom Jasmin has offered us, I would like to return home before the end." He pauses, looking at Mama, then back to me. His next words are angry and in our home language. *"But if she doesn't break the curse soon, I will die in this castle."*

His words strike me. I didn't know his condition was so bad. It's just like them to not tell us something this important. We were always kept in the dark. When we first came here, we didn't know until the day before we left. Then it was months after we learned we were sold with the horse because we were just fucking chattel to Jasmin's parents. Fear of losing him is tangling with the anger of his admission. I don't want to deal with this now.

I don't need this from him. I don't need this from Mama. She doesn't know Jasmin the way I do. She doesn't love Jasmin the way I do. What I have with Jas isn't something I can just give up because she found her true love. Well, that sounds like a terrible thought, but the sentiment is there. I'm not giving Jasmin up.

I decide to take a walk to the greenhouse. Being surrounded by jasmine is quite relaxing. It gives me a sense of accomplishment; something came from my nine years of being cursed, and the aroma is my favorite. I could smell it daily for the rest of my life, and it wouldn't be enough. I spend a long time in the greenhouse, considering what Mama and Baba said.

I didn't know Jasmin offered protection to Zander and Tomas. I don't know what their life will look like in the future, but I am glad they have her on their side. Mama is wrong about Jasmin. She would do everything in her power to protect me. I know she would. I'm sure Mama knows that also. Jasmin loves me as much as I love her. She is just struggling with Clem right now. He should travel the kingdom to check in all the gardens. That would take a few weeks. That's more than enough time for me to get closer to Jasmin. I will tell her that tomorrow.

Baba's admission hurts. I'm scared of him dying, but I'm also tired of them treating us like little children that can't handle hard news. They seem to forget that my whole life has been hard news. Nothing is easy for me. Nothing except being with Jasmin. At least when Clem isn't around, it's easy. Dealing with him is another issue altogether.

I've spent enough time in the greenhouse. I will walk in the gardens to clear my head before finding somewhere else to sleep tonight. I need to ask Jasmin about getting a room of my own. I've been sleeping on the large sofa in Mama's suite, but that is getting old. There are other people in the gardens tonight. It sounds like they are doing dirty things. What better way to clear my mind than snooping on someone else. There are grunts, then a long moan. It seems as if I have missed all the fun.

"Mm, you smell like me, whore, because you belong to me."

Oh, someone is pretty rude. Wait, was that Clem?

"Put your fucking breasts away."

It is Clem! He is fucking someone, and I need to get closer to see who. There is no way Jasmin would tolerate him speaking to her like that.

"No, you can carry it, my little slut."

They are walking away from me, heading back toward the castle. Clem seems to support most of her weight; she is leaning into his side as they walk. He's clearly close to whoever it is. She's short and wearing a dress. Her hair is dark, but I'm unsure who looks like that. I'll just have to tell Jasmin what I know. Clem is fucking someone, saying terrible things, and it's not her. This will be enough to get him out of the fucking way for me.

At breakfast, I scan everyone there, looking for any woman that fits the description of the woman I saw Clem being terrible to last night. I don't find any that fit perfectly, but it was dark. I list who it could be, including one man I haven't seen before. He may not technically have breasts, but I won't rule out Clem's ability to insult anyone.

Clem tells Jasmin how he plans to go to the fields to help Mikhail today. Perfect. There's my opening. As soon as Clem stops speaking, Kian and Emmeline ask Jasmin to help them. Kian is doing more research and wants to access certain information he can't get to without a key. Emmeline is planning the summer solstice masquerade ball and wants Jasmin's input. I offer to help all three, and they accept. Clem gives me a suspicious glance from beside Jasmin, and I return his gaze with an angry stare. I know what he did, and he won't get away with it.

Clem gets up to leave after everyone is finished. He gives Jasmin a long, passionate kiss as if he'll never see her again. If it's up to me, that will be the case. So he better enjoy it, as it could be his last. He finally leaves, and the four of us go to the library. Kian is walking with Jasmin, but she splits off to find the key he needs. I will stay with Emmeline; she may have more information on Clem.

"Emmeline, what do you think of Clem?"

"Hm? Oh," she turns her attention to me instead of the pad she is taking notes about the ball on. "Clem is a great guy. You should get to know him better, Dahlia." I roll my eyes at her.

"That's what everyone says," I mumble beneath my breath, but she still hears me.

"Then there must be a reason for it." Cue more eye-rolling.

"Okay, but how is he without Jasmin, like with other women?" Emmeline knits her eyebrows in confusion, pursing her lips at my question.

"What does that even mean?" I shrug casually. I won't accuse him of being a man whore to anyone but Jasmin, but it concerns me that Emmeline doesn't see it. I thought she saw everything. Before we can continue the conversation, Kian and Jasmin return, laughing at something together. I try to tamp down the jealousy, but it courses through my body, heating me from the inside.

We spend the next hour or so in the library. I help Jasmin and Emmeline plan the masquerade ball. Kian works quietly, reading books, grabbing more, reading, then grabbing. He doesn't speak to us again after getting access to the section kept under lock and key. I didn't realize an area was locked in the library. It's a small section containing texts about the kingdom's history. I have no interest in ever reading those, and I can do without them.

Jasmin announces she is going to take Finn out for a walk. While the massive white dog isn't my favorite, I offer to go with her. We leave Kian and Emmeline alone in the library. I ask her about what she plans to wear to the masquerade ball. She has yet to get an idea, but I ask to help when she sees the tailor. We are quiet while we let Finn outside. There are lots of people around. The castle is always busy and bustling with people. I want to tell her what I saw with Clem, but I don't want to do it while many people are around. Finally, Finn tires out and trudges over to us. We go inside the castle, walking toward her room. That won't be the best place to tell her, either. Clem could return, or Emmeline could. I finally spot the room we used a lot when we were young and tug her into it.

"Dahlia, what are you doing?"

Finn follows us in, collapsing on the floor, snoring within minutes. He'll be out for a while now. Perfect for me. The room is mostly empty. Some furniture is stacked against the wall, covered with protective blankets, precisely like before. I step in front of her, close enough to hug or catch her if she falls from shock.

"I have to tell you something," I say somberly. "Something about Clem." She nods, showing she is listening. "He is fucking some other woman." She looks startled but doesn't say anything else, so I elaborate. "I saw him in the gardens last night with some woman. I don't know who she is, but I have a few ideas. Possibly even a man. It was dark last night." She looks even more startled at that claim, more surprised than angry. "He was doing terrible things to her, or him. And said things even worse. He was so awful." I grab her shoulders, offering her support. "I'm sorry, Jas. But he's a terrible man." When I finish speaking, she bursts out laughing. Now it's my turn to be startled. I drop my hands, watching as Jasmin struggles to breathe through fits of laughter. I cross my arms over my chest, frustrated with her reaction.

"That was me!" She finally exclaims, still laughing, though. Then she smacks my arm. "A man, Dahlia? Are you serious?" I chuckle at that comment but quickly stop. This isn't a laughing matter.

"Wait, he said that shit to you?"

"Yes, and I let him. It's a thing we do."

"What the fuck, Jas? That's not okay!" I'm practically shrieking at this point. There is no fucking chance I will let Clem talk to her like that.

"No, Dahl. It's…" She pauses, searching the room for the words to explain her thoughts. "I like when he says it." She finally admits sheepishly.

"You like when he says those things?" She shrugs, nodding her head at me. She has always been a sexual deviant. While we never got rough, it's not typical to prefer women when you are a woman. I suppose if she likes whatever he does and she wants him to do it…

"He's not forcing you to do that? You let him? Because I swear to all things holy, Jas, I will end him if he forces you." She shakes her head, finding a relaxed stance. Her arms cross on her chest, forcing her breasts out toward me. Ugh, does she realize what that does to me? She's teasing me, and I think she knows it based on that twinkle in her eye.

"He's not forcing me, Dahl. He's a good man." That's the second time she's used my nickname like that. It sounds like music to my ears. No one else calls me that. Just her. She shortened my name to that when I first moved here. It's my favorite thing she ever says. I need her. My core is aching with need. I want her so badly.

"So, you like when people say degrading things to you?" I prowl toward her as she walks back until she bumps into the wall. Fear and arousal are written all over her face. Her arms fall to her side, her chest heaving under the thin tunic she wears with leggings. I wish she had worn a dress, but that doesn't matter. I'm going to claim her regardless.

"Kian said we need to experiment. Maybe I should call you my little slut." She gives a small gasp as her hands grab my arms. I press my body against hers, my hands on the wall behind her head. She whispers my name, sweet, pleading music to my ears. I lean in, pressing my lips against her neck. I can hear the lightning crackling in the air around us.

"So you like when people say terrible things about you, hm? That's fine. This cunt is still mine." I drop one hand to cup her pussy over her leggings. It's so warm and moist; I want to touch her directly. I want to know if she still tastes as perfect as always. My lips skim her neck, pressing delicate kisses to the column. Her breathing is hard and heavy. Her nipples are pebbled under her tunic. She still wants me, and she wants me now. I rub my hand over her pussy, giving her some friction where she wants it. She moans, grinding her cunt against my hand. Her eyes are closed tight, her fingers still wrapped around my arms, just above my elbows. I nibble her collarbone, causing her to stretch her neck, giving me better access.

I grab the loose collar of the tunic and tug it down until her breasts are exposed. She gasps as the cool air hits her sensitive, already hard nipple. I quickly wrap my lips around it, not wanting her to get cold. She groans, moving her hand to the back of my head. Her fingers trace between my braids, massaging my scalp.

"Dahlia, wait..."

"No." I suck her nipple in my mouth, then pop it out. I love the way her skin tastes. There's a hint of her floral soap mixing with her natural flavors. She's exquisite.

"I can't sit by as he kisses your skin." I press several kisses across her chest, feeling the hard bone beneath, next to the soft skin at the top of her breasts. "You were mine first. Look at this lightning." My fingers press against her core harder as a large burst of light blasts behind my head. She closes her eyes, both to protect herself from the light and because of my fingers on her pussy.

I create a trail of kisses up the middle of her chest, straight up her neck, and under her chin. Just before I round her chin, the door opens then slams behind us. Jasmin gasps, but I just slowly turn my head to look back. In the doorway, his shoulders are heaving as Clem shoots daggers at us with his eyes.

Chapter 13

Oh fuck.

Clem is furious. His face is hardened in anger, hands clenched so tight his knuckles look white from across the room, even covered in dirt from being in the fields. Dahlia has the sense to stop kissing me, but she hasn't moved away from me. I can't be sure who Clem is staring at, but his eyes would kill if they could.

Just as I realize the hurt I have caused him, a memory floods back into my brain from years ago. This same situation, but my mother. She stood in the doorway. She was so angry that she banned Dahlia from my life. She banned a person, a whole-ass person. I didn't see Dahlia for months after she did that. Crippling fear courses through my body. I can hear my mother screaming at me. She's calling me a whore, a slut, a terrible princess, unfit to rule or even serve my kingdom. She is yelling at the servants to remove the tramp that tainted me. The yelling, there was so much yelling.

Clem stalks toward us. Dahlia turns to face him, standing directly in front of me. I can still hear the harsh, loud words of my mother. Some tiny, quiet part of my brain is trying to tell me that's not how Clem would act, but it's barely audible under her screaming. It's hard to breathe. I can't get a breath in; my chest is heaving. I'm terrified at this moment.

Clem stops in front of Dahlia and demands, in a calm, rational voice, that she move. She doesn't; he steps closer. My breath catches again; I'm trying to breathe, but it's so hard. Where is the air? Why is there no air in here? It sounds like I'm underwater, but I hear someone call my name. I try to look around and realize I am underwater. No, wait, those are tears. I'm crying.

I touch my cheek, finding it soaked with tears. I wipe them away to see Clem push Dahlia to the side. Instinctively, my arms rise defensively in front of me. I'm backed against the wall here. Dahlia is standing on one side, furniture on the other. I'm trapped. My mother's voice increases its volume in my head. She is still screaming obscene names at me, trying to make me feel terrible. It's working; she does her job well.

Hands grab and pull me from my position. I can't stop the shriek that comes from my mouth. I close my eyes as my hands go over my head. The hands drop me, but the fear remains. I don't feel safe here, despite the part of my brain that knows I am. Guards rush into the room. I need to tell them I am fine, but all I can hear is my mother. All I can see are the months without Dahlia. All I can sense is anger from Clem. All I can feel is the fear of how this situation will turn out.

Dahlia is talking to the guards, trying to usher them out of the room to give us privacy. Clem is standing over me. I can hear his voice now. He is sad, scared, hurt, concerned, and so full of love. The door closes somewhere in the distance, then Dahlia returns. The delicate beads in her hair clink together as she walks toward me. I can finally hear things other than my mother's voice. I'm not ready to open my eyes yet. Dahlia's hand rubs my back.

I finally open my eyes to see Clem. He looks so hurt, so worried. His shoulders are tense, and his eyebrows are pulled together slightly. He speaks my name softly, and I rush into his arms. I cry out, telling him how sorry I am. He squeezes me tight, tangling his fingers through my hair as he shushes me.

"It's not your fault, Jasmin. It's okay."

"Like hell are you gonna put all the blame on me. I didn't force her."

"You are to blame. Maybe you didn't force her, but you certainly took advantage of her!"

"Took advantage!?! Listen..."

And just like that, they are fighting. They are yelling. My whole body hurts. What is happening in my life? Will it always be this difficult? I try to pull out of Clem's arms, but he doesn't let me go. His hand stays on my arm. They are still yelling about whose fault this is, who loved me first, who loves me most, who deserves me.

"Please," I whisper. I just want the fighting to stop. Finn is now next to me, glaring between Clem and Dahlia, unsure where the threat comes from or how to react. He knows he needs to protect me, though. I slide one hand lightly across his back, letting him know I am okay.

They both stop talking but glare at each other. I'm worried Dahlia will learn a spell to shoot actual daggers from her eyes. Then we will all be fucked. Everyone will be dead at some point if there is a spell out there for that. I take a deep breath and another. Their attention slowly turns from each other to me. I must make this right, but I can't do this with both here. I need to sort through this shit show.

"Dahlia, can you please leave me alone with him?"

"While he's this angry and wild? Fat chance in hell." She retorts. Her accent is always thick and heavy when she is emotional. Every word is harsh and stacked with anger.

"While I'm angry? You're the one in danger of my anger!" Clem raises his voice, not quite to a yell, but loud nonetheless. I shudder at both the command and anger. He notices and barely contains the flash of a smirk. My stupid body would betray me in that way now. Dahlia sees his smirk but not my reaction. Before she begins to yell, I raise my hands to halt her. Finn growls from his position beside me.

"Please, Dahl. I need to talk to Clem first. Please." I'm begging; it's unbecoming of a queen to beg, but Dahlia is stubborn. Sometimes I need to pull out the big tricks, like begging. She finally agrees, swearing if I don't find her before dinner, she will find me and won't settle for begging. I simply nod as she walks out. I watch her, trying to decide what to say to Clem, how to make this right with him.

When I turn back to face him, he looks hurt and sad. Gone is the anger he showed just minutes ago. I bite my lip, struggling not to release any of my emotions. I ask if he wants to go to our room to chat in more privacy. He simply turns and walks away from me. I follow him, stopping to let the guards know I am okay, apologize, and thank them for their concern. We walk silently through the halls, me a few steps behind him the whole time. Finn stays next to me, glancing between Clem and me. Finn has grown really fond of Clem, and I hate that he feels torn between the two of us now.

Clem heads straight to the bathroom to wash his arms. I sit on one of the sofas, waiting for him to return. He takes a seat across from me in one of the armchairs. His action stings more than I want to admit, but I can't blame him.

"I'm sorry." I start weakly. I know it's not enough, but too many other things rush through my mind to form a full apology.

"For getting caught?"

"Yes." No, that's not the right answer! "No! I'm not; I mean... Clem." I sigh. There are so many things I need to say, but one thing I need to know before I can move on. "What brought you inside? You were clearly busy in the fields." He scoffs at me, looking away. His shoulders are slumped. I hate seeing him like this, yet I feel it's a consistent look between us. We are either doing well or fighting like this. I would like more of the good days, but even just more in between; regular days where nothing crazy is happening would be nice.

"The lightning. Why were you doing that with her, Jasmin?"

His words break my heart. Part of me knew he wouldn't be happy about this, but part of me hoped he wouldn't mind so much if it meant breaking the curse.

"Kian suggested we see how strong the lightning would be depending on how much we are together." Clem's look indicates he's ready to kill Kian for that. "But, Kian mentioned I should tell you first. I'm so sorry, Clem. I wanted to tell you. I really did, but things were going so well for you. You've been so happy the last few days. I didn't want to ruin that for you." He sighs, standing to pace the room.

His hands rub through his hair. I wish he would let me do that, but I know I have lost that right for now.

"What else have you done with her?" He turns sharply with his words, anger and fear coursing through his body in tightly clenched muscles.

"Nothing. She kissed me at the pond, but not today."

"No. Today she just had your cunt in her hands." I wince at his words. I don't mind them during play, but there is a line, and this is over it. I stay silent for a few minutes, gathering my thoughts. This is not how I wanted this conversation to go. This isn't how I wanted this day to go.

"I don't want you to be alone with her." Clem pauses as shock flashes across my face. "I know better than to try to keep you from her. But you broke my trust, and I don't trust her to keep her hands off you." I jump up, taking a step toward him.

"She is important to breaking the curse!"

"How do you know that?"

"You've seen the lightning."

"How do you know that isn't the border resealing? An opposite reaction to the thunder." He waves his hand between us to emphasize his point. I open my mouth to respond, only to realize I don't have a response. He is right; I don't know what the lightning actually means. Kian is the one who suggested it, but he could be wrong. He could be wrong about Clem, too. No. I refuse to entertain that idea. He is right about Clem. He is my true love. The curse has been breaking with Clem being around. I just don't know why Dahlia is here now.

"Then we need to go to Greynon," I tell him.

It's been a week, a long week. Clem won't leave me alone, but he doesn't want to touch me. I've had enough weeks that are the longest of my life. There is always something frustrating going on. My life is a remarkable string of frustrating years, months, or weeks. Some ridiculous amount of time for shit to be so difficult.

Today we are finalizing the plans from Greynon. I'm both excited and nervous. I'm excited to travel again. To travel with Clem. I'm excited to see more of the covens. We are spending time there to build better relationships. They have been so strained with the past rulers; I refuse to let that be my legacy. I'm nervous about what Matron Maud will say about this curse. She is the strongest witch in Sweet Briar now. I hope she can shed some light on the curse and tell us how to break it. We will meet with her about the curse a few days after we arrive.

Today, we are discussing the final timeline and travel plans. Kian and Emmeline are coming with us. I want Erik to come, but given that he is off chasing Bea, I don't expect him to. We have several guards going with us, along with Lord Alwyn. He returned to the castle a few days ago to help make final travel arrangements. He tried to convince me to stay in his village instead of the covens. I was outraged by his suggestion. I will spend a day in the city proper, but not the whole time. The witches have assured us they are capable of hosting us. We are about to walk into this meeting to determine what Dahlia will be doing. Clem and I are divided.

I've tried to persuade Clem that Dahlia should travel with us, but he refused to listen. I understand his point, but she should be there to meet with Matron Maud. I reach out to hold his hand as we near the meeting room. He looks back at me but doesn't hold my hand or slow his pace to allow me to hold his. I drop it, feeling defeated already. I stare down at the ground, not wanting to hold my own head up at this moment. I bump into Clem because he stopped outside the door. He turns to face me, and I lift my face to him, feeling more hopeful than I should. Clem sighs and presses a kiss to my forehead. It's progress.

"Sorry," he mumbles before turning to walk in before me on an ominous current. This isn't going to go well.

We take our seats after bows and pleasantries have been exchanged. Henry recounts the itinerary that has been made, listing the number of guards and people traveling, minus Dahlia.

"Which brings us to the topic, should Dahlia travel with this group?"

"No. She cannot be trusted with the Queen." Clem's response is quick and measured. I sigh.

"We need her to speak with Matron Maud about this curse." My response is less measured. These emotions have taken a toll.

"We can't take her," Kian adds, sending a wave of shock through me. He's been on my side since the beginning. He holds his hands out to stop anyone else so he can explain. "There isn't enough room for her. Many witches are still displaced, and they don't have an extra room for her." Well, that solves that problem, then. Clem releases a heavy breath, turning to look at me. I don't meet his gaze, though. We discuss a few final details, then mention a few items relating to the summer solstice celebration before we end the meeting. I ask Emmeline to find Dahlia and bring her here. She nods and walks off.

I rise to get a glass of wine. Clem stays in his seat.

"I plan to tell her, but Emmeline can stay with me." I pour the wine into my glass, turning to take a sip. He doesn't look back at me, just remains in his seat.

"I'll stay. I've nowhere else to be right now."

"Clem, please. Give me five minutes with Emmeline and Dahlia. She won't do anything with her here."

"Emmeline needs to help with packing and getting ready for tomorrow. You know she has lots to do for you to travel. I can stay."

"Fuck, Clem." He's right. He's made me feel both selfish and terrible for even suggesting this. Maybe I am those things, but I wouldn't be if he weren't being so overprotective and jealous. I pour two more glasses of wine and walk to the table. I place one on the table before him, harder than I should. I set the other in the spot next to mine. We wait in silence for Dahlia to arrive.

When they walk in, I let Emmeline know Clem will stay and she can tend to whatever duties she needs to. I hug Dahlia and offer her the seat next to mine. I explain why she can't travel with us and tell her how long we'll be gone. I ask her to read over some books Kian is leaving for her. At this point, I'm surprised there are any books he hasn't read. She isn't happy, but she doesn't put up much of a fight. Secretly, I wonder if she is planning something. She would always be more reserved when scheming. Nonetheless, we leave for Greynon in one day. It's time to prepare for that trip.

Part Two

GREYNON

Chapter 14

JASMIN

The first stretch of road to Greynon is beautiful. We ride along the path that leads to Arkaley but turn before going into the mountain range. We ride through the foothills of the Beinn Mountains. Most snow caps are melted, and the trees are turning vibrant shades of green. The mountains alone are breathtaking. They stand against a bright blue sky with clouds scattered throughout. The day is warm, and the ride is relatively easy. We ride for many hours until we reach the base of the Crescent Mountain range. Before heading up the mountains tomorrow, we will stay in a small camp reserved for royalty.

Someone is already set up at the base as we near the camp. This is odd since it is meant for royalty. Clem and I wait while the guards ride ahead to check it out. We are soon called forward. We ride over calmly, only to find Erik and Bea at the camp already. Clem nearly falls off his horse, trying to dismount quickly to get to his sister. I climb off Vesper much more gracefully, approaching the couple. Bea is wearing a ring, as is Erik. I'm so excited to hear about their time together.

After Clem tackles Bea, we settle around a fire Erik started, ready to make dinner shortly. Some of the others take over that duty while we catch up. I snuggle close to Clem, glad to be off Vesper. I love the horse, but riding for a long time can get tiring. Kian and Emmeline join us as Erik tells us how he finally convinced

Bea to marry him. Clem seems sad to have missed his sister's wedding but doesn't show it much. He does his best to look happy. I'm glad he finally lets me touch and snuggle him again. It's been such a long week without that.

"The boy is doing well; his arm is healing nicely." Erik changes the conversation to discuss the other duties I asked him to fulfill.

"Oh, good. And his family is being compensated?" Erik nods in response. "What of the guards in Greynon?" He takes a deep breath, looking between Kian and me.

"They don't work well with the covens. They mostly function independently. The witches have fortified the barrier touching their lands, leaving it at that. The rest of the guards cover the barrier in the manner that has been requested, but there is little communication between the two groups." I tsk, shaking my head.

"I wish they would work together more. How did they fortify it?"

"I don't know. I didn't ask and didn't go see. It would have been another 3-4 days to my trip."

I nod, accepting his answer. I must ask the witches what they did when I see them. Clem kisses my cheek as someone brings us over bowls of rabbit stew. I thank them, diving into the delicious food. I love our cook at the castle, but this stew is delicious. We all sit around, chatting until the sun begins to set. With the summer solstice so close, the sunsets are later than usual. We enjoy the last of the fading sunlight before going to bed. Clem is more relaxed around me now that Dahlia isn't here. I hate that reasoning, but I am glad for the contact with him again.

In the morning, we bid farewell to Erik and Bea. They leave in the opposite direction, returning to the castle to spend time together before settling into their routine. Bea has agreed to oversee the animals while Erik continues working with the guards. He told us he offered to quit, and I nearly had an attack. I understand why he said it, but I wouldn't let him quit. He is too valuable to me to lose him. I tell Bea how happy I am to have her at the castle. I hope she is as satisfied as Erik and Clem are there or as happy as I think they are.

Today's ride is more strenuous but no less beautiful. We wind through the mountains, dipping low in the tree-filled valleys, then high to the crest, where we can see for miles. I absolutely love the mountains. The beauty against the land's harshness reminds me how resilient life can be. We finally near the covens' land, and Kian rides ahead to let them know we are near. I swear a flash of longing appears on Emmeline's face, but if it does, it's gone before I can be certain.

The covens have learned to live with the land instead of changing it to their advantage. Their homes are built into the side of the mountain. Many homes have been made with pine trees that grow everywhere. The buildings look surprisingly rustic for a place that has magic. I expected the villages to look more like Vadried or a more prominent display of their abilities. They have decided to focus their magical efforts on other areas.

We are staying in the same inn we visited during the coronation tour. This one is built into the side of the mountain, but Clem and I have been given a different room. This one is smaller but is on the far side of the mountain and has a balcony overlooking the valley below. Matron Maud leads us through the winding hallways carved in stone. Most of the walls are plain, allowing the beauty of the stone to shine through. A few panels are carved with intricate designs. I will come back and view them soon, as we are moving too quickly to enjoy them now. Once in the room, Matron Maud briefly explains everything, then leaves us, letting us know dinner will be in a few hours. Despite the long ride, they are waiting until sundown for dinner. I don't mind as it gives us time to relax or do other things.

Clem is standing out on the balcony, overlooking the mountains beyond. I walk up, resting against his arm and leaning against the railing.

"I like the castle, but your predecessors were morons to pass up a location like this." I chuckle at his observation.

"My predecessors had no natural skills in the mountains. They chose a strategic location they could defend. Besides, they probably would have ruined this view." I sigh contentedly as he makes a noise in agreement. We stare for several more moments, enjoying the quiet of the mountains. The peaceful birds chirping and the wind blowing, rustling leaves and needles. Matron Maud said our balcony was spelled to keep most sounds out while all sounds are contained within. I love the uses they have found for the magic.

I place a kiss against Clem's arm, tugging him lightly to turn toward me. He hasn't rejected any of my advances today and was more giving with his touches yesterday. I gently kiss his lips, and when he doesn't pull away, I deepen our kiss. My tongue traces along his lips, pressing inside his mouth. He accepts me, swirling his tongue with mine. He tries to push his body against mine, but I hold him at a distance. I put his hands on my hips, intentionally keeping space between us. I may have hurt him when he found me with Dahlia, but he hasn't so much as stroked my head in a week. He's not getting off that easily.

I groan into his mouth, hoping to distract him so he doesn't realize what I'm doing with my hands. When I finish, I tug the rope hard, jerking his hands away from my hips and pulling them together at the wrists. He snaps back from the kiss, very confused about what happened. He sees his wrists tied together, the tail in my hands. His eyebrows raise in curious disbelief, and I shrug playfully.

"I may have asked the guards how they restrain someone, and I may have also found some spare rope," I swoon teasingly, then bite my lip. "I may also have a plan for how we will spend the next few hours." I turn away from him, tugging the rope behind me as I reach the bed. Thankfully it is a four-poster, similar to my own, but this one does have curtains and materials all over it. I asked one of the staff if the fabric is important or expensive. I was informed it was moderately expensive but not important. One current benefit to the disconnect between the covens and royalty is some anonymity. The kid that answered the question didn't recognize me.

I climb on the end of the bed, pulling the rope over my head to the top post. It's not a graceful or sexy move, but it will get us there. I tie the rope with his hands above his head. He watches me curiously, hungrily, but also silently. Once the rope is secured, I climb down, standing before him.

"Hope you weren't attached to this shirt." I grab the collar, pull it hard, and quickly rip it from his chest. His breath hitches at the action, his dick already straining his trousers. I didn't expect him to be so responsive, but that makes this better. I fiddle with the material until his chest is bare. I lick across his chest, then from one nipple to his neck. I tongue down his abdomen, tracing the softer lines of his muscles. At his waist, I nip the skin just above his pants. He jerks back as I giggle at his reaction. I look up at his intense stare, almost losing my train of thought. His eyes express his deep need for me. It strikes me how deeply he wants me at this moment. Maybe his recent distance is helpful.

I drop to my knees, slowly pulling his pants down. He steps out of them, and I toss them to the side. I press a small kiss to the side of his cock, then stand and take a few steps back. My eyes devour his nude body in front of me. Every dip and muscle. The tuft of blonde hair just above his cock. The sun-kissed shoulders with his long blonde hair just brushing them. I could get off just staring at him, but that's not the plan.

"Can you snap?" I ask. He looks confused.

"What?"

I snap my fingers at him. "Snap, can you snap?"

"Oh," he snaps for me, showing me he can, but his head is already focused on the end game. I saunter up to him, pressing a seductive kiss against his cheek, then whisper in his ear.

"What a good little cock you are."

My fingers glide across his penis in a feather-soft touch before I walk away to stand in front of him again. I remove my top, the dress with the part that allows me to wear pants and ride easily. I'll wear an actual dress for dinner, but I prefer these for riding. I remove the pants slowly, bending at the waist so he gets a good view of my ass. He bites his lip, his cock leaking. This is going to be fun since he is already so aroused. I walk smoothly to our bags, finding a handkerchief.

"Do you know how wet I am right now?" He shakes his head as I amble in front of him. I grab his face with my fingers, squeezing tightly.

"Use your words when you address your queen."

"No, Queen." I shiver, loving the way that sounds on his lips. "Open your mouth." I squeeze again before releasing him. I drag the handkerchief through my aching core, then shove it in his mouth. I push in all the material to form the makeshift gag. "Now, do you know how wet I am?" He nods, and I pat the side of his face. "Good. No more talking for you."

I drop to my knees in front of him, taking the head of his cock in my mouth. I bob up and down slowly, ensuring there is enough spit to coat it properly. He groans as I finally bottom out. I swallow him down, pressing my tongue against his cock. I swirl my tongue along the head as my hands stroke his length. He groans when I cup his balls lightly in my hand. I remove my hand from his length, sliding up and down his stomach again. He groans, and I feel his balls tighten. He's about to release, and that just can't happen. This is a punishment for not touching me for a week. I remove my mouth, stand up, and walk over to get a cup of water. As I sip, I struggle not to laugh at his face. The cloth is hanging out of his mouth. His eyebrows are pulled together from confusion and hurt. His shoulders are slouched despite his raised arms. He looks distraught as his cock jerks for release.

After my water, I walk back to our luggage, finding another sash. I twist it around my wrist, letting the tails dangle low. I trace my fingers across Clem's stomach, then glide behind him and caress his shoulders, letting the sash trail just below my touch. He groans, low and desperate. I climb on the bed, untying his hands. He leans back against me, rubbing his back against my chest. I chuckle, letting him do what he wants for now.

When his hands are down, I drag him onto the bed on his back. I secure his hands above his head again on the headboard this time. I hover on his chest, rubbing my wet pussy against his chest. I pull the handkerchief out of his mouth, quickly replacing it with my lips. The kiss is searing and desperate and short. I use the cloth to wipe my wetness from his chest, then make another pass across my pussy before I shove it back into his mouth. He moans my nickname as I shove the cloth inside his mouth again. I unravel the sash from my wrist and secure it over his eyes, ensuring he can't see. I climb off the bed and tiptoe around to the other side. I don't want him to know what I'm doing yet.

I gently crawl across the bed until I am beside his ear and whisper, "I'm going to fuck myself on you now. And you don't get to watch." I mount him quickly, sinking over his cock. I moan out his name as his thick length fills me completely. I pause at the bottom, letting us adjust to this new sensation. If I'm not mistaken, he won't last long. So I need to be quick.

I lift myself up, dropping down again. I bounce over Clem, setting a pace I like. It hits that spot deep inside that feels so good. "Oh, gods." I moan. My tits bounce against my chest, and I wish he would grab them. Then I remember his hands are tied, and he can't see me. So I grab them myself but get an idea.

"Oh, I wish you could squeeze my tits for me," I grunt as I thrust him deep inside me. "I need your rough hands." His hands jerk against the restraints, causing the headboard to groan under his pressure. I pound faster, realizing he is probably close. "Don't worry. I'll play with my clit." I drop one hand to the bundle of nerves and swirl my fingers around it as my pussy clenches around him. My orgasm is so close, but he distracts me by jerking against the bed.

Finally, his hands break free, moving faster than I can comprehend. He jerks the mask and gag off, then flips me over before I can react. He thrusts twice, then pulls his cock out, spilling his seed across my stomach and chest. His hand is on my clit, sending me soaring into orgasmic bliss. I might yell or scream or stay silent. All I know is my body is flying through ecstasy, and I don't know where I physically am anymore. Lips are on mine as my body slowly, so slowly, returns to the world. I can't return the kiss, though. My body isn't responding to my commands. Maybe I'm not actually sending commands. I'm just stuck in orgasmic purgatory.

Clem collapses beside me as I do finally return to the present. I turn my head to look at him, and we both burst into giggles. He wipes his mess from my body while I am sailing in pleasure. He pulls me against him, his warmth encompassing my now chilled body. I snuggle against him, enjoying the intimacy of touching him. I kiss him properly this time, glad to have some control of my body again.

"What possessed you to do that?" Clem questions, propping up to hover over me. His fingers skim my body as I stay close to his chest.

"You did! You haven't touched me in a week, and I won't let that slide." He chuckles but insists he didn't do that. I assure him he did.

"Well, I'm not sorry then. I may just have to not touch you for another week." I smack his chest, snuggling tighter against him. We need to get dressed for dinner soon, but at this point, I just want to take a nap. I want to stay snuggled against his chest. All the other problems can wait until later. I don't want to worry about the witches, the curse, or what dress I will wear. I will just sleep in the arms of my true love and be content.

Chapter 15

CLEM

She took control and made me lose my mind. I've never been forced or restrained like that before. I loved it but needed more quickly. I probably could have let her finish how she wanted, but where is the fun in that? I would much rather take control, but watching her make demands and tease me ruined me. I didn't know my body could even handle not erupting when she stopped sucking my cock.

She's dressing for dinner now, and I can't focus on anything but her. The way her ass sticks out as she bends over. The way her hair falls to the floor as she laces her shoes. The way she yells at me to get dressed. Maybe she should use that dominating voice again. Suddenly, a pillow flies at my head. I try to dodge it, but it still hits me. I laugh at her, but she just yells more about getting ready. Someone has already knocked on the door once. I'm surprised Emmeline isn't in here yelling at us.

As if on cue, Emmeline walks in, griping at us for being late. She balks at my state of undress. I couldn't get ready while I was watching Jasmin. I am so enamored with her now. I just want to watch her and touch her and not do anything else.

"I don't know what you did to him, but I'm not touching him like that." Jasmin sighs while a goofy grin spreads across my face. She rolls her eyes, tossing my trousers at me. I slip them on while Emmeline complains about the size of the room. It is much smaller than what we are used to. It's about the size of the room I had as a bachelor. There is a bed, a wash table, a desk, and two chests of drawers for our clothes. There is a private bathing area, but it's not nearly as lovely as ours. The balcony is spectacular, though.

Jasmin leaves the room to find Kian while I get ready. Without her in the room, it only takes a few minutes. Emmeline helps me with the clothes since we have opted for more formal wear, and I'm unfamiliar with this style. I thank her and compliment her own clothes. She leaves me in the room to recenter myself briefly before I go too. I take several deep breaths but can only smell Jasmin, her floral scent. I try to think of things other than Jasmin, but everything circles back to her.

I am so in love with the woman I can't handle it. I want to be with her all the time. Being away from Dahlia has been a breath of fresh air for me. Jasmin loves her and wouldn't intentionally do anything to hurt me, but I realize how difficult that position is for her. Being here, though, without the threat of anything happening, has me in a joyful mood. I just want to shower Jasmin with love. I feel bad for the past week that I have ignored her. I really have been unfair to her. She didn't do anything, but she didn't stop it either.

I shake my head, clearing Dahlia from my thoughts as I search for the woman I love. I find her waiting with Kian and Emmeline, who wear suspiciously matching clothes. I walk into the large room with Emmeline and Kian, Jasmin trailing behind us, entering last as her position demands. The room is carved in stone, with images engraved in each panel. There are images of witches, flowers, and animals, but I'm unsure what they mean. The room has a large U-shaped table set up. People are sitting on either side of the table on the two legs. On the connecting table, people are only sitting on one side. Jasmin and Matron Maud are at the center. An older woman sits to the left of Matron Maud; I am on Jasmin's right.

Kian is beside me, a interesting spot since he is a witch. I'm curious about the meaning behind his placement and will ask Jasmin later.

We stand next to our seats while others find theirs. Matron Maud welcomes everyone, then Jasmin shares her appreciation for the beautiful arrangements and delicious-smelling food. With that, they both sit, and everyone else follows. Wine is brought around as we fill our plates from dishes on the tables. The food is unique, with more local cuisine than we saw last time. I chat with Kian about some of it. Jasmin continues to flit in my peripheral vision. She is so regal and gorgeous tonight. She looks like an angel, living perfectly. She chats with the Matrons and servers, using the same kind demeanor with everyone she talks to.

"What?" She grins, leaning toward me to whisper.

"Hm?"

"You keep staring. Is there something on my face?" Her fingers rise to touch her lips. I'm not used to being insanely jealous of fingers, but here I am.

"You... I love you, is all." Her grin grows widely. She grabs my hand, squeezing it firmly before returning to her food. I try not to stare at her for the rest of the night. I'm not entirely successful, but I try.

After food, the Matron of every coven introduces themselves to Jasmin, offering some gift, a token of appreciation. Some offer spells, such as healing lotions, magical items to help find things; one coven offers a blank music box for her to use when she wants, having heard from Kian how much she enjoys those. Other covens offer spices, materials, animals, or services. Jasmin is thrilled with every gift, no matter how small. I admire her ability to show the same excitement for each item.

Once all the covens have been introduced, Matron Maud informs us there will be a band and a casual gathering in a few moments once the room is cleared out. We all rise to leave while servants and other witches begin clearing tables and chairs and food. Jasmin walks away to talk with the covens, and I find Kian.

"So, this band, can you make one of those magic music boxes for her?"

He pats his chest, where a slight, barely noticeable bulge appears under his fingers. "Already planned to." He winks at me, adding, "You can give it to her later. But I want to know what she did to prevent you from getting dressed before dinner." I laugh, tossing a glance at Emmeline. She is suddenly a deep shade of red and turns away to look at the engraved wall.

"I'm not one to kiss and tell." Kian takes in my response and Emmeline's reaction with consideration.

"Oh, but you should," he swoons, but Emmeline shoves his arm playfully. Thankfully, they announce the ballroom is ready, and we can enter. People start filtering in as I find Jasmin and take her arm. We wait until everyone else is in and walk in together. I kiss her cheek, unable to stop. Matron Maud announces the first song will be one from the castle, then more traditional witch songs will be played. I'm excited to hear their music, but glad there will be something I am familiar with.

The music starts playing Jasmin's favorite piece. Before I say anything, Kian walks past us, whispering, "You're welcome." He finds a spot with Emmeline, and I take Jasmin in my arms. We start dancing, laughing, and enjoying our time together. She lets down her regal persona, laughs, and celebrates much like everyone else. She is still somewhat reserved from what she would be at the castle, but she is obviously having fun and genuinely enjoying herself.

The next song is a traditional witch piece, so we find seats and wine and watch while they move through the dances. We chat with the Matrons for a while, then Jasmin mingles with everyone. My favorite thing about watching her is seeing how she treats them all the same. The Matrons and Lords receive the same respect as commoners and servants. I have no experience with royalty, but I don't think that's normal behavior for them. She never ceases to amaze me.

After the song ends, we are asked to find seats for a middle-aged witch in long dark robes. Stars and swirls are sewn into the robe, giving it a magical appearance. Jasmin and I settle into a small couch near the wall. She snuggles into my side, trying to hide a yawn by leaning into my chest. It has been a long day between the ride through the mountains, our afternoon tryst, and the late dinner. I don't know how long the celebration will last, but I hope it wraps up soon. We could both use some rest.

The witch introduces herself as the second in command in Matron Maud's coven. She tells how each panel in the room represents the covens. The story of her coven is one of the first panels you see when you enter the space. It is just off-center and covered with flowers and stars in the sky. Their coven is one of the oldest in Greynon. The witch tells more of their history as Jasmin wiggles beside me, fighting to stay awake.

The witch's story ends, and she announces the party will continue for those interested in staying, but the royal party is welcome to retire after their long ride in. Thank the gods for that. Jasmin and I rise, saying goodbyes and promising more time during the trip. We have nearly a week planned to stay in Greynon, with only one day dedicated to the village below. We won't be able to visit every coven, but we will see many of them. Tomorrow, we are starting with breakfast, then taking a tour through some of the closer covens before having dinner with everyone again. We're both excited to learn more about this land.

Despite being smaller than our usual room, Jasmin and I fall asleep quickly and sleep all night. Not having Finn with us has also been fantastic for my sleep. I love the dog, but he is so big, furry, and hot. I wanted him out of bed when I started sharing a room with Jasmin, but that will never happen.

The witches have prepared more of their preferred foods for breakfast. Tiny quail eggs fried with seasonings I am unfamiliar with are stacked on a plate. A variety of fruits and some vegetables fill bowls, along with many spiced jams and fried bread. It all looks delicious and tastes as good as it seems.

"Matron Maud, I haven't had a chance to ask how the repairs are going. Kian has updated when possible, but I want to hear more." Jasmin asks. I lean closer to listen to the response. This room is larger than the dining hall at the castle. More people are making noise, so it is louder than we are used to during breakfast.

"They are going slower than we would like. Thankfully, no one was seriously injured since most of us were at the castle." Matron Maud has a wise but harsh-sounding voice. I would think she is always angry if I didn't know any better. "The two injured people are healed now, but we are having trouble rebuilding in that location. It was a building with multiple homes. There are only so many places we can erect buildings that large here."

"Do you need, or want, assistance from our builders? We can send others to help survey the land for you. I don't know if ours would be as beneficial as yours since we don't typically build in the mountains, but we can arrange to have them come out quickly."

"Oh, no thank you, Your Highness. We can manage on our own. This isn't our first collapse. While we hope it will be the last, we will rebuild." Jasmin nods for a moment, then the words sink in.

"This isn't the first?" She takes a deep breath before speaking quickly again. "I'm sorry; when did the others happen?"

"The first building collapsed about six years ago; the second about two. They were more devastating, but we have rebuilt and are doing better now." Kian huffs on my side. He looks angry, which is unusual for him. I'm not used to seeing him express such emotion. Jasmin notices, too, but Matron Maud speaks up again before she can say anything. "Oh, this isn't a proper discussion for the breakfast table. Let's discuss something happier, like the upcoming summer solstice." Jasmin hesitantly switches the conversation to the summer solstice, turning back to face Matron Maud and Matron Celeste, head of the largest coven. As they chat, I turn toward Kian, worried about his reaction. Emmeline seems to have the same concern as she is already whispering to him. I lean close, wanting to hear what he says.

"No, Matron Maud is correct. This is a story for another time. I'll tell you then. I do have a surprise for both of you today, though." He gives a wink before sipping on his tea. He continues eating, not giving us any more details about said surprise. What kind of surprise could he have for both Emmeline and me?

Once breakfast is over, we gather at the main entrance, waiting for everyone before the tour of the area begins. Jasmin is on edge now. She was relaxed before breakfast, but the comments about the other buildings set her on edge. I step behind her, placing my hand on her back.

"What's wrong, little flower?" I whisper into her ear. She turns to look at me.

"I'm upset I didn't know about the other buildings. That is something I should have been told about when it happened. Now I'm mad at Alwyn, too. This trip will not go well when I see him." She sighs, so I squeeze her side in a half hug. Court protocol prevents me from showing too much affection. I hate that rule the most.

"Wonderful," Matron Maud calls to the crowd. "Let us begin the first tour for a royal member in generations!" She claps loudly and walks out the door. Jasmin struggles to restrain a wince as she follows quickly behind Matron Maud. As much as she wants to repair the stifled relations, she doesn't want reminders of her predecessors' failures either. Maybe that will be the only comment made. Hopefully.

Chapter 16

CLEM

Matron Maud is undoubtedly making a big deal about the Queen taking a tour of her lands. She has mentioned several times that Jasmin is the first in a long time, the first that Maud has ever seen. Her comments are wearing on Jasmin. She is becoming more reserved by the minute. I do what I can to keep the mood light, but there is only so much I can do in this situation. I take Jasmin's hand, wrapping it around my arm. It's not a favorable position within the court, but still allowed.

Jasmin wore one of her new dresses with an open front. She paired the green dress with dark leggings and boots that are better for walking. The sleeves are loose but still warm in this weather. Thankfully, the mountains are heavily shaded. The sun is warm when it breaks through the trees, but the shade is cool. Matron Maud leads us through her sector of homes and buildings. A few facilities are shared by all covens, but most have structures and function as a small village within Greynon. The area is beautiful, with flowers blooming, bright green trees, and birds and animals flittering around. This area is full of life.

"Matron Maud, can you tell me how the curse has affected your area? It seems to be doing very well," Jasmin asks.

"We have seen smaller crop output, and our livestock hasn't fared as well. We have used our magic to sustain ourselves better than some villages."

"Hm," is all Jasmin says in return, but I know that look. She's upset that they have fared so well while others have struggled. Jasmin does not like having villages unwilling to do their part for the kingdom. It also doesn't help that she didn't know that information beforehand. I fear the lashing Alwyn will receive for this. I still want to be there for it, though. He elected not to come on this tour with us, insisting he is already familiar with the lands. I have a feeling that is a lie.

We come to an area with logs and stones scattered everywhere. It is a mix between destruction and construction. This is the place of the most recent building collapse. Matron Maud turns as if to walk away, but Jasmin inquires after it. Maud explains the building fell, and they have temporarily relocated the families to the inn. The construction is going well; just taking time. After her comments, Matron Maud does turn away, leaving no room for further questions. Jasmin sighs but follows along. She wants answers about what happened but isn't getting them.

We reach the end of a road, and another stems off the side but is not meant to be part of this road. Matron Celeste speaks up at this moment.

"This road leads back to my coven and toward the inn." Matron Celeste is even older than Matron Maud. Her grey hair is in a knot on top of her head. Today, she is wearing a long dark dress, similar to the robes she wore last night, but not quite as thick. Her skin is wrinkled and covered with age spots. She hunches slightly as she walks.

"Matron Celeste," Kian speaks calmly, "If you don't mind, I would like to show them to lunch, then I will bring them to your coven for a tour." Celeste nods, waving us away as she turns back toward her coven. Maud gives an angry look to Kian, but she follows behind Celeste, walking away and leaving us alone. Two guards remain after everyone else goes.

Kian leads us down a path in the opposite direction of everyone else. The trail is small, covered in some places. Pine trees mix with grand oak trees while grass and wildflowers grow. The sound of running water grows until we hear the waterfall.

Kian leads us further, taking us to several rocks on the edge of a small pond. On the far side of the pond is a roaring waterfall. It splashes over its ledge, nearly twice as tall as me, crashing into the pond below. It's far enough back that we can still hear each other when we talk.

We settle on the rocks, Jasmin between Kian and me and Emmeline on Kian's other side. Kian removes a pack I hadn't noticed before and pulls out some sausages, berries, and cheese for all of us to share. We snack quietly, listening to the birds and crickets chirp. After eating, Jasmin lays down, putting her head in Kian's lap and lifting her feet into mine. I don't know why I'm stuck with her feet. Jealousy weaves through my body; I bite my lip to hold down the feeling. Kian chuckles, tapping Jasmin's ribs quickly. She looks at him, then follows his eyes down to me. She laughs, sitting up to wrap her arms around me.

"Oh, Clem." She giggles, squeezing her arms tight around her body. "You're so jealous." We all laugh at her comments, though my laughter is tighter than theirs. I know it's true, but I don't know how to stop it. At least Dahlia isn't here. I can handle Jasmin around Kian because he won't make a move. Especially not when he seems to be secretly interested in Emmeline.

"How long do you think we can stay here?" Jasmin asks in a soft, content voice. I shrug under her arms, wrapping mine around her, too. She kisses my cheek and then leans back on her hands. Kian suggests we can stay away for another quarter hour before they search for us.

"Will you tell me about the repairs and why you were upset by your grandmother's comments?" We all look to Kian, who has his eyes trained on Jasmin. He releases a deep breath, turning back toward the water.

"The first building fell six years ago. It only housed 4 families; it wasn't a large building. In fact, most of the families were actually out during the day when it collapsed. One woman was home with her children. She provided care for other children who couldn't attend school or training or work with their parents in the village. At the time, my mother was working with a volatile new potion and didn't want my four-year-old brother around it. He was in the building when it collapsed. There were 8 children and 4 adults. All perished in the building." Jasmin gasps while Kian takes a deep, shaky breath.

"Kade was only four. Matron Maud doesn't like us to talk about him. Or anyone from any of the buildings, for that matter. In the second, the building was larger but housed primarily adults. It was in a smaller coven, but they lost 20 witches that day. We rebuild and press on like the people didn't really matter. The other coven recently placed a sign to honor the loss of the witches. Maud still ignores ours. My mother fell into depression. She hasn't created any potions since that day. My father began drinking. He stayed drunk for years but has since sobered. He works in the fields but refuses to use any magic also. I believe the buildings fell because our own magic is weakening. Since we can't use it as regularly as before the borders fell, it isn't as strong as it used to be. Our crops haven't suffered as much as in other areas, but our magic has.

"Mother is the oldest of Maud's children; I am the first grandchild. She was disappointed to learn I was not a woman, but I still have more magic than many other witches. After Kade's death and my parent's struggles, some questioned her leadership ability. Her hold on her position was rocky, but she maintained it. Now that Father has sobered, she has used that to her advantage. Sending me under the True Love Edict was another chance to reclaim our family's glory. None of Mother's siblings were as magical as her, and most aren't as powerful as me. Maud was devastated when she learned Clem is your true love. I was meant to redeem the family, but I didn't." Jasmin huffs, making an angry face.

"If anything, Kian, your position now is more powerful than Clem's, at least regarding the covens. You are my direct link, and you got me here, something that hasn't happened in 'generations.'" Jasmin says the last word the way Maud has been all day. We all burst out laughing at her impression. Kian thanks her for the kind words as we settle down.

We all sit quietly, considering everything Kian just told us. Jasmin takes Kian's hand, squeezing it. Emmeline rests against his side, her arms draped over his chest and back in a comforting manner. Kian's story is heavy and hard to process. I can't imagine losing Claire at such a young age. She was so innocent and sweet. She still is, but maybe a little less sweet now.

Kian finally tells us we must leave to return to Matron Celeste's area. Jasmin thanks him for telling her his story. He simply nods, gathering everything in his pack. The walk back to the covens is quiet and subdued. Jasmin is reflecting on everything. It's evident on her face. She is usually good at hiding her emotions, but sometimes she doesn't. Now it's apparent she is trying to work through some problems. Before we reach the path that turns back to the covens, I grab Jasmin, pulling her into a tight hug. I kiss her gently, hoping to soothe some of the aches she feels.

Kian leads us to Matron Celeste's coven for our tour with her. On the way, we pass a witch a few years older than us that has been hovering outside our group since we arrived. Kian speaks with her briefly, then introduces her as Lucia, a powerful witch from Elemental Grove Coven, the smaller coven the second building collapsed in. Jasmin takes her hand, greeting her and apologizing for her loss. Lucia thanks her and asks if she can tag along. She has always been interested in court and would like to learn more. Jasmin accepts. She wants to bring more witches into the court that rules the kingdom.

We find Matron Celeste, who walks us through her territory. It looks similar to Maud's. Large, covered with trees, witches buzzing everywhere. Aside from a few small plaques and displays, it seems the same. We head back to the inn, where Maud suggests we get the magical flower and take time to discuss the curse. Jasmin nods but asks me to walk with her back to the room. She seems nervous, probably a mix of what she heard from Kian and what Maud may tell her.

I grab the box we found to store the flower. With some of the petals falling off due to the curse weakening, it was safest to travel with it packed by itself. I hold the box out to Jasmin, but she hesitates, staring at the box, then up at me.

"What if..." She doesn't finish her thought, but I know what she is thinking. What if we're wrong? What if I'm not her true love, and Kian read the signs wrong? What if we aren't doing enough or are doing too much? So many what-ifs are floating around; of course, Dahlia is part of them. Jasmin's eyes snap to mine, tears building in them. "What if they judge me for what they see? What if they tell my secrets?" I set the box aside, pulling her into a hug.

I don't know what the witches will do. Maud does seem power-hungry, but to what extent will she go? Can she be trusted? Kian suggested we bring this to her. He knows Jasmin's whole story; he would know if Maud shouldn't be trusted with this. It can be hard to trust in a situation with such dire risks, but it's all we can do.

"Kian still trusts Matron Maud with this," I whisper. "All we can do is trust him now." She nods against my chest, sighing deeply. I kiss her forehead and turn to grab the box. We walk out together with the box tucked under my arm.

Maud, Celeste, Lucia, and Kian are waiting in the room for us. The guards have been instructed to wait outside the doors. We want to limit the number of people in the room as much as possible. Despite having just met Lucia, Jasmin seems to trust her with this. Kian hasn't said anything against her, so she must be trustworthy. I offer the box up, sliding it across the table to them, but Jasmin puts her hand on it.

"I cannot let this begin without preparing you for what you will see. I am not innocent in this curse. I have made poor choices. My past is ugly and somewhat violent. I ask that what you learn in this room, stay here. These are secrets I am trusting you with." Her pause leads us to believe she has more to say, but instead, she opens the box, exposing the dahlia to the witches. They look at it with intrigue.

Maud reaches first, touching the flower, then jerks back. She glances at Kian and then over to Jasmin.

"I've never actually seen a curse with the visual effects." Jasmin leans over to remove the flower, placing it on the table in front of all three. She settles back next to me, holding my hand. She isn't masking her nerves during this meeting.

The three witches reach simultaneously to grab the flower. As soon as they touch it, their eyes glaze over and dart back and forth. This must be what Jasmin saw when Kian and I were watching the images. Their faces change through a range of emotions over several minutes. When their eyes return to normal, Lucia slides back in her seat. Celeste stares off past us while Maud looks between Jasmin and me. Neither speaks for several minutes, then Maud asks to hold our hands. Jasmin and I reach out, taking her hand in ours. Maud breathes deeply, then drops our hand.

"Something is missing. This dark-skinned girl, tell me about her." Jasmin tells a brief story of who Dahlia is and what role she has played in our lives so far. Maud speaks again when Jasmin is done. "The magic has decided she is linked to you, but I am unsure how. True love indicates one person. I don't know why she would be involved. I'm not even sure of the extent of her involvement. Have you two made a formal commitment, similar to the wedding, but in private?" We think for a minute, but Jasmin shakes her head no.

"Not anything as formal as a wedding. We've confessed our love and desire to be with each other."

"Might I suggest a formal commitment, in private, with maybe one or two witnesses? I don't know that it will break the curse, but it will provide insight on how to move forward if it doesn't."

Kian speaks up, "Emmeline and I can attend. We can decorate one of the atriums. We can hold the small ceremony tomorrow night, and it will give us time to work on phrasing." Jasmin nods, turning to me.

"Ready to make a lifelong commitment to me?" A smirk spreads across her face.

"Always," I whisper before pressing a kiss to her lips. Thunder rumbles outside the building, bringing my own mouth into a smile. Maud claps her hands.

"Yes, this will be very helpful. Tomorrow night, then. We shall see what happens."

Chapter 17

JASMIN

One day.

One night.

One day until I commit myself to Clem and possibly break the curse. After the meeting, I sent a rider to deliver a letter to Henry to alert him of the situation. He must be ready if we break the curse and the border comes down. That's why I'm terrified. It's the border. That's all. I'm not fearful of committing myself to Clem. Especially not while Dahlia is at my castle. No. The border is why I'm terrified. Yep.

I feel terrible. Clem is ecstatic to make some progress in both the curse and our relationship. He didn't say anything, but postponing the wedding upset him. Maybe it was just Dahlia like he said, but I don't really believe that. He's practically bouncing down the hallway now. I feel terrible that I am not as happy as he is. He's not King yet; he doesn't think of the kingdom first. He's not thinking about the border. I hope he can keep that excitement as he takes on more responsibility in the kingdom.

I will meet with Lord Alwyn in the morning. I am beyond pissed with that man. To learn about all these buildings collapsing so long after they happened, and from other people, is insulting. I didn't even find out if Alwyn was paying them survivors' benefits, but I highly doubt it. Now I get to deal with that on this big day for us. At least tonight, I just get to sleep.

Clem and I help each other out of our clothes, but I soon realize he isn't as ready to sleep as I am. He stalks toward me with his cock sticking straight out. I suppress the sigh I want to release. I take a deep breath, closing my eyes as I imagine how good it will feel to have him buried deep inside me. I'm not quite aroused, but it is a start. While my eyes are closed, he grabs my jaw between firm fingers and gently kisses my lips. That'll do it. I moan into the kiss, letting my body twist beneath him. He pulls me up to stand with his fingers still planted on my jaw.

"I'm gonna fuck you over this bed. I'm in control this time." I can't help the smirk appearing on my face. I wasn't sure how he would like being restrained by me, but it seems to have struck a chord with him. I'll have to try that again sometime with better knots. Or maybe not. It was exciting when he broke free and finished on me. A chill of excitement runs through my body. The worries of earlier are stored for a later time, arousal cascading through my brain and body. He guides me to the bed until the back of my thighs bumps against it. He snatches the hem of my shift, ripping it over my head violently, leaving red marks on my arms and back where it pulled. His hands spin my shoulders and shove me down on the bed. He notches his dick at my entrance and slides in smoothly.

"Oh, your cunt feels so good." He mumbles against my back before standing to thrust inside me. He grabs a fistful of hair, arching my back as he pounds deep. I grunt as he hits the spot that causes my eyes to roll back in my head. Even not being interested in sex a few minutes ago, I'm ready to explode now with his few actions.

"Yes. Take my dick, little flower. Take it hard." He slams in with so much force my feet slip out from under me. He wraps his arm around my waist, lifting me back up and using his fingers to seek out my clit. I moan as he makes a small circle around the bundle of nerves. I won't last long like this, which he probably wants. He presses hard, pinching me as I wiggle beneath him with my impending orgasm. My body spasms as his cock slides in and out of me. The intense pressure builds deep in my cunt, clenching around his thick dick as it relentlessly pounds inside me.

"Come for me, Jas. Fall apart on my cock."

I moan as I do as he says. My muscles clench as my body soars through my orgasm. My breasts are pressed hard against the sheets, almost chaffing my nipples. The sensation is surprisingly divine. He thrusts a couple more times then I feel his cock jerking and emptying deep inside me. His hands hold onto my hips as he buries his seed in my pussy. I can feel it drip onto my thighs when he finally slips out. The warm liquid sliding down my already wet legs. We both collapse on the bed, tangled together and settling in orgasmic bliss. He kisses my forehead, whispering how he loves me, then moves to get cloths to clean up. I grab his arms, tugging him back to bed.

"We'll clean up later. Just hold me now."

He looks at me curiously but does as I ask. He pulls me into his chest. I wrap one arm around his back, toying with his hair. I love playing with his hair. It has a calming effect on me. As I drift off to sleep, my mind is clear of everything that will happen in the next few days. A welcome break from stress and worry.

I asked Clem not to come to this meeting. He refused, stating if I have to be here, he will be here, too. It's not going to be a pleasant meeting. He's been to less-than-ideal meetings before, but this could be worse than the others. I requested Lord David and Lord Thurston attend also. They arrive just before the meeting begins. They are in the room waiting for me now. We are still in the covens' territory. I haven't been to the village yet but didn't want to wait for this meeting. I don't know what the people of Greynon think of Lord Alwyn, but I'll deal with that tomorrow.

Clem and I enter the meeting room we have secured for this purpose. It's small, only large enough for the table and six chairs. One remains empty. I debated asking Kian to come, but Alwyn and Thurston will likely find his presence insulting now. So the chair remains empty. A server brings over tea, but I ask for wine instead. It may be early, but wine is definitely needed for this meeting. None of the Lords speak before me this time. Thank the gods they have enough sense not to do that. After the wine arrives, I take a long drink, staring at the men. Thurston and Alwyn seem annoyed. Only David has the sense to look somewhat nervous about this meeting. Clem is surprisingly stoic. Maybe he has too many emotions to show just one. Perhaps he is improving; either way, I need to ensure he knows.

"Lord Alwyn," I sigh. I haven't entirely settled on how to proceed. Do I give him another chance? How many has he had already? How long do I overlook his disregard for the covens before I refuse to accept that? "What do you have against the witches?" I don't expect an honest answer, but I want to try anyway.

"I don't trust them, your majesty. We're living in a hell created with their witchcraft. I can't trust that another witch won't do the same."

"And how many curses have you seen in your time as Lord of Greynon?"

"One that I am aware of." He speaks confidently as if that answer justifies his behavior.

"That you are aware of?"

"Yes, milady. There have been several strange occurrences that I believe were curses but couldn't confirm." David rubs his head in disappointment. Thurston remains neutral while Clem shows his surprise. He almost looks giddy at this point. Regardless of what the people actually think of him, Alwyn believes he is being cursed by his own people. That speaks volumes about how he treats them.

"For fuck's sake, Alwyn." I sigh, standing before him. "I hereby relieve you of your duties as Lord of Greynon." He jumps up, yelling at me about how I can't do that. David tries to quiet him while Thurston watches in surprised horror. I continue on. "You are relieved immediately. I will find a suitable replacement for you within the next few days. You will not have any contact with the new Lord of

Greynon. You are stripped of your benefits and must vacate the property within a fortnight." I pause, considering what to say next. I never saw Father relieve anyone of duties, and I can't remember everything I am supposed to say. It's been ages since I covered this topic in my training.

"Queen Jasmin, why is he being relieved?" Lord Thurston asks with a hint of anger in his tone. Ah, yes, that's what I am forgetting.

"He has continuously overlooked a huge portion of his population. He refused to update the census correctly. He lied about securing help from the witches during the curse. He not only didn't help but didn't report damage the witches received to their property due to the curse. His duty is to report to me about everyone in his territory. He knows nothing about the witches, which make up at least a third of his territory. He is being relieved for dereliction of duty."

"Please let me try again, Your Majesty," Alwyn cries. "I can do better." A single humorless laugh escapes from me.

"No. I'll be down to Greynon tomorrow to pick a new successor. You are to tell no one of this. I will announce this situation after I have chosen someone."

"Shouldn't he recommend possible successors, Queen?" Lord David is always quick to remind me of the proper actions. I would probably drive this court into the ground if he didn't remind me of these procedures.

"No, Lord David. I don't trust his judgment. I will find one without him. Thank you."

With that, I rise and leave the room with Clem behind me. The Lords are yelling, but I don't care now. I have said my piece and am not changing my mind. Walking through the inn toward my room, I ask Emmeline to find Kian and Lucia while she is at it. There are a couple of hours until the ceremony tonight. Things could change drastically at that point, or not at all. I need to be as ready as I can be before that point.

Kian and Lucia join me in my room. Lucia is uncomfortable with the close, private quarters, but she'll have to get used to that if she wants to be in court with me. After Lucia joined us for the coven tour, she made quite an impression on me. She has studied court protocol on her own, even going as far as researching the history of witches in our kingdom and others, how they work and don't work. She's well-read and knowledgeable on how witches can fit into the kingdom. She has excellent ideas to improve our relations. She reminds me of a female version of Kian. Even Kian was impressed with her knowledge. She garnered enough trust that I invited her to view the flower. We chatted for a while that evening, sharing ideas and experiences. Despite the short time I have known her, she has made a great impression on me.

I explain what just happened and leave the floor open for ideas. Clem suggests Dominick, the other bachelor from Greynon. Kian agrees even if he isn't a good option for Lord, he can offer insight. They both seem to trust him. I didn't spend as much time with him as others. He chose to go home after the winter solstice. I just hope that's because he realized he isn't my true love, and there are no hard feelings. Kian leaves the room to find someone to send for Dominick.

"Milady, Queen?" Lucia meekly speaks.

"You can just call me Jasmin in private. In public, Queen or Milady is fine." She nods, gathering some confidence. People with limited real-life experience with royalty usually do more than is necessary regarding titles. It would be funny if it didn't happen so often.

"With this change, would you consider separating the witches?" Kian walks in as she finishes this, though, freezing near the door.

"As in creating a sixth village for the witches?" She nods in response as Kian tentatively moves closer. Clem sits on the bed, watching everything with no emotions on his face again. I sit next to him, whispering so only he can hear. "You are doing so well hiding your emotions, Clem. I'm really proud of you." A smile grows across his face, breaking his stoic streak, and we giggle.

"You'll get used to it," Kian murmurs to Lucia.

"I can't do that from here; it will take time." I turn back to Lucia and Kian. "What do you think?" I ask of Kian.

"It would create a more direct path to the witch community, but we would need to discuss how they would be governed. Their systems function differently than the other villages. Placing a Lord over them would not go over well." I ponder his statement, understanding some of their hierarchy. Matron Maud would not answer to a lord.

"What if there was a Lady? And she didn't govern them but simply reported to me." I ask, watching Lucia. Kian looks at her, then back to me.

"So, my position?" Shit. Actually...

"Yes." He looks hurt, but I haven't finished yet. "Yes. Your position. We could give her the Lady of the Covens title instead of Advisor. Her time would be split between here and the castle, depending on what is required. She would have the same rank and duties as the other Lords but wouldn't govern her people."

"Yes, that would be a wise idea. The witches will respond better to a woman in charge than me. I can convince my grandmother this will be good as my final act." I chuckle at him.

"It could instead be your first act as Advisor to the Crown." His eyes go wide, mouth slightly agape, showing every bit of shock he is feeling. "I've long thought Coven Advisor wasn't enough for you, Kian. I also hate that you need to travel. I want you close to me because I value your opinion."

"And not because she wants to fuck you anymore," Clem adds jealously. I roll my eyes, smacking him in the chest. We chuckle at his comment, but Lucia looks horrified.

"Don't worry. Fucking me isn't a requirement for being in my circle." We all laugh loudly at that comment. She chuckles nervously along, obviously uncomfortable. "I know we don't know each other well, but I would like to work closely with you to establish this new position, possibly even consider you for the role. We need time to know each other better, to build the trust needed for a new role like this. You have already proven to be more than valuable in your short time. I believe I can use you to benefit our covens." Kian nods approval as Clem watches anxiously. Lucia's eyes go wide.

"Oh, Milady, I would be honored!" She cries out, covering her mouth with her hands. I laugh at her response.

"Perfect. It will take time and resources for me to work through this. I think this will be a good role for you. Kian, I do want to change your official title now."

He bows his head solemnly, accepting his new role. Relief washes over my body, relieving some of my tension. Kian is easily my most valuable advisor. He has even more texts to study, as he'll need to brush up on court protocol. He'll be busy for months. I get the impression that he will appreciate that, though.

There is a knock on the door informing us Dominick has arrived. We bring him in, filling him in on all the changes we have made in the past couple of hours. We chat with him, getting his opinion. He wants to be considered for the Lordship but also gives other suggestions for the position. I regret not spending more time with him when he was at the castle. He is a wonderful man and would be a great leader within the community. I'm positive Alwyn didn't think he would bring his replacement to me with the True Love Edict. I plan to meet with a few other contenders before deciding.

We wait until morning to inform the covens of the changes we plan to make. There isn't enough time before the ceremony to thoroughly discuss the changes. There is just enough time for us to rest before going to the atrium. Emmeline was involved with the decorating, so I am sure it is beautiful. As Dominick leaves our room, promising to gather the contenders in the afternoon, I collapse on the bed, just wanting a quick nap. Clem is being touchy, but inform him I am in no position for that. He settles with cuddles and small kisses.

After a couple of minutes, there is a knock on the door. It's not time to leave yet; why is someone knocking?

I open the door, finding Emmeline looking nervous and scared. Her fingers are fidgeting with the hem of the bodice of her dress. Before I can say anything, Dahlia waltzes into the room, carrying her bags and dropping them on the floor.

"Hello, my love. I'm here now!" She sings out.

Fuck.

Chapter 18

CLEM

What in the fuck is she doing here?

The audacity of this bitch to show up now, talking about "her love." Jasmin is shocked but not nearly angry enough. She is not going to ruin a second ceremony for Jasmin and me. I refuse to let that happen.

"Dahlia, what are you doing here?" Jasmin's voice is sheepish, unsure of what to really say. I notice Emmeline backing out of the room. Part of me wishes I could slink away too, but I am not leaving those two alone again. I'm still hurt over Jasmin's actions last time and won't give her or Dahlia a chance to repeat them.

"I was bored at the castle, Jas. I left early this morning and rode hard to get to you today. I missed you."

"We've been gone less than a week. Surely, you can go that long without seeing her. And why the fuck are your bags in here?" I seethe, unable to control my anger at her.

"Clem!" Jasmin's voice is a warning, but I'll be damned if I'm going to let this go. Another quick rap on the door draws our attention, and Jasmin opens it again, having not moved away. Kian walks in, assessing the situation.

"I've been sent to help with sleeping arrangements, but the inn is full." This information isn't helpful.

"What the fuck. What about the fucking barn?"

"CLEM!" Despite her opposition, Jasmin's voice is much closer to yelling.

"What, Jasmin? I'm just supposed to welcome her into this room?" I wave my arms around the small room to emphasize my point. "I don't want her in the castle, let alone this tiny ass room. Why doesn't she room with Emmeline?"

"Emmeline is already with me," Kian adds. Huh, well, that piques my interest. I didn't realize they were sharing a room this time. But I don't have time to focus on that. I am angry, seething, furious.

"Emmeline doesn't really like me anyways." Dahlia spouts as if that will help her case.

"No fucking shit. It's because you're a bitch." I state. Now Jasmin is angry, but I don't think we're mad for the same reasons. I can't fathom why she isn't more upset over her showing up like this. Kian chooses this moment to speak up.

"How do you want to proceed tonight? We should be getting ready now."

"Then let's get ready." Jasmin sounds determined, which sends my heart soaring. Affection swarms through my body, coating the anger temporarily. My muscles relax slightly. She still wants to marry me, and she isn't going to let Dahlia ruin another ceremony.

"Really?" I ask, giving her my best puppy dog eyes. I've spent enough time with Finn to know that look works on her. She doesn't get a chance to respond before Dahlia interjects. Even thinking her name makes me want to sneer.

"Ready for what?" Dahlia questions as I glare at her. Jasmin speaks before I say something else.

"Clem and I are having a private ceremony tonight in place of the wedding we stopped. We need to get ready, and I need you to stay here until we return."

"No, I won't do that."

"Dahlia," Jas uses the same warning tone she used with me. At least she is consistent in her warnings. "You will not ruin another ceremony for us. We halted the last one; we will not postpone tonight."

"Fine, but I'm coming." She grabs her bags and makes her way into our bathroom to change. Jasmin walks to stand in front of me, and I look down at her but quickly turn my attention back to Kian. "Is there nowhere else she can sleep?" He shakes his head sadly.

"The guards are three to a room. Even Emmeline and I have a third. This is the only room without three people or more." Shit. I didn't realize that. Jasmin wraps her arms around my waist, resting against my chest. I drape my arm around her loosely, unsure what else to do. It isn't fair to ask others to take on a fourth person, but I don't want her with us, either.

"Couldn't we swap her and Kian?" Jasmin huffs a laugh.

"You were jealous of me putting my head in his lap yesterday, Clem. Is that really a better option?"

"He didn't have his fingers on your cunt recently!"

"Define 'recently.'" I step back, eyes wide, as my mouth drops open. She and Kian are both chuckling. "I'm teasing, Clem. We're not going to force Kian to change rooms for us. It will be fine." She pulls me back into her arms, but my mind now lists all the people potentially wanting to touch her cunt. The list is unacceptably long, even if entirely fictional.

Jasmin whispers my name as I turn my attention back to her. She is still pushing this ceremony, so at least there is that. I kiss her before releasing her to get dressed. I try to suppress my jealousy and anger. I want to focus on this joyous occasion, not that bitch that always shows up at inopportune times. Kian exits the room as Emmeline returns to help. We aren't wearing anything regal but have opted for better attire than usual. We all remain silent as we dress.

The only sound we hear are clothes rustling, then the bathroom door creaks open. I'm standing without a shirt, just my trousers are on. Jasmin, thankfully, has a shift, and Emmeline is pulling her dress over her head. Dahlia stops in the doorway but is staring at me, not Jasmin. Why is she staring at me? Is that lust in her eyes? Surely, she isn't lusting after me. She is beautiful, and under different circumstances, I might even find her attractive, but I can't stand her. I tug on my shirt as her trance breaks. Are her cheeks covered in rouge, or is that a blush? She walks toward Jasmin, gushing over the beautiful dress she has. She avoids looking at me again.

"Dahlia, tonight is for Clem and me. You must be on your best behavior, please?" Dahlia, surprisingly, nods in agreement with Jasmin. If Jasmin can get her under control, maybe she won't be so bad. I pull Jasmin into a tight hug, kissing her deeply. She returns the kiss, wrapping her arms around my back. While I love kissing Jasmin, this is a show of possession. She is mine, and no one will take her from me. Once I break the kiss, I glare at Dahlia, hoping to silently convey she needs to back off.

Emmeline and Kian guide us to the atrium, with Dahlia tagging behind. The atrium is decorated with flowers and greenery from the surrounding plants, different from the ones at the castle. These flowers are a blazing array of colors, bright oranges, brilliant reds, and radiant purples. Candles are glowing around the sides. An extra glow creates an ethereal feel. Magic has been used to give it a boost of romance. We step into the center, under an arch decorated with ribbons and strands of greenery. Jasmin and I face each other as everything else fades away. She is the only thing in my vision, the only thing I need in my life.

We discussed what to say to each other earlier. We settled on a vow to love and respect each other forever. Despite my confidence in this move, I still feel nervous butterflies fluttering around my stomach. We didn't have time to get rings or anything else. There won't be an item to represent our vows this time, but maybe in the future. We have mentioned another ceremony for the kingdom. Here, tonight, this is just for us, and I don't need a ring to signify forever with her.

"Clem," Jasmin starts, holding my hands and staring into my eyes. "I love you so much. You are everything I have ever hoped for in a true love. You are kind, generous, and work hard for what you want. Even though you are jealous and possessive at times," we both chuckle softly, "I still love you and will do anything for you. You are mine for the rest of my life, Clematis Byrne." My eyes water as my emotions threaten to overwhelm me. "I promise to love and support you for all my life. None will be more important than you through every phase of our life."

"Jas, you are my favorite person ever. For so long, I didn't think I would find anyone to call mine. Then Finn tackled me, and I saw you for the first time. Even then, when you lied about who you were, I knew you were mine. I love you as Tia, Jas, or Queen. You are mine for the rest of my life, Jasmin Reis." I squeeze her hand, taking a deep breath before repeating the vow we agreed on. "I promise to love and support you for all my life. None will be more important than you through every phase of our life."

I press my lips against hers as everything else fades away. The thunder and the wind blowing branches around us quieten. There is only Jasmin and me, kissing deeply. I wrap my arms around her, holding her tightly. We break briefly, but she stays in my arms, staring at me. We each whisper, "I love you," but she seems nervous to break away.

It occurs to me for the first time that this could have been what we needed to break the curse. If we just did that, there could be pure chaos at the border. Apparently, my face gives me away because Jasmin smirks. "I already notified Henry. It will be fine. Let's see what happened."

We turn together to find a misty-eyed Emmeline, a happy Kian, and a confused but quiet Dahlia. Jasmin thanks them for putting this on for us. I mumble something to that effect, not sure what to do now. If this were the wedding, we would have an evening of meeting with villagers before retiring to do unspeakable things. With our new roommate, we won't be able to do those. Kian invites us to walk outside to see the border. He says we can't go up to it, but there is a spot where we can see the top well. We follow him out of the main room, down a small path for a moment or two, then see the border in the sky. It is flashing shades of purple and green, thunder crashing around us, but it still seems in place.

"Could it just take time to come down? Didn't it take a while to set?" Jasmin looks around, desperate for a response.

"I think it set pretty quickly, but it took a few hours for everyone to realize what it was." It crushed my father, who wasn't one to linger in the face of the unknown. It had to have caught him by surprise.

"Of course. I'm sorry." She apologizes, even though it isn't necessary, then wraps her arms around me.

"Why don't we get to bed? We can get an update in the morning." I press my lips against her forehead and bid the others good night. We silently walk back to the room, Dahlia just behind us. I pause in the room, realizing there isn't anywhere for Dahlia to sleep. In the face of everything else, I didn't think to ask about an extra bed. The one bed is large enough for another person to sleep comfortably, but that doesn't mean I want her in the bed.

I help Jasmin undo part of her dress before she heads to the bathroom to clean up. She has been subdued since we came back in. I hate that the border is still there. Dahlia removes her shoes and sits in one of the chairs.

"Thank you," I start awkwardly, "for not interrupting." I don't want to thank her for anything, but I will concede some gratitude for her silence. She pauses, looking up at me.

"Why do you think it didn't work?" Her accent is thick, each syllable separated from the others. I shrug, honestly unsure why it didn't. I expect her to have some witty remarks, but instead, she returns to her shoes and then stockings. I untuck my shirt, keeping it on for now, not wanting her to stare at me again. I walk to the balcony, watching the lights fade across the border. The lights aren't as bright as they were, and the thunder has mostly stopped.

When Jasmin comes out of the bathroom, she asks where everyone is sleeping. Dahlia perks up and says that Jas should sleep in the middle. Over my dead body. I tell her I'll sleep in the middle, keeping Dahlia from doing anything ridiculous. I don't like being in the middle, but the thought of Dahlia snuggling up to Jasmin is too much for me to handle. They don't argue with me, but no one is happy. We soon settle into bed, with me in the middle, between two beautiful women, even if one is a demon.

"It's been a long time since I've slept with a man," Dahlia whispers seductively. I sigh, gritting my teeth, but Jasmin giggles. Before I can say anything, she speaks up.

"Did you ever sleep with a man?"

"Once, back home. Well, he wasn't a man." Both women burst into a fit of giggles. I'm left uncomfortable between the two. I turn on my side to face Jasmin as the two women continue chattering about past trysts, not something I want to hear about, especially since they are mostly Jasmin's.

"Please stop," I mutter after a couple of minutes. Jasmin apologizes, giving me a quick kiss. Her kisses always help recenter me.

"Do you two fuck a lot?"

"No. No," I respond quickly, "no, we're not talking about that."

"Okay, but I can always help. I still know all her spots. You don't forget someone like Jasmin."

"No!" And here is why I didn't want to be in the middle. I want to get up and away from this, but do I scoot off the edge? Climb over Jasmin? Or worse, over Dahlia? I sit up but decide against it and just lay back down. Jasmin snuggles in, pressing kisses to my face, but I don't want it right now. I turn my face away, and she stops, settling against my chest. Thankfully, Dahlia doesn't say anything else. We eventually fall asleep, despite how uncomfortable all of this is.

Chapter 19

DAHLIA

I will never admit this out loud, but I see the appeal of Clem now. Holy hell, his body is impressive. He's warm and treats Jas well. Shit, if I wasn't obsessed with her, I could see myself happy with Clem or someone like him. Even though he hates me, he still isn't terrible to me. He called me a bitch, but didn't make me sleep in the barn. He hasn't tried to ban Jas and me from seeing each other. They are lovely together. It's not going to stop me from wedging my way in somehow.

I couldn't wait another week or more before she returned to me. I need her every day. My soul screams for her. The distance made it hard for me to breathe. My chest ached with her absence. I gave her as long as I could before leaving to find her. Clem may be angry, but I'm sure he understands my feelings. We have similar feelings regarding Jasmin.

Sleeping next to Clem was both exciting and nerve-wracking. I was so nervous I would fall asleep and wake up wrapped around him, or worse, trying to grab his junk. Not that I would mind that; I'm sure his junk is as fabulous as the rest of him. I have an idea of how he would react, but I'm not sure what Jasmin would do. She's never really been jealous, but she might be angry that he is upset. I imagine it's probably worth it, though. If Jasmin is so swept up with him, she won't even spend time with me; that dick has to be good. She wouldn't avoid me for some meager sex.

Whew, I need to bathe and wash away the filth on my mind. I roll out of bed, still exhausted from not actually sleeping. I barely slept between thoughts of Clem, Jas, and paranoia about groping him. Jasmin is still asleep, but Clem watches me as I move to the bathroom. He tugs Jasmin close to his chest, and she just rolls into him, sighing happily. I hope she at least slept well.

I start the water, needing time to wake up. The witches have spelled this bathroom to allow water to run in. The tub is small, but it will take several minutes to fill. The towels are kept near the door, so I grab one, wanting it closer to the tub. I realize I didn't shut the door all the way, but before I close it, I hear Clem whispering. His whisper is surprisingly loud.

"Hey, little flower, I need you, please." Is he begging her? "She's in the bath; she won't hear."

Jasmin moans and rolls over, kissing him deeply. I can see them from my spot in the bathroom without being completely exposed. This is my chance to see what he is working with and what I am up against. Without considering any other option, I settle into a comfortable position to watch. I've never actually watched two people fuck before. This should be interesting for several reasons.

He flips her over and drags her to the edge of the bed. He stands behind her, squeezing her ass several times before he drops his hand behind her ass. I can't see what he is doing with his hand, but based on her reaction, he must be playing with her clit. She arches, shoving her ass against him. He grabs a fistful of hair, pulling it tight enough that she rises off the bed, her perky tits exposed to me.

A deep ache grows in my core. I had only planned to watch, but this need is becoming unbearable. I have to touch my own cunt. Clem smacks her ass, and the sound causes my pussy to clench. I didn't know I would react like that. I quickly pull my shift, sinking my fingers deep inside my soaking entrance. I press my thumb lightly against my clit. I don't want to orgasm too soon and miss whatever he is doing.

Clem releases Jas, and she collapses on the bed, writhing under her growing pleasure. I love when she is like that, out of her mind with pleasure. I can see her face in my mind; I know her eyes are glazed over. She's probably biting her lip, trying to see what's happening. Clem drops his trousers, and his massive cock stands out. I almost squeak at the size of that thing. Holy gods, the size alone explains Jasmin's desire not to piss him off. I sink another finger in with my first two as Clem plunges deep inside Jas.

She groans, burying her face in the blankets as he slams into her. I try to match his pace with my fingers, but he is ruthless. He is so fast and hard that I can't keep up. So I do what I can to bring my own orgasm. My eyes are focused on the two, though. His softly defined muscles are tight as he slams into her pussy. Her ass high in the air, jiggling perfectly under his motions. He slaps her again, and I feel my pussy clenching around my fingers. Clem massages the space where he just hit but grabs her hair and jerks her up again. He is focused intently on her. There is nothing else in the room but her for him. That realization causes my cunt to clench again. He really does love her.

Her eyes find mine as her head rises from him, pulling her hair. Panic briefly flashes through my mind, but then she bites her lips and moans. She drags her hand down her side, underneath her, until she finds her own clit and begins to rub it while he pounds behind her.

"That's it, slut. Take what you want." His voice is deep and gravelly.

She moans at his words. I don't care for his words, but I can understand the appeal of his timbre. I would prefer to hear kinder words, but I can't pretend that voice isn't also a turn-on. My body is clenching and twisting, so close to orgasm. I bite my lip, wanting to see when they come, but unsure if I can hold out. Suddenly, Jas yells that she's coming, which sets me over the edge. My pleasure barrels through me; lightning flashes behind my eyes as my body convulses ecstatically. I ride the waves, teasing my clit and pussy until it calms down.

Jas and Clem are lying on the bed, touching each other sensually. I take that as my cue to actually get in the bath. I need to clean my own body now. I'm covered in sweat and my own fluids from watching them. I didn't see Clem come, but at least I enjoyed an orgasm with my girl. It's not what I want, but it's enough for now.

I wash quickly, unsure if Jasmin will say anything about how long I take. Both are dressed when I come out, but they head into the bathroom together to finish readying for the day. Neither says anything to me, nobody acknowledging what I just did. We soon head to breakfast together. I walk just a few steps behind them, unsure what to do now, knowing I masturbated to them fucking.

"I have to go to the village center today and plan to go alone," Jasmin informs us.

"What? No, let me go." Clem sputters out his response. She just shakes her head.

"No. I have to replace Alwyn today. While they like you, you are still not officially involved in these proceedings. It will be difficult enough as it is. So please, stay here. Get to know Dahlia."

"Dahlia is the reason I'm not officially involved. I don't want to know her."

"Clem, don't be rude." He huffs but doesn't say anything else.

"I don't mind getting to know Clem." I coo sweetly, trying to garner some good graces with Jasmin. She looks back at me, slightly confused at first, then throws me a wink. Clem doesn't see. My cheeks burn with blood rushing toward them. I didn't imagine her seeing me, then. I had hoped maybe I just imagined it, but no, not based on that reaction.

"Clem, didn't you say you want to improve your penmanship? Dahlia could help with that today."

"No," he says before we reach the dining hall. He is sulking now, but I don't care. At this point, I will do anything for Jasmin and pretty much anything to be around Clem and figure him out more. Jasmin obviously loves his massive cock, but is there more to him?

Emmeline and Kian greet us as we find our seats at the table. There isn't a spot for me, but someone brings in a chair and places me by Emmeline. Kian, who is sitting next to Clem, offers to swap. I consider taking him up on it but notice Jasmin shaking her head no at me. I do the responsible thing and listen to her. I expect her to appreciate my good choices later, preferably with kisses. I cast her a glare that hopefully reads, 'You're welcome for this decision.' She got the message based on the happy but playful smirk she gives me back.

"What were the three of you up to this morning?" Kian asks.

"Nothing," Clem answers quickly, and I wonder if he saw me too. I thought he was obsessed with Jasmin, but he was behind her. He could have seen me, too. Did I make noise when I came?

"Oh, there was lightning and some thunder. I thought maybe the one bed you shared had something to do with that."

"No." Clem is really digging the word 'no' lately. Has he said more than that ever? He uses that word a lot. Jasmin doesn't add anything, so neither do I.

After breakfast, we escort Jasmin to the front door, where guards are waiting with Vesper to take her to the village.

"I'll be back by dinner. I have to meet with the men Dominick recommended and make a decision. Wish me luck." I do as she asks but refrain from hugging and kissing her like I want. I'm irate that I came all this way only for her to leave, but that is on me a bit. Clem pulls her into a hug, kissing the top of her head. "You don't need luck, little flower. You'll make the best decision." She smiles at him in the sweetest, almost sickening manner before kissing him equally sweetly. After she leaves, I turn to Clem, who is walking back toward the room.

"Do you want to work on your penmanship?" I offer, following behind him.

"No."

"Okay, do you want to find a library?"

"No." There's that damned word again.

"Do you..."

"No, Dahlia. I do not. I'm going to nap alone because I'm fucking exhausted after spending the night next to you. Find somewhere else to be." He walks into the bedroom, making it clear he's shutting the door behind him. Before he does, he sighs, then says, "Please." I take a moment to appreciate his manners. He didn't have to ask nicely; I certainly wouldn't have. The door closes in my face, and I feel so dejected. I didn't expect him to want to fuck me right away, but I thought maybe we could get to know each other better. I want to spend time with him, learn who he is, and find out if I can work my way onto his cock. Surely he could hate-fuck me, right? I could use a good hate-fuck. I shiver at the thought, turning to find somewhere else to be for a while.

Clem comes out for lunch, which is even more relaxed than breakfast. With the matrons not in attendance, we all sit in a cluster instead of the more formal lines from breakfast and dinner. Kian talks about some of his discoveries during research on the curse. None pertain to our specific curse, but some are pretty cool. I chat with him about the research, wanting to learn more about magic and hone my craft. Emmeline and Clem talk about plans for the summer solstice next month.

After lunch, Clem makes for the room again. Is he going to take another nap? Surely he will do something other than sulk in the room until she returns. I rush in front of him, stopping him before he can enter the room. Shit, now I'm here; what do I say? I look around for any signs of something to talk about.

"Dahlia, move."

"No. Um, Kian told me about a waterfall you went to. I want to go but don't know where it is. Will you show me?"

"Why? So you can fuck Jasmin there later?"

"You offering to let me?" He deadpan stares at me, entirely unamused with my antics.

"Look, Jas wants us to spend time together. Take me there, and we can tell her we did something. We don't even have to talk."

"Fine." He turns and stalks off toward a side exit, apparently taking me up on the vow of silence. He leads me down a path, not walking slowly. I struggle to keep up with him, and this dress doesn't help. His trousers and boots are appropriate for this type of walk, and my long gown and soft slippers are only suited for indoor use. I should have worn something better for outside, but that wasn't in my plans this morning.

The trail turns quickly. Clem easily takes the sudden change, but my dress catches on a branch and tugs me awkwardly. The sudden jolt causes me to fall hard on the ground. I land with an oomph, scratching my knees, elbows, and wrists. The hurt to my pride is worse than my skin, but even that stings. Clem curses softly, turning back to help me. He holds a hand out, and I hesitate but decide to take the help.

When our hands connect, the instant need smashes into me again. All I want is to ravish him right here on this trail. As soon as I stand, I snatch my hand back, rattled from the fall and my desire to fuck Jasmin's lover. I dust my dress off, trying to think of anything but the sounds of him slapping her ass as he buried himself deep in her cunt. I'm definitely not thinking about how massive he is.

"Sorry for walking so fast. That was a shit thing to do." Fuck, now he's apologizing.

"It's fine. I should probably wear more pants like Jasmin," I chuckle weakly, needing to lighten the mood. "She never wore pants before the curse, but damn, her ass looks great in them." I offer a feeble smirk, rubbing my aching palms. He sighs, turning away, but quickly turns back, taking a step toward me.

"Why do you have to say shit like that? It's not your place to talk about her ass."

"Why can't you just let me say that and accept that she does have an amazing ass?"

"Because she's mine." He growls at me, and my traitorous body clenches. Why am I so attracted to him? It's just because of his cock. And watching him fuck. That's all. It's purely physical. God, I need to get laid. I wonder if things are serious between Kian and Emmeline. Kian is pretty handsome. I bet he has some skills hiding up his sleeve.

"She was mine first, jackass." I try to storm past him on the trail. My soft shoes prevent me from effectively stomping. I have got to wear better shoes from now on. He grabs my elbow before I get past him, snatching me back to him. I slam into his chest, staring at him as my breath hitches. His gaze is intense, mere inches from my own face. His lips are so close I can almost taste them. I want to taste them. No. I don't want that. I fight the urge to lick my lips. His are close enough that I could lick them, but the action would also betray my thoughts.

"She may have been yours nine years ago, but she is mine now, and I'm not leaving." He releases my arm, storming off in the direction of the waterfall. His boots are heavy enough to create the stomping sound I wanted. My body is reeling, torn between lust and anger. Each stomp of his feet sends a new wave of desire and hatred through my body. I've never hated someone I wanted to fuck, but damn, I bet the sex would be phenomenal.

I follow behind him, unsure whether I can trust my voice not to say something embarrassing. We soon reach the waterfall. He settles on a rock, watching the water crash into the small pond. It's cool next to the water. The sound of the waterfall is louder than everything else. I can't hear the birds or bugs or even the wind blowing through the trees. I take a spot near him, but not close enough to touch him. I don't want what the fuck ever that feeling is to happen again. I don't want to like him. I want to take Jasmin from him. I want her for myself.

"I was in that room for nine years," my voice is tender but still firm enough for him to hear. "Not by choice. I didn't willingly give her up then, and I'm not now. We feel the same things for her." He doesn't speak for a while. We just stare at the water, contemplating everything we have said. I know he loves her, and maybe it is unfair of me to expect him to just leave and let me have her. I wouldn't do that.

"Would you fuck her?"

"In a heartbeat," I respond with the truth. I would give anything to claim Jasmin again as mine. Clem stands from the rock, walking toward a tree. He grabs a rock and thrusts it through the air into the water beyond. It lands with a satisfying plunk. He holds another but turns to face me. I nearly flinch but manage to pull in the fear of him hurling the rock at my head.

"And would you be fine sharing her?"

I shrug, not opposed to the idea. Jas was with other suitors when we were younger. Ideally, I would have her to myself, but I am aware of what things are like in our society. We are not allowed to be free with our love. Clem turns, throwing the rock into the water again with the same force. He repeats this several times with more stones, but his vigor decreases with each throw. He picks up a small rock but doesn't throw it in the water. He bounces it in his hand, thinking, delaying saying whatever is on his mind.

"I...if...will. Hell." He huffs, turning to face me. "Will you help me with my penmanship so we can get to know each other better and come to a truce for Jasmin?" His words are rushed and forced out in one breath, then he quickly turns and launches the rock across the pond. The rock lands behind the waterfall, a testament to his discomfort in asking the question.

The idea of working with him closely thrills me. This will allow me to get to know him, explore this damned arousal I feel, and work my way into Jasmin's good graces again. It's a win-win for me. I nod yes, adding that we should probably head back soon. It doesn't escape my attention that he doesn't offer to help me. I can't help but wonder if he feels the same attraction to me. Is he as thoroughly aroused as I am by our touch? I haven't checked for an erection when we touch, but I've never noticed him adjusting. Maybe his feelings aren't quite as strong as mine. Whatever the case, I want to get to the bottom of this.

While we walk back, we make a plan for his penmanship. He needs nice handwriting when he sends correspondences in his position within the kingdom. Jasmin will be busy changing lords and creating a new territory for the witches in the next few days. We decide to start with informal letters he would write to Jasmin or his family. Then we will move on to practicing more formal pieces. I can ask Kian to give me some of the texts on magic. I can brush up while he is writing, then help when needed. Then we all retire to the bedroom at night. Maybe one night, Jasmin will slip into the middle. Perhaps I'll get to cuddle with her. Hopefully, I will work into both of their good sides and can spend time with her alone soon, preferably in said bedroom.

Chapter 20

CLEM

Jasmin rides in just before dinner is set to begin. Her meetings ran longer than she anticipated. I'm glad she is back. Spending all day with Dahlia has been a mind fuck. She's trying to steal my woman, but she's also her best friend and is helpful at the moment. I don't know what to think about any of this anymore.

Jasmin explains her meetings during dinner. She met with Dominick plus two other men for the position of Lord of Greynon. One man is a witch, while the other is not. Dominick's father has witch lineage but is not a witch himself. Dominick is the top contender for the position. Lord David and Thurston want an older man. Jasmin doesn't. She wants someone that can be counted on for most of her own life. Ultimately, Jasmin has the final say but doesn't want to snub the other lords either. She plans to return to Greynon for the next few days to work on the lordship. The plan wasn't to stay this long, but it has become necessary.

After dinner, I ask if she will walk with me. I don't know my way around anywhere, but I want to spend time with her alone. Seeing as Dahlia is in our room until she leaves, that isn't private anymore. She agrees to walk with me, and we leave the inn. We walk on a trail with pebbles and pine trees surrounding it. Owls are hooting in the distance, and small animals are scurrying around the ground. Jasmin holds my arm as we walk down the path as the sun sets.

After walking for nearly half an hour, we come to a small clearing with a bench. All other sounds from the inn and covens have faded. It's just us and the guard who is trying to stay a discreet distance away. I stop, pulling her into my arms. I kiss the top of her head, holding her tightly.

"I missed you today."

"I missed you, too. Those meetings were so boring without you there. Normally, I either watch all of your facial expressions," Jasmin flicks her fingers against my cheek playfully, "or I daydream of what I want you to do to me later." This time she winks, giving me a deep, passionate kiss.

"Is that so?" I question when she breaks the kiss.

"Mmhmm."

"Did you daydream of me today?" She shakes her head no.

"It's not as fun when you aren't there." I chuckle, pulling her tightly against me. I love this woman so much. I don't know what I would do without her. I would give her anything and everything. I pull a small box from my pocket, holding it out for her to see.

"Kian made this for you the night of the celebration here. Would you like to dance with me?"

The way her eyes light up is breathtaking. She is so excited by the simplest things, which is one more reason I love her. Despite everything going on, she can still find pleasure and enjoy activities that make her happy. She places the box on a nearby rock before she returns to my arm. I hold her close, knowing this is where she belongs. She should always be in my arms, but at least I get these opportunities with her.

There is a slight breeze in the air, and the area we are dancing around is small but moonlit. Leaves rustle in the breeze while pebbles crunch under our swaying feet. Tall pine trees cast moonlit shadows around us, swaying with the gently blowing air. I don't know if this is a magically enhanced area, but it feels magical now. A soft ballad comes on, and Jasmin rests her cheek against my chest, near my heart. She is listening to my heartbeat, another of her favorite activities that always brings her joy.

We stay together until the music stops, but I tighten my hold when she tries to pull away. I'm not ready to let her go. Once I let her go, we have to go back to her room where Dahlia is. Then I'll have to share my time with her, and she will be in our space. I just want Jasmin. I want to relax with her in our own room, with no one else.

"Sorry, Your Majesty," the guard watching us speaks hesitantly, "we should get back to the inn. It's getting too dark to stay safe." I sigh, kissing her quickly before I release her. We walk back hand in hand. At least we have these moments together until we return to the castle.

Dahlia is asleep inside the room, taking up nearly half of the bed. There is no way for either of us to sleep without touching her. Jasmin tries to wake her but to no avail. She tells me Dahlia can sleep like the dead at times. If only she were one of them. Okay, that was harsh. I don't wish Dahlia dead, just not in my bed. Or near us. Maybe in another kingdom. Jasmin offers to sleep in the middle, but I would bet my own life Dahlia will touch her or grope her or even worse once she realizes. Even the dead can wake for a beauty like Jasmin.

If I sleep next to her, I have to deal with those zaps that come with touching her. The unusual arousal I get every time I touch her. I usually try to cease all touching immediately. Last night was so bad I had to fuck Jasmin this morning. I wouldn't normally fuck her with someone just washing up, but my cock was so hard I had to. I don't know if I can go through another night like that. I suggest we try to move her, but even as we do that, the little stings hit my hands. With every move we make, Dahlia undoes. I have a hard time believing she is actually asleep at this point.

I eventually give up, insisting on sleeping in the middle again. Fucking Jasmin in the morning isn't the worst thing I could do to start the day. I try to stay wrapped around Jasmin as much as possible but don't want to make her uncomfortable or keep her from getting sleep. I'm just working on writing letters tomorrow. I don't need nearly as much sleep as she does.

Dahlia is moving so much, and she bumps me every time she moves. A caress of my back. Her foot nudges my leg. An elbow to my ribs. Eventually, she starts snoring, but it's too late for me. I'm fully aroused, unable to sleep. I'm on my side, facing Jasmin. I can't sleep on my stomach, and if I roll onto my back, anyone could see how fucking hard I am. There is no way I am going to face Dahlia at this point. I don't understand why she has this effect on me. I don't want to be with her. For all intents and purposes, I can't stand her. She is trying to steal Jasmin from me. We aren't friends. So why is my body betraying me like this? Jasmin rolls into me, snuggling against my chest. I push my hips away from her, only to bump into Dahlia and get another current of arousal sent straight to my already straining cock. I bite my lips to stifle the groan.

"Clem?" Jasmin whispers. Her hands trail my sides, sliding closer to my hips and my secret arousal I don't want to deal with. "Why are you so far away?" She mumbles as she moves her body quicker than I can react. "Oh," her hips press against mine, then her hand slides from my hips down to my cock.

"Shh, go back to sleep, Jas," I whisper against her forehead. "Don't worry about me." In defiance of my request, she begins stroking my cock. I close my eyes, pressing my forehead against hers, breathing deeply to contain the groan. She releases it, only to slip her fingers inside my trousers and wrap them around my aching dick. I breathe her name out, trying to focus on not bursting into her hand so soon. I don't know how long I've been this hard, but it's been too long.

She pushes me onto my back, shifting the covers over us. I glance at Dahlia, worried she will wake up. Jasmin crawls on top of my body. Her lithe form covers mine as her lips cover my ear. She presses several kisses before telling me to be quiet. Several more kisses have my cock jerking in her hand. I can feel her smile against my neck. She slides down my body, wrapping her warm mouth around the tip of my member. I bite my lip to avoid groaning, but it's more challenging than anticipated.

I watch the covers rise and fall as Jasmin bobs up and down on my cock. She isn't taking me all the way in the back of her throat, probably so she doesn't gag and make a lot of noise. The concern over Dahlia, who is snoring softly beside me, waking up, adds to the sensation of Jasmin's lips around me. I am not going to last long at this rate.

She wraps both hands around my length, twisting and pulling as her mouth covers the head of my cock. I grab the blanket in one hand, reaching under with the other. My fingers trace through Jasmin's hair as my body tingles with the telltale sign of my impending release. I grip her hard, forcing her down twice before I empty deep in her throat. She struggles not to make any sounds, but a few still sneak through. Each little squeak sends another pulse through my body. All thoughts are focused on Jasmin and her glorious mouth swallowing my orgasm. As I finish, she licks off any remaining mess, then crawls next to me again.

"You didn't have to do that, little flower," I whisper against her lips, giving her several small kisses.

"I want to sleep too, Clem." She chuckles, snuggling against my chest. I debate trying to touch her, to get her to release also, but she is already drifting off in my arms. As sleep consumes me, I realize I should probably tell her what's happening. It's only fair that she knows the whole truth. She has told me everything that happened between her and Dahlia, and it's not like I did, or want to do, anything with her. Things are just happening.

I manage a few hours of sleep before we need to wake for the day. Jasmin is moving around with Emmeline, getting ready for another day of meeting with prospects and working out the details of the new lordship. I want to go with her but understand why they don't want me there now. I'll spend the day working on my penmanship and being miserable near Dahlia. I'll find a way to keep my distance. I'll sit across from her, slide my paper to her, something. I can't take another day of touching her.

"Can I have a few minutes with Jasmin before breakfast?" I ask Emmeline and Dahlia just before we are all ready to leave. Emmeline nods, walking out immediately. Dahlia hesitates initially but decides to follow suit and walks out behind Emmeline. I stand behind Jasmin in the mirror, where she is checking her hair. My arms wrap around her waist while I rest my chin on her shoulder.

"What's wrong, Clem?" She eyes me anxiously, picking up on my nervous demeanor.

"Thank you for last night," I mumble, kissing her jaw. I don't know how to tell her that her best friend was the cause of that rock-hard erection last night. Just the thought makes me feel like an ass. I step away, but she grabs my arm, stopping me.

"What is it?" She presses, knowing there is more. Either she knows me too well, or I really need to work on my facial expressions. Probably both.

"There's a reason I was so hard last night." She just nods, waiting patiently for my response. I sigh, "Every time Dahlia touches me, I get this...sensation that runs through my body. Enough of them leads to that." I motion toward my waist, looking away from her, embarrassed by my confession.

"Touches, how?" I can hear the concern and anger in her voice, though she is trying to keep it out.

"Any way. Shaking her hand, her bumping against me all night, grabbing her arm to help her up. It all affects me the same way." Jasmin lets go of my arm, taking a few steps away. She is rubbing her chin, considering what I have said to her.

"When did it start?"

"When she came back." I shrug my shoulders, thinking about the first time I actually touched her. "It was at dinner when you formally introduced her to everyone. That was the first time I touched her."

"And it happens every time?" She turns toward me, looking concerned. I nod to her, but she seems so confused and upset. I question whether I made the right decision in telling her.

"Does she feel the same way?"

Another shrug from me. "I haven't told anyone else, and it's not something I really want to admit."

"Do you feel that way with me?" She questions sheepishly, looking nervous all of a sudden. Shit.

"Jas," I start, unsure what to say. I don't get the same zaps with Jasmin, but that doesn't mean I don't want her. She turns away from me, but I walk in front of her, grabbing her arms so she can't move away from me. "I don't want her that way; it's just how my body reacts to her. You are the only one that I want. Not her. I don't want anything to do with her. I know she's your friend and all, but I don't particularly like her." Jasmin chuckles at my confession. It isn't meant to be funny, but at least she isn't entirely angry at me. "I may not have sensations of instant arousal coursing through me at every little touch from you, but I'd have to live with my dick buried inside of you all the time if I did because you are the one I want to touch."

She steps into my arms, letting me hug her tightly. I don't know what this means, but I can work through anything with her.

"Could it be part of the curse?" I chuckle slightly at her question, shrugging my shoulders.

"Why would Dahlia's touch causing arousal be part of the curse? I don't think we can keep blaming things on the curse." She shrugs in my arms, stepping away from me.

"You're right. Let's go to breakfast." I nod, taking her hand to walk her to the door. "You are working on your penmanship with her today, right?" I nod again in response. "Just keep your hands to yourself, okay?"

"Who's jealous now, little flower?" We both laugh, kissing quickly before leaving the room. I fully intend to keep my hands to myself. I don't want to spend the day with tented pants. Or be attracted to Dahlia at all.

Chapter 21

JASMIN

Clem makes a point of avoiding Dahlia at breakfast. It is awkward, but I may be projecting because I don't know how to feel about his confession. I'm glad he told me. Not only did he want me to know, but he trusted me enough to tell me something personal and awkward. I'm relieved in that sense but unsure about what to do next. I want to talk to Dahlia and find out if she has the same feelings, but I need to get to the town center early today.

Lords David and Thurston have been giving me a hard time choosing a successor to Alwyn. I'm still beyond pissed at him. He has had the decency not to attend any of these proceedings. I'm leaning heavily toward naming Dominick. He is perfect for the role. I didn't spend much time with him while he was at the castle, and virtually no time alone. He is well-rounded, though. He can be diplomatic when necessary but also knows how to relax. He also cares about the witches and everyone in his community. I'm surprised Alwyn selected him to come under the True Love Edict last year. I almost expected someone worse.

I leave Clem with a gentle kiss as I head down to the village center. My entourage is large, but we know this path well. The journey is quick and easy. I am set to meet with one other contender, then follow up with Dominick before I name someone. The other contender is just a formality, and I can't imagine anyone being better suited than Dominick.

Thurston and David are waiting on me when I arrive; seeing as they are staying in the village center, they can get here faster than I am. We start with a brief recap of the previous men we have met with, then discuss the new one coming in. His family is wealthy and well-known. He walks in with an air about him, and I instantly don't like him. I can do without this.

Within his first four answers, I already know I won't consider him. His replies are pompous, and he isn't thinking of everyone within the village. We have a list of nearly thirty questions to sit through. My mind drifts to Clem, wondering how he is faring with Dahlia. I look at the list of questions and look back at the man before me. He is halfway through an answer that I hate. Thurston nods because this man talks about increasing taxes on the lower classes to increase the village's wealth. Of course, he has not mentioned where those taxes would go. David seems more reserved, but he hasn't stopped this madness.

"What are your ties to the covens?" I interrupt. There is no reason to sit through hours of endless droning when one or two questions will tell me everything I need to know.

"The witches keep to themselves, and I'm content to follow the status quo." He seems proud of his response, while both lords have the decency to look nervous.

"Thank you for the time. You are dismissed. You will not get this position." He has the gall to look appalled like he will argue, but Thurston shakes his head, encouraging him to leave. Smart man. He goes, and both of the Lords turn to me.

"Do you think that was wise, your majesty?" Thurston asks.

"Do I look like I want to waste my time, Thurston? I am not looking for another Alwyn. I want a better kingdom than my father had, and I cannot do that with the same kind of people." I give him a pointed stare, indicating his job is at risk now. "I will no longer stand by as taxes are pilfered from lower-class villagers. Maybe I should plan a visit to Vadried after the summer solstice."

"No, milady. That isn't necessary. We will alter our taxes upon return." He nods, but I am outraged that he admitted his taxes are being pilfered. I will need to follow up on that. I stand, walking to the back table to pour my own wine. I send a servant to find Dominick. Getting here could take him time since his meeting isn't for a few hours. I want to finish this ordeal and get back to the castle soon. I miss my own space, and everything is wearing on me. I need Finn and my large room and to not worry about Dahlia and lords and this damned curse. Maybe I'll go to the pond by myself when I'm back. I could use that.

"So you are settled on Dominick?" David asks, watching me curiously. I nod and take a sip of my wine. I don't need to elaborate; it will all be explained when Dominick is here anyway. "For what it's worth, I think you are making a good choice in choosing people your father wouldn't approve of. He had many great qualities but did tend to overlook certain groups within his kingdom."

I nod my thanks to him. My father had been my role model until the curse started. Being thrust into his shoes made me realize there were many things I wasn't proud of that he did, including owning slaves, avoiding witches, and ignoring lower-class people. I love my father, but he didn't raise me precisely in his own image, which will hopefully be better for our kingdom.

"At least he didn't go around firing people to get some dick," Thurston whispers to David. David has the sensibility to look surprised by his comment. I'm sure it's not the first time Thurston, or other lords, have made snide comments. But to do so in my presence, in an already quiet room, is quite bold of him.

"I already got some dick this morning, Thurston. No need for your concern. You are dismissed from these proceedings. I believe Lord David and I can wrap things up. I expect you and your court financier to be at the castle three days before the summer solstice with proof of how you have reformed your taxes." I take another sip of wine, remaining nonchalant in my attitude. "You can consider this your first warning. Pray you are as lucky as Alwyn to receive as many as he did." I down my wine and return to my seat. Thurston doesn't argue with me but does rise and leave the room angrily.

I am tired of dealing with their attitudes. I am now crowned ruler of Sweet Briar and plan to act as such. They prevented me for years from taking my rightful title. I wandered as a ghost, allowing them free reign of the kingdom. It took finding Clem to break me from the trance I was under. I would like to blame the curse for everything, but honestly, I just took the easy way. Letting them rule their own land was simpler than getting involved. Because of that decision, the living conditions of many of my people have devolved, and I can no longer sit idly by. I don't want to replace most of the staff, but I will if they no longer match my goals for the kingdom.

Dominick finally arrives a few minutes after Thurston leaves. I tell him to sit, then inform him I want him to be Lord of Greynon. He manages to suppress his excitement, remaining aloof during the meeting. We spend the next couple of hours discussing his duties and what I expect of him and answering any questions he has. Dominick is an attractive man. He's a year younger than me with light brown skin and sun-kissed brown hair. It is shorter than Clem's but has a bit of length to it. He keeps it combed but occasionally runs his fingers through it, rustling it up. His nose is broad with golden eyes. He is still unmarried but probably has many prospects once his position is official. I ask him to report to the castle two days before the summer solstice to check in.

The rest of the afternoon rushes by, filled with discussions of duties and requirements. We are soon back on the trail to the inn in coven territory, no earlier than if I had continued with the meeting with the last contender, though. I am interested to hear how Clem has fared, but I hope he won't mind if I can have a talk with Dahlia alone. I am concerned he still won't let me, but I need to speak with her about what is happening to him. I can ask Emmeline to join, but it's not ideal.

As we near the inn, nothing is burning; everything is still in one piece. This is as good of a sign as I'll get. At least they didn't have a catastrophic fight. One of the guards takes Vesper to the stable for me while I enter and head to our room. I don't know that they will be there, but I want to wash up and change out of these clothes. I love these mock dresses the tailor made for me, but between the ride and sitting in the room all day, I just want to bathe and put on fresh clothes.

I find a note on the bed with my name written outside. I don't recognize the handwriting, leading me to believe it must be from Clem. It strikes me that he hasn't written me a note before. I've sent a few to him, and he received some from his mother, but he never did respond in writing to any of them. I open the letter to read it. There are ink marks across the page where the quill dripped or he pressed too hard.

My little flower,

I have missed you today. My time with ~~Data~~ Dahlia has been long and frustrating, but she has been helpful. I look forward to your return and hearing about your day. I hope you have decided to name Dominick as Lord of Greynon. I will see you at dinner.

Your true love,

Clem

His note is short, sweet, and messy. I love it so much. I fold it up and tuck it into my luggage to save before climbing in the bath. I savor the warmth of the water surrounding my body, letting it soothe my stress. When I get out, Emmeline has clothes selected for me, leggings and a loose tunic. I thank all the gods for both my comfortable clothes and Emmeline.

During dinner, Clem does his best not to bring attention to how far away from Dahlia he is staying, but it's still noticeable. It doesn't help that she seems to be teasing him. She must have realized the sensations he gets when she is near. Otherwise, she is torturing him for fun, which I cannot rule out. Dahlia would absolutely do that. I recount my day, explaining that Dominick is the new Lord of Greynon. Everyone is very excited about this new appointment.

As we return to the room, I grab Clem's arm and slow to distance ourselves from everyone else. Dahlia is so wrapped up in telling her story to Kian and Emmeline that she doesn't notice us fall back. When we're out of earshot, I ask how his day was. He confirms my suspicions that Dahlia knows what he feels when she touches him and has been torturing him all day. I curse under my breath, offering a kiss as an apology. I suggest I sleep in the middle so he can rest tonight. He tries to argue but eventually concedes. He needs to get some sleep before he goes crazy.

The rest of the evening is uneventful. We spend an awkward hour getting ready for bed, chatting, and being uncomfortable. When we finally go to bed, Dahlia immediately notices our new sleeping arrangements and begins to cheer.

"I swear to all the holy gods, if you touch her, I will end you," Clem seethes at her. I'm not used to seeing him so angry, but I don't hate it either. It's kind of hot when it isn't aimed at me. My pussy agrees, based on the new wetness pooling there. I take a deep breath, trying to calm my body, knowing we all need actual sleep, not just more sex. I snuggle into Clem's side, swatting Dahlia's hands away several times. We quickly all drift off to sleep. She takes up a lot of space for sharing a bed with two other people. Clem and I will spread out on some nights, but we are more content being wrapped around each other. We get a good night's rest for the first time in days. I fall into a deep sleep and stay that way until morning.

I wake with a warm body underneath me. Oh, how gloriously comfortable it is. So soft, so cozy. I wiggle my head but don't open my eyes, not ready for the day to begin. There is a pebbled nipple next to my mouth. Who can say no to that? I suck it between my lips, swirling my tongue lazily around it. My fingers drift across the small body to the other side.

Has Clem been gaining weight? This feels softer than usual. He has been more sedentary than normal, not working in the field. I squeeze the skin beneath the other nipple, sucking on the one in my mouth. A deep groan sounds from the chest beneath my face. It doesn't sound like Clem, but it's been a while since I was on his chest when he groaned. I'm usually a little lower. Fingers lace through my hair, holding me close. I love being handled like that.

"What in the actual fuck, Jasmin?" Clem's angry voice sounds from behind me. That's not where he is supposed to be. My eyes fly open. My hand is on Dahlia's breast; her nipple is in my mouth. I jolt up, popping her nipple out and causing her to groan again. Oh, this is bad.

"Clem, it's not...I didn't..." What am I even trying to say here? He's standing next to the bed, his hands clenched by his side. He turns to start pulling on his clothes. This isn't good. He is so angry right now. He's not wrong about being angry, but I need to wake up before I can adequately explain what happened.

"Ha, it's not what I think? A nipple in your mouth is pretty clear, Jas. You trying to tell me you feel the same shit I do now?" He huffs as he snatches a shirt over his head angrily.

"So you do feel that!" Dahlia sits up quickly, but it goes unnoticed as he stomps into his boots.

"I need some air." Then he storms out of the room.

"No, wait!" I call, but it's too late. He's already gone. I wasn't trying to do anything with Dahlia. I just thought it was him in my sleep-induced horniness. Dahlia wraps her arms around me, whispering about continuing what I started. I shove away from her, getting out of bed.

"I'm so tired of hurting him because of you, Dahl. We have to figure out a better arrangement." A sigh slips out of my mouth, frustrated with this whole situation. She walks over to wrap her arms around me in a hug. "We'll sort it out, Jas. Promise. You'll get your happily ever after. I'll make sure of it." She squeezes me tightly, and the promise she makes causes my heart to skip.

Chapter 22

DAHLIA

Clem said he is feeling shit. Did he mean he feels the same pull I do? That incessant arousal every time our skin gets too close? If he's feeling it too, maybe I'm not crazy; maybe it means something else. I need to talk with someone about this. Jasmin seems to know nothing about the curse. She's more clueless than I am. Clem is the same way. Fate really nailed the similarities between them in that respect.

I need Kian. He is the one with the knowledge of the curse.

I seek him out during breakfast. He is in deep conversation with Jasmin. From what I remember, she is due to spend the day with the witches, preparing for the separation from Greynon. Kian has been buttering up the matrons to the idea; now they need to work out the official details. More boring crap I don't really care about. Politics and court musings were never of interest to me.

He mentions the meetings he will be in with Jasmin, and I interrupt.

"Wait, you're going to be busy today?"

He gives me a confused look but answers, "Yes. As Royal Advisor, this will be an important meeting for me to attend."

Well, fuck. I need to talk to him about the curse. I glance around the table, he and Jasmin are watching me, but everyone else is preoccupied with their conversations. Clem hasn't shown up to breakfast, and Jasmin suspects he grabbed something and went for a walk. He'll probably turn up in the library later. That's his regular routine. I lean close to Kian, wanting to be close enough that others can't hear.

"Let me ask you a hypothetical question then." My voice is hushed so no one else hears. "Hypothetically," I repeat for emphasis, "If Jasmin or Clem were feeling an attraction to someone else, that maybe the other person was also feeling, do you think it would mean anything?" Both Jasmin and Kian eye me suspiciously, but Kian considers the question.

"Hypothetically," he repeats. He knows this is an actual situation, but he has enough experience not to mention it to anyone. He will be good in the courts. "I wouldn't worry about it if it is a normal attraction. They are still human, after all. Fate can't suppress desire. However," he pauses, glancing at Jasmin, then back to me, "if the hypothetical arousal is more than normal, if it feels magical or unnatural, I would encourage them to explore it. Something is missing, and that is why the curse hasn't been lifted." Jasmin's eyebrows furrow as she considers what he is saying.

"You mean the two who are feeling the attraction should explore it? Hypothetically?" Jasmin questions, and I chortle over the repeated use of 'hypothetical.' I'm glad we're all on the same page. Kian nods in response.

"Yes. Or maybe all three if there is attraction between them."

"How would that work?" Jasmin questions. My mind is still stuck on exploring things with Clem. I could touch his body, his hard cock. Let him fuck me the way he fucks Jasmin...

"Like a triad, I suppose. It could be the missing piece."

"Fuck." Jasmin hisses. "Clem is going to hypothetically be angry." We all giggle over her statement.

"No one says a word of this." Jasmin gives us a pointed stare, and we nod in agreement. "Please let me tell Clem," she begs of me. "Leave him alone today, and I'll talk to him when I'm done." I nod to her. I don't think he would take that information well from me anyway.

I spend the day avoiding the room and the library, the two places I suspect Clem would be. I find a few witches and question them for a while. They let me work with them on some spells they are piecing together. I have always loved magic but have never been very good at it. In my homeland, magic was illegal and couldn't be used. Mama and Baba forbade us from messing with it since we were slaves. I dabbled when we moved to Sweet Briar. It took me a year to master the spell for the pond, though. I needed more guidance, but the books still did the job. Using magic can be tricky since it varies from person to person. Even the location can affect it. The castle has a natural pocket of magic for anyone to use.

Jasmin and Clem are sitting at the dinner table when I enter the dining area. I take my usual seat next to her. Something about sitting on her side feels so right. I love being beside her. They are in deep conversation, and it doesn't look delighted. She finally sits back, holding his hand beneath the table. She greets me calmly, but he ignores me. It hurts more than I want to admit. I didn't think the sensations had infiltrated my feelings. I still want him gone, but if we can work things out between us for Jasmin, we have to try.

After dinner, they walk back to our room. She asks Emmeline and Kian to give us privacy tonight so we can talk. They nod and leave, whispering together as they walk away. I can only imagine what those two have to say about everything. Emmeline probably knows more secrets than anyone in the kingdom. Kian knows how to learn that information and more and holds many secrets.

We all enter the room; Clem sits on the bed while I lean against the wall, and Jasmin stands between us. She takes a deep breath, looking at Clem, then over to me.

"Tell me about the feelings, the touches, or whatever it is." I glance at Clem but explain what I feel when he touches me. His eyes go wide. He really can't hide his emotions. I suppress laughter over his expression. Jasmin rolls her eyes at me, knowing me well enough to know I am doing that.

"You feel it, too?" He asks nervously. I nod, crossing my arms over my chest. I feel exposed and on display talking about this so openly. Apparently, he feels the same way because he crosses his arms. Then realizes he is mimicking my movements and uncrosses his arms. He finally stands and walks out on the balcony. There is too much distance for us to continue the conversation now. Jasmin goes to talk to him alone. I remain by the wall, knowing they need some time together.

He may be annoyingly jealous over her, but he is the one experiencing attraction to someone else now. He will undoubtedly need time to process that information. After several minutes, they walk back in, neither looking happy. He stands like he might walk over to me but turns to Jasmin, taking her hands.

"I can't do it. You are my true love, Jasmin. Not her. I only want you." She sighs, wrapping her arms around him. Jealousy of my own courses through me. Jealousy over him being in her arms, where I so desperately want to be. A sudden need to be in his arms spikes through my emotions. A metaphorical knife slices through my chest at watching the two of them embrace. The woman I love and the man I loathe and desire are embracing in a way I can't experience. Jasmin sighs in his arms but holds him tightly. She understands his feelings. None of us were expecting him to change instantly. I wouldn't have been upset with it, though.

"I'm going to bathe. Maybe you two should talk," she suggests. He looks at me but turns away, unsatisfied with that suggestion. Oh, the knife twists in my chest. He clings to her, but she finally tears away and goes to take a bath. Hopefully, she doesn't take a long one. I don't want to have this conversation with him.

"How long have you been feeling it?" I inquire, not sure what else to say. He looks at me but sits on the bed, avoiding any type of contact. I can't pretend that his behavior doesn't hurt. I understand it, but that doesn't change how it feels.

"Since the beginning," he huffs out, fidgeting with some string on his shirt. My mind runs through different ways this could play out, and I feel it won't end in me getting fucked. I settle on the bold path and stand in front of him. I reach out, moving slowly enough he can stop me at any point. I press a lock of hair away from his face. He hisses a breath out, closing his eyes. That attraction is flitting through my body.

With his eyes closed, I lean down and press my lips against his. It's light, barely a graze. His lips are soft and full, and I want so much more. He jerks back, shaking his head.

"I can't... I can't."

"Then what are we supposed to do?"

"I don't know. But I can't love her and be with you."

"Why not, Clem? What is your issue with sharing? Weren't you taught to share as a kid?"

He huffs a laugh, standing to walk away from me. He refuses to be anywhere near me. "Not my woman." This is going to get us nowhere.

"Then let's just go to bed." I glance back at the bathroom, where Jasmin is still locked away. "I need your help with this dress." I don't, really. "I can't reach the ties." I don't need them to take off the dress. It's more work to undo them, but maybe having him close and touching will help my cause. He sighs, moving behind me, ever the gentleman willing to help. He loosens the ties and grazes my skin as the material falls away. I groan as arousal courses through my body. He jerks his hand as I turn and drop my dress, standing in front of him with my chest exposed. He hisses a breath between his teeth.

He stares at my body momentarily, then turns and walks out of the room. The door shuts behind him with me standing stark naked and confused near the bed. Eventually, I grab a shift to sleep in. Jasmin comes out of the room later, searching for Clem, and I tell her he left without saying anything. She sighs, looking between me and the door. She soon walks over to me, tracing her fingers along my face. She rises on her toes to kiss my forehead. I close my eyes, savoring the feeling of her lips against my skin.

I don't feel the same way about kissing Clem and Jasmin. Jasmin is a more worn in attraction. There is still excitement, knowing what I can get with her. With Clem, the excitement comes from the unknown. Both drive a deep desire, though.

"I'm sorry, Dahl. We'll figure this out." She presses a quick kiss to my lips, leaving all too soon. She walks out of the room, searching for Clem. I fall asleep on the bed, sleeping through the night. At some point, both return, snuggling into their side of the bed. My own damn jealousy is eating away over both of them and their relationship. I wish Clem had never said anything about these damned sensations. I could have kept pretending nothing was going on and been perfectly fine.

We're all super awkward in the morning, and it's so much fun. Ugh. Clem is again going out of his way not to touch me. Jasmin keeps sighing but isn't trying to be more comforting for either of us. Clem tells us he will grab a bite on his way to the library. He's apparently found some alcove he likes and wants to claim it for privacy before anyone else comes. His tone implies I am 'anyone else.'

Kian and Emmeline are already waiting for us in the dining area. They ask how things are going, not explicitly mentioning Clem's absence. Jasmin gives a brief recount without giving too many details.

"How do we make him realize he needs to accept this situation?" I huff out in a frustrated voice.

"I don't think you can," Kian reasons, but that's a stupid reason.

"Get him drunk," Emmeline adds saucily. "That man will do anything with some wine in him."

"'Emmeline!" Jasmin scolds as I grin. This is what we need. He needs to relax. Hell, we could all stand to relax. I ask Kian and Emmeline to bring wine to our room tonight under the guise of us celebrating a successful trip. Jasmin feigns attempts to stop, but it's weak. She wants this as much as I do. Both she and Clem are so damn stubborn. Luckily, I'm more determined than both. I will get what I want, which is both of them, apparently.

Jasmin leaves for the day, heading to the covens to work with them and all her monotonous duties. Clem stays in the library, I assume. He doesn't come out for lunch, and I don't spot him at any other point. He has mastered the craft of avoiding places he doesn't want to be. It's probably a good skill for a partner of a queen.

Later that evening, Kian and Emmeline show up with wine. We are all in our room, drinking, laughing, and relaxing. We bring several blankets and pillows to the balcony and pile them on the floor under the stars. Clem is in the middle of the group, with Jasmin between him and me. Kian and Emmeline are on his other side, sitting closer than strictly platonic friends usually do. I grab another bottle of wine, topping everyone's mug. For now, the conversation is light and casual. We're reminiscing about stories from before the curse. We all led very different lives before the curse, as one would suspect, with a queen, a witch, a lady in waiting, a former slave, and a farmhand. It's quite an eccentric group.

After another bottle of wine, both Jasmin and Emmeline are getting handsy. Jealousy once again courses through my body. I need to play tonight just right. If I push this too soon, Clem might get nervous, but too late, and he would be too drunk. As I make plans, Kian rises, taking Emmeline with him, and wishes us a good night.

"Don't forget, the balcony is spelled, and no one can see or hear what happens here." He winks as they return inside and then leave the room. I stare up at the stars, wondering if I'm good enough to figure out a spell like the one around the room.

"Clem," her voice is sultry, pulling my attention to her. She is kissing his neck, her hands roaming his body. His eyes are closed, savoring whatever she is making him feel. He still wants her touch even after all this and all they have been through. My heart clenches in my chest, so in awe of their relationship.

"Let me fuck you," she whispers, sliding over his legs to hover over his body. "While I eat her." My eyes go wide at her suggestion. It sounds like heaven, but I'm surprised she went with that. I watch him, waiting for his response with bated breath. He bites his lip, looking between the two of us. Jasmin grinds her hips against his in a slow, smooth rhythm. Just watching her gyrate against his dick is making me wet. Her hands drag the side of her body, pulling her shirt over her head. Her breasts are exposed in his face. His eyes are locked on her body as heat burns through his eyes. He grabs her hips and gives the slightest, barely noticeable nod. Jasmin crashes against his lips, kissing him deeply and thoroughly.

She breaks the kiss and turns away, removing her leggings and pulling his dick from his pants. Without speaking, she motions me to move in front of her. She grinds her hips, rubbing her wet slit against his cock. She raises her hips and then sinks down on his cock, with her back to his chest. His hands grab her breasts, twirling her nipples between his thumb and forefinger. She picks up the pace as I sit and watch, arousal coursing through my body. My brain is frozen with desire, but I soon remember his agreement.

Once my mind wakes up, I strip my clothes, tossing them to the side. I sit before Jasmin with my legs open as she bounces up and down on Clem's dick. Her eyes roll back in her when one of his hands drops from her breast to her clit, circling the bundle of nerves in the way she likes. Watching his fingers so deftly work her body is causing my own pussy to clench. Not wanting to detract from them but unable to resist, I slide my fingers down to my wet core. I spread my legs, accidentally bumping Clem's. A jolt goes straight through my cunt. I drop my head, moaning out loud as need pierces my body.

I lift my head just in time to see Clem pushing Jasmin forward while managing to thrust inside her. Her hands creep up my legs while my skin tingles under her touch. Her eyes stay on mine until she reaches my core. She places a soft kiss on my wet cunt, and that alone nearly makes me orgasm. I've waited so long for this, and I'm not about to lose it this soon. Her tongue travels along my slit, swirling around my clit. Okay, I'm not going to make it long. Hopefully, she'll just give me more than one orgasm.

"Put a finger inside of her."

Clem's voice is gravelly and more profound than I'm used to hearing. I have faint memories of hearing his voice, similar to that in the gardens. Before I can focus on his strong voice, Jasmin teases a finger through my opening, and I crack. My orgasm crashes through me. Her lips wrap around my clit, sucking it tight as my eyes roll back in my head.

"She's so sweet, Clem." Her words against my cunt cause it to clench around her finger again. Part of me doesn't believe I came with only one finger inside me; part of me is surprised I lasted as long as I did.

Suddenly, Clem is pushing forward, shoving Jasmin into me. I wrap my arms around her, holding her off the ground.

"Move over her," he demands. She shifts onto her hands and knees, crawling over me. She licks her lip, a devilish grin spreading across her beautiful face. Just as she leans in to kiss me, her head is snatched back, causing her to gasp. His fingers are wrapped in her hair. "I didn't say you could kiss her. Put your legs together." She does as instructed, and he pulls her back away from me. The cool air brushes against my wet cunt, reminding me of how exposed I am. All I can focus on is how he is manhandling her and how much she likes it, based on her hard nipples, rolling eyes, and glistening pussy.

He pulls her back against his body, kissing her neck. He finds her lips, kissing her deeply, then licking her lips. He is licking my taste off of her. He groans, returning to kiss hers deeply. I take the opportunity to sit up, taking one of her breasts in my mouth. My fingers caress her wet pussy, but I graze Clem's cock, which is just behind her. He hisses at the touch, then forces her forward onto me, thus forcing me back so I can't reach him. He smacks her ass so hard that the sound vibrates off the wall. And my girl moans. She fucking moans over being spanked. Why have I never spanked her?

"Fuck her while I fuck you."

He shoves her head to me again as she kisses me desperately. This is everything I have wanted. Her with me again, her body against mine. Her fingers find my cunt again, slipping two inside instead of just one. She breaks the kiss, moaning against my neck as Clem enters her from behind. She wedges her hand between us as he begins to fuck her. Jasmin tries to find my nipples as he pumps behind her, but she keeps moaning too loudly. I chuckle but quickly stop as she hits my clit, and it becomes a moan. I pull her face to mine, trying to kiss her.

My body is clenching with the threat of a second orgasm, but I want to hold out longer. I need to come with her. She is also on the cusp but likely holding out for Clem. He slaps her ass again, and my own cunt clenches around her fingers. She slips a third inside me, filling me so perfectly.

"Make her come, slut. Make us both come for you."

His harsh words throw me, but I feel Jasmin groan underneath me and re-member she likes when he says shit like that. As that realization hits, her finger rubs the spot inside me that sends stars dancing around my vision. Just before my orgasm takes over, I grab her nipples, twisting as hard as possible. She always liked that before, but I'm sure she likes it even more now. As if on cue, we both release, moaning loudly as our bodies twist and turn against each other. Her body collapses on top of mine as Clem pounds inside her. Moments later, he grunts, his own orgasm barreling through his body. Jasmin stays on top of me as her breathing regulates, but Clem settles back against the wall. He could collapse next to me, but we'll get there.

We stay on the balcony for several minutes as the sky flashes bright with lightning and thunder sounds in the distance. It's not as loud as before, but the lightning is still pretty. The lightning is shades of green and purple instead of the typical white we see in storms. It looks like stars streaking through the sky. The barrier isn't breaking tonight, but it was still fun. Jasmin shivers under my arms. I stroke her body, trying to warm her up. I'm not ready to move back inside yet, but I also don't want to move to grab a blanket. Clem could warm her, though.

"Clem, come cuddle with Jas. She's chilly."

He huffs and turns to the side to avoid looking at us. I thought for sure asking him to do something for her would work. His stubbornness runs deep.

"I said, come warm her up, Clem." I use a firm voice, not giving any room for arguments. Jasmin is trying to adjust under my grip, but I tighten my arms. She realizes this is a battle Clem and I need to have, so she just lays there quietly like my good little girl. I press a kiss on her forehead for behaving. Clem crosses his arms over his chest, and I've had enough. I grab his leg tightly, knowing the sensations still run straight to his spent cock. He groans at the touch, his body distorting to stop it.

"Don't make me repeat myself."

"Fuck."

He does as I say. He's by my side, arms wrapped around Jasmin. She wiggles happily, settling between us. She kisses him gently, thanking him for warming her. He sighs but presses a kiss to her head. I have power over him. For now, who knows how long these feelings will last. But I'm damn sure going to make the most of this newfound ability.

Part Three

Antirrhinum

Chapter 23

CLEM

Tonight is the summer solstice masquerade ball. The castle has been buzzing for the past week since we returned. Flowers and plants have been spread everywhere throughout the castle. The halls are decked with garlands of green leaves and bright ribbons. Painted suns and stars are hung on walls and columns. I had no idea the castle celebrated so strongly, but I suppose they would. In Arkaley, the celebrations were always meager. Maybe someone would buy a round of ale at the pub.

Emmeline insisted I get dressed separately from Jasmin. Again, more theatrics I am not used to. Though I must admit, after seeing Jasmin in the foyer at the winter solstice and wedding, I am excited to find her after she gets dressed without me. Kian invited me to his room to get ready. He is especially chatty today. I haven't been listening. I have been lost in my own thoughts. I'm excited to see my girl and dance the night away with her again. Any excuse to hold her body next to mine...

"What are your thoughts on something like that?"

Kian's words break me from my own thoughts. Unfortunately, my thoughts are not on whatever he was talking about.

"I'm sorry, Kian. I wasn't actually paying attention. I am lost in my own thoughts tonight."

He shrugs nonchalantly, letting me know it's time to go anyway. I feel terrible for not listening to him. I tried to focus, but my brain kept circling back to Jasmin. We haven't fucked since we were with Dahlia on the balcony. Even a week later, I still don't know how to feel about it. The taste of Dahlia on Jasmin's lips was unlike anything I have ever experienced. Seeing her enjoy such a gorgeous woman with me inside her was surreal. Part of me wants to do it again. But it's Dahlia. Why couldn't she be in love with Emmeline? Or anyone else?

Between her duties to the kingdom, starting a new territory, a new lord, and planning this solstice, Jasmin has worked late every night since we returned and has been exhausted by the time she made it to bed. She is working so hard; I hope tonight is a break for her, and she can relax. We could all use a break from the stress of everything.

We reach the foyer, where she is waiting on the stairs for me, much like the winter solstice, but Dahlia is beside her this time. They wear similar gowns, but Dahlia's is fuller than Jasmin's. Jasmin's dress is a deep navy with silver thread stitched into intricate designs to look like stars and smoke. The dress is slim against her body with sheer sleeves that flow down but gather at the wrist. The dress clings to her body, making my mouth water at the thought of what is underneath. She is wearing the smaller tiara I had made for her and the necklace I gave her six months ago. My heart flutters that she wears it as much as she does.

Dahlia's gown is a similar color with the same stitching, but it is gold instead of silver. She isn't wearing any sort of jewelry except for her mask. Jasmin's is silver to match her dress. Dahlia's is gold, but the color against her dark skin is stunning. It almost looks like it is glowing against her face. Her hair has been braided again, with gold and silver strands intertwined with her hair. The long colorful locs fall straight down her back. Her beauty is equal to Jasmin's at this moment. The air is suddenly thick as I stare between the two beautiful women. My heart thunders at the image of them side by side.

My eyes reach Jasmin's. She stares at me with curiosity but also patience. I clear my throat and saunter to them, unsure how long I have been staring. As I move, my awareness of my surroundings also comes back. I realize there is loud thunder outside. Is this what everyone heard at the last solstice when I was so oblivious to it?

I kiss Jasmin's cheek, careful of the powder and rouge Emmeline has applied. I take her hands, wanting to tell her how beautiful she is and how much I love her, but my mouth is startlingly dry. She understands what I want to say and gives a slight smirk. She turns toward Dahlia; my eyes follow the movement.

"Isn't she beautiful?"

Jasmin reaches one hand to take Dahlia's. As soon as they touch, all three of us connected through Jasmin, an overwhelming wave of emotion crashes through my body. Desire, love, longing, lust, then confusion when Dahlia drops her hand. I watch her momentarily for any sign of her feeling the same thing I did. She turns, announcing she'll see us inside.

I could love her.

I try to hide my shock and confusion over that thought as thunder crashes behind us. The sound pulls Jasmin's attention away from me long enough I can reign in my expression. I don't know where that thought came from or what the fuck it means, but now isn't the time to sort it out. I finally manage to whisper how beautiful Jasmin is. She blushes at my kind words and hands me a mask to wear. It is a navy mask to match our clothes but has swirls stitched into it. The thread is silver on one side, but as it spreads across the mask, it blends into gold. I eye her suspiciously at the potential meaning behind wearing a mask that matches both hers and Dahlia's but don't say anything. I simply turn as she helps me tie it behind my head.

Everyone is wearing extravagant dresses and fancy suits, and intricately designed masks. My own suit is more regal than anything I normally wear. The material is thin to account for the heat of summer, and the trousers are fitted while the tunic is looser. It is in dark colors to match Jasmin's dress. Mine doesn't have the intricate stitch work, though we obviously match.

Jasmin and I make our way around the room, greeting everyone. I am much better with names this time, but I still don't know nearly as many as Jasmin. I am in awe of her ability to make everyone feel welcome. People have already started dancing, but Jasmin said she wants to mingle for a while before dancing. I offer to get wine, giving her a quick kiss when she accepts. I saunter over to the table, feeling elated in this atmosphere. Everything is beautiful and perfect. I have the woman I love. Thunder is rolling outside. The castle is decorated exquisitely. What more could I ask for?

I pour two goblets of wine and turn to find Jas. She is surrounded by people, and I soon realize Dahlia is one of those people. I bite my cheek, unsure how to feel about her being so close to Jas without me. I'm still deciding if I like her. She ruined my wedding, tried to steal my girl from me, crashed my second wedding, then my bed, and moved into the nursery across the hall. Jasmin was all too glad to give her that room and have it remodeled. At the same time, Dahlia is beautiful and strong, and Jasmin loves her so much. She clearly has something to do with the curse. I just don't know what.

"What are your thoughts on something like that?"

"Oh, fuck, Kian. Have you been talking to me?" I startle at his sudden appearance. I know I was zoned out, but I didn't even hear him walk up. He chuckles, shaking his head.

"No, but you had that look on your face. You don't want any bread this time?" I chuckle, remembering my behavior at the last solstice celebration when I came to terms with my feelings for Jas. How many solstices will I go through with roiling emotions?

"Did I have the same look just now?" Kian nods in response, sending my mind reeling again.

"What the fuck does it mean?" I question, leaning against the table behind me for support. "And can't we get a solstice we can just enjoy for the fun of it?" Kian huffs a laugh at my question.

"Can I tell you something that you won't like?" I eye him suspiciously, and he adds, "I think you can handle it now." It's my turn to huff at him.

"You have come a long way from when you first arrived, then ignored Jasmin for weeks." I cringe internally, remembering how I behaved then. I was just so angry and upset; I needed time. I finally nod to Kian, wanting to hear what he says. He is more insightful than he gets credit for. "You can love them both."

"How? It's man and wife. Not man and wife and other woman." I drink from one of the goblets, watching Jasmin and Dahlia talk with other people from the castle they know. Maybe it would be easier if it could be all three of us. It would be easiest if Dahlia would back off. I don't see how I could love both, though. I love Jasmin. She is my true love. Dahlia isn't my true love.

"Do you only love one of your sisters?"

"What? No!'

"Only one parent?" I don't respond to that question. "Only one friend?" I huff, giving him a pointed stare. "My point is you have the capability to love more than one person at a time. The only thing holding you back is you."

I stare at him again, considering his response. He makes a valid point, not a good point, but a valid one nonetheless.

"Are you saying I need to love Dahlia, too?"

"Maybe not, but you are expending a lot of energy on hating her." He presses something to my chest and starts to walk away. I wrap my arm around the item, then look down when he steps away. It's a loaf of bread. I break off a piece of the bread while chuckling and pop it into my mouth. As I chew, I watch Jasmin and Dahlia and consider Kian's words.

Could he be on to something? Is there a reason I feel all these sensations and emotions when Dahlia is around? I want to make Jasmin happy, but Dahlia is such a force. As I'm lost deep in my thoughts again, I feel a cool, wet item press against my hand, startling me again. I really shouldn't be this absorbed in my own thoughts. I look down, finding Finn sniffing at the bread I am holding. I tear off a chunk, tossing it to him. He clearly missed us in the weeks we were away. While I was glad to get a break from sleeping with the large dog, I'm delighted to have him back now. He still tries to sleep between Jasmin and me, but I don't mind that as much now.

I finish the bread and grab the wine, realizing I need a refill. As I fill my goblet, I glance back at Jas. She is still talking with people, Dahlia still by her side. Maybe this is a good opportunity to get on her good side and see if all these feelings could lead anywhere. I grab a third goblet and fill it, carefully carrying all three. Finn follows closely as I walk toward the group Jas is with.

"Look who I found."

Jasmin takes one of the goblets from me, giving me a suspicious look before kneeling to pet Finn. Even though he was in her room while she was still getting ready, she acts like she hasn't seen him in ages. No wonder he is so spoiled. I hold the extra goblet out to Dahlia, and she takes it, also eyeing me warily.

"It's not poisoned."

They both laugh, but Dahlia takes a drink. She rolls the liquid around in her mouth, then pretends to choke but just bursts out laughing at her own joke. I roll my eyes at her, unable to suppress the smile blooming across my face. Jasmin looks up with a large grin, then stands by my side. I wrap my arm around her, holding her close. She and Dahlia continue chatting as the other people wander away.

Kian is always making some bullshit comments, but he is usually right. He has more experience with things than I do. I've never met people that were in a triad. I know plenty of men that take lovers behind their wives' backs, but I don't think the wives typically know. It's not a consensual relationship for all involved. This with Dahlia, though, whatever this is, would be completely different. Jas would love to be with both of us. She was over the moon when we were together in Greynon. I was just glad to fuck her without sneaking around.

I don't know that I want to have a relationship with Dahlia, but I have always been curious about a threesome. It would be hard to pass that up, especially seeing how much pleasure Jasmin gets from both of us. If Dahlia stopped trying to steal Jasmin from me, I could tolerate being her friend. If that would make Jasmin happy, I could start there with Dahlia.

Dahlia bursts out laughing at something Jasmin says. I don't know what is so funny, but Dahlia throws her head back with raucous laughter. She is beautiful in her gown and mask, genuinely happy right now. Jasmin looks at her with love and affection, a partial smile on her face, half humor, half adoration. That's how she looks at me, too. A soft swirl of jealousy tingles in my body, but it is also mixed with a desire to keep that look on her face. Maybe I can give that to Jasmin. She gives so much to everyone else. As their laughter dies down, Dahlia looks at me. There is a look in her eyes I haven't noticed before. She has a desire to make Jasmin happy, too. She offers me a gentle smile as she sips from her goblet of wine.

I could love her, too.

Chapter 24

Jasmin

Clem has that far-off look in his eyes. He's been deep in thought for a while now. Knowing him the way I do, it either means he's going to disappear on me, or he's going to be stuck up my ass for a few days. I wonder what has him so consumed.

He brought wine to Dahlia and didn't actually poison it. Maybe this is his peace offering to her. Gods know we could use some peace between the two of them. They are too stubborn to be around each other for long. And I love them both for it.

Despite all the Lords being here tonight, I plan to relax and have a great evening. I have been busy restructuring the kingdom the last few weeks and need an evening without worrying. So far, the Lords have left me alone. We will see how long that lasts, though. I finish off my wine and pull Clem out to dance with me. An upbeat march is playing, and I'm glad to have the chance to move my body without thinking about it.

Clem is much better at dancing than he used to be. He's definitely come a long way. I love him so much. He struggles with his emotions but works so hard for me. I'm so relieved he doesn't run away from me like he used to. I couldn't handle that distance from him for that long now. The smile on his face as we dance is intoxicating. He's so happy here. I want to do everything possible to ensure he always feels this way.

We dance through several more songs, enjoying each other and the people we are dancing with. Everyone is in such high spirits tonight. The atmosphere is joyous. People are dancing, drinking, chatting, and enjoying the fading sun. I laugh along with Clem as we miss a few steps and have to catch up to the music. No one around us minds that we aren't in sync. Many other people aren't in sync with the music. Everyone is just having fun, with no qualms about decorum.

Dahlia is standing beside the wall, lonely and out of place. Around the room, our other friends are all dancing together; Bea and Erik, Tomas and Zander, and even Emmeline and Kian are dancing. Dahlia stands alone, sending a pang of sadness through my chest as the song ends.

"I'll be back," Clem whispers as he leaves me on the dance floor. The next song starts slowly, so I sway in my spot, letting the music move through me until he returns. My eyes close as the beat courses through my body, tangling with my very being.

"Clem said you need a new dance partner," Dahlia whispers as her fingers trail my skin. I almost don't open my eyes, wanting to feel her touch. It can't be real; I must be imagining things. I finally open my eyes to realize she is in front of me, taking my hands as the dance starts. My eyes find Clem across the room. He gives a slow nod, turning to get more wine. Finn sits next to him, clearly begging for more scraps. A chuckle escapes over my large dog's antics.

My attention turns back to Dahlia in my arms as the music rises. We glide through the dance effortlessly. Before the curse, I always made her practice dances with me. She was my first favorite dance partner, the one I always wanted to dance with. Our bodies know this routine from memory and flow so well together. I step, she steps. She spins, I spin. We're in better sync than Clem and I. A slight sadness creeps through me at the thought of him. I love him, but I love her so much too. I don't know that I could pick only one now that she is back. It was easy when it was just him, or just her for that matter, but with them both here? My life feels unnecessarily arduous.

I push those thoughts aside to enjoy the time Clem has given me with her. We dance through several more songs, laughing together, enthusiastically enjoying the party. After several songs, Clem cuts in, and he wants to dance with me, but I need a break.

"Dance with Dahlia."

I press a kiss to his cheek as I make my way to the chair that has been set up for me. It's not quite a throne, but it might as well be. As soon as I sit, Kian finds me, giving me a goblet of wine. Finn joins me next, resting his large head on my lap. This giant baby always needs attention. I scratch his head, making idle chat with Kian as he stands by my side.

He kneels down, rubbing Finn's back absentmindedly. "She could be the key to breaking the curse." I inhale deeply, following his gaze to where Clem and Dahlia are dancing. They look very awkward but are still dancing together. They miss more steps than either did with me, but as time goes by, they loosen up. They still miss steps but laugh more when they do. It brings a smile to my face to see them enjoy themselves. Kian slips away without my notice, and I'm the one left absentmindedly petting Finn, lost in my thoughts.

After a couple more songs, they join me in my chair. There is another chair for Clem, but Dahlia plops down on the floor next to Finn without missing a beat. He eyes her warily but doesn't move away from me. More wine is brought over to us as the party continues. None of us speak for a while. Clem reaches out to hold my hand, squeezing it lightly. My heart is whole now, holding Clem's hand, Dahlia beside me, and Finn resting on my lap. I couldn't be more content than I am right now.

As if on cue, the sky outside lights up in bright colors as thunder crashes. The room is illuminated with flashes of green and purple, yellow and orange. The lightning is very colorful tonight. I just sit, taking in my castle and my people, dancing and enjoying their night, bathed in colors from the curse. It's not all bad here.

As the party winds down, I bid everyone farewell. Usually, the party will continue until the sun rises again, but I am too exhausted to stay out that long.

I'm ready to get back to my room and remove these clothes. While they are more comfortable than my formal wear, the dress is still stiff. My entourage of Clem, Dahlia, and Finn follow me as I leave and return to the room. At some point, Clem makes his way in front of me and opens the door to our room, letting Finn in, then holding it for me. Dahlia hesitates in the hallway, wondering whether she should follow or not. I grab her hand and pull her into the room with me. I hear Clem's breath catch as we walk past together.

In the room, Clem is left staring after Dahlia with a very unsure look. I call him over, breaking whatever thoughts are careening through his mind. I ask him to get me undressed, not that I need help, but I want him to do it for me. Slowly, with an eye toward Dahlia the whole time, he undresses me. His fingers brush my skin lightly, sending chills down my body. I close my eyes as he finally removes the dress, leaving me bare in front of him and Dahlia. Now, his attention is solely on me. His eyes caress my body, hunger and lust shining through his face.

"Get her undressed, too."

His eyes slowly drag away from my body, moving over Dahlia's. I motion for her to walk over to me, putting her back toward Clem, so he can unbutton her dress. After a moment, he finally starts removing her clothing. I try not to release the breath I am holding too loudly. I didn't think he was actually going to. Clem is being less hostile toward her tonight, so I'm using that. Being with both of them is heaven; I want that feeling back. He slowly and methodically removes her dress, my eyes trained on hers the entire time. Once her dress falls to the floor, I turn her so we face him.

"Now it's his turn."

At the same time, Dahlia and I reach for the hem of his shirt, tugging it over his head. Clem's face is blank, not letting me know what he thinks. I hate that he is getting better at hiding his emotions. I love knowing what he is thinking. Once his shirt joins the rest of the clothes on the floor, Dahlia unties his pants. While she does, I step up, wrapping my arms around his neck. I press my lips to his in a deep kiss, wanting to connect with him. One of his hands lands on my side, gently squeezing my hip. I groan into the kiss, feeling moisture pool between my legs. I need them both so badly.

Dahlia hums in approval once Clem is naked. I glance down at his body, loving every inch. The way his stomach muscles are defined but not overwhelming. His skin is smooth and creamy, leaving me wanting to lick every inch of it. Dahlia feels the same way because she is already pressing kisses against his chest. He watches her with curious eyes. For a moment, I just watch too. The sight of them together sends a wave of arousal through me, my pussy clenching as I watch. I match Dahlia's movements, kissing his other side the same way she is. He finally groans, clearly enjoying what we are doing to him.

After a minute, I grab their hands, leading them to the bed. While I thoroughly enjoy caressing and kissing Clem, I want them to do that to me. I climb in the middle, pulling each of them on either side of me. As soon as we lie down, Dahlia is on me, kissing my collarbone, chest, breasts, and gods, her lips are glorious. Clem is watching her with a mix of jealousy and lust. We didn't have as much wine tonight as last time, and I worry his thoughts will run away with him. I grab the back of his neck, pulling him into a searing kiss. I don't wait for him to part his lips as I force my tongue into his mouth. He groans, opening for me. Despite my concern over his willingness, he isn't holding back. He seems nervous but not unwilling.

Dahlia's hands are all over my body. Her fingers graze my ribs, across my stomach, over my hips, down my thighs, but never right where I want them. My hips lift and sway under her, wanting her to move her hand to my core. Clem breaks the kiss, noticing my writhing. He watches her hand drag across my body for a moment, then a sly smirk appears on his face. Oh, fuck. I'm in trouble. His hands begin to match her movements, teasing my body, driving my desire to new heights, my aching core clenching around nothing.

"No, please," I whine. I hadn't planned on them teasing me when I started this.

Clem chuckles as his fingers trail down my side, over to my core. I take a deep breath, preparing for him to finally touch me. Instead, he taps my clit, causing my whole body to jerk in reaction. I moan as he continues to tap against my slit too.

I turn my head toward Dahlia, and she catches my mouth in a kiss. Gods, I love her lips. They are full and smooth and feel like they were built for me. Dahlia's tongue grazes my lips, and I open my mouth for her, needing more contact. I'm so desperate right now.

Clems slides one finger through my opening. One single finger. It does nothing to quench my aching desire, and he knows it. He drags his finger along the entrance, teasing me so thoroughly that I whine against Dahlia's lips. I hear Clem chuckle at my response. Dahlia's hand squeezes my breast tightly, causing my cunt to clench around Clem's single finger. I break the kiss, twisting my upper body toward Dahlia and my lower half into Clem's hand.

"Please," I beg. "Please."

"Use your words. What do you want, Jasmin?" Clem's voice is deep and husky. His lips are on my body, and my brain misfires. I don't know what words are anymore.

"Need…" I groan as his lips skim my hips while Dahlia is still twirling my nipple in her fingers. "Need you inside me."

Clem bites my hip, sending a wave of pleasure and pain through my body. His hand cups my ass as he returns to my side.

"On your side." His hand guides my ass as I shift onto my side, facing Dahlia. His fingers trail my thigh, moving to the inside. He lifts my leg up, wrapping it over Dahlia. I haven't been wrapped around her like this in so long, and to have Clem guiding me there is both nerve-wracking and exhilarating. He kisses my neck when my leg is wrapped around her and whispers, "Touch her." I groan at his words but don't need to be told twice. My hand is at her core, dragging a finger through her wetness. She moans, closing her eyes as I make a small circle around her clit.

I shift, adjusting my arm under me to grab Dahlia's breast this time. Her hand is on my ribs, slowly caressing my side. Clem slides his fingers through my core, letting me enjoy this time with Dahlia. I grab her breast, rubbing my thumb over her pebbled nipple. Two fingers slip inside her cunt, exploring the soft, wetness of her pussy. I begin sliding my fingers in and out of her, feeling for that small rough spot that sends her up the wall. Just as I find it, Clem lines the tip of his cock up with my entrance, slowly pressing inside. My head tilts back, my mouth falling open at the pleasure.

I caress the spot inside Dahlia as Clem gets into a good position, then slowly presses inside. I rub my thumb over Dahlia's clit, and her lips catch mine, kissing me deeply. Clem begins to thrust harder inside of me. My entire body is tingling with my looming orgasm. I increase the pressure on Dahlia, feeling her clench around my fingers inside her.

"Come for me, Dahl," I whisper to her.

Clem kisses my shoulder several times. I'm relieved he is allowing this to happen. I love fucking him, but having two people worship my body is twice as nice. As that thought runs through my body, Dahlia slips her hand onto my clit. She presses it, not going easy on me. Within moments, my orgasm crashes through me, and I cry out. My body distorts with pleasure, and I feel Dahlia follow me over the edge. Clem continues pounding inside as Dahlia and I slowly return to our bodies. Then she kisses me deeply.

"I love you." She mumbles between kisses.

"I love you, too." As soon as the words leave my mouth, I realize my mistake. Clem is just accepting that she is here. He will not be okay with me openly admitting to loving her. Fuck. I quickly add, "Clem." Maybe he'll think I thought it was him that said it first. But his name sounds unnatural on my lips. My body tenses, unsure of what he will do. Dahlia is still, whether from her orgasm or my words, I don't know. Clem presses a small kiss to my shoulder and then pounds relentlessly inside me. Dahlia notices his pace and returns her hand to my clit. I groan at the intense sensations so soon after an orgasm. My body tightens with my growing pleasure. I moan out as the two continue to work my body.

"Not yet," Clem mutters between clenched teeth. He is close to his orgasm but not as close as I am. Understanding his words, Dahlia removes her hand from my clit, stopping my orgasm.

"No," I groan, wanting the release she was about to give me. I do everything I can not to cry over the loss of her fingers. Then they are back on my clit. Clem is filling me so thoroughly, and Dahlia is driving me right up to the edge. I get back there quickly, breathing heavily as my orgasm builds again. Just as I am about to come, Dahlia removes her hand again. I cry out, unable to stop the sobs of my disappointment. Clem chuckles in my ear, still relentlessly pounding inside me.

"You feel so good, wrapped around my cock, clenching like the needy little slut you are."

I groan, arching my body fruitlessly to get more friction where I want it. Clem slides his hand up my body to my throat. He rests his fingers there, then says, "Are you ready to come like a good little whore?" I nod my head, desperately wanting to come again. My body is on fire, and I need to release this orgasm they have built up. His hand tightens around my neck while his thrusts become more erratic. Dahlia's hand is back on my clit, and I cry out at the sudden touch. She rubs my clit unforgivingly, driving me closer to the edge. Finally, my orgasm tears through my body. My soul is floating somewhere above the bed. Clem releases my neck as he releases deep inside me. Dahlia doesn't let up her ministrations, extending the length of my orgasm. I have died and gone to heaven. This is the most glorious feeling in the world. I can't think of anything besides the pleasure coursing through my body. Dahlia and Clem finally remove themselves from my core, holding me close between them.

Slowly, my soul returns to my body, settled between them. They are kissing and stroking my body gently; the only response I can give is to moan in pleasure. Dahlia whispers in my ear, pressing tiny kisses around her words.

"You are such a good girl."

I swoon at her words, a shiver coursing through my body. She chuckles while Clem grabs the quilt to pull over us. He stays by my back while Dahlia is at my front, my leg still wrapped around her. I slowly drift off to sleep, unable to fight the exhaustion of several weeks of stress and being smushed between my two favorite people.

Chapter 25

CLEM

The morning sun is creeping into the room through the cracks in the curtains. Jasmin turned to face me during the night, and Dahlia pressed against her back. As I slowly wake, I realize I have one arm on Jasmin's side, my other wrapped under her neck and around Dahlia's back. That's an interesting position. Dahlia has an arm draped over Jasmin and me. We are very tangled together for a group with such animosity.

Jasmin nuzzles into my neck, trying to block out the increasing sunlight. Joy spreads through my body as she snuggles with me. I love these little moments I get with her. Dahlia's arm slowly strokes up my back, then back down. I tense under her touch. She hasn't realized she is caressing me, though I'm unsure who she thinks she is touching. Suddenly, her hand stops and then jerks away from my side. She did finally figure it out.

Now for the awkward part, where we all have to face the consequences of our actions.

"Um..." Dahlia hops out of bed, nervously looking around the room. It's such a fun experience to see her out of her element. I should aim for this more often. She finally grabs her clothes from the floor and darts out of our room. I can't hide the chuckle at her reaction. Jasmin swats my arm, suppressing her own laughter poorly. I squeeze her tightly, glad she is still in my arms.

"Clem," she starts nervously, "I'm sorry I said "I love you, too" last night. It just slipped out, and it didn't mean anything."

I'm surprised she brought this up. I was startled when she said it in response to Dahlia, but as I sunk deep inside her pussy, I realized my place with her wasn't threatened by Dahlia. We can exist equally within Jasmin's world. So I didn't mind that she announced her love for Dahlia because I knew her love for me was still there.

"'Didn't mean anything'? So you don't love her?"

"No, I love you."

"But you love her, too, right?"

Jasmin doesn't respond. She just looks nervous, unsure of what the correct answer is. It strikes me that her uncertainty is likely due to my reactions in the past. I don't like that she feels she must give me a correct answer. I shouldn't be causing that feeling for her.

I trace my fingers across the scars on her cheek, taking in the ragged edges. "I know you love her and me, too. It's okay. I...I want you to be happy as long as I am still with you." Her body is still tense as she considers my words. Her eyes meet mine, caution and uncertainty showing there. She nibbles on her lips as she figures out what she wants to say.

"So, I can love her, too?" I nod, pressing a reassuring kiss to her forehead.

"What about being alone with her? Do I still have to have a chaperone?" She's teasing me, giving me a hard time for my previous reactions. I tickle her sides in response, causing her body to jerk as she giggles. As she settles, I speak softly.

"You can spend time alone with her. I'm sorry I was so jealous before. I know now I don't need to be." Her face presses into my chest as I wrap my arm around her, holding her close. I don't know why I thought my place with her was threatened. She loves me as deeply as I love her. "I still need time to adjust to you being around her. I...I know you love me, but it's not always easy to convince myself you won't leave me for her."

"I won't, Clem. I love you so much," she whispers into my chest.

Finn crawls on the bed as we snuggle, sliding up to Jasmin. He whimpers, wanting our attention now. He must be pretty upset he was forced to sleep on the floor. There isn't enough room for him when Dahlia is here too. Jasmin flips over, petting her oversized dog. I stay wrapped around her, holding her close. We lie like this for several more moments before Emmeline comes in.

She informs us Jasmin only has one meeting this afternoon, but we still need to go to breakfast and see other people. She gathers our clothes and the things we will need, then leaves them on the bed as she walks into the bathroom. Even after all these months together, Emmeline still refuses to see me naked. Once she leaves the room, I climb out of bed, slipping some trousers on. She prefers me fully dressed but won't throw a fit over not wearing a shirt. I scratch Finn as Jasmin walks into the bathroom, getting herself ready.

Jasmin leaves early to chat with Dahlia while I take Finn outside. After he has done his business, I meet her in the dining hall for breakfast with everyone else. Surprisingly, many people are missing. Tomas is here, but not Zander. Erik is moving through the food tables with two plates; Bea is nowhere in sight. Emmeline and Jasmin sit with Dominick and Lucia, but Kian and Dahlia aren't in the room. I'm not used to so many of our group not being around during meal times. I get my food, joining Jasmin.

"Where is everyone?" I question, flummoxed, why we rushed out of bed for breakfast if no one else did. Jasmin looks around as she begins recounting everyone's whereabouts. "Erik said Bea isn't feeling well. Zander and Dahlia are with their parents. And I don't know where Kian is." She looks to Emmeline, who shrugs casually as if there is no reason she would know something about Kian. She continues eating instead of giving us an answer. I'm sure he will turn up soon. I chat with Lucia and Dominick about their usual solstice celebrations. They are both thrilled with the masquerade ball from last night.

Halfway through breakfast, Kian bursts into the dining hall, pulling everyone's attention to him. He looks rumpled and tired, not like his normal self. His eyes cut straight to us, then he makes a beeline to our table. His eyes are wide with excitement, and papers are crumpled and held tightly in his hands. Wherever he has been has provided some interesting information. When he gets to the table, his eyes dart back and forth between Jasmin and me and the rest of our group.

"Where is Dahlia?" His voice sounds rough, like this is the first time he's spoken in hours.

"With her parents," Jasmin answers casually. Why is she not freaking out about his state?

"Fine, you two, come with me. You can tell her later." He points at Jasmin and me and turns to walk away.

"What, now? We're in the middle of breakfast, Kian." Jasmin answers because I am too dumbfounded by his appearance and behavior to know what to say to him. What has him in such a mess?

"Yes, now. It's important." He doesn't say anything else, just turns and leaves the dining hall in the same fashion he entered. I don't know what he wants, but my curiosity is piqued. I grab a breakfast roll and follow him out of the dining hall, more curious than hungry. Jasmin sighs behind me, finally tagging along. We follow Kian to the library in silence. I munch on my breakfast roll, wanting to finish it before being around all the books.

Kian walks purposefully, not even looking back to see that we are following. Apparently, this information he has found is good enough that he just knows we want it. And I do. I can't deny that right now. He leads us up the stairs into the reference section of the library. We walk by the table Kian typically works at and into a dark corner of the library. Even with the bright summer sun beating into the library, there still isn't much light back here. Several candles provide some light, but not enough.

"What is all of this, Kian?" Jasmin is annoyed, which is fair. She's probably still hungry, and we definitely didn't get enough sleep last night. I don't understand why she isn't more curious, but I have the same question for Kian. I would use a different tone.

"The answer," he chuckles dryly, as if he knows it isn't funny but still finds it hysterical. "After the celebration died down, I wanted to do some reading.

Something..." his fingers run through his already tousled hair, giving him a crazed look, "I've been missing something. And couldn't..." He looks unhinged, and now I am getting worried. I've never seen him in such a state. He is always composed. His eyes lift to ours, but he isn't really looking at us. "I've found it." He laughs again, with more emotion behind it, but not a matching sentiment for the sound. "The reason the curse hasn't broken. It's here." He points to the book spread out in front of us.

"Read it." He settles in a chair across the table from us, looking like a weight has been lifted from his body. "Read it," he mumbles again, a smile creeping across his face. Jasmin turns the book toward us cautiously.

"Antirrhinum, that is what Sweet Briar was originally called, as a kingdom." Jasmin looks to Kian, who just nods. She sits beside me, pulling the book closer to her. I also sit, feeling nervous about this situation now. Jasmin begins to read out loud from the worn text but stops short. She whispers a string of curses and then slides the book to me, nervousness and uncertainty written on her face. I read the story, trying to figure out what I am getting into.

Antirrhinum was a large kingdom before Sweet Briar came to be. It was ruled by a king and his two wives. They held equal power over the kingdom, leading the expansive mass of land with grace and benevolence, offering protection to the people within their lands. The three were powerful rulers, holding their own land and not allowing their kingdom to fall to ruin.

But their reign was short-lived. Several years into the relationship, one of the women became pregnant, offering an heir to the new kingdom. The king and new mother doted on the child, but the king was also careful to spend time with the other wife. He was fearful she would be jealous of the new baby. She had always been ambitious and wanted more for their kingdom.

The king spent time with her, ensuring she never felt alone or neglected. However, she began to feel jealous when the mother became pregnant again, without a pregnancy for the other woman. She began to build an army behind the king's back. Once it was large enough, she announced that she was leaving and claiming most of the land as her own. The king wanted to fight but soon realized the army he was left with would never hold against hers. He didn't want to risk his people's lives, so he conceded her demands.

She took over half of the land from him, creating a new kingdom. The king and his pregnant wife were heartbroken over the separation. They stayed with the now smaller domain, renaming it Sweet Briar. The namesake flower represents an emotional wound. The king and his single wife raised their children and kingdom but never quite recovered from losing the other wife.

The other kingdom, aptly named Hollyhock, representing ambition, grew more robust, blocking Sweet Briar from any other kingdom. Sweet Briar was forced to build a navy to trade with other realms. Sweet Briar accomplished that, but they never gained the size or notoriety Hollyhock had. With the triad split, Sweet Briar became a small kingdom with generous rulers and a strong line of heirs. Hollyhock gave way to more ambitious leaders, leaders always looking to gain something, to take over another kingdom. Sweet Briar was left alone, remaining stagnant in size as Hollyhock expanded.

I turn the page, expecting more to the story, but it ends there. The next page lists the rulers and their heirs. I look to Kian, trying to understand how this answers the curse. Jasmin seems to understand, watching me for a reaction. I shrug, sliding the book to Kian.

"It's the triad. That's why Dahlia is back. You two need her." My body freezes at his announcement. I may have just told Jasmin I won't stop her from spending time with Dahlia, but that doesn't mean I want to discuss a triad. Sure, the sex with her is excellent, phenomenal even. But a complete triad? That's asking a lot. Jasmin squeezes my hand, drawing me back to reality.

"I have to love her too?" My voice sounds weaker than I want it to, but that's the least of my concerns right now. Kian nods, and I jump out of my chair, needing to move my body. Nerves are crashing through me, unwilling to accept this.

"Why? That triad ended a kingdom. I don't think Sweet Briar can stand another loss like that."

Kian sits forward, pulling the book toward him. "Did you ever hear the words of the curse?" I nod, remembering the words I heard in the vision from the flower, but unsure how that is relevant. "There is a line that mentions bringing the kingdom to glory. It's vague enough that maybe I'm entirely wrong. But I think the magic took that line as meaning back to its original glory under the triad. Look," Kian laughs, running his fingers through his hair again. He is utterly unhinged today. "This story is so long forgotten we don't even have records of the names of the original rulers. Our kingdom tried so hard to forget what happened that it actually worked." He shakes his head, reclining in his seat. I look to Jasmin, unsure how to feel about all of this, Kian's appearance, this story, what he is telling us.

Jasmin is eyeing Kian with a mixture of concern and intrigue. She nibbles on her lip as thoughts crash through my head. Being in a triad means falling in love with Dahlia. It's one thing to fuck Jasmin while she fucks Dahlia. It's another thing altogether to actually love her. I know I'm not there yet, but could I be one day? Is that what it will take to save the kingdom?

"How would we know if this is the answer?" Jasmin asks. Kian shrugs, pulling his attention to her.

"The same way you did with him. There will be signs." Now Jasmin leans back in her seat, and I realize she is contemplating whether this could work. Shock runs through me, realizing she wants this. This is what Jasmin has wanted the whole time. She has always wanted a triad. Maybe she never said it, but it's been there. I turn quickly, bumping into a table I didn't see.

"I can't...I can't love her."

Jasmin is startled by my sudden movement. She rises, holding her hands out to calm me down. "Just sit for a minute, Clem. Kian, you need to go get some sleep and bathe. I need you at the afternoon meeting, but not in this state. Go, now." I don't sit down but watch as Kian gathers his things to leave. "The book has to stay, Kian." He gives her a confused look, then realizes he is collecting the book to take with him. They don't allow specific historical texts to leave the library. He leaves the book, making his way out of the library, hopefully to do as he was told and not get distracted by something else along the way.

Jasmin wraps her arms around me in a hug. Being in her arms always settles the anxiety from my doubts and worries. I take a deep, soothing breath as she tightens her arms around me. I press my lips to her cheek, enjoying the calm moment of intimacy.

"You could love her, though." I sigh, dropping my face into the space between her shoulder and collarbone.

"I know. But I don't want to." Jasmin giggles at my response, sliding her hands up and down my back.

"Would you try?" Her hands find my hair, her fingers caressing my head. I stifle a moan under her touch. She knows I would never say no to her while she's rubbing my head. I groan out a response, causing her to giggle with delight. I may not want to deal with Dahlia, but I will do anything to keep Jasmin making happy noises like that. I have already had thoughts careening around my head about loving Dahlia. Maybe it wouldn't be so bad. I found a way to love Jasmin while other men were still trying to win her love. The only thing I can do at this point is try.

Chapter 26

DAHLIA

Waking up and realizing I was caressing Clem was awkward. I don't know how I wound up in that position. His skin is soft, so soft. I really do just want to touch him more. As much as I want to touch Jasmin, I want to touch him. This desire to be with them both is nearly overwhelming, but he doesn't want that. Waking up to that idea is a brutal one. Sneaking out of their room without getting dressed? That was a dumb idea.

My room is just across the hall now. I thought I could go from one to the other, with maybe only the guard seeing me, but that isn't actually my luck. Zander was waiting near my door for me. Jasmin added a few extra names to the list of people who could enter the hallway for me. While I'm glad for the additional protection, I could use more as I sneak, naked, from Jasmin's room back to mine.

"Dahlia, there you are. You need to come to breakfast with Mama. She is requesting it." Requesting always means we don't get a choice. Zander finally takes in my appearance, eyes Jasmin's door, then me again. He shrugs but says, "Just don't let Clem catch you." It's cute that he thinks Clem isn't involved here.

"Okay, I'll be down in a bit. Go on, so I can get dressed." He rolls his eyes at me but walks off. I finally sneak into my room, ready to get some food. I really worked up an appetite last night. I can definitely tolerate working up an appetite like that more often. I would prefer to go to breakfast with Jasmin and Clem, but I haven't seen much of Mama and Baba since we returned from Greynon. It will be nice to spend the morning with them.

Baba isn't doing well. He hasn't been doing well for a while but seems to be declining more rapidly. He moves slowly, doesn't talk, and is in constant pain. I'm devastated each time I remember how much time I lost with him. I lost so many years under the curse, and now that I am finally free, he is almost gone.

I sit with them through breakfast, my own thoughts running wild. My mood sours between whatever this is with Clem and Jasmin and the realization that my father is dying. I spend my time fighting my thoughts while trying to enjoy my time with my father. Today is the first day he isn't going into the stables to work. He sends Zander ahead to tend to the horses. I stay to sit with him. I tell him stories about Greynon, what it looked like, and what the witches were like. He seems interested but also very tired. After a while, Mama returns and ushers him to bed, insisting he needs sleep. I give him a long hug, fighting off the tears that are threatening to spill.

I have been so focused on Jasmin that I didn't stop to take in everything else I have. Mama and Baba have been through so much. I am thankful I awoke before something happened to Baba. I have been given a chance to spend more time with him and need to try to do that now. As much as I love my new room, I may have made a mistake by moving. No, I need my own space, and they need theirs. Mama and Baba should also get time together without Zander or me there.

I feel so lost and unsure right now. Jasmin is in her meeting, and I can't seek her out for comfort. Emmeline doesn't like me much, but is probably equally difficult to find. I am not in the mood to deal with Clem. I know he can be nice; I've seen him do it with Jasmin, but he is so rarely nice to me. Unsure what else to do, I decide to stay here. Mama asks if I want to go to the gardens with her, but I decline. Instead, I sit on the couch, staring at a painting from our homeland.

The painting is of the coast. I never understood why Mama had this painting. We didn't live anywhere near the coast. We only saw the coast when we were sold with Vesper. It is a lovely picture, but it doesn't represent where I grew up. I understand Baba's desire to return there. While I don't share his desire, I know I would do anything to find my way back to Jasmin if we were separated. She is my home. She is where I want to be. I don't fault Baba for wishing to return home.

I wish I could say I use my time on the couch wisely. I could spend my time dreaming up spells or thinking through incantations. I could spend my time considering the worth and merit of Jasmin and Clem's relationship. Maybe even reflect on what I have learned in my short time as an adult. Instead, I stare at the painting with a blank mind. Baba eventually wakes. I help him settle on the couch, getting him water and pillows to make him comfortable. We sit in silence. I offer to read to him, but he just waves his hand at me. So we sit. My mind is disturbingly blank.

Mama returns, surprised I am still here, and makes dinner. I eat with them, not wanting to go to the dining hall. After dinner, Mama reads a book about plants while Baba sips tea and writes on parchment. Mama said he has been making notes to send home. My mood doesn't lift, but I don't try to do anything to improve it either.

Shortly after dinner, there is a knock on the door. Mama answers, calling me over. At this point, I don't even question her. My body moves of its own accord. I feel numb. I kiss Baba on the cheek before walking to the door. Jasmin is there, looking lovely in a light pink tunic and dark leggings. She looks like a warm spring day. I force a smile at her, but it's not genuine. Mama walks away as Jasmin steps into the suite. The door is closed behind her, but she doesn't say anything. She just stares at me. She takes my hand, pulling me down to Zander's room. She wraps her arms around me, hugging me tightly. Her hair brushes my cheeks, covering me with her scent.

"What's wrong, Dahl?"

I open my mouth to speak, but only sobs come out. We both tighten our grip around each other. Her concern is overwhelming. I want to tell her Baba is dying. I want to tell her I love her and I need her. I want to tell her to leave Clem and just be with me. I want to tell her I'm selfish enough to want that, knowing it would prevent my father's dying wish of returning home. I want to tell her I don't like myself right now and don't know why she likes me. There are so many things I want to say to her. Only tears fall instead.

She holds me for a long time before asking if I will come to her room. I shake my head, not trusting my voice. She simply nods, remaining stoic. I don't know if she is angry or upset, but I can't be around Clem and her right now. She offers to give me space for a while but says we need to talk soon. She doesn't elaborate, clearly concerned about my current emotional state. She kisses my cheek before leaving the room, promising to find me in a day or two.

It's been three days since I last saw Jasmin and had my emotional breakdown. I spent that time with Mama and Baba, reading, writing, and being near each other. Zander joined us more while I was there. It was nice to have our whole family together. I spent the nights in my room but was careful to sneak by, not wanting to run into Clem. I wanted to see Jasmin but wasn't ready to face Clem. I can't handle his anger.

I don't know what either of them are doing now. I have debated going to dinner tonight with everyone else. I am undecided on that, but I plan to find Jasmin afterward. I want to spend some time with her now. These past few days have brought solace and acceptance of this situation. I am not ready to lose my father, but I understand it is his time. I'll be a wreck when he is gone, but I will never regret the days I have spent with him. He is napping again, and Mama is back in the garden. Not wanting to skulk around their suite any longer, I settle on going to the pond. That is always a relaxing and refreshing way to spend an afternoon.

I love the walk to the pond; it's the reason I chose this location. It isn't far from the castle but is still pretty. There are trees everywhere, with bushes of flowers scattered between. The road is rough, with signs of heavy traffic. I love that so many people travel by here and never know the gem I have created for Jasmin and me. The small red flower that somehow stands out and blends in appears on the side of the road. I glance around to be sure I am alone, then turn off the road. I step around the overgrown leafy plants, following the trail to the pond. I am so engrossed with all the flowers blooming that I almost miss Clem lounging on the large rock beside the water.

"What are you doing here?" I snap, angrier than I mean to be. I don't want him here, though.

"Just lounging." His voice is smooth and calm, like he doesn't have a care in the world. Meanwhile, mine seems to be collapsing around me. Then Finn comes bounding toward me. I gasp, holding out my hands to stop him. He will knock me on the ground, and I don't particularly want to be laid out on my ass by an overgrown puppy in front of Clem. I try to tell Finn to stop, but he keeps running. I hear Clem move, shouting at Finn, but it's too late. The dog crashes into me, knocking me flat on the ground and causing the air to whoosh out of me.

Finn spends an eternity sniffing, licking, and stepping on me. Clem steps closer, shoving Finn away. The giant dog finally turns and runs off, chasing a butterfly, frog, or whatever he has found. I stay on the ground, eyes closed, trying to reign in embarrassment and overwhelming emotions. The urge to cry is almost too much.

"Here, let me help." Clem's voice is soft, like he genuinely wants to help. I shift my arm away from my face so I can see him. His hand is outstretched, and his face is soft and relaxed. He actually wants to help me. He is being kind to me, and as far as I can tell, no one else is around to see it. He's had moments of kindness before, but this feels different. I take his hand, and he easily pulls me to stand. He knocks a few leaves off my dress. Tears threaten to spill from my eyes because of his kindness. I can't do this today.

He notices my face and then asks if I am okay. His concern sounds authentic, sending another wave of emotions through me, forcing the tears from my eyes. He wraps his arms around me, pulling me into a warm hug. It feels like nothing else matters in his arms, like I can face anything. His hug feels magical, which is unfair because I don't want that. He presses one forearm against my mid-back and the other against my shoulders and head. He has me encapsulated in his arms. It's so warm and safe here. I wrap my arms over his shoulders as my tears spill onto his shirt. He squeezes me tightly, and I have a brief flash of panic that he will let me go, but he doesn't. He just loosens his grip enough that it's comfortable. We stay like this for several minutes until Finn prances back, sniffing our legs. Clem chuckles, rubbing his head as he releases me. I rub my eyes, wiping the tears away.

"Did I ever tell you about the first time I came to the castle?" His words are soft again, but his eyes stay on Finn, not turning up to me. I wonder if he realizes I am crying.

"When you met Jasmin, but she told you she was Tia?"

He chuckles but nods. "Yes, but when I first walked into the castle, there weren't guards or anything, so I was just standing in the foyer with my pack. Finn came around one of the corners and tackled me before I ever saw him. I was laying on my back, probably screaming like a child, because I thought I was being attacked. Jasmin called him off me. I was mortified at what happened."

I give a weak laugh, unable to produce the whole emotion right now. I can imagine Clem lying on the floor in the foyer after Finn attacked him. That would have been a good sight to see. Clem finally looks at me, nervousness on his face.

"Well, I'll leave. You probably want to be alone."

I do want to be alone; that's why I came here. So I'm shocked when I open my mouth and say, "No, you can stay. I just want to soak in the water for a bit." I don't know where that came from, but I can't take it back now. Without hesitating, I remove my dress, leaving it beside the rock as I enter the water. Clem takes his spot on the rock again, grabbing a book to read quietly.

He stays on the rock, quietly reading. This calm, quiet mood between us is so at odds with every other interaction I've had with him. Does Jasmin see this side of him a lot? Is this why she loves him? She probably doesn't get much of the angry side I typically see.

I float on my back, staring at the sky above me. I watch birds fly by as my body settles into a calm state. I focus on my breathing, letting all the thoughts leave my head. I just need some quiet now. I feel the water slipping through my braids, gently tugging them in the gentle currents. My hair connects me to the earth, to this pond, to my magic. I am here, now, alive and in this space. I am no longer trapped in my curse.

I lay in the water for a while, long enough that my fingers are wrinkled. Clem is still on the rock, reading his book. I have no idea how long we have been like this. I'm unfamiliar with being with someone without talking or doing some activity together. Being in this space with Clem, without doing anything, has been incredible. It's nice just to know he is here with me. I drop my feet, lifting my head out of the water to look at him. His long hair is falling over the rock, spilling down like a waterfall of blonde hair. He is focused on the book he is holding above his face. While his body is relaxed, his face shows every emotion he reads in his book. I love that you can always tell what he is feeling.

On a whim, I swim up to the rock he is resting on. I get a closer look at the book he is reading. I haven't read many, including that one. So I have no idea what his book is about. He notices my appearance, placing the book on the ground beside him. He turns to look at me. The full force of his attention feels overwhelming right now.

"Sorry, I didn't mean to disturb you." He shrugs, turning to drop his feet in the water next to me. It occurs to me that I am completely naked next to him. I fold my arms, propping them on the rock next to Clem's thigh, leaving my body submerged in the water. I close my eyes, enjoying the smoothness of the stone. I savor the way the cool water feels against my body. Birds and insects are chirping in the distance. It's so quiet and peaceful here. I love this spot so much.

I startle when Clem's fingers caress my arm. He either doesn't notice or care because his fingers continue moving across my skin. He trails his fingers over my arm, across my shoulder, up my neck, then down my jaw. My breathing increases as his fingers move. I'm unsure why he is touching me, but it feels intimate. I want more but also less. The conflict over Clem being the one to touch me is profound. There would be no hesitation on my part if this were Jasmin. But it's Clem; he's been so angry and removed from me except lately. What changed? I realize the twinge of desire isn't as strong in his touch anymore. I still feel some desire for him, but it's more comparable to what I feel with Jasmin than what I have felt with him before now.

"I want to kiss you." His words are soft as his eyes stare at my lips. I want him to kiss me too. That realization comes as a shock, but I really do want it. I slowly push myself out of the water toward him. He leans down until our lips finally touch. It feels awkward at first, but we adjust. His lips are soft, and he uses just the right amount of pressure. Clem drags his fingers into my hair, massaging my head, causing me to moan under his touch. He deepens our kiss, pressing his tongue against my lips. I open my mouth, letting him explore. I lift my hand to his cheek, wanting to run my fingers through his hair. This feels right, as much as kissing Jasmin does. Why does this feel so perfect with him? I need more. I want to know why this feels so good.

Before I get the chance, he pulls away from the kiss, putting some distance between us. His hand drops from my head as his eyes open, looking at mine. Now, I can't tell what he is thinking. I am feeling a lot at this moment. I want more of those lips against mine. I want his lips on my entire body. I want more time alone with him like we just had. I want that with Jasmin. I want her to be here now. There is no end to the list of things I want now.

"We need to talk to Jasmin." His voice is soft, like he knows his words are valid but doesn't want them to be in this moment. Does he want to do more with me right now? Instead of questioning him, I simply nod, climbing out of the pond to get dressed again. I didn't bring anything to dry myself with, but apparently, Clem did. He gives me the towel, letting me dry myself before putting my dress on again. He yells at Finn, telling him to come back to the castle. The large dog rushes ahead of us, pounding through the bushes.

I stop him at the edge of the magical barrier around the pond just before we pass back into regular space. He looks down at me with these soft, affectionate eyes, and I need more. I can't stay away from him at this moment. I wrap my arms around his shoulders, pulling him close to me. My lips meet his, kissing him desperately. I need more from him. I can't go back without another kiss. His arms wrap around my body, and suddenly we're the only two people in the world. I finally run my fingers through his hair, his arms pressing me harder against his body. He strokes my back as I push my tongue into his mouth. He parts his lips for me, letting me deepen the kiss. It feels like I belong in his arms. Something settles in my soul, letting me know this is where I belong. I don't know what this means for Jasmin, but I need him like I need air.

Chapter 27

JASMIN

I'm lounging in my room, content to just be here. I don't know where anyone is. I haven't seen Clem since breakfast, and Dahlia has been with her parents for several days. Kian has also taken a few days of much needed rest and relaxation. Emmeline has assured me he is reading for pleasure, and Clem has ensured he isn't just hiding in the library, reading more books about curses. Despite his exhaustion, he is still so accommodating. I haven't even seen Finn in a while. He is probably with Clem, though. Those two are like peas in a pod now. If I didn't know better, I would think Finn likes Clem more than me. I'm not going to entertain that notion, though.

Everyone else is busy, and I have some peace. As soon as my body collapses on the couch, the door opens. Finn prances to me, nudging his head in my lap for attention. Clem walks in next, with Dahlia close behind him. It's odd to see them together and not scowling. They look surprisingly happy, but why are they together? And both happy? Finn slinks away in search of food. I watch as Clem carelessly plops down next to me, giving me a quick kiss. There is something about this kiss...

"Did you kiss Dahlia?"

She gasps behind me, looking terrified at my question. Clem just has a goofy grin, very pleased with himself. He did kiss her! He presses his lips against my cheek and then settles into the couch, pulling me against his chest. His demeanor now is so at odds with how he has been around Dahlia before that I don't know what to do now.

"You should tell her what Kian said," is all he responds with.

"Me? Seems like you should be the one to." I feel the anger simmering beneath my skin. I'm mad that he is being so nonchalant now when he hasn't been for months. I'm shocked to see Dahlia here with him. The last time we spoke, she couldn't even find the words to tell me what was wrong and refused to come back with me because of Clem. What the hell have they been up to that they are in such good spirits now? He senses my anger and kisses my cheek to try to soothe me. He fills in Dahlia with the story of Antirrhinum. After he finishes the story summary, he adds his own feelings.

"I've been irate and upset at the thought of losing Jasmin to you. I have noticed my feelings toward you changing, which made me more upset. To think I couldn't give myself fully to Jasmin wasn't something I could come to terms with on my own. Kian has helped me understand and process those feelings. I...I can see how this could work between us now. The three of us."

I'm surprised. I knew Clem was struggling with his emotions, but I didn't realize how conflicting they were for him. I thought he was just jealous this whole time. I didn't know he was developing feelings for her. I wish he had told me, but my anger subsides. He looks down at his hand in his lap, not making eye contact with either of us. I glance at Dahlia, who is staring straight ahead but not seeing anything. She is clearly lost in her own thoughts. As much as I want to push this conversation, I should give them both a chance to process this.

"So, the three of us are meant to be together?" Dahlia looks to me for confirmation. I nod, wanting to reach out and hold her but not wanting to leave Clem's side to do so. I could ask her to come to me, but I don't want to put her in a place where she feels she has to. She collapses in the chair beside me. It's still too far away for my liking, but at least I can reach out and touch her leg. I squeeze her knee and smile softly when she meets my gaze.

"How does it work?" She looks between the two of us for an answer.

"We have to talk to each other," I start. "We need to be open and honest with our feelings." We sit in silence for a long time. All of us thinking about what this means and how this will work. We all want it to work; we just have to put in the effort now.

"Are we to just forget all the bullshit that has happened in the last few months and be in love now?" Dahlia gives a bitter glare at Clem. His jaw flexes, clearly annoyed with feeling singled out. We have all done horrible things to each other in the past couple of months.

"No," I start slowly, glancing between them. "We can't forget all the atrocities we committed against each other." I give both a pointed stare, placing guilt on all of us. "We can agree to move forward in a better manner, talk to each other when we have strong feelings, and develop a relationship without animosity." Clem has a solemn look on his face. Dahlia looks more reserved, unsure about this new information.

"I am sorry for my behavior, Dahlia." I do my best not to gasp at Clem's words. "I felt threatened and chose to react through anger instead of kindness and understanding." Now, I'm trying my hardest not to swoon at him. Sexy, smart, and emotionally healthy? Yes, gods, please!

Dahlia stares for several minutes but doesn't say anything else. I don't expect her to right now. This is new information for her, while Clem and I have been discussing this for a few days. Maybe I'll get some time with her soon, and we can work through some of her emotions around this situation. We fall into a heavy silence, each lost in our thoughts, trying to sort through a vast yarn ball of emotions.

"It's time to go down for dinner," I speak gently, not wanting to startle them after the long silence. We silently go down to the dining hall, get our food, then sit with our friends. Dahlia and Clem are on either side of me, where they belong. I can't deny how unparalleled their presence on my side is. Dahlia keeps her thigh pressed against mine while Clem's arm is settled on my other thigh. This is what I want, both touching me. Dahlia is still somewhat removed but not too removed to be uninvolved in conversations. The chatter is light and casual, like usual. Bea didn't come to dinner again. I ask Erik about her, and he says the healer will visit her tomorrow. We didn't get a chance to spend much time together, and I hope to change that soon.

Once dinner is over, Dahlia and I rise to leave, but Clem calls all the others and asks if they want to stay for a drink.

"The ladies can go off, and we can have a night at the pub or here, where the ale is." He laughs at his own joke, clearly in a joyful mood. The other guys agree, heading toward the casks to refill their mugs. Before I walk off, he grabs my hand and pulls me close. He whispers in my ear.

"As an apology for my jealousy, I want to give you and Dahlia some time alone. I'll be here for several hours." Is he really saying what I think he is saying?

"I need you to be perfectly clear with me, Clem," I whisper to him, not wanting anyone else to hear, even though they have all walked away. "Are you saying I can fuck Dahlia?" He chuckles, grabbing my face with both of his hands. He pulls me back so we can look at each other.

"Yes, Jasmin, that is exactly what I am saying."

I can't contain the smile growing on my face. I've tried so hard to suppress my feelings for her for Clem's sake but was never fully able to get rid of them. I've wanted time alone with her since she returned and have come so close to throwing caution to the wind with her. And now I get to. I never needed his permission, but to know he won't be upset and hurt by my actions this time is astounding. I crash my lips into his, practically falling into his lap. His arms wrap around me, kissing me with equal intensity.

"I love you," he whispers before pushing me away. I skip down the hallway, catching up with Dahlia.

"What are we doing tonight, Jas? I snagged a couple bottles of wine." She shows me the two bottles, not realizing what Clem intended when he let us go. I glance around the hallway quickly, not seeing anyone. I rise on my toes, pressing a quick kiss to her cheek.

"Let's go to my room."

Her eyes go wide with understanding, and she follows me quickly. We start giggling, glancing down halls and open doors, checking for anyone that might see us. We aren't doing anything wrong, but it feels very familiar.

She places the wine bottles on an end table. The second they touch, I jump on her, wrapping my arms around her and crushing my lips against hers. I have no desire to take this slow. I've been waiting for her far too long to go slow this time. Her arms snake around my body, then grab my ass, hoisting me in her arms. I wrap my legs around her waist as our lips part and slide my tongue into her mouth. I take a moment to marvel at her strength, carrying me across the room. She takes a few steps to the bed, collapsing atop me. My fingers caress her arms, taking in the grooves and planes of her muscles.

She breaks the kiss, pressing her lips along my jaw, then down my neck. Her hand circles my throat, and I groan under her touch. Her smile against my skin sends chills down my body. I slide my hands down her ribs, then up her back.

"Too many clothes," I pant. "We have too many clothes."

She chuckles, stepping back from me to pull her dress over her head. Then she is standing naked in front of me. Seeing her breasts and the smooth skin of her stomach, then the patch of hair above her cunt causes me to clench with desire. One good thing about wearing a dress is how easy it can be to remove it. Now I have to deal with a shirt, trousers, and my shoes. Dahlia helps remove the clothing quickly, taking every chance to skim my sensitive skin with her lips.

She crawls back over me once our clothes are piled on the floor. Her mouth latches onto my breast while her hand massages the other. Her touch sends currents of arousal flowing through my body. I moan as her tongue swirls my nipple. I can't wait any longer. I need to taste her.

"Dahl," I moan, "stay there."

She's on her hands and knees, so I slip out from under her. She tries to protest, but I tell her to trust me. I kiss her quickly before climbing under her, with my head between her legs. I slip my own legs around her head, then lift my head so I can kiss her pussy. We snuck around so much when we were younger. We didn't get to be completely naked and pleasuring each other. We always took turns. Tonight, here in my bed, we don't have to. We can savor each other at the same time.

I have every intention of doing that now that her cunt is in my face. It's wet and so ready. I drag a finger down her slit as she catches on to what I am doing. Her lips find my clit, and it takes all my restraint not to buck in her face. Her tongue slides down my length as mine twirls her clit. We're both moaning, our bodies aching with arousal and desire. I need her more than life itself.

I slip a finger inside of her, savoring the way her cunt feels so soft, warm, and inviting. I would stay here all the time if I could. I add a second finger and begin fucking her. I suck her bundle of nerves into my mouth, eliciting a low moan from her. I could probably orgasm just from that sound. My body is so tense, my orgasm so close. Dahlia tongues my nub while her fingers tap against my core. The feeling causes me to clench around nothing, desperate for an orgasm. She growls deep in her throat, not breaking away from my clit. Her pussy is clenching around my fingers, so I add a third one. Her hips press into my face, and I suck on her clit, pushing her into an orgasm.

She crawls away from me as she comes down from her orgasm. I'm a little sad initially, then realize she is focusing on me. I prop up on my elbows so I can watch her. She lifts her gaze, staring at me just above my pussy with her dark eyes and skin. I slide my hand across her braids, pulling her closer as she slides two fingers inside me. I can't help thrusting against her face this time. Her tongue is still working my clit as her fingers change the way they are stroking. I arch my back, throwing my head back as I fuck her face harder, my orgasm growing stronger by the second. There is a pulling feeling deep in my stomach, telling me this orgasm is going to be more intense than usual. I open my mouth to tell her, but her hand clasps over my breasts, twisting violently.

My orgasm crashes through my body. My soul leaves, and for a moment, I can see the past, present, and future simultaneously. It's glorious and colorful and feels so divine. A gush of liquid leaves my body, soaking Dahlia's face. She doesn't stop her ministrations, and my body continues to tense, pulse, and cycle through a never-ending orgasm. My body begins to shake as my soul returns. Dahlia is staring up at me as she continues to swirl my clit in her mouth. It's so sensitive and overworked I collapse with another orgasm. I close my eyes as a giggle escapes. Then I can't stop the giggles. My body feels so light and tingly. Dahlia is still sucking, but it's just making me giggle more. I finally have to push her head away before my clit gets over-sensitive and starts to hurt. She shifts to lie down beside me, pulling me into her arms.

"That was different." She giggles, pressing a kiss to my cheek. "I've waited so long to do that." Her hands gently skim my body. I absolutely love this feeling. I curl into her, enjoying her warmth.

"Do you think Clem will be upset when he returns?" Her question is valid, and honestly, I don't really know. He's usually a happy drunk, but I don't know how much he is drinking. He's not had a night out drinking without me since he came to the castle, not like this.

"I don't know, Dahl. He said he was okay with it, but this is new." She nods, kissing my forehead.

"Maybe I'll sleep in my room. This has been great, but I don't want him to change his mind again." It's not what I want to hear, but I understand. I don't particularly want any more drama between us, either. I sit up, kissing her gently once her dress is back on.

"I love you," I whisper, unwilling to keep that suppressed any longer.

"I love you, too."

"I will find a way to make this work, Dahl. There has to be a way," my words are soft, making a promise I intend to keep. She gives me a gentle kiss. With that, she leaves the room, and I relax in bed.

My mind runs over everything that happened in the past few days. Clem really seems to have reached a turning point. I hope he doesn't feel resentful at some point, like he was forced into this. I debate this topic with myself before I drift off to sleep. Just before I completely fall asleep, Clem enters the room, clearly drunk.

He bumps into a chair and curses. I giggle at him, finding humor in his actions. He walks to my side of the bed, pressing a kiss on my cheek. He was aiming for my lips but missed. He just rolls with it.

"Did you have fun?" His words are slurred, but I can still understand him.

"Yes, did you?"

"Yes, but," he looks around the bed, then the room, "where is Dahlia?"

"She went back to her room."

"Well, that...*hicc*...won't do."

Without any explanation, he leaves the room. I follow him, grabbing a robe first, unsure what he is doing but he is very drunk and should not be left alone at this point. He walks into Dahlia's room, which is surprisingly quiet. She's already asleep in her bed. For a brief moment, I'm envious that she fell asleep so quickly. Clem moves to her bed, then starts to grab her. She instantly fights back, unsure of what is happening.

"No, shhh...*hicc.*" Clem is trying to calm her, grab her, and talk while very drunk. I know I should intervene, but it's quite a sight. Dahlia is trying to push him away; he is persistently grabbing her from her bed.

"Dahlia, it's me...*hicc*...Clem. You're in the wrong...*hicc*...bed."

She seems to settle at his voice, despite how drunk he sounds. He scoops her up in his arms and starts walking toward the door. She is very unsure but is going along with him. I rush over to the door and open it for him. Dahlia gives me a confused look, but I just giggle and shrug. I sneak past them to open our bedroom door. Clem carries her straight into our room and places her on the bed. He climbs in, wrapping his arms around her waist and settling his head against her lap. She sits back against the headboard, holding her hands up so she doesn't touch him. I would be more concerned if the two didn't look so funny together. Clem seems so sure of himself, despite how drunk he is. Meanwhile, Dahlia is uncertain, not knowing what to do right now.

I climb onto the bed, rubbing Clem's back.

"She should...*hicc*.. she should always be in here."

"You think so?" I question, settling to press kisses against his back. He is still now, just holding her close.

"Yeah...*hicc.* She's ours now." I raise my eyes to look at Dahlia. She is staring down at him with affectionate curiosity. Her hands lower to rest on his shoulder and arm. She nibbles on her lip, doubt clouding her features. She can be so strong and stubborn most of the time. I love that I get to see this softer, more fragile side of her. She just wants to be accepted and loved for who she is. I grab her hand, kissing her wrist to reassure her. No matter what Clem feels in the morning, I will do whatever it takes to keep both of them in my life. It's my turn to fight for what I want, and this is it.

"Do you mind sleeping in here?" I want her here, but I won't force her to stay.

"I don't," she says slowly, considering this situation. "It's weird, you know. It's been so tense lately. This feels sudden." I lean over and kiss her cheek.

"Clem has had several days to think about this. He'll be nicer now." She gives a huff full of disbelief. "He is wonderful, Dahl. And I still love you." I grab her face, pulling her close and kissing her deeply. Regardless of how things play out, I will always love her. "Let's get some sleep."

Dahlia nods, but as soon as she tries to move, Clem snores softly, and I laugh at the timing. I tug on his shoulders, lifting him off her lap enough for her to slide down next to him. Once she is settled, I let him go. He grunts, tightening his arms around Dahlia.

"Dahl's mine," he mumbles, holding her close as he snorts softly again. Dahlia watches him curiously for a moment, then relaxes in his arms. I snuggle up to his back, wrapping around him to rest my hand on Dahlia. I love being in this position, with both of them within reach. This is all I want in life. At this point, I don't care about the curse, the kingdom, or anything else. I just want these two in my arms as much as possible.

A breeze blows the curtains open, and I realize it sounds like a storm outside. Thunder is booming loudly in the sky. Lightning strikes outside in an array of colors. The barrier is breaking down. While this is a stronger reaction than we have seen before, I don't think the barrier will entirely disappear. While I want to believe it, I don't think Clem is there yet. Or Dahlia, for that matter. I've loved them both the whole time, but I got time alone with each before we started this. Now it's time for them to come together.

Chapter 28

CLEM

Waking up, sandwiched between two soft bodies, and neither is Finn, is the most fantastic feeling in the world. My head is pounding from all the ale I drank last night, but that doesn't matter now. I keep my eyes shut to keep the light out, enjoying the warmth encapsulating me. I slide my hands across the body under me, unsure if it is Jas or Dahl. Doesn't matter either way to me.

The body underneath me is warm and soft. I drag my hand across her ribs, cupping her breasts. My thumb strokes over her nipple as it buds slightly under my touch. A slight moan escapes from her as an arm wraps around my stomach then chest, pulling me closer to the woman at my back. I never thought I would wake up surrounded by two beautiful women. Of course, it was always a dream I had; I just never imagined it would be real. Or that it would be the Queen.

We lie in a bundle of arms and legs for several more minutes until Emmeline comes in. She throws open the curtains, showering the room with bright morning sunlight. Both women beside me groan while I close my eyes tighter, trying to settle my stomach. There has to be a better way for her to wake us up than opening the curtains that wide. Surely she can come in with soft, kind words and tea, right? That sounds like a much better plan.

Jasmin climbs out of bed, moving around to get dressed and ready for the day. I tighten my arms around Dahlia, not wanting to get up. It's warm and soft, and she smells nice. Why would I ever want to get out of bed? She doesn't return my tight grip, but she doesn't push me away, either. She hasn't had the same time to adjust to the new relationship as Jasmin and me. I was developing feelings for her when I heard the triad story. Maybe she wasn't there. She'll get there, though. I'm a perfectly lovable guy. In the meantime, I will take all the cuddles I can get with her.

"Clem, when are you going to see Bea?" Jasmin calls from the bathroom.

I groan, shifting to sit up. Dahlia slides out of bed as soon as I am up, standing awkwardly for a minute. She squares her shoulders, then calmly walks out of the room. I open my mouth to reply, but a wave of nausea crashes through me. I drop back on the bed, draping my arm over my eyes to block out the light. Emmeline just laughs, tossing some trousers and a shirt toward me.

"Kian had a similar response this morning." Emmeline chuckles.

"So you and Kian, huh?" Jasmin steps out of the bathroom, taking in her friend with waggling eyebrows.

"Is Dahlia going to be here more often?" Emmeline matches Jasmin's tone with a pointed stare at her. I snort at her response, just peeking under my arm, unwilling to let all the bright light in but still wanting to see their reactions.

"Yes." I stretch my other arm out in search of my clean clothes. I slept in the ones I wore yesterday and feel dirty and uncomfortable. "Now, tell us about Kian." Emmeline rolls her eyes, walking to the bathroom and running water in the tub. Jasmin comes to sit on the bed beside me. I wrap myself around her, burying my head against her stomach to block out the light. My stomach is still upset from drinking, but being wrapped around Jasmin comes to the forefront of my thought, and everything else fades away.

"She's not going to say anything about Kian. You'll have to broach that with him." I groan in response. He won't tell me anything, either. He's too philosophical to give me a straight answer. Not that it matters. It isn't my business, but that doesn't stop me from wanting to know. "I want to know when you will see Bea, though." Her arms caress my shoulders and back, soothing the aches and pains from my night out. I start to feel better under her touch.

"Will you come with me?"

"No, you should go by yourself today. Take her some flowers, though."

"Bath is ready," Emmeline announces, promptly leaving the room and taking Finn.

"Who's going to bathe me now?" I question. Jasmin laughs, shoving me off her. She walks through the room gracefully, looking more at peace than in a long time. It reminds me of our time in her room after the winter solstice. Things had been so difficult at first, but then she was happy for a while. Now she has that same dreamy look in her eyes. I stand slowly, taking up the space behind her. I place my chin on her shoulder, slipping my arms around her stomach.

"Are you happy, Jas?" Her head drops back against my shoulder, and I kiss her cheek. She sighs under my touch, closing her eyes. She doesn't even need to speak at this point. I know she is happy. She is blissfully happy right now, and I have something to do with that.

After breakfast, I make my way to Erik and Bea's suite. I haven't been since they moved in, only meeting with them in public spaces since we returned from Greynon. I knock on the door, uncomfortable, just barging in on them. Erik opens the door with a wild, frazzled look on his face. He doesn't acknowledge me, just steps to the side and lets me walk in. It's as if he doesn't even see me. He is staring straight ahead, his eyes unfocused.

"Hey, I came to see how Bea is, but how are you?"

"Yeah. She's in there." He points absently to a door behind him and shuts the door behind me. I debate talking with him more, but I did come here to see my sister. I'll check in with her and follow up with him before leaving. She is sitting on the bed in her room, looking slightly stunned but also pretty sick. The room is warm, and the air feels heavy. The curtains are pulled tight, and the bed is rumpled. She has been holed up in here for a while. A sudden pang of regret rushes through me because I haven't come here before now.

Her room is smaller than Jasmin's but still a good size. She hasn't said anything to me, just glancing at me when I first walked in. She looks tired and worn down. Her short hair is longer than I am used to seeing it, indicating she hasn't cut it in a while. I'm not sure what is going on with these two right now, but if this is what marriage looks like, maybe I don't want that. What is happening in this suite? I fill a mug of water on a table and hand it to her, sitting on the bed near her.

"What is happening in here, Bea? You and Erik both look crazy today."

"Oh, thanks. I can always count on you to lift my spirits." Her words are clipped with laughter as she takes a drink.

"Erik didn't even look at me when I walked in, and I haven't seen your hair this long in years." I lightly grab a strand and tug it away from her head to make my point. She swats me away, rolling her eyes at me. "What's going on? What did the healer say?" As I ask, Erik enters the room, staring at his wife. There is some emotion in his eyes that I can't place. Is it joy? Fear? Excitement? He finally nods at her, and she turns to me. A smirk crosses her face, then fades to uncertainty.

"I'm with child, Clem."

Holy shit. I did not see that one coming.

Although, I should have. They are newlyweds, after all. Suddenly, my mind is running at top speeds, trying to process this. My sister is having a baby, and I'm going to be an uncle. Their wild reactions make more sense now. That's probably how I would look too. Oh, this is exciting. I jump off the bed, looking between the two of them.

"Seriously?" A huge grin spreads across my face as the possibility of being an uncle starts dropping into my mind. I get to watch them raise a baby, and I get to be close to the kid. We had aunts and uncles growing up. One of my uncles always took me to the river and taught me how to catch fish. I'm going to be able to do that. A little baby running around the castle. I'm overwhelmed with joy and excitement at the possibility.

"Oh, my gods." I bounce as I wrap her in a hug. She laughs as I squeeze her tightly. "Jasmin is going to be so excited. And obviously, you can name him Clem after his uncle. It's a great name, after all." I elbow Erik, who is slowly coming out of his stunned silence. He huffs at my blow, rubbing his side absently. "I can teach him to fish and garden. And oh, Finn will love him! We can teach him to ride horses and..."

"Wait, Clem," Bea chuckles but turns serious. "Don't get too excited. It's still early. Anything can happen."

"Too late. I'm already too excited." I bounce on my toes, my hangover long forgotten. My sister is having a baby. What's more exciting than that? "Ma never had any issues carrying. I'm sure you won't either."

"Ma was younger than me, though."

"Not when she had Claire." Bea pauses momentarily as if she forgot about our younger sister. Hope seems to light inside of her. Erik takes my spot beside her, sliding closer to wrap his arm around her. He whispers in her ear. The look she gives is so loving. Warm joy spreads through my chest seeing my sister so in love. She wasn't unhappy before I came to the castle, but she was never this happy. I never would have imagined how huge of an impact coming to the castle could have on my sister too.

"Do you plan to continue working?" I question, knowing what she will say.

"Yes."

"No!" Erik shouts, "You cannot keep working with the animals! They will endanger the baby."

"Plenty of women tend animals and raise babies. I can continue to work." Erik eyes me but doesn't say anything else. This argument isn't over between them, though I don't think he has a strong chance of winning this one. I ask if I can tell Jasmine and offer to leave them alone. They just found out some life-altering information. They need some time alone without me making things worse. I go after giving Bea a long hug and congratulating Erik. I can barely contain my own excitement over having a niece or nephew. This is just the best information.

I walk through the castle feeling elated. Colors are brighter; sounds are more cheerful. I never thought about how it would feel to become an uncle, but this is absolutely the best feeling in the world. Jasmin is in meetings with guards. She is preparing for the border to come down, readying men for whatever may be waiting. As happy as she is in private with us, I know that doesn't extend beyond our bedroom. She has many concerns facing her at this time.

I stand awkwardly in the foyer, unsure of what to do. I'm too excited to sit and read, which is something else I will get to do with my new niece or nephew. I want something more than just taking Finn out to run. I love playing with him, but it's not a very stimulating task. As I settle on what I want to do for the day, I spot Dahlia roaming through one of the halls. I'm glad I'm not alone in this purposeless wandering. She turns down the hall without seeing me, walking away from me. I decide to have some fun with her.

Quietly, I creep down the hall until I am closer to her. Once in range, I jump, screaming and wrapping my arms around her in a sneak attack. She screams and drops to the ground, flailing her arms to stop me. She slams her elbow into my stomach, knocking the breath from me. I roll off her onto the floor, grabbing my stomach where she just hit. She realizes I am not attacking her and calms. She stands regally, dusting off her gown as she looks down at me.

"I'm not apologizing," she states matter-of-factly.

"Me either," I groan, rolling onto my side to stand up. Dahlia picks a piece of dirt off my tunic, tossing it on the floor, maintaining her composure the whole time. It looks comical, but I don't laugh at the situation. I just give her a warm smile, keeping a cautious eye on her elbow now. My stomach has really been through the wringer today.

"I'm going to pick summer berries in the fields. Would you like to join me?"

I don't know what passes over her face. It's a brief look before she glances around to see who is near us. She assesses me again, seemingly unsure how to handle my request to spend time with her. I have been the one fighting this relationship; now, she is the one making things more complicated than they need to be.

She nods, motioning for me to lead the way. I guide her to the storage shed. We collect several baskets to gather the fruit, and I lead her to the rows of strawberry plants. Some people are already working, but only a few are in the berries today.

More people are tending to the other plants. The berry fields will be full of people in the coming days, but we get the first pick primarily to ourselves today.

We creep through the rows of small strawberry plants. I spot several plants with large red berries ready to pick and settle in to pluck them. I walk Dahlia through the process, and we begin collecting berries, still in peace. My mind has settled from the excitement of this morning. Dahlia is focused on her task, not giving me any attention. I would like to talk with her, but I am unsure what to talk about.

She looks lovely today. Her dress is a light yellow color, almost glowing against her skin. Yellow is a good color for her. Her long braids fall down her back, accentuating the seriousness of her face. Watching her work is as enlightening as the work itself. I could watch her for hours and not grow tired of the sight.

The sun is shining bright above us. The dirt beneath us is soft from watering but not muddy. The sweet scent of the berries fills the air. It's warm out but not overly hot. Several bees buzz around us, hopping from blooms, traveling between the plants growing in rows. It's a perfect summer afternoon, one of my favorite days. This is the reason I love working in the field.

"You can eat some if you want."

Dahlia glances at me, considering the words I just said. She was focused on her task, enjoying the warm summer day.

"These are the juiciest berries you'll ever taste."

"Is that so?" Her voice is teasing, but I watch as she lifts a fat red berry to her lips. Her full lips close around the fruit, biting into its tender flesh. Juice slides down her chin, dripping down her throat, leaving a red trail I want to lick. She chuckles, bringing her hand to her mouth to catch the juice.

"I told you. It's how they water the plants. Best berries around."

My eyes are transfixed on her mouth as she finishes the berry, more juice coating her lips and chin. She takes another, biting into it, sending juice dripping down the other side of her neck. She knows I am staring. She is putting on a show for me, and I'll be damned if it's not working. The only thing I can think about now is licking the trail of strawberry juice from the side of her neck. Tasting the sweetness of the berry mixed with the taste of her skin. She grabs a third berry as my breathing grows more shallow. Her eyes are fixed on me as she brings the fruit to her lips. Her lips open, and her tongue wraps around the end of the fruit. My cock jerks in my pants, envisioning her doing that to me. Instead of biting the strawberry, she turns it to me, holding it for me to bite into. I slowly slide closer, grabbing her wrist and sinking my teeth into the berry. The liquid slides over my chin like when Dahlia bit into it. Her eyes follow the trail down my chin, lust filling them.

I tug her wrist, pulling her closer to me. I can't take the distance any longer. My other hand wraps around her neck as my lips find one of the juice drips. I lick and suck the flavor off her. It is as sweet as I imagined. Her taste, combined with the sweetness from the berry, is everything I want it to be. I drop her wrist, grabbing her back to pull her body closer to mine. My tongue follows the trail from the fruit leading to her lips. I don't ask permission as my tongue dives into her mouth, searching, craving more of the sweetness mixed with the taste of Dahlia. I've long thought I would only have these feelings for Jasmin, but Dahlia is driving my desire now.

She moans into the kiss, pressing her body into mine. Our bodies meld together as sweetly as her taste and the berry's. She breaks the kiss to lick the juices from my own chin. She follows the trail down my neck, but her tongue is soft and playful, and I can't help the laughter that escapes. I squirm under her touch, laughing at the ticklish sensation. I fall on my back, pulling her on top of me. She straddles me, still trying to lick the juices off my neck. I tickle her ribs, making her squeal in delight. We twist together between the rows of strawberry plants, giggling and teasing each other.

Someone coughs loudly in the distance. I lift my head, noticing we have drawn the attention of some other people out picking berries. Dahlia moves away from me quickly, straightening her clothes as she returns to picking berries.

"Thank you for getting the sticky juice off me, Dahlia." My voice is a little louder than it needs to be, but it still has a playful ring. She smirks at me as she drops fat berries into her basket. We work for another hour until thick summer berries fill our baskets. We sneak playful glances and touches occasionally but remain separate for the rest of our time in the fields. We drop one basket in the kitchen and take the other to our room for an afternoon snack, hoping Jasmin has returned to share in our bounty.

"Thanks for taking me out today. Mama never let us work in the fields." Her statement confuses me. Why wouldn't she be allowed to work where she wants?

"Why not?"

"Before we came here, Mama and Baba were field workers for their last owner. He made them work long hours in the sun, burning their skin and giving them inadequate water and breaks. She swore she would never let the same happen to us." Fuck. That was terribly insensitive of me to not even consider the implications of taking her to work in the fields with me. It's something I've done willingly for so long it didn't occur to me how cruel it could seem.

"I'm so sorry, Dahlia. I didn't even think about that. Fuck, Sunette is going to hate me." She laughs at my statement.

"Don't worry, Clem. She loves you already. Besides, she knows I'm strong-willed enough you wouldn't have stood a chance against me." She bounces off toward the kitchen to drop her basket. I am left staring after with concern but also admiration. She has been through so much in her short life. Yet she is here, so full of energy and determination. I can't help but savor the warmth spreading through my body as she walks ahead of me.

Chapter 29

Jasmin

From my spot in the meeting, I can see out the window. We have them open to allow a breeze through the room, but that's not what has my eye. The sun is high and bright, sending heat down on the castle. There is lightning, colorful lightning, flashing across the sky. Only a few clouds float lazily as the border shimmers with bright purples, greens, reds, and oranges glaring bright.

Lord Dominick, which will take me a while to get used to calling him, is sharing an update on some changes he plans to make within Greynon. I am ecstatic with his work and enthusiasm. I hope the job doesn't crush him in the long run, but he is more than capable. Lucia sits beside him, listening intently, taking notes, and occasionally adding her thoughts. The thrill of having a woman in my governing courts brings me so much joy, and she has adapted to this position so quickly. I haven't officially offered Lucia the role, but I plan to eventually. She proves herself worthy every day.

I glance around, taking in my changing array of court members. Kian, Dominick, Lucia, Erik. I am finally excited about running this kingdom. I have started curating a team that will assist me in improving our kingdom. Not all older Lords are as thrilled as I am, but they will either get on board or be replaced.

This meeting only lasts briefly, mostly a formality before everyone returns to their villages. We'll meet again before the summer ends, but I hope for an easier autumn and winter this year. Doubtful if we will break the curse, but who knows when that will happen. I leave the meeting, wandering leisurely through the castle. I chat with a few people I pass, making my way to the gardens, wanting to enjoy the summer blooms in the daylight. I haven't had much time to walk through them this year, and I don't want to miss one of my favorite parts of the castle.

"Milady!" Mikhail walks toward me anxiously, scanning the area for people around us.

"Hello, Mikhail. How are you?"

"I need to take a moment of your time. Privately." He looks nervous, and he has never been one to be shy in front of me. I glance around, realizing we are closer to the greenhouse than the castle. We walk in together, calling to see if anyone is in the room. When no one responds, I face him, offering a soft smile and motion for him to speak.

"This isn't easy to say, milady." He keeps his eyes down on his hands, not meeting my eyes. "Clem came out to the strawberry fields today with Dahlia." This is interesting. Neither told me what they were doing today, but I wouldn't have expected that. "They were picking strawberries at first, friendly and such." His voice is so cautious, like he doesn't want to tell me. I remain quiet, letting him work out the words. He sighs heavily, looking up to meet my gaze finally. "They began kissing and rolling around between the plants. Several of my workers saw them." He drops his gaze again. Of course, he is nervous about telling the Queen her true love is fooling around with another woman. I would be worried about telling someone that information, too.

I do my best to reign in my laughter. This is the second time someone has accused Clem of being unfaithful to me, and the second time they were utterly wrong. We need to discuss how we will present this in public. I have been so focused on how it would work between the three of us I didn't consider how it would work in my kingdom.

"How far did they take things?" I'm less concerned about what they did and more concerned about what the people around them saw.

"Just kissing and tickling."

"Thank you, Mikhail. I know that wasn't easy for you to tell. I appreciate your concern and will deal with this matter privately." I offer him a reassuring smile, but before I turn to leave, curiosity gets the best of me. "Do you know anything of Emmeline and Kian?" He considers my question but shakes his head.

"Is she close with him?" It's my turn to shake my head in response.

"No, they just work well together." If she hasn't said anything to her father, there must not be anything going on. She's close to her father and wouldn't keep information from him, especially not if something serious between her and my favorite advisor. As I walk back to my room, I decide to drop the Emmeline and Kian topic. I'm sure they will tell me if they want me to know something.

I appreciate the warmth of the halls as I make my way back to my room. It's an encompassing warmth but not overwhelming. The kind of warmth that leaves me wanting a nap under a tree, with a slight breeze rustling leaves. I'm wrapped up in my daydream when I enter the room and don't register the devilish grin on Clem's face. My mind is still hazy as someone grabs my hands and pulls them behind my back.

Everything becomes clear quickly as Clem stalks toward me. His eyes are focused on me, sending waves of different heat rolling through my body. My mind is so focused on his muscular body prowling in my direction I've forgotten about my hands restrained behind my back. A warm body presses against my back as lips find my ear. Dahlia's scent hits me as my eyes stay focused on Clem's slow, intent walk.

"We've got a surprise for our queen."

Now I need a change of clothes as these are soaked. Clem finally reaches me, and his lips go straight to my neck. I tip my head back, forgetting the reason I came here in the first place. Nothing else matters when I'm wedged between these two. Clem is nipping and sucking my neck, hitting all the spots that send pleasure soaring through my body. Dahlia still has my hands in hers, but she is pressing kisses along my shoulder. My eyes close as the two work me over, savoring their lips against my skin.

Clem pulls away and says, "Ready?" I give him a confused look but realize he is talking to Dahlia. Arousal and excitement flood my body. Holy gods, they're working together now. My pussy is dripping at that realization. Without another word, they pull me toward the bed. Clem takes my hands as Dahlia removes my clothes, working with Clem so that I am not released at any point. Once naked, Dahlia walks to the sitting area, where I can see several sashes and a basket of strawberries. Clem's lips are on my neck again. I have a fleeting thought of something related to those strawberries, but it doesn't stick. My brain is swamped with desire and curiosity.

Dahlia returns with the sashes as Clem guides me back onto the bed. She hands him one as he secures my wrist to the headboard, then they do the same for the next wrist. They don't restrain my legs this time, leaving me wondering what they are planning. I also want to know how long they have been planning this. Who is the ringleader here? Clem has a knack for devious plans, but I can't put anything past Dahlia, either.

Dahlia rips off her dress as Clem walks to the sitting area. Before I can see what he is doing, her lips are on my body, kissing, sucking, nipping. She covers my nipples to my belly button, then back to my neck. I moan under her mouth, loving every single touch she gives me. The bed shifts as Clem climbs next to me. He lounges beside me, tracing his fingers over the spot Dahlia's mouth just was. She sucks my nipple, then he pinches it. She kisses my ribs, and he trails his fingers over the same place. This continues for several minutes until I am wriggling under their touch.

My eyes are closed as they continue to work in unison. I'm surprised by how well they are working together now. It's hard to believe these are the same people I have been with for months. Suddenly, a cool, wet thing lands on my nipple. I jerk up, gasping at the sensation. Clem watches me with a knowing smirk as he circles a juicy berry over my skin. He removes the berry as Dahlia's lip covers my breast, sucking the juice off. He does the same to the other nipple, then feeds me the strawberry while Dahlia sucks my other nipple. She grabs a berry next, biting the tip off, then rubbing it against my neck. Clem sucks the juice off me this time. She trails the berry down my chest as Clem follows the trail with his tongue, licking the sweet juice from my skin.

She stops at my belly button, bringing the fruit to my lips as Clem licks the juice off me. I bite into the fruit, surprised by how much liquid still spills. Some spreads down my face, but Dahlia quickly kisses the juice away from my cheek. My core is starting to clench with my need and desire for them. While I love this slow, planned action, I'm ready for it to go to the next step. As if reading my mind, Clem grabs another berry, making a trail from my belly button down to the top of my hips. Dahlia leaves me to trace the line he just made. He slides the berry over my clit, and Dahlia follows. I moan once her lips brush against it. Seeing Clem bring the fruit to his lips to taste sends a wave of tingles over my pussy. Dahlia begins to lick my opening, swirling her tongue inside, taking her time as if I am the most enjoyable thing she has ever tasted. Clem continues rubbing berries against me, then licking the juices off.

"You get one." Clem growls at Dahlia. She lifts her eyes to him, gives a devious smirk, then dives back into my pussy. She brings her thumb to my clit as her tongue works my entrance. Unable to restrain myself longer, I moan so loudly it's almost a shout. Clem clamps onto my nipple, dragging his teeth across it as my body tenses with my nearing orgasm. Dahlia switches her fingers, shoving two deep inside me, and her lips clamp on my clit. At the same time, Clem sinks his teeth into my neck. I scream as my orgasm tears through my body. My body flexes and releases then flexes again. Light flashes behind my closed eyes as my spirit soars through every plane of existence. Before I have even returned to my body, Dahlia and Clem are both moving. Their hands are on my body, soothing and praising me.

"You're such a good girl." Dahlia coos.

"So perfect," Clem claims.

My body calms in a state of pure bliss. As my mind returns to normal, Clem slides his cock inside me completely, bottoming out against my hips. I twist my head at the sensation, my body wracked with pleasure. Dahlia is sitting next to me, but she's too far away for me to do anything with, especially since I am still restrained. Clem knows my thoughts and already has a plan for that.

"Dahlia, lift your legs over her face and sit on her." My eyes widen with excitement, remembering when Clem licked me while I was above him. The thrill of doing that to her sends a wave of pleasure through my body. "But face me," he adds quickly. I don't know what he's doing, but I don't care. It takes another minute to get Dahlia in place, but I start licking her thoroughly once she is there. My tongue caresses her entrance, swirling her clit before returning to plunge inside her. She keeps raising up off me, though. I follow her but can't keep her close. Now I see why Clem kept his hands around my hips. I snap my fingers several times, hoping to get Clem's attention.

"Oh, stop. Dahlia. Move off her." He also pulls out of me, and I instantly regret snapping.

"No. No, don't stop." I groan, then remember why I snapped in the first place. "I just want my hands free to touch her." Clem chuckles, reaching over to untie one hand while Dahlia undoes the other. Once my hands are free, I motion for Dahlia. "Come back over here. I want your pussy back." I stick my tongue out as she climbs back over me. Clem enters me again, causing me to moan against Dahlia as she slides over my face. My arms wrap around Dahlia, holding her tightly as Clem pounds into my pussy.

My hands explore her body, keeping her close. I savor her taste, understanding why Clem liked this position so much. Dahlia groans, but it sounds subdued. Is she kissing Clem? My hands glide over her body, bumping into one of Clem's on her breast. He is enjoying her, too, while fucking my cunt. That sends a thrill through me, causing me to clench around him.

Dahlia drops one hand to my clit, circling it slowly. I wrap one of my arms around her waist, dipping my finger to her clit, matching her movements. I won't last much longer at this rate. My entire body is tensing, ready for release. We all work together, driving the other two closer to an orgasm. Dahlia presses her finger harder against my clit, and I match her pressure. Clem's thrusts become more erratic. I drive my tongue deep into Dahlia and feel her clenching with her orgasm around me. I follow her, and a second, more powerful orgasm rips through my body, causing me to cry against her cunt. Clem slams into me, emptying deep inside me. We are all jerking and moaning against each other as we experience intense orgasms.

Dahlia is the first to move, climbing off me to sit beside me. Then Clem collapses with his head on my chest, lying on my side. I drape one arm over Dahlia's thigh, keeping her close. The other wraps around Clem's shoulders, running my fingers through his hair. None of us speak for a long time, just enjoying the peace and post-orgasm catharsis. Eventually, Clem looks up, meeting my gaze and then Dahlia's. We all burst into a fit of giggles, holding each other as we laugh over the immense joy we feel at this moment.

"So, you picked strawberries today, huh?" I ask. Dahlia rests her head on the pillow near mine while Clem nods from my chest. I remember I am supposed to talk to them about that, but I don't want to bring that up now. We can talk about that later. Clem is tracing his fingers across my stomach. He stops, tapping me as he looks up.

"Bea is pregnant."

"What? Really?"

He looks so happy right now. Part of it is definitely the orgasm he just got, but I can tell he is also excited about this news. A slight pang of hurt hits my chest, knowing I can't give him that same excitement. I take a deep breath, pushing that thought from my head. Dahlia moves first, getting up off the bed. Clem reaches for her, but she steps away from him.

"I need to bathe before we go to dinner." I realize it is that time, but we all need to.

"We can go in my bathroom together." She just shakes her head and grabs a robe before leaving my room. It's an odd exit, not matching the afternoon we spent together. Clem and I head to the bathroom to bathe. He tells me about seeing his sister this morning and how crazy Erik and Bea looked. His excitement is shining through him. I can't stop the thoughts of wondering how he would react to his own child. He has told me several times he doesn't need his own. I do my best to match his excitement over this situation.

We find Dahlia slipping her shoes on in her room and go to the dining hall together. Dahlia seems in better spirits than when she left our room earlier. I'm unsure what got into her but don't worry about it now. That isn't a question we want to discuss in public. Everyone is already sitting at our table when we come in. Lucia and Dominick have joined us instead of sitting with the other Lords at a different table. Both Erik and Bea are at dinner tonight. I give her a quick hug, whispering congratulations to both. Clem didn't say if they were telling people, and I don't want to be the one to spoil that announcement.

Dinner passes pleasantly; everyone is in good spirits tonight. Chatter is light-hearted and fun, nothing severe or awkward. These are the nights I live for when everything is calm and easy. As the evening wears on, Tomas and Zander wander off, followed by Lucia and Dominick, leaving only Kian, Emmeline, Erik, and Bea. Once the others leave the dining hall, Kian leans in, speaking softly so only we can hear.

"That was an astounding storm that rolled through late this afternoon." His eyebrows raise as he looks between Dahlia, Clem, and me. Not gonna lie; I'll be thrilled when this curse is over, and there aren't magical storms occurring every time we fuck or have some major breakthrough in our relationship. I roll my eyes as Dahlia blushes. Clem just chuckles, shrugging.

"I picked some delicious berries this afternoon." Bea groans, grabbing her stomach like she'll be sick. We all chuckle at her response, but she bids us good-night, saying she no longer wants to be involved. Everyone laughs harder, but Erik stands to leave with her.

"Wait, Erik. Can you stay for just a few minutes? I have a matter I need to discuss with you here. Bea can stay if she wants, but I imagine she wouldn't want to hear this topic." She shakes her head, giving Erik a kiss before leaving. Contentment fills my body, seeing how happy those two are. Even though it was less than a year ago that Erik was technically courting me, I'm so glad he found her. They are perfect together.

Everyone waits for me to start the discussion. While I probably need to talk with Clem and Dahlia first, I also want Kian, Emmeline, and Erik's opinions on this topic.

"So, Kian believes the three of us together will break the curse." I wave my hands between Clem, Dahlia, and myself. I bring Erik and Emmeline up to speed on the triad story Kian found in the kingdom's history.

"I want your input on moving forward from a political standpoint. Today, Mikhail reported that certain activities were happening in the fields between two people." I give a pointed stare at Dahlia and Clem, who both have the decency to look bashful and nervous. I chuckle, patting their legs on either side of my own. "We need to decide how we will present this to the kingdom."

"So you plan to see this through?" Kian asks, looking between us. I nod but look to Clem and Dahlia, not wanting to speak for them. Clem also shakes his head. Dahlia watches, then realizes we are waiting on her. She nods quickly as if she doesn't want to admit this. Everyone is quiet and thoughtful for a minute.

"If you went public with this, you would change the tone of the kingdom." I nod again, having considered that before in wild daydreams about Dahlia from my youth.

"Would we face a lot of backlash from that?" I look to Kian and Erik for that answer. Erik wiggles in his seat, considering but also slightly uncomfortable. I'm glad Bea didn't stay for this. She would not have enjoyed talking about her brother's love life this openly.

"Possibly," Erik starts. "There are many that would frown on something like that, but I wonder if there aren't more that would be pleased to see a change." Kian nods along in agreement.

"It could be a good change for the kingdom, more open and accepting of all people." I hope Kian's words are true, but I always worry when we discuss so many people at once. I look to Emmeline, wanting her opinion too.

"I think you might be considering the wrong people." I give her a confused look, unsure who else she could mean. "I love you, but can the three of you honestly say you could keep this hidden?" Without missing a beat, Clem speaks up.

"No."

"And we already know you and Dahlia can't either," Emmeline adds. Shit. She's right. We've all been caught in various situations before. We would never be able to keep this hidden, and I hadn't even considered that. I chuckle at that thought.

"So, what do we do?" I ask, looking around at everyone.

"Can we think about it for a few days?" Kian loves having time to process and research. I glance to Dahlia and Clem.

"Can you two keep it confined to our room for a while?" Clem laughs but kisses me on the cheek, swearing he will.

"Not off to a good start, mate." Erik roars with laughter at his own comment. We all laugh, but Clem, Dahlia, and I promise to keep our hands to ourselves for the next few days until we figure out something. In public, anyways.

Chapter 30

CLEM

Dahlia says she wants to say goodnight to her parents before bed. Jasmin and I avoid kissing her before she leaves, but that isn't easy for either of us. We both love touching and being close. Not sharing our affection that way will be difficult until we sort things out.

I didn't even consider how it would look to be intimate with Dahlia while we were in the fields. The idea passed through my mind, and I acted on it. I should apologize to Mikhail for putting him in that position, but that also means telling him about this situation. I'll find him when we sort this all out. Being with Dahlia now that I know I am not in competition with her seems much more feasible. I can see why Jasmin loves her so much. She is strong and daring and knows what she wants.

Jasmin and I climb into bed, whispering and giggling, enjoying each other's company. Dahlia doesn't come back to our room, though. We both doze off at some point, only to wake later and realize she still isn't back.

"I'll go get her," I whisper, not wanting her to sleep anywhere but with us now. Jasmin chuckles, kissing my cheek.

"Yes, please go get the woman you hate to come sleep in my bed," she teases, but I still leave the room to do just that. Jasmin knows I don't hate her, and I don't think I did at any point; I was just very frustrated and annoyed and angry with her behavior, and jealous. Just a little bit jealous.

I tap on her door but enter before waiting for a reply. She is lying in bed with her back turned away from the door. It's odd seeing how much they changed this room. The crib and rocking chair are gone, replaced with a large bed and vanity. The pink walls were taken down, replaced with a soft grey. A colorful rug has been placed in the middle of the floor. Even the candles and journal Jasmin always kept here were removed, tucked away in our closet.

Dahlia sniffles from the bed as I draw closer, realizing she isn't asleep. I sit next to her, placing my hand on her hip. She doesn't shove me away but doesn't acknowledge me. It's hard to guess what is wrong with her in this state. Jasmin might be able to tell since she is closer to her. I don't know her well enough to guess the problem, though.

"How are your parents?" My words are soft, worried about startling her. She just shrugs, not giving me an actual answer. I may be out of my league on this issue.

"Will you come back to our room?" She finally turns to face me. Anger and hurt are written across her face as tear stains cover her cheeks. She has been in here for a while crying. This is a surprising realization. Why didn't she come to us straight away? Doesn't she know we would help her with anything?

"I can't do this," her hand waves between us while she sits up in the bed. "Everything is fucked up, and it's all my fault." I cock my head to the side, confused by what she thinks is her fault. Nothing has even happened in a few hours at this point. I can't understand what she is upset about.

"What is your fault?"

"Don't be so insulting, Clem." She huffs, crossing her arms and looking away from me. Frustration rises at her actions, but I try to remind myself she is upset about something and doesn't need my anger. I take a deep breath, forcing air through my body to relax.

"I'm not trying to be insulting, but I don't see how anything is your fault." Her eyes turn to glare at me. Thankfully, this isn't the first time she has given me that look, and I am unfazed by it. If she wanted that look to be effective, she shouldn't have used it so much when she returned.

"Well, let's count everything then." She holds her hands in the air, ticking off one finger for each point. "Jasmin is cursed and it's definitely related to the pregnancy concoction I gave her. Oh, and she's infertile. And sure, you both say it's not a big deal. But I saw your face when you were talking about Bea's baby. You would be ecstatic to have your own." Her fingers rise, counting as she continues. "I was the reason we were caught in the field today. Now Jasmin has to potentially change the entire fucking kingdom for me. Not to mention you two aren't even married because of me." She huffs, slamming her hands down on the bed. "Just leave me alone, Clem. Go be with her, break the curse, and get married."

My initial thought is to call her a dimwit, but thankfully something in the back of my head tells me how horrible that would be right now. I try to process everything she just said. It was a lot, and I understand her doubts. I have similar feelings of my own. This whole curse business is a complete fucking mess. Jasmin and I have been through so much because of it, and now we have a third person to add to it.

I was unaware Dahlia was so upset about the fertility issue. We haven't discussed it much since there isn't anything we can do about it. Obviously, I am excited about being an uncle, but that doesn't mean I will resent Jasmin or Dahlia for not being a father. I don't need my own child to be happy. In fact, I think being an uncle might be even better. I get to sleep at night without worrying about the baby.

"Slide over." I push her side as I slide under the covers next to her.

"What? No...Clem," she sighs but still moves to the side. I wrap my arm around her, holding her tight. I'm not entirely sure what to say to make her feel better. I never know what to say but always think of something. Her arms still cross her chest, despite me trying to hold her close.

"Claire was born when I was 17. My father died a year later. I spent so much time helping Ma with my baby sister. I love her, but gods, she is exhausting. Do you know, the last time she was here at the castle, she practically begged for details on what I did to Jas to cause so much thunder? She was relentless in her quest to know every single detail about how I spent my time with her. And you can imagine what we were doing to cause that much thunder." Despite her angry demeanor, she still chuckles in my arms.

"I am undoubtedly, unbelievably excited for Bea and Erik. And I will spend as much time as I can with the baby when he is here. But you better believe I'm gonna be happy to return him to Bea and go to bed with Jas and you." She remains silent, staring off into the distance. "I've never really cared for having kids, and Jas said she doesn't either. Neither of us has a choice, but you know what that means, right?" She looks up at me this time, hesitation but curiosity gets the best of her.

"What, Clem?"

"It means I get to fuck her however and whenever I want without worrying about getting her pregnant." She scoffs at me, shoving my side. I don't let her go, though, holding her close.

"Is that all you think about?"

"Yeah, basically." I shrug nonchalantly as Dahlia laughs in my arms. It's not a lie. I would much rather spend my time thinking about fucking than doing anything else. We stay silent for several minutes. From my spot, I can still envision the rocking chair that was in here before. I can still see Jasmin kneeling before me, telling me every horrid detail of her story before I met her. What I would give to go back and change so many things. Stop things from happening, and change the outcome for her. But I know I can't do that.

"Jasmin was always going to change the kingdom for you." My voice is softer than I intend, but it matches the feeling in the room. "That's why I was so scared and angry when you showed up." She turns her face toward mine. The soft light from the moon outside her window highlights her face. Her strong cheeks look smoother in the pale light. Unable to stop myself, I press a gentle kiss on her cheek.

"I know the fear you are feeling now. I felt the same thing. But we want you, Dahlia. We both do." I give a gentle shrug, gathering my next thoughts. "I can't make you stop thinking all those things. I probably can't even say the right things to make you believe me. But I will tell you, every day if I need to, that you are ours, and we won't let you go, even despite all those things you mentioned." I grab her fingers, tapping each one for every point she made. She watches my fingers against hers, not saying anything but not shoving me away, either.

The door opens, and Jasmin steps in, holding a burning candle. The soft glow lands on us, snuggled up on the bed. She huffs at us but walks over, putting the candle on the bedside table before crawling over us. She settles in on Dahlia's other side, snuggling under the covers.

"What are you doing now?" Dahlia sighs at her but drapes her arm over Jasmin's back, caressing her side softly. Her love for Jasmin is written across her face while she is also wrestling with her fears and doubts. It's easy to get so wrapped up in fear and doubts when dealing with fate and an entire kingdom.

"I'm going to sleep. If you won't come to our room, I'll come here. I'm not sleeping without you two." Dahlia stares down at Jasmin in disbelief. I kiss her ear, whispering as gently as I can.

"Told you."

I blow out the candle and tug Dahlia down with me. We all snuggle under the covers, pressed tighter together since Dahlia's bed is smaller than ours. We won't complain, though. This is where we are meant to be. We will figure out all the craziness together. It should be easier with the three of us, right? Sharing one bed is more pleasant now than it was last time. We are all here willingly. Dahlia may not be as willing, but she isn't pushing us away, either. She won't say it out loud yet, but she wants us here.

I suggest going on a hike the next morning. The fresh air and sunshine will help lift our spirits. A change of scenery will be nice, too. We've all been working on various tasks around the castle and haven't left the immediate area. Dahlia has been working on her magical skills with Lucia and Kian when he has time. I've been working with Mikhail and corresponding with other farmers in the kingdom. Jasmin has been busy with her royal duties, especially now that she has replaced Alwyn and created a village for the witches.

We crunch through the dry ground, walking the path toward Arkaley. It's my favorite for obvious reasons, but it's always a beautiful walk. It isn't overly taxing until you get into the mountains, which I don't plan to go that far today. Large trees block the sun with their leaves, keeping the grounds cooler. Flowers and green shrubs blossom throughout the entire forest. Animals scurry to and fro, collecting food or just frolicking in the warm weather.

As we walk, I tell them about some of the legends we share of the mountains. Extravagant stories of ogres and werewolves. I'm not as good of an orator as Kian, but I can still keep the story interesting. I resist the urge to hold their hands. The path isn't wide enough for us to walk three wide. I also point out animals I see occasionally and need at least one hand to do that. Finn started the hike with us but quickly decided this wasn't right for him, and he turned back to the castle. We'll find him fast asleep outside the castle when we return.

"Why don't we stop for a picnic?" I suggest after we have been walking for a while. Jasmin and Dahlia pick a spot for us, and we settle in. I drop the pack, pulling the blanket, then the food I packed. Once my girls are settled in, I take some extra food to the guard. He stands a few feet away from us, leaning against a tree. There is also an extra water sleeve that I brought for him. He nods thanks, stating he didn't bring anything. This isn't the first time we have gone out with a guard that wasn't entirely prepared for our activities. Now, I always make sure I have extra supplies for them.

"What are you doing?" Dahlia asks.

"Making sure Aelric has lunch, too."

"Aw, that's kind of you, Clem." Jasmin swoons, grinning at me as I turn back to them. The sky flashes above us, bright red and orange colors high in the sky. I turn my head to look at the lightning, then look back at Dahlia with a wide smirk on my face. I saunter over to the blanket, way cockier than I should be.

"Fuck," Dahlia mumbles. I collapse on the blanket beside her, resting on the side with my hand on my head.

"Hey, Jas?" I pop a grape in my mouth, unable to stop the grin on my face.

"Yes, Clem?" Her grin is apparent, unable to suppress her amusement with this situation.

"I think Dahlia is in love with someone." Jas snickers as Dahlia curses again.

"Yeah, myself," she retorts in a sassy tone. This is too much fun.

"Hmm, no. I think it's someone else." Jasmin tries to hide her laughter behind her hand, but her whole body is shaking.

"You're right. I love Jasmin and me, that's it. That's the whole list. Me and her."

"No, that doesn't seem right. I think your list is growing by one." I trace my hand along her thigh teasingly. Dahlia groans, turning to Jasmin.

"Why did fate choose such an insufferable twat?" Dahlia sighs, grabbing an apple to eat.

"But that's an insufferable twat you love," I sing out.

Jasmin laughs out loud at my comment this time. Dahlia huffs at her, but a slight grin spreads across her face. "It's okay, Dahlia. You can love me. I'm a wonderful person. Just ask Aelric, who has lunch now." With that comment, Dahlia and Jasmin burst out into giggles. Thunder and lightning crash above our heads. Bright colors flash through the sky, and loud thunder rumbles through the earth, seeming to shake the very ground we sit on.

"Fuck, I'll be glad when that is over," Dahlia mumbles. I lean up, pressing a kiss against her cheek.

"Me, too," Jasmin responds, but she stares into the sky with wonder. I will be glad when there isn't an obvious sign that we have done something significant in our relationship. I'm not quite ready to confess my love for Dahlia, but I can feel myself getting closer. I never wanted to be in a triad or share Jasmin. These last few days with Dahlia have been fantastic, though. She really does bring something to our relationship that I never thought possible. I am excited to see what the future holds with the three of us together.

Chapter 31

JASMIN

Sitting in this meeting I called has me debating the merits of replacing all the Lords. Kian, Emmeline, Erik, Dominick, Lucia, Clem and Dahlia are in the meeting room with me. They are all here to discuss what to do with my relationship with Clem and Dahlia. We explained the potential of needing a triad to break the curse. I want to hear their thoughts on presenting this to the kingdom. Kian has been researching relentlessly since we last spoke, and I'm almost scared to break the curse for his sake. What will he spend his time doing once we don't have the challenging questions about magic?

The people in this room give me such hope for the kingdom's future. They are debating the best course of action, the potential consequences, and if the benefits outweigh them. They are bringing up points I haven't even considered. There are topics that the other lords wouldn't even mention in front of me, let alone actually consider for the kingdom's sake. Several conversations concern the merit of announcing a triad as the rulers. They debate for several minutes, with me just listening and absorbing what they were saying. I finally stand, ready to give my own thoughts.

"I appreciate all of your thoughts. I value each opinion you have shared in such respectful ways." They stop talking and listen to what I have to say. "There is much to consider in announcing such a non-traditional relationship to our kingdom. I don't know that we will ever find the correct answer to that. I have something that I would like your thoughts on." I open the journal I brought, sliding a copy of my idea to each person in the room. They all scan the page as I continue talking. "I would like to make a new law that I think will pave the way for our relationship down the road without exposing us now. This law will punish all discrimination toward people in non-traditional relationships."

Everyone is silent as their eyes bounce between the page I gave them and me. They take several minutes to process what I am saying. It could be huge for our kingdom. Since we are trapped, I have no idea what other territories are doing regarding their people. Everything could be the same as nine years ago when people were forced to hide and pretend they weren't different. I don't want that for my kingdom, regardless of what others do.

"Non-traditional, like Zander and Tomas? Or me and you?" My eyes meet Dahlia as she speaks softly, her voice shaky and uncertain. Clem told me her doubts about changing the kingdom for her. He was right; I was always going to do something like this. It took me a long time to get to the point of enacting it.

"Yes," I say to her, then turn to address everyone else. "For too long, people have been persecuted for who they love, and it shouldn't be that way. It never should have been that way. I have wanted to change this since I became aware of the problem." There is so much more that I want to say, but I decide to stop there. Not everyone knows my past, and this isn't the time to drag it out.

Lucia speaks first. "I believe this is something the witches would accept with open arms. We are already more accepting of differences and wouldn't bat an eye at a non-traditional relationship. This won't be an issue for us." Kian nods along as she speaks. The witches have always been more accepting than others. I try not to consider the possibility of it being due to their own treatment. There are many things I need to atone for on behalf of my predecessors.

"Greynon will have some upset by this," Dominick starts. He is deep in thought, considering what he knows of his village given his new position. "I think once we have set a precedent with a few, the rest will not cause a problem."

"Many in Arkaley will not like this," Clem has sorrow in his eyes as he looks at me. "They like to hold to their traditions and values and will take issue with this. After the trial with Jackson, many may be hesitant to act, but I can't promise no one would." This is what I fear, that some will cause problems. There was rioting when the border fell, and it was deadly and dangerous. Arkaley was the worst of the rioting, and I don't want to repeat that time. It's hard to say if many would riot over this, but some in the village would. The real question is whether they would garner enough support to cause lasting damage.

"Vadried won't have a problem with this. There will be some shock, maybe some outrage," Erik speaks, "but I think we will find more trying to use this to their advantage. It may be a false front, but it would be a start."

"How will the guard handle this? We will need them to intervene if things turn violent." Before Erik can answer my question, Dahlia speaks up again.

"Will things get violent?" A moment of silence settles before Erik answers the questions.

"I would expect some violence. Most of the guards will be equipped to handle this change. I recommend giving us time to prepare them for that possibility before it goes public." I nod, considering all that has been said. Overwhelming support on a topic like this would be ideal, but their thoughts have given me more hope than I had before mentioning this.

"Very well. Let's meet with the Lords and guards in a few days to officially discuss this with them." Erik nods in response. The air is still heavy with the complex topic. "I want you all to know how deeply I value your opinion and willingness to speak candidly. I truly believe we can make this kingdom a better place for all." Everyone smiles, the mood lifting slightly.

"Now, I have one more topic to discuss. I promise this one is more fun. But, I need Clem to leave." I turn to him; his face is aghast at my suggestion. I give him a quick kiss and then shove his shoulders. He is outraged at my proposal.

"What...I'm not leaving. Anything they can hear, I can," he waves his hand around the room before crossing his arms. His petulant mood causes me to giggle. The others are watching the interaction with humorous curiosity.

"Trust me, Clem. You do not want to stay for this." He huffs, sitting up straighter in his chair.

"Well, I am."

"Very well," I shrug. I knew he wouldn't actually leave. I debated for a long time on how to get him out of the room at this point, even considering two separate meetings. I didn't want to have two different sessions, though. My days are already filled with so many meetings, and there are other things, specifically people, that I want to do. Now it is time to implement my plan to get him out of the meeting room and piss him off.

"As you all know, Lughnasa is approaching and strongly celebrated at the castle." It's not. It's a holiday once celebrated many generations ago but faded with other traditions. No one I know has actually observed it. It is occasionally mentioned with harvest but usually only in passing. Emmeline gives a confused look, knowing this information. Everyone else has a mix of intrigue and interest.

"I am now crowned, so I want to bring back the bachelor judging competition." Clem, my poor jealous jester, has an unfortunate mouthful of wine when I say this. He sprays wine across the table, choking on the rest. I do my best to look more irritated than humored. Erik and Kian jump into action, grabbing rags to wipe up the mess.

"Clem! You told me you could handle this!" I fake outrage as best I can, but it's hard to stay in character with Emmeline and Dahlia snickering.

"What the fuck is a bachelor judging contest?" Clem is wiping his shirt with a rag from Kian. His face blistering red with anger, and his breathing is heavy. Seriously, I deserve a medal for not laughing at this.

"It's a competition where all the eligible bachelors come to the castle. They perform feats of strength, usually without shirts, for my benefit," I shrug casually, trying to downplay this situation to anger him further. "You wouldn't be able to compete since you are no longer a bachelor, and neither would Erik." I turn with a sigh to look at him. His cheeks are red as the beets pulled from the earth. I didn't intend to embarrass him this way, but I do love toying with the men. "Though Kian and Dominick can participate."

"Like fuck they will!" Clem is shouting, so angry and jealous. I know I shouldn't, but I can't help but love this reaction. By this point, Kian and Erik have caught onto my scheme. I do feel bad for not filling in Dominick and Lucia.

"Well, Clem, if you had just left when I asked you to, I'm sure they would have talked me down from that event. But seeing your silly reaction, now I feel even more eager to host this competition." He is so angry that he can no longer form words. "If you will leave this meeting room, I will discuss the rest of these plans with them. I'm sure they can persuade me to make an acceptable choice." He seethes, his shoulders rising and falling with his deep breaths. He turns to where Kian and Erik are standing, both watching this situation unfold. Erik has a nervous look in his eyes, but Kian is filled with delight. He loves fucking with Clem more than I do.

"I swear to all the holy gods if you let this happen," Clem starts. Erik looks slightly terrified at Clem's tone, but excitement is dancing in Kian's eyes. Before either can say anything, my arms drape over his shoulders, bringing my lips close to his ear.

"Please just go, and I'll make it up to you later," my voice is light and promising as my lips brush his ear. He is still tensed, glaring at the others in the room. He doesn't acknowledge my presence as I lean back, meeting his gaze.

"Are you fucking with me?" His voice is soft but still angry. A smirk spreads on my face as I shrug coyly at him. His hand slides to the back of my head, fingers tangling in my hair. He jerks it tightly, pulling me closer to him. Wetness pools in my core at the promise of his violence. His lips are next to my ear, his words soft. Though the room is so silent, I can't be sure anyone else can hear. "I will fuck your throat later to make you pay for this." Oh fuck. I have to stay on my feet and fight every urge in my body that wants to drop to my knees in front of him now. The desire to giggle is almost overwhelming, causing my stomach to turn and flip inside me. He hasn't been as rough with me since Dahlia joined us, and apparently, my body misses that.

He releases me as quickly as he grabbed me, sulking out of the meeting room. I watch him leave, my back to everyone else in the room. I need a moment to compose myself before turning around. I send a silent thanks to the gods that I don't have a dick because my arousal would be even more apparent now. I take in a deep breath, turning back to my friends. They all watch in various states of aversion, interest, and confusion.

"Clem's birthday is in a few days, and we need to plan a celebration."

Erik guffaws loudly. His laughter is always so joyful, so sincere. Everyone else chuckles as I offer a brief apology for not filling them in before; I just didn't have time. We haven't celebrated a birthday in a long time. Some people within the castle hold smaller celebrations for friends or families, but they are never official events. Dahlia's birthday is in the winter, and mine is in the spring, but most people have forgotten. Since I haven't been celebrating, people don't remember. It's not written in many places to protect my privacy. Kian probably knows, and Emmeline, but few beyond them know.

We spend the next hour discussing activities and food for the celebration. This will be smaller than our holiday celebrations. Erik mentions bringing in Ada and Claire, which I love. Clem would be thrilled to see them. Everyone offers ideas of what we can do, even Dominick and Lucia, who don't know Clem as well as the rest of us. I'm so overjoyed with this group of people by my side.

Dahlia and I leave the meeting, making our way toward our bedroom. We are talking about some other plans I have for Clem that only include the three of us. She seems more hesitant to agree to some of that, but I think she will come around once we start. She still has a lot of doubt about being with Clem, especially sexually. It has more to do with her inexperience. For all she touts, she doesn't actually have much experience, especially with men.

We enter the room, and Clem stands in front of the fireplace, his arms crossed over his chest. His eyes still promise the violence he spoke of in the meeting room, and my core throbs at the sight.

"Stop there," his voice is deep and gravelly, sending butterflies through my stomach. Dahlia and I stand just inside the door. My eyes are focused on his. His muscular shoulders are brushed by his hair, which he has left down tonight. He knows how much I love when his hair is down. It's tousled as if he has been running his hands through it since he left the meeting. He probably has, angry at the words I said. Dahlia is tense next to me, looking between Clem and me. His eyes stay glued on mine while heat spreads throughout my body. He stands up straight from the chair he is leaning against. The height difference in his new position is overwhelming.

"Jas is going to pay for her comments in the meeting." My body literally shivers as he speaks. Yes, gods! I want to pay, and I'll pay so much right now. "You can leave now, Dahlia, or stay quiet and watch. But I'm not going easy on her." His words are laced with threats of pain and pleasure, and I want it all. We still stare at each other, increasing the tension in the room.

Dahlia is torn next to me. She glances between the two of us, unsure of what to do. She isn't fond of Clem's deviancies, having made several comments about them. He has toned down some of his actions when she is with us, which is all the time now. I love her, and I love that he does that for her, but I am so fucking glad he isn't going to hold back tonight. My body has started to crave his form of violence. She finally walks over to the couch, sitting sideways so she can still see me. Clem finally breaks eye contact with me to look at her. A wicked grin spreads across his face. I can see the gears turning in his head, making a new plan now that he knows Dahlia is staying. Wetness pools between my legs, realizing she will be watching. Clem turns his attention back to me.

"Strip down and drop to your knees." He leans against the chair again, crossing his arms across his chest. His strong arms are on display, causing me to nearly forget the words he just said. It is such a simple command; I'm almost disappointed. I remove my clothes slowly, his eyes never leaving my body. Dahlia is also watching but is more stoic in this situation than Clem. Clem is oozing power, lust, savagery. I want every bit of it. I finally drop to my knees, waiting for my next command. He stares for a moment before speaking.

"Do you want to be involved?" He looks at Dahlia, who seems startled by his question. "I won't be rough with you, but I have some ideas to punish Jas." She glances at me, and I try not to look too eager, but I would love to see what Clem is imagining. She looks back at him and just nods. That wicked grin returns as my core clenches with anticipation.

"Jas, what's your safe word?"

"Flower."

"And when I gag and bind you?"

He said when, not if, and I suppress a groan. I snap each hand once, letting him know I remember. He gives a thoughtful look to Dahlia. "This little slut tends to say 'no' when she doesn't want me to stop. So we use other methods when she means 'no.' Do you want a word?" The simple act of explaining this to help her understand and feel more comfortable warms my heart. Dahlia shakes her head at him as he turns back to me.

"Crawl to me, whore."

I'm stunned at his demand at first but drop to my hands, crawling across the room toward him. The further I move, the more awkward I feel in this position. I can't see his face from this angle, and not having his intense gaze on me makes my confidence waver. I stop at his feet, sitting back on my knees. I can finally look up to see him, but his hand wraps around my throat as I lift my eyes. He lifts me to my knees, thumb stroking across my chin as his eyes follow the movement. Without any warning, his lips crash into mine. The kiss is forceful, demanding, charged with lust. My hands move to his arms, but he jerks away as soon as I touch them.

"Bend over this chair." He waves to the spot he has been standing in since I entered the room. "You want to show off? Do it. Put your ass on display for me." His words are laced with a barbaric tone, leaving me wanting to rebel and follow through simultaneously. Curiosity wins this round, and I do as he says, bending over so my ass is perched in the air. I lean into the chair until my breasts touch the seat. His hand caresses my ass, rubbing one cheek then the other. His finger starts at my tailbone, dragging straight down over my opening to my soaking cunt. A moan slips out into the cushion of the chair at his touch. It does nothing to release the growing ache, but it feels so good. Suddenly, his hand is gone. Before I have time to react to the absence, his palm connects with my ass. Pain sears through my ass while his hand returns to massage it again.

"You want to be a bad girl? I will treat you like one."

The ache between my legs is growing more as he caresses me. Then he smacks the other side with the same intensity. It isn't a hard hit, just enough to sting. I manage not to yelp this time, savoring the feel of the sting under his hand. Wetness drips down my thighs from the ever-present ache in my core. I rub my thighs together, searching for any kind of relief. Clem notices and kicks my legs apart, forcing them wide so I can't get any sensation. Once he is happy with my new position, he spanks me twice, once on each side of my ass. He uses both hands to caress me as I moan beneath his touch. I squirm beneath him, needing relief from my growing desire.

His hands connect with each of my ass cheeks again, harder this time. I cry out, turning my head to the side. The pain is getting more intense, but so is my desire. This orgasm, whenever he allows me to have one, will be stronger than I am used to. I am already accustomed to really intense orgasms from him, but this will be even more. I open my eyes to find Dahlia staring at me. A wave of embarrassment washes over me, realizing she is watching me get spanked. As soon as that thought settles, Clem hits me even harder. My pussy clenches, no longer concerned about my embarrassment. Clem is standing behind me, pressing into my ass. His hard cock is pressed between my cheeks but still covered with his trousers. I groan at the sensation. I want his pants gone. I need him buried deep inside me. Either hole. Any hole. All the holes. I just need more. He backs away from me, and I whimper. Dahlia is watching, flushed with her own arousal. Her eyes are focused on mine. My eyes are glazed over with desire.

Clem's hand connects with my ass again, and I yell this time. He massages gently, bending over to place a kiss on my cheeks. With his mouth so close to my holes, I wiggle, trying to encourage him to slide over just a few inches. That's all I need from him, and I need it desperately now. My entire body is tensed with arousal. He smiles against my ass, and I can feel his lips spread in a devious smirk.

A quick kiss lands on my ass before he stands. I whine as he presses his cock against me again.

"Stand up, my little slut."

I do as I'm told. Clem turns to grab something from a table behind him. I didn't notice he already had items pulled out. It makes sense; he's been thinking about this for an hour or more. With his back turned, I slide my hand down to my aching, dripping core. Just as I reach the apex of my thighs, Dahlia rises and walks over to me, passing behind Clem. He turns to look as frightened excitement passes through me. Dahlia grabs my hands, pulls them behind my back, and restrains me. She copies Clem's move from earlier and kicks my feet apart. I groan, arching back to touch her, but she is too far away.

"Oh no, my precious girl," she whispers near my ear. "You aren't getting release that easily." Holy hell, I'm in trouble. They've teamed up against me! This isn't how this was supposed to go. She is supposed to be on my side! The look on Clem's face can only be described as the devil incarnate. They'll never bury me in the royal cemetery. At this point, the only thing that could kill me is orgasm denial, and Clem is promising that with his grin.

He brings over a rope, stepping behind me to take Dahlia's spot. She walks to my front, kissing my neck, my chest, my shoulders. While her lips work my upper body, Clem pulls my arms tight, tying my forearms together behind my back. The position forces my breasts right into Dahlia's face. He makes sure I can still snap before he walks to my front. I don't frequently snap, but he always ensures I can. He kisses Dahlia deeply, right in front of me, teasing me with his affection. My juices are dripping from my cunt by now, so ready for release. He tells her to strip and returns to the table with all his supplies.

I watch Dahlia remove her dress slowly, seductively. She knows what she is doing to me, and it's working. My mouth waters as her breasts are exposed. My eyes follow her hands as they slide down her stomach, pushing the dress out of the way. The dark tuft of hair between her hips has me licking my lips, wanting a taste, wanting to offer her release. Her clothes are kicked toward mine as Clem comes around. He tosses his shirt over with ours, removing it while we watch each other. He turns the chair I was just leaning over around, instructing Dahlia to sit. He walks to me with a metal bar in his hand, cuffs on either end. My eyes go wide; not sure what he intends to do with that.

"I may have asked the guards what are some tricks to restraining a challenging person. Then I may have found some spare devices lying around." He is repeating my words from the time I tied him up and teased him. I didn't think he would let me off easily tonight, but I may be in for more than I anticipated. He kneels before me, giving me a smirk that assures me I'm not prepared for him. He cuffs one ankle, then positions the other to cuff it too. My legs are forced into a spread position. There is no way I can rub my thighs together. I am stuck in this position with my legs apart and arms tied behind my back. He leans in, running his tongue over my opening. He presses his tongue flat, swiping entirely across me. I groan at the touch, knowing it's not enough to get me off, but it feels so damn good anyway. He has been planning this for far longer than the past hour.

He walks over, claiming Dahlia's mouth again. She can taste me on his tongue. She groans under his lips, but he breaks away quickly, not lingering on the kiss. At this point, even Clem denying Dahlia is driving my own needs. He returns to the table, slips something in his pocket, then walks back to me. This time he gags me, pressing a quick kiss to my cheek. He circles me, grabbing one tit, then the other, eliciting another groan from me.

"Dahlia, have we told you how much of a whore our queen is?"

She doesn't answer, just keeps her eyes on Clem as he talks. He walks behind her, placing his hands on her shoulders, caressing her in a way that makes me jealous.

"For Christmas, she convinced Kian to cast a spell on a device to make it vibrate." He holds his hand out, showing the magic fun ball to her. This is another item that hasn't been used much since she came back. I completely forgot she didn't know about it. She stares at the smooth wooden cylinder, trying to discover its secrets. "Our little slut loves this item greatly. So I will show you how it works while she watches, tied up and unable to feel it." I groan, my core clenching with need.

Clem taps the device, sliding it over Dahlia's breasts. Her nipples peak as her breathing becomes shallow. His hands caress down her stomach, between her legs, pushing them apart. He lifts her knees, propping them over the arms of the chair. She is completely exposed for me now. My mouth waters as I can see how wet she is from here. Spit dribbles down my chin from the gag in my mouth. Dahlia watches my face. She is enjoying all of this too.

With her legs separated, Clem places the magic fun ball on her clit. She arches her back, her head going over his shoulder as the item vibrates against her bundle of nerves. He leans around, latching his mouth onto her nipple. My own nipples are peaked, wanting the same sensation. Her body undulates under him, her pussy clenching under his hand. He realizes this at the same time I do, and he sinks two fingers deep inside her while holding the cylinder in his palm. He pounds inside her as her breathing becomes irregular. She is so beautiful, writhing under him in pure pleasure.

"Open your eyes and look at your queen." His words are soft in her ear. Her eyes open and find mine. A wave of pleasure washes through me, not an orgasm but a joyful feeling. I must be quite a sight, gagged, bound, breathing heavily, and covered in sweat and arousal and spit. Her eyes search mine for a moment before they roll back into her head in ecstasy. Her body tenses and releases with her orgasm. Her cunt grows wetter as Clem continues his ministrations, guiding her through her powerful orgasm. I whine, wishing I could touch or feel or have my own release. Her body calms down, and Clem helps her lower her legs. He circles the chair, pulling her into his arms. He holds her close, pressing tiny kisses to her face while her breathing settles to normal. I'm left standing behind them, forced to watch a tender moment that somehow makes my own need even more intense. He whispers softly in her ear, but I can't hear the words. She finally nods, climbing off his lap and onto the floor. He stands and walks in front of me.

"Tell me, my slut queen, are you going to try to make me jealous again?"

I shake my head, but we both know it's a lie.

"On your knees."

I bend my knees, and Clem grabs my upper body, helping me lower smoothly. I'm thankful, not wanting to hurt myself while restrained like this.

"You've been a good girl tonight," he whispers as his hands untie the gag. I whimper at his words, loving the way they sound. "What do you think, Dahl? Should we let her come?" To my surprise, Dahlia responds to him.

"Not yet. She hasn't suffered enough." Loud thunder rumbles outside, shaking the window. I never thought Dahlia would be so sadistic. I guess Clem is starting to rub off on her. I love it so much, but I'll never admit that to them. Clem smirks as he finally pulls the gag away, tossing it to the side. His hand quickly unties his pants, releasing his own leaking cock. I lick my lips, opening my mouth for him. I don't need to be told what to do. We both want this. He presses his cock against my tongue. The heavy weight makes me groan as my tongue swirls over it. I slide my tongue around, wetting his cock before he fills my throat.

"You know how much I love you, right?" His words are soft, not his normal deep, sexy voice. I meet his eyes, but they still promise pain. I nod, wrapping my lips around his cock and sinking down on it.

"Because this is going to hurt."

His hands lace through my hair as he slams to the back of my throat. I gag, shutting my eyes at the roughness. His hands are wrapped around my head, holding me in place as he pounds into my throat repeatedly. When I think I won't be able to handle this any longer, Dahlia appears at my side. Her hands caress down my body while Clem's cock fills my throat. Dahlia places the magic fun ball against my clit, and my body ignites instantly. I moan around his dick in my mouth, eliciting a low growl from him. My hips undulate in Dahlia's hand, seeking release from the vibrations. My body tenses, right on the verge of orgasm, when Clem mumbles, "Wait."

Dahlia pulls the vibration back, and I groan. The tears leaking down my face are now from my denied orgasm instead of the pain caused by his thrusting. His thumbs stroke them away while his fingers hold my head tightly. I gag again as he thrusts, and he groans.

"Now," Clem forces out through clenched teeth. The vibration is back on my clit as my body tenses, already on the cusp again. As I prepare for another denied orgasm, Clem releases his hot fluid down my throat. His taste sends me over the edge into an orgasm more substantial than I have ever felt. I can hear time. I can taste color. My body is soaring through an ethereal plane. I can see sounds. They look like purple clouds and taste like honey. I float on a cloud, my body tensing and releasing with pleasure. My soul watches Clem and Dahlia release and soothe me, but I don't register the touch. I'm in such a state of bliss that I never want to return. I can fly through the clouds with eagles and sparrows and bats.

The thunder and lightning crash around me, but I know I am safe here. This isn't dangerous for me. The lightning is bright pinks and greens, yellows, and blues. The clouds are deep purple and red, rumbling with the booming thunder. I can feel their vibrations and strikes. Or maybe that's my body shaking and quaking from the orgasm.

Clem carries me over to the bed as my soul slowly, unfortunately, returns to my body. The pleasure is still coursing through as Dahlia wipes my core with a rag. My muscles convulse at the touch, sensitive and overworked. Clem is saying words, but I don't know what they are. I will my head to turn to look at him, but it won't respond. Instead, I close my eyes, enjoying the fading feeling of clouds around my body. Clem pulls my body against his as Dahlia snuggles in behind me. I regain enough control to pull Dahlia's arm around me before I drift off into a deep, peaceful sleep.

Chapter 32

CLEM

Jasmin is up to something, and I don't know what it is. I also don't like it. I prefer to avoid meetings, but it irritates me when I'm told I can't attend. They have yet to tell me why I can't attend recently. They've had me working with Mikhail or writing correspondence with Dahlia for the past week. I just want to go to the meeting with Jasmin and figure out what she is up to. Is that really too much to ask for?

Jasmin is getting ready for a meeting she has this morning. We will all attend another event this afternoon that requires more formal wear, but until then, I have nothing to do.

"Let me go with you. Please," I've resorted to begging. This is how desperate I am to learn what she is doing that I am not allowed to know. I've asked Emmeline and Kian. I even bugged Erik and Dominick, but everyone is tight-lipped about whatever Jasmin plans. I hate being left out so much. Jasmin gives an exasperated sigh but looks at Dahlia. They have some silent conversation, making faces and turning their heads in different directions. Great, there's something else I'm excluded from.

"Okay, but you'll need your formal wear on now." I jump up, rushing to where Emmeline has my clothes laid out.

"Done."

Dahlia and Jasmin chuckle as I start putting on the clothes. Dahlia helps Jasmin with her hair but doesn't get ready herself. I don't question Dahlia's reasons. I'm just glad Jasmin finally gave me permission to join the meeting. I'm ready to know what's going on.

"You look nice." Jasmin's words are soft as she wraps her hand around my arm while we walk together. Her hand on my arm always makes me feel more powerful than I am. Having her by my side makes me feel invincible. I kiss her temple quickly, complementing her in return.

"So, what's this meeting about?"

"The non-traditional relationship proclamation."

I sigh, not getting the information I want. Based on the grin spreading across Jasmin's face, she knows what I want and is just fucking with me. Well, two can play that game.

"Good. I'm very excited for it to be enacted. It's a brilliant bill, Queen." She squeezes my arm, pressing a kiss to my elbow. These gentle kisses are everything to me.

"Why isn't Dahlia coming to the meeting?"

"I'm not ready to inform all the Lords of this situation. If we decide to try to get married or make our triad official, then we will come out with everything. But for now, I just want to keep that tidbit to ourselves until we figure out the curse. Plus, several of the old Lords despise Dahlia and will immediately blame her for this change." Since the meeting she kicked me out of so rudely, she has been referring to the Lords as old and new. She is so focused on making her kingdom a better place for everyone. I don't mind that she is in meetings constantly. I just mind when she is hiding things from me. Like I know she is now. This thought continues to grate on my nerves as I walk through the halls.

We pause outside the door of the meeting room. Jas is deep in thought, trying to solve whatever problem she has.

"What are you hiding from me?" My head can't take the unknown any longer. I need to know. Why she's been so distant, why we are in formal wear now, what she's been doing that I can't be part of. Her eyes find mine as a soft smile spreads across her face. She steps in to hug me, wrapping her arms around my back. I hug her back, hoping for an answer this time.

"Oh, Clem," she whispers into my chest. "You'll find out soon."

The guards pull the door open behind us as she steps out of my hug. She would time that perfectly so we can't talk about it. I debate not walking in first, but then she would just leave me in the hallway. I give her an unimpressed look as I turn and walk into the meeting room in front of her. Jasmin takes her seat, beginning with the usual pleasantries and greetings.

She begins the meeting by explaining the proclamation and what she expects. Everyone is silent as she describes how punishments will work, what needs to change, and what she wants from the Lords. Those of us who already knew this listen intently. I marvel at how well she composes herself. Even if the meetings are dull, it's always fun to mentally compare her posture here to when I have her bound and gagged. Images of her reddened ass appear in my mind. Her bent over the chair, wiggling as my hand connected with the tender flesh of her ass...

"This is an outrage!" Lords Gustavo and Erland are shouting a multitude of reasons why this is the worst thing she has ever done. Thurston is adding in a few quips every now and then. Lord David is calm, reading the proclamation over. The rest of us sit silently. Jasmin has told me enough about meetings that go poorly to know she just lets them yell for a while when they get like this. Apparently, she has filled in the others. While the Lords continue yelling, the rest of us watch in various states of boredom. Lucia looks irritated at the comments, like at any minute, she will start yelling back. She is barely able to restrain herself. Dominick's anger is quickly growing.

This group has an odd divide between those yelling and those not. Jasmin watches calmly as if she might be absorbing every comment they make. For the most part, the men are just angry about the change and not receiving time to prepare for such drastic changes. Aside from the tone of voice, they aren't really being disrespectful. Jasmin does not like being yelled at but handles this gracefully and with poise. Lord Gustavo shouts something about dimwits, and I notice

Jasmin flinch. It's a tiny, barely noticeable movement. One that would only be recognized if someone was explicitly looking.

"That's enough." My voice is deep and threatening, but Lord Erland responds before I say anything further.

"Calm down, farmhand. You have no power here." Erik slams his hand on the table, rising as he does so. The guards snap to attention, readying their weapons to fight. Erland has the decency to look appalled but takes his seat.

"There will be no insulting the crown," Erik glares at Erland, balling his hands into fists. Jasmin stands, motioning for everyone to sit.

"To improve our kingdom, we must do so as a united front. Erik, please sit." He does, and the guards assume a neutral pose in their positions. Several still watch with intensity but are not in a battle-ready stance. Jasmin starts the discussion more calmly, addressing several issues the Lords raised. The arguments seem to drag on, but eventually, the Lords concede to enacting the new bill. The meeting is tense and takes longer than ordinary meetings, but good progress has been made. Unfortunately, before the end, Henry, the Head of the Guards, stands.

"Queen Jasmin, in the past day, we have noticed movement on the northeastern border in Vadried. Hollyhock has sent several foot soldiers to set up camp near the border. They seem peaceful now, but we believe they have been stationed to watch the border and make contact when it falls." The silence in the room is deafening. Jasmin stares at Henry as she processes what she just heard. They knew we could be attacked when the border fell. She has been worried about this since I arrived at the castle. Probably since the border was put in place. She finally clears her throat, speaking softly.

"Please keep me updated on their numbers. Increase our own. How are our troops doing?"

"Very well. Erik's training has been beneficial, and we are ahead of schedule with the new recruits." She nods, her hands tightening against her chair. I drag my fingers across hers, offering her a slight touch. She rises, dismissing everyone with instructions to implement the new proclamation. She leans over the table as everyone leaves, staring at the proclamation and documents Henry gave her.

Once the last guards have stepped out of the room, leaving only her and me, she plops back into her chair, looking defeated. I push her chair back from the table, kneeling before her.

"How long until we need to be wherever requires these formal clothes?"

Jasmin glances down at her gown, sighing softly. "Not long. Maybe a half hour?"

"Good."

My hand grabs her ankle, sliding up her leg under her dress. She looks ready to stop me but bites her lip instead. I take this as my cue to continue. With both hands on her legs, I caress her calves, knees, then lift the hem of her dress up as my hands reach her inner thighs. My lips find the soft sensitive spot just inside her knees, causing her to shiver with desire. I wrap my arms around her ass, sliding her closer to the edge. She gasps softly as I press her thighs apart with my face. Her thighs shake under my hands as I massage her strong muscles.

Her scent engulfs me when I move her thighs, exposing her cunt. I groan, pressing my forehead into her stomach. The smooth material of the dress glides over her stomach, giving me access to the parts I desperately want. Jasmin runs her fingers through my hair, massaging my scalp. I hum under her touch, never wanting her hands to leave my head. I hoist her thighs over the arms of the chair, propping her open for me.

I drag my nose along her, breathing in her sweet scent. Swirling her clit lightly, I finally taste her, sliding my tongue down her opening. She moans and adjusts her hips to give me better access. My hands cup the side of her ass, keeping her right where I want her. I lick her from back to front again, then suck on the nub at the top. As I work here, I remember I forgot to shave today, leaving rough stubble on my face. She notices, grinding in different directions than usual, getting all the friction she can. I suck her clit harder, pulling it between my lips. She cries out, groaning loudly when I plunge my fingers deep inside her.

I twist my hand around several times, spreading my fingers inside her. My tongue is working her clit, switching between flicking and sucking. Her hands wrap around my head, holding me close as her orgasm grows. I turn my hand upside down, wiggling my fingers in a 'come hither' motion that sends her soaring. Right on cue, her tight cunt clenches around my fingers as she cries out with her orgasm. She is so beautiful with her head turned toward the sky. Her body tenses and jerks through her orgasm. My fingers work her gently down, letting her ease back to reality.

Slipping my fingers out of her, I grab my handkerchief, wiping off my fingers first, then wiping her cunt. I don't want to leave her dripping while we have a formal event to go to, not this time, anyway. I adjust my trousers, trying to will my own erection down. Now isn't the time to deal with that. I fold the handkerchief up, slipping it back into my pocket. Knowing that her fluids are tucked away safely in my pocket brings me more joy than something that devious should. We stand, and I help her adjust her clothing to a presentable fashion. She wraps her arms around me, trying to kiss me, pressing her body against mine. I groan, pushing her away.

"I love you, little flower. But if you keep that up, we'll be late for your formal event."

Her eyes light up as she remembers the plans for the rest of the evening. She giggles, and I can't help but kiss her, erection be damned. I can pull off tented pants at a formal event. I'm certainly going to at this rate.

She wraps around my arm as we make our way to the door. Erik is waiting for us on the other side, looking disturbed.

"Oh, shit, Erik. I'm so sorry," Jasmin starts. "I forgot you were taking over for us." She cringes through her apology. I feel bad, too, but at this point, I'm pretty sure it's common knowledge we're going to fuck everywhere.

"It's okay, Queen." Erik flashes her a quick grin, "I understand the feeling." Jasmin laughs loudly, but it takes me a full minute to realize he is talking about Bea. My sister. That he is fucking. I whine loudly as we walk through the halls. Their laughter grows louder at my reaction. I don't need to hear about Bea. Though, I suppose he also doesn't want to stand guard while his wife's brother fucks someone. Maybe we should be more careful with the guards around, but that doesn't sound like something I'll stop and think about.

"Where are we going?" We're walking through the halls, headed toward the dining area. It doesn't make sense that we would wear formal clothes to go to the dining hall. All the formal events have taken place in other areas. We stop outside the door, leaving me with a perplexed look. Jasmin wraps her arms around my shoulders, pulling me down to her face.

"I love you," she whispers. Then Erik pulls open the door.

Suddenly, loud noises and strong smells fill the air. People are yelling, "Happy Birthday!" Colorful streamers and banners decorate the room, with matching tablecloths and napkins. The aromas are overwhelming. It's one of my favorite meals, seared duck with fresh vegetables. There is even cake on the table, with a few other desserts. Everything smells amazing. So many of my friends are in the room, and everyone is wearing formal clothing. Mikhail and several people that work in the fields. All of our friends here in the castle. Then I spot Ma and Claire. Jasmin drops her arms, pushing me toward them.

Ma and Claire rush to me, and I hug them tightly. I've missed them so much since they left. After living with them my entire life, it's a strange feeling to only see them every few months. They both wish me a happy birthday, and it occurs to me that this is all for me. I haven't celebrated my birthday in years and honestly forgot when it was. It isn't a big deal, not something that needs to be celebrated, but this party is terrific.

I glance around, looking for Jasmin. She is with Dahlia, deep in conversation. She is probably recounting the meeting, so I'll leave her alone. Ma pulls me over to the table with Bea; Erik sits by her side, his arm loosely draped over her shoulder. The novelty of my older sister being in a serious relationship with a man is starting to wear off. I feel uncomfortable realizing he could hear me eating Jasmin's pussy earlier. At least he can ignore that fact and act normal.

As if she can hear my thoughts, Jasmin walks over and sits on the other side of Claire. Dahlia follows, sitting on Jasmin's other side. Jasmin and Claire start a conversation, chatting so comfortably you wouldn't know they aren't actually sisters. Ma and Bea are talking about the baby. Ma is undoubtedly very excited, while Bea is still more reserved about the news.

Around the room, other people chat, enjoy each other's company, and have a lovely time. My heart fills with warmth at the people here to celebrate with me, even something as mundane as another birthday. We eat dinner and the most decadent cake I have ever had. Jasmin says the cook used to bake everything before the curse. It makes sense because this is the best thing I have ever tasted in my entire life.

After dinner is cleared, the tables are pushed to the side, and people begin dancing. A small band is set up in the corner I overlooked before, and they create joyful music. I try to get Jasmin or Dahlia to dance first, but Claire beats them to me. I can't deny my baby sister a dance, so I sweep her away onto the dance floor. She is surprisingly good at dancing. I ask her where she learned to dance, and suddenly she has nothing to say. I begin pestering her with questions about boys and girls. She gladly whisks away when the song is done.

Jasmin is dancing with Kian now, and I'm unsure where Dahlia is. Ma comes over, and I dance with her for a few songs. She comments that she hasn't been dancing since Da died. My heart aches at her statement. She deserves happiness, too.

Finally, I get a chance to dance with Jasmin. We circle around the dance area in a fluid motion, matching the music perfectly. These dances aren't as structured as formal events. These are more fun, though. We get to move the way we want to. I sneak kisses with Jasmin as we dance, thrilled she planned all this for me.

Soon, the band winds down, and people wander off independently. I can't explain how happy this evening has made me. Everyone is so willing to celebrate with me, for me. And my family is here. I am overwhelmed with happiness and gratitude. Jasmin instructs me to walk Ma and Claire back to their room, and they will meet me back in ours. I kiss her cheek and Dahlia's, as I can no longer avoid touching her. She had a hand in this party, too.

Ma is staying in the room I was in as a bachelor, and Claire has her own room beside Ma. I help Claire to bed first, tucking her in and promising her more fun tomorrow. She is asleep before I even leave the room. Ma is leaning against the door, watching me as I walk toward her to exit Claire's room.

"I've been thinking, Clem," she starts as we enter her room. "With Bea being pregnant and you and Jasmin being serious, maybe we should relocate." My eyebrows shoot up at her. I would love for them to be here. I practically begged for months, and she always said no. Of course, Bea getting pregnant would be the trick. "Your father loved the house. He worked so hard for it. But I would be remiss if I kept that over time with my grandchildren. I imagine Jasmin will have lots of support, but with her parents gone, your children deserve loving family members." Oh, that's right. I have yet to tell her about that.

"Oh, Ma," I glance through the hallway to be sure no one is around and Claire is still in her room. I don't want this information to be widespread. We've managed to keep a wrap on it, but that will only last so long if we aren't careful. I close the door and walk into the room, moving closer to her. She looks confused and concerned about my actions.

"Clem, forget I said anything. It's fine. I have a charming home and can still come to visit frequently. I didn't mean to overstep."

"Ma," I chuckle softly at her doubt. I guess I come by that honestly. "Sit down. I need to tell you things. You are obviously more than welcome at the castle. We have invited you before, and that invitation still stands. But I need to tell you some things first." She sits on the bed next to me, listening intently. She is such a great listener. Whenever I have a problem, she is always a good person to talk to. I have missed her so much.

"Jasmin is infertile." Ma doesn't react, but I give her a moment to process that. "We won't be having children together." Ma is deep in concentration, processing this information. She finally nods, bringing her eyes to me.

"What will she do about an heir?"

I shrug. "We haven't discussed it, really. We plan to break the curse, deal with the aftermath, and later, in the future, we'll worry about that stuff. It isn't important right now." She drops her hand to mine, squeezing it tightly.

"Of course, Clem. I'm just glad you are happy now. I'm sure those things will work out in the future." I nod, squeezing her hand back. I'm relieved she isn't upset by this. I knew she wouldn't be devastated, but she has talked about grandchildren for years since Bea and I were old enough to consider marriage. At least she still gets to be close to Bea. Maybe Claire one day, especially if she is already learning dances with boys.

"There's one more thing, too." Her eyes show caution but also curiosity. "This isn't public knowledge. Only about ten people know; we want to keep it that way. But you'll notice whether I tell you or not, so I might as well explain it." Now she is more frustrated with my rambling. I snicker at her expression before explaining. "Jasmin, Dahlia, and I are in a triad. We believe it's needed to break the curse, and we have gotten closer than Jasmin and I have at breaking it." Ma looks shocked now. Her eyes are wide as she stares at me. I'm not even sure if she is still breathing at this point.

"A triad? The three of you, together?" I nod, giving a casual shrug. I do not want to go into much detail on that topic with my mother. There are some limits to what I want to discuss with her. "How do you know the curse is close to breaking?"

"The border has been weakening. Many smaller aspects of the curse are changing, too. Jasmin's hair was short because of the curse, and it's growing. Harvests have been better than we have seen in years. And we learned Dahlia was asleep under a spell. That's why she woke up during our wedding. We were as close as the two of us could get then." Ma nods, understanding what I am saying but still processing all this information.

"So the thunder and lightning are part of the curse?"

"Yes." I don't need to elaborate beyond that. Hopefully, she doesn't ask. We sit in silence for several moments. Ma is staring off at the wall, deep in thought.

"Okay," she starts, but it sounds weak. "Okay, thank you for telling me." We both stand, giving each other a hug.

"Do you still want me to tell Jasmin you want to relocate here?" She hasn't said anything about that topic, but I just dropped a lot of complicated information on her. I don't want her to feel forced or in an awkward position. She looks up at me, smiling, shaking her head clear of her thoughts.

"Yes. Yes, of course. Bea's baby needs a grandmother, and it sounds like you will need a mother to help you through all this." She chuckles, brushing some hair off my face in a loving manner. I give her a soft smile, glad she still wants to be here. I could definitely use a mother around here.

"Good. I'm sorry things are so difficult, but I'm thrilled you are here." I pull her into a hug again, wrapping my arms around her as she places her over my shoulders.

"Life is difficult, Clem. Don't ever apologize for doing what makes you happy."

Chapter 33

DAHLIA

I can still see her in my mind. The young dark-skinned girl that lived on the farm with her parents. She had no idea they were underpaid and used purely for profit by the farm owners. She didn't know that her parents were barely valued more than the cattle and lands they cared for. She didn't realize the light-skinned girls she played with outside in the evenings had been in a schoolhouse all day, learning from people with proper educations. She didn't know mothers weren't the ones to teach their daughters to read, write, add, and subtract. She didn't know any of that.

She did know that her family wasn't the same as theirs. She knew something was different when the light-skinned girls went home to a massive house, and she stayed in a tiny one-bedroom hut with her exhausted parents and little brother. She didn't know they were treated better there than they would be when they were sold with Vesper. That wasn't something she knew at the time. Her parents did their best to hide the darkness of their lives.

What the young girl with the long braids knew was that boys kissed girls. And sometimes girls kissed girls, but you couldn't tell anyone. It wasn't right to kiss other girls. But she knew, even at that young age, that she wanted to kiss the girls. Sometimes she wanted to kiss a boy, but kissing girls was always what she wanted to do. She wanted to lift their dresses and discover what was beneath. She wanted to kiss their lips, taste their soft, delicate skin hidden beneath layers of lace and cotton. She always knew that.

But if you had told that young girl that she would move away and meet a short, light-skinned girl that wanted to kiss girls, too, she probably wouldn't have believed you. If you had told that little girl that she would kiss and fall in love with the short girl, she definitely wouldn't have believed you. Then if you told her that girl would be a queen one day, that would change the entire kingdom for her; the dark-skinned girl would have called you crazy, asking if you need to be sent to the asylum. And if you told her that her story doesn't end there, that it continues with a tall, strong farm hand that would love both girls fiercely and equally? Well, that young girl would have laughed at you. She would have told you fairy tales don't exist in the real world. That little girls like her don't end up in stories like that. She knew that wouldn't be her happy ending.

Now, I sit in this ornate chair, in a silk robe, in the Queen's chamber, waiting for that strong, tall man to return to us. My logical brain knows this is my reality now. This is all real. I am living in this fantasy, and it's lovely and agonizing. However, my unreasonable brain says this can't be real. I can't have Jasmin and Clem; that is just absurd. I chuckle at the thoughts running through my mind: doubt and uncertainty. I'm not familiar with this much doubt. I have always been confident in my decisions. Clem and Jasmin are both sure of our relationship. But now that I can have it, my unreasonable brain is drowning me in doubt and disbelief.

She steps out of the bathroom, also wearing a silk robe. Her dark hair brushes her shoulders as she slinks through the room, looking relaxed and comfortable in this space. We have been working on the details of this specific part of the night for days. She convinced Emmeline to keep Finn for the night, giving us some privacy. She mentioned several activities she wanted to do for Clem, but my unreasonable brain fills me with doubt at every suggestion.

She kneels in front of me, placing her hands on my thighs. My chest squeezes as she rubs my legs. From the first time I saw her, I loved her with everything I had. That isn't something I have ever doubted. I've always known Jasmin was it for me. I lean down, pressing my lips against hers in a soft kiss. Butterflies soar around my stomach as she kisses me back.

"You ready for this?" Her words clank through my mind as she settles back on her feet. I sigh while she slips her hands under my robe, sliding her fingers closer and closer to my cunt. I may not be ready for everything she wants to do, but I am always ready for her to touch me like that. I scoot down in the chair, her hands rising closer to my hips. I just need her to touch me.

Clem's voice sounds from the hall, wishing the guards a good night. Jasmin's grin grows to epic contagious proportions. Even with all my self-doubt, I can't help but feel some excitement over her plans. She gives me a quick wink as she walks toward the bed, ensuring everything is in place. It is; we both know everything is where it needs to be. I adjust my position as Clem finally opens the door and walks inside.

"Stop." I use a voice as stern as I can muster. He freezes, looking at me, confused about what is going on.

"Stay where you are and remove your clothes." His eyebrows rise at me. In my peripheral vision, Jasmin is grinning, giddy with excitement. Clem glances at her but does as he is told, removing his shirt slowly. He takes his time undoing each button and then tossing it aside. His muscles are strong, defined but not intimidating. Jasmin says his skin was more golden when he worked in the fields last year, but he is still beautiful. He finally removes his trousers, standing naked near the door. Both Jasmin and I take a moment to appreciate his form. She saunters over to him, pulling the tie from his hair, letting it fall down his shoulders. He hasn't cut his hair in a while, and it falls down his back, longer than Jasmin's but not as long as mine.

I walk over to the two of them. Jasmin has her fingers tangled in his hair, but his eyes focus on me. Jasmin asked me to take charge of the activities tonight, but I'm not as confident as Clem and don't know what to say or how to say it. Instead of speaking, I pull him into a kiss, letting my fingers brush against his hardening cock. Jasmin circles around him, dragging her hands all over his body.

"Bed, now." I incline my head in that direction, giving him clear but straight-forward instructions. His smirk says he knows I'm uncomfortable, but he won't make things difficult for me. He climbs onto the bed, settling in the middle. I pull Jasmin to the end of the bed with me. I feel more confident and willing to take control with her, but I still don't use many words. I untie her robe, brushing it off her shoulders. It drops to the floor, piling at her feet. My lips find her's in a fiery kiss. Her small tease earlier wasn't enough, and I want more now. Plus, Clem is watching. He enjoys watching us together. He stretches back, propping one arm behind his head. With the other, he slowly strokes his cock, watching us intensely.

"Hands off!" My words are quick and short, startling Jasmin. Clem holds his hand up in defense, then places it behind his head with the other. I turn my attention back to Jasmin but realize he probably won't follow my instructions for long. He has self-control when he wants it, but only when he wants to maintain that. I nod toward him, silently telling her to deal with him. She crawls across the bed, hovering over his body. Her ass is in the air, wiggling for my pleasure. My core throbs with desire as I watch her. Gods, I can't wait to get a piece of her.

Jasmin restrains his hands, tying them to the headboard. We practiced knots when we could get away from Clem to make them tighter and more secure. We don't want him to get away before we say he can. Once he is secure, I slip my robe off, letting it fall with Jasmin's. She slinks down the bed to me again, pulling me into her arms. Her lips close around my nipple. I wrap my hands around her head, holding her close. My eyes shut, enjoying the feeling of her tongue on my budding nipple.

Clem is biting his lip, cock standing straight up while his eyes focus on us. A wry grin spreads on my face. I pull Jasmin's head back, looking down at her. Her eyes are glazed with lust, and her lips are pink and puffy from their ministrations. Unable to stop myself, I kiss her deeply, holding her in place as my tongue explores her mouth. I've never been particularly rough with her, but holding her head in my hands, having that control over her...I definitely see the appeal of such actions.

I break the kiss and push her in Clem's direction. It's a soft push, not very forceful. I still can't bring myself to be harsh to her. She may like it, but I don't, really. She crawls over him, stopping when she is just over his thigh. I join her on the other side, pulling her back into a searing kiss. Clem groans as he watches, unable to touch or join. I slowly guide her down until we are hunched over Clem's waist. I finally break my kiss with her, a bit unwillingly, if I'm honest. Her lips instantly wrap around his cock. Clem moans, tipping his head back in pleasure. I caress my hand on the inside of his thigh, brushing my fingers against Jasmin's breasts and up to cup Clem's balls. I have no experience with men's pleasure. I've watched Jasmin enough to get an idea of what to do, though. Based on his response, this is the correct action.

Clem is tugging his wrists against his restraints, trying to break free. I'm glad Jasmin insisted on practicing so much. The rope is holding now. She swallows him down more while I continue to massage his balls. I would love to take care of Jasmin, but we agreed to focus on him tonight. After a moment, she pulls off, looking at me. She wipes the corner of her mouth, giving me a devilish smirk. She kisses me, tasting slightly of Clem. When she pulls away, I lean down, pressing a soft kiss to the tip of Clem's cock. I've never had a dick in my mouth. The thought still makes me nervous, but the look in Clem's eyes leads me to believe I can do no wrong at this point. I wrap my lips around the tip, swirling my tongue around the top. He groans as his hips wiggle under me. He only moves side to side, but I'm positive he would prefer to thrust deep into my mouth.

Jasmin moves back onto the bed with the extra sashes we brought out. I lick the length of his rigid member as she ties one over his eyes. He huffs in frustration but doesn't say anything. As she wraps one around his mouth, I instruct him to snap. He does, understanding that is his way of communicating with us now. Once his eyes and mouth are covered, Jasmin and I climb off the bed. We don't want him to know where we are and who is doing what to him. As soon as we are away from him, she pulls me tight with one arm around my shoulders, the other going straight to my pussy. She kisses me deeply as her fingers plunge inside me, eliciting a moan in our kiss. She swallows the sound before breaking free. She gives a quick peck to my nose, then climbs back on the bed, leaving me desperate for more.

Jasmin settles on Clem's chest, with her back to his face. She grinds against his stomach, wrapping her hands around his cock, stroking slowly. I climb up from his feet, bringing his legs together while rubbing them teasingly. I straddle his thighs, watching Jasmin for our next move. I should have drank more wine. My nerves are tangling with my desire, leaving me with this overwhelming feeling. She grabs my cheek with her free hand, bringing me in for a gentle kiss.

At some point, I mentioned interest in having Clem inside me. It's not an experience I have had before. The boy I was with before barely got the tip inside, and it wasn't a pleasant experience like Jasmin has with Clem. Jasmin decided tonight is the night, and I couldn't agree more. But as I watch his huge cock slide through her tiny hand, I worry about how this will feel. I've never had more than a couple of fingers inside me. He is impossibly larger than Jasmin's fingers. Her fingers move off his cock, reaching out to my pussy. She slips two fingers inside me. Gods, she feels so good inside me. I close my eyes, savoring the feel of her touch.

She tugs her hand inside me, guiding me up and over Clem. My breathing increases with nervousness, excitement, and arousal. Jasmin presses the tip of his cock against my opening as she pulls her fingers out. I bite my lip, unsure how this will play out. Her hand wraps around the base of his cock, rubbing it around my opening. It feels so good. I want more. I want to know what it feels like inside me. She holds it still as I lower myself just a fraction, notching his cock inside me. It's so big; I'll never be able to fit him. Just as I'm about to pull off and move away, Jasmin wraps her arms around me. Her lips find my ear, whispering that I can do this, giving soft kisses and nibbles. One hand cups my breast, flicking my nipple with her thumb. Her other hand finds my clit, circling it slowly.

I moan softly against her shoulder, sinking lower on him. I feel so full but so good, and he's not even halfway in. Jasmin's hand drops from my clit to his hips, pressing down on him. He was about to thrust inside me. As good as this feels, I am not ready for that. Jasmin's lips find mine, distracting me from those thoughts. Her soft lips, combined with the fullness in my cunt, are overpowering. I can't think of anything else. Her hand grabs my hip, guiding me until I reach the tip, then presses me back down. I take more of him in this time but pause when it stings. Her thumb circles my clit again as I adjust to the sensation of a cock inside me.

Her hand guides me up and down several more times until I sink a little lower. I can't take any more of him. I pause momentarily, wrapping both hands around Jasmin's face as I kiss her, swirling my tongue with hers. Clem moans, clenching his muscles to stop from thrusting. Jasmin breaks our kiss, grinning at his reaction. Her hands find my hips, but I grab the magic fun ball before I start moving, tapping it to start the vibrations. I slip it between her and Clem, letting it settle against her clit. She grinds against it on his stomach, then guides me up and down over his cock. She sets the pace, wiggling my hips in different directions. Her lips find my neck, biting lightly. I grab her breasts, squeezing them in my fingers as I bounce on Clem.

Jasmin wraps her fingers around the base of Clem's member, covering the part I can't. Her actions also provide extra pressure on my clit. This is entirely different from anything I have ever done; Jasmin takes her hands off my hips, letting me move in the best ways. I continue in the way she set, enjoying it more than I ever thought I would. Her free hand is all over my body, tingling my skin, driving me insane.

"Snap before you come, Clem." Jasmin has the headspace to remember that. I am wholly absorbed in this feeling of ecstasy and haven't even considered his orgasm. I'm just busy chasing mine. It's getting so close. Jasmin's hands and Clem's cock are almost too much for me. Just as that thought settles, Jasmin presses her thumb against my clit. My entire body lights up, sending shockwaves through every vein, every muscle, every inch of my being. I drop against Jasmin, unable to hold my own weight. She supports me by keeping her hand on my clit through my orgasm. Just as I am calming down, Clem snaps several times. Jasmin guides me off Clem. I slide off, laying down beside him. Once I'm out of the way, Jasmin wraps her mouth around his cock, swallowing him whole. He yells out behind his gag as his hips thrust into her mouth. He doesn't hold back as he jerks wildly beneath her. She keeps her lips around him, gagging several times as he thrusts.

The magic fun ball has fallen on the bed. I grab it, placing it back against Jasmin's clit. She groans around his cock, causing Clem to jerk and moan again. I stroke Jasmin's pussy, feeling it tighten with her orgasm. I hold the toy against her, letting her ride out her pleasure as Clem calms beneath her. When she settles, I remove the item, tapping it off and tossing it aside. I rub my hands over her back and ass, soothing her pulsing body. She releases Clem's cock, and her face is just resting on his thigh. She rests with her eyes closed as her breathing slows down.

Clem snaps his fingers several times. Jasmin and I look back at him, giggling because we forgot he was tied up. She unties one hand while I remove his blind-fold. Jasmin removes the gag while I free his other wrist. When free, he quickly wraps his arms around me, pulling me tight against his body. His lips find mine in a searing kiss. I'm caught off guard at first, not expecting such a strong reaction from him. My arms finally settle over his shoulders as I return the kiss. It becomes more tender, more intimate. Jasmin chuckles as she climbs off the bed. She returns a moment later. Clem breaks the kiss, looking down at his lap. Jasmin is wiping him up. She reaches to do the same for me, but I grab the cloth from her. My pussy is already sensitive from the orgasm and the extra stretch to accommodate his cock. I want to be as gentle as possible.

We crawl back into bed after we are all cleaned or somewhat clean. Jasmin and I lay on either side of Clem, his arms wrapped around us. We sit for several minutes, and Jasmin holds my hand on his chest. Being connected with both brings a peace I never knew I could have.

"Best birthday ever," Clem says slowly, sending all of us into a fit of giggles. He kisses mine and Jasmin's forehead as we settle against his chest again. This is the happiest I have been in years. These two are my world. I would have never thought I could say that about Clem. I didn't think my animosity toward him would ever disappear, but he is remarkable. I look at both of them, taking in the relaxed, happy looks on their faces. I know deep in my heart this is the way things are supposed to be. It was always meant to be the three of us.

"I love you." My words are soft, almost as if I don't believe them. Jasmin squeezes my hand in hers. Clem turns his head until his lips land on my forehead. He presses a soft kiss before speaking.

"I love you, too." Butterflies soar through my stomach, giddy with excitement at this new chapter in our lives.

Part Four

OLEANDER

Chapter 34

JASMIN

Dahlia just confessed her love for Clem, and he returned the affection. My eyes close as I let my imagination run, just for a second, and pretend that the curse isn't real. People aren't judgmental, and the three of us can be together and be happy. I bask in the idea of the moments we could share together, the experiences, the joys, and upsets. I revel in the thought of a full life of love with the two people that mean the most to me.

Outside, the thunder is booming in the sky. The lightning is so bright; the crashes are nearly deafening. Even with the curtains pulled, knowing it is the middle of the night, light filters in through the cracks in flashing spurts. It's beautiful and breathtaking and utterly terrifying. I close my eyes, breathing in Clem's familiar scent, letting him calm my raging thoughts. As happy as I want us to be, I don't get that reality. The curse is still in place, people are still assholes, and I still don't know what kind of life I can offer them.

As if sensing my doubts, Clem's arm tightens around me. Dahlia drags a blanket over the three of us. Clem removes his hand to pull the blanket higher around my neck. I nuzzle into him, burying my face in his neck. Dahlia's hand begins to stroke my side, soothing my nerves. My mind slows, drifting off to sleep as Clem and Dahlia start whispering. They are discussing the storm outside, but my body is falling too hard for me to stay focused.

The bedroom door slams open, startling me out of my drifting slumber. I sit up suddenly, looking around to figure out what burst into my room.

"Jasmin!" Kian is practically shouting at me. He looks disheveled, his clothes wrinkled and not appropriately tied. "You must come outside now!" Emmeline rushes in behind him in a similar state. A cool draft flows through the room, causing my nipples to peak. Due to the state of sleep I am in, I can't process that I'm naked and exposed in front of everyone. Sure, they've all seen me, but Kian is officially my advisor now. He shouldn't see me in this state.

While my mind tries to catch up to what's happening, Clem pulls the blanket back over my shoulder.

"Jasmin! I need you to move faster! Now!" Kian's tone is urgent as he and Emmeline rush around the room, gathering clothes for us. My brain is starting to function again as she brings a thin dress over to me. Kian tosses Clem trousers and a shirt. Emmeline hands a dress over to Dahlia as they fret over getting us dressed and out of bed. Clem and I begin whining, and Dahlia does what she is told. None of us are in the proper headspace for this sort of interruption.

"Okay, Kian. I have clothes on. Now tell me what this is about."

"No," he shakes his head, grabbing shoes from our closet. "You need to be outside." I groan, annoyed with his theatrics, slipping on the flat shoes he hands me. Emmeline has the decency to give me a mug of water and surprises me by placing a crown on my head. What in all the holy gods has gotten into these two? Without saying another word, the five of us walk outside at a pace far faster than I would like in the middle of the night.

Kian leads us outside by the gardens. I was aware of the storm brewing outside, but I was entirely unprepared for the reality of it. The ground feels as if it is shaking beneath our feet. The sky is flashing as bright as the sun at high noon, except in spectacular colors. Reds and oranges and blues and purples dash across the sky. The air feels magical, the lightning and thunder kissing our skin playfully. The magic is in full force, putting on a brilliant show.

My eyes rise to the sky to see where the lightning is dancing. A circle has formed around the zenith with jagged edges and is widening. I watch for several moments, convinced my eyes are deceiving me. I turn my head to look around at the crowd forming in the grass. Many of my friends, workers, and others living in the castle have come to view the fantastic storm outside. Clem's family is near the wall, not far from Dahlia's family. Erik and Henry are surrounded by several guards while Bea approaches us. Lucia is in a group of witches who are huddled together, whispering and pointing at different areas in the sky. My breath quickens as the reality of this settles in my stomach.

"Kian?" I grab his arm to get his attention and steady myself. "Is this what I think it is?" His wide smirk tells me everything I need to know, but I want to hear him say it. "Answer me with words, Kian!" Clem steps next to me, taking his hand in mine. I squeeze in acknowledgment but don't take my gaze off my advisor.

"Yes, my Queen. You've done it. You've broken the curse." A loud boom sounds behind us as a flash of purple explodes through the sky, briefly tinting everything in the yard. Tears well in my eyes, making it hard to see anymore. I look around the yard, wiping my eyes with my free hand. I'm searching for Dahlia, who is no longer by my side. I turn back to Clem to see he has pulled her close, tucking her into his side. A chuckle bursts from my lips, then another, and another, until I devolve into a fit of laughter.

Clem pulls me into his chest, and Dahlia wraps around my back as the laughter turns to tears. For nearly ten years, we have lived in this cursed kingdom. I stayed confined to my castle for years, unwilling to face what had happened. Years of my life were spent in confinement and solitude as a form of atonement, self-inflicted punishment. The whole time, the people I needed most were closer than I ever could have imagined. Dahlia and Clem squeeze me between them tightly, whispering soft words of love and adoration.

Fear strikes my body as quickly as lightning bursts through the sky. I pull away from Dahlia and Clem, searching the yard again. As wonderful as it is that the curse is broken, our borders are opening. There is a band of soldiers north of Vadried, and that's only what we know of. I frantically scan the area, finally finding Henry and Erik.

"Are we prepared?" My words are rushed as I reach their position. Both turn to me with grave looks but not fear. Neither man is scared, but that doesn't bring me enough comfort.

"Yes, my Queen." Henry looks more relaxed than I anticipated. This also doesn't calm my raging nerves. "We have instructed every post to send out extra guards when there are signs of the border falling. We have been preparing for this moment for months. Spend time with your loved one, Queen Jasmin. We will update you in the afternoon." He offers a warm smile. I take a deep breath, trying to settle my emotions, but I can't find a way to make it work.

I turn back, looking around for Kian. Surely he has some other update that I need to deal with. The border certainly cannot just be falling without any kind of chaos. Clem is standing with his family, all smiling and laughing about something. Dahlia is with her family, but they look more somber. Maybe they need some assistance with some crazy situation. Just before I reach her, I spot Kian standing with Emmeline. Both watch the skies, not talking or touching but standing together.

"Kian, what do we need to do? Are there any concerns over the magic lifting? We should probably gather everyone for a meeting to discuss what happens next." He slowly lowers his eyes to me, confused about what I said to him.

"Milady, there are no concerns. We do not need a meeting as we have already had many. The Lords are prepared to deal with their villages to avoid chaos. The guards have already been told what to expect and how to handle it. Their numbers are more than enough to handle this situation." He pauses, assessing me, then Emmeline before speaking again. "The only thing left for you to do is enjoy your accomplishment. Mingle with your people. Let them congratulate you. Then try to sleep before we meet with the guards for an update."

Outrage courses through me. The border is finally collapsing, and everyone's answer is to spend time with my people?? We need to be prepared! Reading my thoughts on my face, Kian wraps his arms around my shoulders, spinning me toward Dahlia and her family.

"You have already taken care of everything. Everyone knows what to do except you, apparently," his chuckle does not amuse me. I cross my arms over my chest in frustration. "You are well prepared for this exact situation. Let your people do their job. It's been a long day. Watch the skies for a few more minutes, then go sleep. I assure you, we will wake you if something catastrophic happens."

I take a deep breath, forcing it out my nose. It doesn't calm me, but Kian has a point. The shock of the curse finally being lifted, combined with my stress and the long day, has left me feeling ill-prepared. I know everything is in place for this exact event. I can let my people do what they have been trained to do. We have discussed this for months since we realized how close we were.

Clem is with his family, all of whom look happy. Erik has joined the group, his arm wrapped around Bea, keeping her close. The two are so wonderful together. Despite my fear and concern for the future, joy spreads through my body at the thought of this expanding family I am part of. I step beside Clem, who wraps his arms around my shoulders when he notices me. He kisses my forehead then I turn to look at him. His smile is contagious. He is unbelievably happy at this moment. He squeezes my shoulders as Ada grins between the four of us. I glance around the area, realizing Claire is missing.

"Where is Claire?"

"Still sleeping," Ada answers softly.

"That child could sleep through canon blasts," Bea laughs. Clem chuckles, his body shaking against my own. I lean into him, letting him support my exhausted body.

"Oh! Jasmin," Clem starts, looking down with an even more excited look than before. I cannot fathom how he is so happy at this moment. Why isn't he more stressed about the border falling? While it is contagious, and I am delighted for him, I am also somewhat dumbfounded by his sheer joy. "Ma wants to stay at the castle with Claire permanently." Ah, that explains his happiness. Ada nods slowly. She looks like she will add something, but Clem continues speaking. "She wants to be closer to Bea and us, especially now that a baby is involved," he nods his head at Bea, who looks surprised by this statement. Apparently, Ada didn't tell Bea this.

"Only if it isn't a problem, Queen Jasmin," Ada adds quickly. "I'm sorry I didn't tell you, Bea. I wanted to get permission before I mentioned it to you." Her face is apologetic. She is such a kind and thoughtful woman. I don't know that she will ever legally be family, but I am so glad to have her in my life.

"Of course, it isn't a problem. In the next day or two, I will arrange a suite to be prepared for you and Claire to settle into permanently. We can probably spare Clem and Erik to help you pack your home and bring things here, but that may be a few weeks." Clem's arms tighten over my shoulders. Happiness and excitement are practically radiating off him.

"Please, don't go out of your way for us, Your Highness. We can sort things out." I wish I had a mother as soft and sweet as Ada. Or anyone close to me. There were always friendly people in the castle when I was a child, but there were limits on how close they could get to me. Even Emmeline, who is as soft and sweet as they come, didn't come into my life until I was older. I would do anything to keep Ada close to me, if only for support and guidance. She will be a tremendous asset around the castle.

Bea announces that she is exhausted and needs to go back to bed. Erik says he will check in with Henry before going with her. Ada tells us she is also going to bed, and Clem offers to walk with her. She tries to stop him, but I tell him to go. He kisses me deeply before turning away to walk with his mother. A deep longing fills me, watching the pair walk away. I was never close to my mother and don't particularly want her back, but I still envy that relationship. Ada's love for her children shines through her every moment. I never felt that from my parents and can only hope that Ada will share those feelings with me one day.

Making my way toward Dahlia, I can see she has tears in her eyes. Sunette told me a while ago how sick Sabeko is. He has handed off nearly all his duties to Zander, only checking into the stables on rare occasions. I have not seen much of him because of my busy schedule. Dahlia has mostly kept me updated, and I got some information from Sunette. They have planned to leave after the border fell for a few weeks, and I suppose now they are finalizing those plans.

I wrap my arms around Dahlia, and she drops against my shoulder, great sobs escaping her. Her body shakes under my arms with the pain she is feeling. I squeeze her tightly, caressing her back in a soothing manner. Sunette's eyes are downcast, showing the sadness she feels right now.

"We will leave on the next boat," her words are simple but sting. Dahlia's arms wrap around my back as her cries grow stronger. I try to hold her tightly, but my exhausted body can only offer so much now. I have been through so many emotions in the past day that I can no longer say what's up and down.

"So soon?" I question. Dahlia pulls against my shirt, trying to hold herself up.

"Yes. It's better if we leave as soon as we can. Dahlia has been trained to take over my job in the greenhouse. It's mostly her jasmine plants anyway." Sunette's staccato accent highlights each syllable, making the words sound harsher than they are. Sunette ensured she covered all of her bases before the wall came down. After all, she did teach me much of what I know. If I am prepared, she is even more prepared.

I offer her a cart, food, and anything else she could possibly need. Zander is staying in their suite, caring for the rest of their things at the castle. We agree on when they will leave, so we can all be there to say goodbye. Sabeko and Sunette walk away, returning to their suite for rest before their long journey. It could take a month or more before they reach their home.

Dahlia and I are left standing, wrapped in each other's arms, unwilling to let go. I finally whisper that we should go back to bed and get some sleep. We will need it for the next few days. We stop by the kitchens, grabbing a couple bottles of wine. We could get in bed and be asleep before our heads hit the pillows, but after a day like today, the alcohol will help numb some of our toiling emotions. Dahlia asks after Clem, but I tell her he's too happy to be concerned with right now. We'll worry about him tomorrow. She chuckles at my comment, taking a long swig from the wine bottle before passing it to me. We barely finish the first bottle before we both collapse in exhaustion before Clem returns to the room. We'll find a way to be happy tomorrow. Tonight, we'll just settle for a fitful slumber.

Chapter 35

CLEM

The past day and a half have been an interesting battle of Jasmin expecting the worst, and nothing terrible actually happening. People celebrated in the streets. There were a few drunken fights across the villages, but there always are. The soldiers stationed near Vadried's border left once the border fell, not making contact. No one has rioted. A few people from each village are packing to leave, but most people are just excited about the possibilities they have now. A few emissaries are being trained to foster trade with other kingdoms, but we haven't sent anyone out yet. Jasmin wants to wait another week before we try to send them to ensure our kingdom is prepared for anything. We are, but she doesn't believe it.

Dahlia, on the other hand, has a reason to be depressed. Today, Sunette and Sabeko are leaving to return to their homeland. Sunette plans to return at some point, but Sabeko will not. He has been sick for a long time and wants to be with his long-lost family in his final days. I respect his decision, but my heart aches for Dahlia. She is losing her father, and her mother's future is uncertain. I do what I can to support her. I tried to remember what I needed when I lost my father, but the circumstances are so different I don't think our needs are the same.

Dahlia spent the day yesterday with her family while Jasmin and I attended the meetings. I don't think Dahlia has stopped crying since the border fell. I never expected it to be such a tragic event. I wasn't aware of her parents leaving before it fell. It had been mentioned, but the information didn't stick due to everything else happening.

Now, we stand outside on the front lawn. A carriage has been prepared to take Sunette and Sabeko to the coast in Tilrade, where they will get on a boat that has already been procured. Jasmin tried to convince them to wait until we knew travel across the sea would be safe, but Dahlia definitely inherited her stubbornness from them. Neither Sabeko nor Sunette would consider delaying any longer. They argued that it won't be safe later if it isn't safe now. I'm not sure their logic is sound, but we've all given up on arguing with them.

I stand on the steps, watching Dahlia and Jasmin say goodbye. Dahlia is fighting against sobs wracking through her body. Jasmin has tears in her eyes but is holding herself together better. Tomas and Zander are hugging Sunette and Sabeko; both also have tears streaming down their cheeks. Sabeko finally ushers Sunette into the carriage. She gives the castle a final, longing look before climbing in after her husband. The coachmen guide the horses onto the drive, leaving the castle behind them. I walk down, wrapping my arms around Jasmin and Dahlia. Dahlia turns into my chest, giving way to more tears. Jasmin leans against me, watching the carriage grow smaller in the distance.

I tug them into the castle, heading toward our room. Kian already agreed to keep things quiet for the morning for us, allowing them time to grieve. Emmeline has brought up food to sustain us for a while. I pull my girls into the bed, giving them mugs of water. They likely won't eat much, but I can insist on them drinking water. I banned wine from the room, at least for a few days. They want the alcohol, and I understand their desire. I want them to stay healthy, though. If their habits of the past day and a half have shown me anything, they won't make good decisions about their health for the next couple of days.

I pull them both against my chest, tugging the blanket over us. It's late summer, and the weather is still unbearably hot. They enjoy the comfort of a blanket, though. I found the thinnest one we have and wore thin clothes so I could still sit with them. I can be hot for a while if they get some comfort from it. I keep my arm wrapped around Dahlia but use my other arm to grab a book I selected.

I haven't had a chance to read to Jasmin the way I used to in a long time. I debated on what to select. I didn't want a love story or one with spicy scenes. They don't need that now, but I didn't want a tragedy. The last thing they need is more heartbreak. I didn't want to bore them with an instructional book. I finally settled on a book Kian gave me about witch folklore. Hopefully, both enjoy the storytelling and appreciate learning more about the witches. And if they don't hear a single word I say, at least they can lean against me for a little while.

Both rest against my chest, listening and occasionally sniffling as I read. I keep a more neutral tone instead of inflecting with the story. I'm trying to soothe my girls, not rouse them. Dahlia falls asleep first, her grief overwhelming her. I stroke her back softly as I read. Jasmin helps turn the page for a while, but soon she drifts off too. I read for a bit longer, ensuring both are sound asleep. Carefully, I maneuver my way out of bed, a tricky task from the middle of two sleeping women. As soon as I move, they snuggle together. I cover them back up with the blanket before leaving the room. I let the guards know they are sleeping and to find me if anyone tries to wake them.

I wander through the castle, noticing how different everything looks for the first time since the curse lifted. It's all the same; nothing has changed, but it seems brighter, as if the color has returned. The curse had placed a damper on the kingdom, and it's now lifted. I never noticed how dull things were before. Now, the colors in paintings are brighter, flowers have more pigmentation and even torches and candles seem to burn brighter.

Ma and Claire are near the library, standing in the hallway. Ma is chatting with the cook, while Claire looks bored and uninterested in whatever Ma discusses. I step beside Claire, nudging her side. She rolls her eyes at me, picking at something in her nails.

"You know, it's not very ladylike to pick your nails in public." Claire rolls her eyes at me again, but this time it's directed at me instead of commentary on her situation.

"It's also improper to roll your eyes at the King." We haven't actually discussed my position within the kingdom recently. Officially, my only title is Master of Gardens, but I have been working on more general tasks with Jasmin.

"You're not the King, Clem. Everyone knows that." Ouch, that hurt more than I am willing to admit.

"Hm, well, fine then. I suppose if I'm not King, then we don't have to keep you in the castle. I hear there are rooms in the stables. Maybe we'll just let you sleep with the horses now."

"You're still sleeping with the Queen, which means we get better treatment." I raise my eyebrows at her.

"Oh, really? So you get special privileges for doing nothing? Guess it's a good thing I'm sleeping with the Queen, then. Since you have no other skills." I tease her, knowing she has plenty of skills that could be useful. She's smart enough to work in the courts with the proper training and time.

She doesn't take to my jesting too well and kicks me in the shin. Even with her soft flat shoes, the impact still stings my leg. I grab my leg, hopping on my other foot to soothe the ache. The woman Ma was chatting with has walked away, and she is looking at one of the books in her hand.

"Ma! Claire just kicked me."

"What, Clem?" She briefly lifts her eyes to me, where I am hunched over, holding my shin. Claire is back to picking her nails again. Ma grabs her hands, forcing her to stop, barely giving me attention.

"Ma," I whine, "I said Claire kicked me." Ma finally looks at me, but her face says she is more shocked at me than Claire.

"Clematis Byrne," I wince at her use of my full name as I stand up straight. "Are you tattling on your sister?" I cringe, unhappy with how this whole conversation is going. Why is everyone against me now?

"Well, yes, Ma. She kicked me!"

"It's unbecoming of an adult, especially one in your position, to tattle on children." She turns and walks into the library without another word to me. I love my mother, but she doesn't offer sympathy when my sisters fight with me. Claire gives me a smug look, knowing Ma would take her side. I stick my tongue out at her, turning to walk away.

"That's fine, Claire. I'll just go prepare that room in the stables for you." I increase my speed just enough to egg her on.

"You better not, Clem." As I expected, she follows me, so I begin to run. She chases me through the halls, both laughing and yelling playful insults at each other as we go. In the front foyer, Finn sits with Emmeline while she chats with Kian. He jumps up, wagging his tail when he sees me. I glance back but don't see Claire right away. I slow enough to engage Finn and get him to run with me. We run through the halls together, racing toward the back garden. I look behind me again, wondering where Claire could be. I haven't heard her in several minutes. I wasn't running at full speed because I didn't want to get too far ahead of her. She should have been able to keep up.

As I slow down, Claire crashes into me from a side hallway. She wraps her arms and legs around me as we squeal over the impact. I wrap my arms around her, lifting her as I run behind Finn until we reach the door. Once I push the door open, Finn rushes into the yard, glad for someone to play with. He finds his favorite ball, bringing it over for me to throw. I set Claire down, tossing the ball. The run from where Claire jumped on me to the door wasn't long, but with the extra weight, I am winded. I lean against the wall as Finn runs after the ball, trying to catch my breath.

"Gods, Clem. I'm sorry for pushing you so hard. I forgot how old you've gotten. It must be tough for you to run short distances now." My shock, combined with the exertion, prevent me from responding right away. Claire reaches up, pushing a strand of hair back from my face. "Oh no, Clem! Is that gray hair already?"

"You little shit." Fuck the exhaustion. This insult will not be tolerated. I jolt to grab her, but she moves quicker, her small, agile body better at making quick movements. She jumps away from me, running through the grass. Finn joins us, running behind Claire. We continue hurling our insults at each other. She is far faster than I realized, racing through the yard just out of my grasp. She makes a loop, rushing back inside the castle. Watching her, I realize she is headed toward the throne room. It just so happens that I know a secret passage used by royalty to circumvent crowds. I dart down the hall, racing at full speed to get ahead of her.

I reach the intersection of the hall where she should be at any moment. I peek around the corner, spotting Claire about halfway down the hall. She turned back, looking for me. I take a deep breath, letting the air course through my pumping body. Then I jump out into the hallway. Claire screams at my sudden appearance, crashing into my chest. I laugh loudly, wrapping my arms around her. Finn barks excitedly, jumping to join in the play. I spin Claire around, causing her to squeal loudly. I finally put her down on her feet. She straightens her clothes.

"Gods, Clem. You're such an ass." Her words are rude, but she has a playful smirk. I feign being hurt, grabbing my chest.

"You wound me, Claire." I nudge her shoulders playfully as we begin ambling through the castle. "Ma may not care how mean you are, but I'm sure Bea will." The look she gives me is one of complete disbelief. She may have a point there.

"Really, Clem? You think Bea would take your side over mine?" She's called my bluff now.

"Okay, but Erik would take my side." Claire gives me a pompous look, puffing out her chest as she points to it.

"Nope. New niece. I'm the favorite now."

"Fuck." She's got me there. I haven't seen Erik interact with Claire much; he is always busy doing other things when they are together. I know Erik well enough to know he would take Claire's side over mine in almost every situation imaginable. I don't bother to correct that she would technically be his sister-in-law, not niece. The age difference between us has always been odd. Claire has a newlywed pregnant sister, while she is at least a decade away from that.

"Fine. Emmeline would... also take your side. Shit." I think for a moment, considering if any of my friends would take my side. Emmeline wouldn't just to spite me, especially in a playful manner. "Kian would take my side."

"Are you sure about that?" Claire has the confidence of someone with the world wrapped around her finger. Suddenly, I wonder if Kian would take my side. He might consider the choices for a moment, but in the end, I fear he would side with my little sister. They love teasing me around here.

"Okay. Dahlia would definitely take my side, though." I think. I'm not positive she would in this situation. She's happy to play along with Jasmin's games. She would probably also side with Claire just out of spite. I know they would all have my back in a serious situation, as they have many times before. But none of them would take my side in a play fight with my eleven-year-old sister.

"I like how you didn't even mention Jasmin." I sigh as we climb the stairs leading to Bea's suite. I didn't mean to come this way, but I'm not upset about it. The last time I saw Bea was when the border fell, and it would be nice to check in on her. Claire bumps into me playfully as we walk by a large window that overlooks one of the roads that leads to Vadried.

I pause, noticing a large caravan traveling down the road, heading toward the castle. Several carriages are surrounded by many guards, each with flags that I recognize as Hollyhock's. This is definitely an official visit from some royal or higher-ranking members of their court.

"Claire," I grab her shoulders, pushing her toward Bea's door. "Stay in there with Bea. If she isn't there, go find Ma and stay with her." She looks out at the caravan, a nervous look on her face.

"Who is it?" I finally look at her, breaking my stare out the window. I shrug in response.

"I don't know, but I want you to stay out of the way for now, okay?" She nods, strolling into Bea's suite. I nudge her, prompting her to speed up. Once she is finally inside, I turn and rush back to my room. I don't find anyone on my way to alert them. I'm sure others have noticed the group's arrival, but I hope Kian and Henry are notified first.

In our room, Jasmin sits in bed, reading a book. Dahlia is asleep with her head in Jasmin's lap. My heart swells at the sight of the two of them together. One benefit to being in a triad is there are more people to offer comfort in difficult situations. I walk over, momentarily forgetting why I rushed here. I give Jasmin a quick kiss, asking how Dahl is doing. I run my hand over her hair as Jasmin explains that she has been asleep since I left. Finn walks into the room, reminding me of my task.

"You need to get up and get dressed quickly. There is a caravan with Hollyhock flags coming down the road." Her face shows a flash of fear before she slides out of bed. We agree to leave Dahlia here, letting her sleep. Finn climbs into the bed, worn out from running with Claire and me. He curls up next to Dahlia, and she settles against him, not waking up. I wasn't sure how Finn would take to Dahlia, but since we've gotten closer, Finn has taken to her well.

Jasmin walks to her closet, rummaging around her things. I grab one of her crowns and place it on the vanity. I rush her along, wanting her to be down quickly to greet the party. She finally sighs from the closet, walking back into the main area.

"Fuck it. This is my kingdom, and I will wear these fucking leggings out." She is in quite a mood right now. I bring over her crown, kissing her forehead before raising the crown to place on her head.

"You look beautiful as you are, but at least wear the crown so they know who you are." Once it's on her head, I give her a quick but reassuring kiss. We walk from the room together, leaving Dahlia and Finn curled up on the bed. I guide her down to the foyer, where Kian is standing.

"Good, I was about to come find you. There is a caravan arriving from Holly-hock. We don't know who it is, though." She nods calmly, taking my arm as we all walk outside together. My nerves ramp up as the caravan moves closer. It's such an odd feeling. We were just here a few hours ago in heartbreaking conditions. Now we are here again, but the tension is high with the unknown visitors.

One of the caravans pulls to a stop in front of the steps. Jasmin squares her shoulders, waiting for whoever is inside to step out. The coachman climbs down from his seat, walking to the door slowly. There is no rush in his step, and he has the confidence of an experienced servant. He opens the door, and a man steps out in full regalia of Hollyhock. He steps to the side, squares his shoulders, and clears his voice.

"Presenting, Queen Oleander of Sweet Briar." What? Who is Queen Oleander? And why does she have the audacity to claim the title of Queen of Sweet Briar? Jasmin sucks in a small breath, squeezing her hand tightly around my arm. A tall woman in a full gown takes the hand of the coachman, climbing down from the carriage. She looks familiar, but I can't place her fast enough. My mind is reeling, trying to figure out why anyone would claim the title of Queen when Jasmin stands beside me. It's a bold move; I'll give her credit for that.

The woman steps down to the ground, adjusting her clothes, and finally looks at us. She wears a dark dress with intricate stitching. Her light-colored hair, I can't tell if it is blonde or grey, is pulled tightly in a bun on top of her head. She wears a small crown, not much larger than Jasmin's, but far less meaningful. It is a detailed design but meant for looks, not representation. Her gaze is cold and calculating.

As soon as I see her face in full, I know where I recognize her from. Anger courses through my body, outrage over her past actions. A surge of confusion follows, unsure how she is here now. I've only seen her in person once before, on the back of a horse as they road through Arkaley. But I'll never forget the face I saw in the vision from the flower that held the curse. The woman that slapped Jasmin nearly a decade ago as she sat bleeding in her room. Jasmin releases my arm, taking a step toward the woman.

"Mother."

Chapter 36

JASMIN

What the fuck.

How is she here? Why is she announcing herself as Queen? Where is my father? Fuck. The thoughts are careening through my mind. My mother looks as cold and calculating as she always has. It doesn't seem like nine years since she last left. She still looks exactly the same. She seems to remember herself and holds her arms out, walking toward me. This is the disaster I have been waiting for since the border started falling.

"Oh, my daughter," she coos. She tries to change her face to look softer, more motherly, and more loving. It doesn't work. I can still see the ice beneath her skin. I step into her arms all the same. We both have roles to play right now. We were always good at pretending to have a loving relationship. Even though I have tried to give up these fake relationships, I will continue this façade for now. Mother's light hug finally ends as she steps back. I offer a soft smile, trying to keep my face neutral. Clem is seething next to me. I can't say what respect he had for my parents before coming to the castle, but he has no respect for them now. I step back and take his hand once Mother steps back.

"Who is this?" Her words are soft and sweet, but the venom swarming her eyes betrays her tone. As happy as I was to realize Dahlia was still alive under the curse, I don't have the same feelings toward my mother. My gut is telling me something is wrong. I don't always trust my gut, as it tends to betray me a lot, but I know with undeniable certainty something is wrong here.

"This is Clem." My words are short and intentional. I don't want to give her any information until I know more about her. Why is she here? Where has she been? I look at Clem, hoping to convey this before he says anything else. He doesn't look at me, though. He is focused solely on her, looking at her like she's a threat. She likely is, but we can't decide that right away. I squeeze his hand lightly. Mother assesses him, then turns back to me.

"Is he your true love?"

"True love?" We haven't spoken to anyone outside of the kingdom yet. This is the first group to come through. We are preparing to send off emissaries in the next few days but are still finalizing travel for everyone. We don't know how much about the curse was spread beyond our kingdom. Did the old hag travel through other kingdoms, telling people what she did? How does Mother know?

"Yes, your true love that broke the curse?"

Men move around the caravan, unload carts, place luggage near the door, and ready the horses for the stables. Zander and Tomas are already out here helping, and Erik and Henry have joined, too, assisting with preparations for guests.

"Mother," I start but am interrupted by her.

"Queen," she gives an admonishing look. She always insisted I call her Queen instead of Mother when I was younger, but she is no longer Queen here.

"Queen Mother," I amend, not giving her exactly what she wants. "Let's go inside. There is much to discuss between us both. We can have food and wine brought to one of our meeting rooms. You must be famished after your travels." I turn to motion her inside, expecting her to walk inside first. This slight will force her to admit she is a guest here, not the reigning monarch. Kian is standing just inside the foyer. His body language is relaxed, but his eyes display terror over this situation. This doesn't help my nerves to see him so frightened. Mother squares her shoulders, standing taller than me as she finally walks in.

"Yes, you are correct." She folds her hands in front of her waist, ever the picture of perfection. "I would like to wash up from my travels. I will visit my room, then we can gather in the meeting room in a quarter hour." I am ready to agree, as it seems a reasonable request. Before I agree, though, Kian speaks up.

"I'm sorry, Your Majesty, that won't be possible now." I briefly squeeze my eyes in confusion but adjust before looking at my mother. I don't know Kian's reason for saying this, but I trust him far too much to contradict him.

"Yes, thank you. I'm afraid the Queen's suite hasn't been cleaned and isn't in proper shape for guests. We can let you use one of our prepared guest rooms while we send staff to ready your suites."

"That won't be necessary," Mother starts, waving toward a couple of women behind her. "I have brought my own servants. They can clean my room for me. I will just show them the way." From my peripheral vision, Kian shakes his head softly.

"I'm afraid I must insist, Queen Mother. You know we must not allow guests into subpar rooms. I'll send staff out immediately." I wave over one of the cleaners that just happens to walk through the foyer. I give them instructions to prepare the Queen's suite and guide Mother to the guest room to freshen up. Mother huffs, pursing her lips in annoyance, but doesn't argue with me further. She follows the young girl as they walk away into the castle.

Once they are out of sight, Kian grabs Clem and me and shoves us into a small sitting room. He closes the door and locks it behind us. He guides us into the middle of the room, pulling out a small item from his pocket. Before I have time to ask, he shakes the item, and a bubble surrounds us. It looks similar to the border that was just around my kingdom.

"What the fuck is this, Kian?"

"I'm sorry," he sounds genuinely apologetic, but his words are rushed. "This is the space we use to keep sounds in. It is similar to the border, but this isn't as strong and won't last nearly as long." He pauses momentarily as Clem and I finish investigating the magic bubble around us. We turn our attention back to Kian. Clem and I open our mouths to speak, but Kian beats us to it.

"She's the witch."

His claim stuns me into silence for a moment. My mother is a witch? That claim doesn't sound as startling as I thought it would. I never saw her perform magic, but the realization isn't shocking. It feels like something I've always known. But Kian didn't say she's *a* witch. He said she's *the* witch, and suddenly my mind is spinning. Clem has caught up quicker than I am.

"Fuck," he breathes out, reaching over to touch me.

"The witch," I repeat the words, trying to process his meaning. A small voice in my mind is screaming, fully understanding the implications. The rest of my brain has become mush, blocking that realization with muddled thoughts and feelings.

"The one that cursed the kingdom." Kian's words are soft but slice through my thoughts, clearing the uncertainty. Of course, it was her. She always punished me harder than she needed to. She was always disappointed in me. She never wanted me to make my own choices. I don't say anything else as I look at the two men standing in this bubble. There are still so many unanswered questions in my head.

"We don't have much time." Kian pulls me from my wandering mind to the present. Of course, we need to deal with this promptly. "We can't let her get to her room. Her urgency indicates there is something she is hiding. With your permission, I would like to take Lucia and maybe a couple of other witches to her room to search it while they clean it for her."

I nod my head, trying to stay focused. My mind is swimming with all the questions I want answered. I can guess why she placed the curse, but why the whole kingdom? And where is my father? What does she want now? I just need so many answers.

"Yes." I shake my head, trying to clear my wandering thoughts. "Yes, search her room. Clem and I will keep her busy with dinner." As I meet his eyes, a thought crashes through my mind.

"Dahlia." I'm gripped with fear now. Mother tried so hard to remove her before. She told me Dahlia was dead. Did she know she was just cursed in my tower? She would have to, wouldn't she?

"We need to send Emmeline to keep her in our room. We need extra guards, and she cannot be left alone while my mother is here." Clem squeezes my hands tightly as the words fall from me.

"I'll find Emmeline and Henry. You make sure dinner is ready and wait for your mother. Kian will find Lucia and search her room." I nod, thankful Clem can think through this mess right now. I can always depend on him when I am crumbling.

"I can't give you long away from my mother. Maybe a few hours at best." I would love to give him more time, but if my mother does have something hidden in her room, she'll be anxious to get to it. There is no stopping her when she wants something. She isn't just stubborn; she's unstoppable.

Kian drops the bubble, and Clem wraps his arms around me in a reassuring hug. A knock on the door draws our attention. Kian opens it, and Lucia steps in with Emmeline just behind her. Before I can even acknowledge them, Lucia speaks to all of us.

"That witch, that's Queen Oleander, correct?" I give a soft nod in response, worried about what Lucia will say next. "She's the one that set the curse." I sigh, cursing under my breath. I knew Kian was right, but hearing that others can sense it, too, is heartbreaking. How is it so obvious now, but we missed it for so long?

"Yes, we are aware." We give her and Emmeline a quick, hushed rundown of everything just said. Within minutes, we are all leaving the room in different directions. Kian and Lucia are off to my mother's suite. Emmeline and Clem walk down a separate hall to find Henry and Dahlia. I make my way slowly to the kitchen to arrange dinner in a private room. The small task gives me plenty to focus on. I take several breaths, trying to calm my mind. I focus on my surroundings, anything but the roiling emotions in my chest.

Once dinner is arranged, Finn saunters into the hallway. I greet him with a big hug and several back scratches. I consider trying to find someone to take him, but

Mother would be outraged by his presence. So I settle on bringing him with me. Setting her out of her comfort zone may help me get straight answers. Not that I expect anything she says to be honest or entirely truthful.

The small meeting room hosts a table with three seats but room for more. I wasn't sure who would actually be at this dinner. I'm much more comfortable with the casual style we take in the dining hall. I don't care for these formal settings at all. Clem meets me in the hallway, giving me a quick kiss on my cheek. He whispers that everything is settled, calming my nerves. I cannot lose Dahlia again. I don't know that Mother still holds a grudge against her, but it's not a risk I will take. Clem pets Finn's head as he tries to wedge in between us.

Finally, Mother walks down the hallway, looking no different than when she stepped off the carriage. Her scowl deepens as she sees Clem and me waiting at the door for her. She knows this game well, having played it with many royal families. She may be calling herself Queen of Sweet Briar, but not having a coronation will prevent her from getting that respect.

She stops before me, adjusting her position to make herself look taller and more threatening. It takes a lot of effort not to square off against her, but I know my place. I don't need to prove anything with posturing.

"Mother," my voice is soft, matching the tone she used with me earlier. A fake tone to express the love we no longer feel for each other. "Thank you for joining us. The cook has prepared a lovely baked fish meal." I wave her into the room. The displeasure on her face is laughable. She clearly expected to be welcomed differently and is very dissatisfied. Oh no! I roll my eyes internally as I watch her walk inside. Clem sneaks a kiss on my cheek as he walks in behind her. Finn follows Clem, and I step next to my giant dog, walking with him. Mother turns once she reaches the table, just in time to see the doors shut behind Finn and me.

"What..." Mother jerks away from Finn, startled by his appearance. Finn growls at her. He has never growled at anyone beyond playtime. Even I am stunned by his response. Clem walks over, petting him and speaking gently to him. Finn calms down but keeps his eye on my mother.

"Jasmin! What is this beast?"

"It is Queen Jasmin." I correct her with a pointed glare, but she doesn't acknowledge me, keeping her eyes on my dog. "This is Finn, my dog."

"This is entirely unorthodox. He should be removed."

Clem and I take our seats, with Finn settling between us. There is no way she will tell me what to do in my own castle.

"Yes, this is unorthodox, but this is my kingdom." I motion to the table in front of her, encouraging her to sit as my butler comes around with wine for everyone. I take a small sip, wanting to keep my head about me for this dinner. The butler brings a tray of leafy green vegetables and a dressing, stating the main dish will be a few minutes longer. It is a bit earlier than we usually dine here, and we don't typically serve plates this way. I thank the butler for his assistance, glad they could adjust to these plans at the last minute. My people are adapting wonderfully despite being out of practice hosting formal dinners.

"Mother, where have you been? We were told you died on the road. The carriage and all of your belongings were returned to us." I cannot take the unknown any longer. I need answers. Mother sips her wine, eyeing Clem and me suspiciously. I'm honestly surprised she hasn't asked any questions, either. She must have her own about what has happened over the past nine years.

"I do not know why you were told we were dead. We were attacked on the road, and they took our carriage. We were lucky enough to find safety with the King of Hollyhock. Then we heard about the curse."

"What did you hear?" Her eyes shift to Clem as he speaks, filling me with unease.

"We heard our kingdom was cursed until you could find your true love." She huffs a humorless laugh, finally bringing her eyes to me. "I thought it would take time, but I never knew it would be so long." That jab hurts more than I want to admit. I already doubt myself over the amount of time wasted. Mother turns back to Clem, plastering a joyful image on her face.

"Tell me about him. Your true love," she swoons, sipping more wine. "Who are his parents? Where is he from? What was your wedding like? I wish we could have been there. Your father would have loved it." Another stab to my already bleeding heart. I also don't overlook her desire to speak of Clem as an object, not someone sitting next to me. So many insults in her first questions.

"Where is Father?" While her return has overshadowed his absence, it has not gone unnoticed.

"Oh, dear. He fell sick shortly after we were attacked and unfortunately didn't make it." My chest is torn with disbelief. I have a hard time believing her when I was told she was dead and Dahlia was dead. But if my father isn't dead, that means he could return. My mind is not ready to deal with another return of someone I've loved and lost. I close my eyes, praying silently to any god that will listen that he passed quickly and peacefully.

"There will be time to mourn soon. Let's not sully our first meal together after so long with sad things. Tell me about Clem." The smile on her face betrays her thoughts. There is evil laced in her gaze. I suddenly feel like I don't know my mother at all. I fear there is an ulterior motive in her words. How could grieving my father, her husband, be a bad thing? I wish Kian were here to help discern what information could be dangerous for a witch to have. I wish I had put more effort into learning about witchcraft in the past nine years. I wish many things at this moment, but none of that will change what is happening. I take a deep breath, trying to decide quickly what to tell her without further endangering us.

"Clem is from Arkaley." I turn to look at him, trying to memorize everything about him. The way his dark blonde hair falls from its leather strap. His strong jaw and full lips. His eyes meet mine, conveying the love he has for me. He has come a long way in hiding his emotions, but some will always shine through. Mother speaks, breaking the trance I am in, staring at Clem.

"Who is your father, Clem?"

"His name was William Byrne."

"Hmm, I don't recognize that name. From Arkaley, you say?" She thinks for a moment as the butler brings in plates of food for us. The scent of savory herbs fills the room but does nothing for my knotting stomach. The cook is fantastic and spent a lot of time and effort making a delicious, stunning meal, but I'm afraid I won't even be able to taste anything I put in my mouth. My nerves have wracked my body, and I want to lie down.

"What position does your father hold? I have forgotten many people from my time away." I fight to restrain any audible reactions. I'm out of practice for dealing with her statements.

"He was a farmer," Clem states plainly. I reach out and grab his hand, offering a small comfort. He squeezes my hand back, taking a sip of his wine. He is doing an excellent job of controlling his emotions and reactions. It's a struggle for him, but he handles this situation beautifully.

"A farmer? You married a farmer?" I decide not to correct her on the marriage yet. That definitely isn't information I want her to have.

"He's my true love, Mother. Fate decided that. I didn't pick his duties. Although he has been promoted to Master of Gardens within the kingdom. He is very skilled at farming and has already improved the farming capabilities of our kingdom." I let my pride for Clem shine through my words. I want Mother to know how happy I am about everything he has done. His self-doubt won't always let him acknowledge how wonderful he is. I certainly will take the opportunity to do that.

Mother just harrumphs her frustrations. She wanted a different reception. Maybe she will get that from the Lords, but not from me. We eat in silence for several awkward moments. As I suspected, the food tastes dry and bland in my mouth. It is neither dry nor bland, but my mind is so consumed with fear, doubt, and anxiety that I can't taste the fantastic food.

Kian walks in, bowing politely at us. I tip my head toward him, asking if everything is ready. He glances at my mother before he speaks. "We were preparing your room when your chambermaids showed up. They insisted on finishing the task for us. They should be done within an hour." I recognize that his words, while spoken to my mother, are also meant to inform me he was interrupted.

Mother simply nods, then stares in confusion as Kian has a chair brought around for him. My servers, familiar with Kian and his position, prepare his spot without being asked. Mother seems appalled that he has this kind of power in my presence. Instead of introducing him, I let her simmer in her thoughts, not knowing who he is. Maybe I shouldn't play so many power games with my mother. But now that I have actual power here, I don't want to cave to her anymore.

"How is the King of Hollyhock?" I ask softly, placing another small bite in my mouth. Despite my inability to taste, tiny bits of food still give me something to do. Mother slowly turns her attention to me.

"He is well. He has a son that is looking for a wife. They are preparing him to run the kingdom in a few years." I nod, vaguely remembering talks of arranging a relationship with said son. I'm surprised he is still unwed, being older than I am. I wouldn't be unwed at this age were it not for the curse. Mother eyes Clem, then Kian. Why does it feel like she knows we aren't married yet? "Perhaps," she speaks slowly, "we can still work out an arrangement with the Prince."

"Negotiations would be wonderful," Kian interjects. "Now that the curse is lifted, we will need to renegotiate trade. If you are close with the King, this will work in our favor." He clasps his hands together, looking excited over the prospect. I smile, nodding to him.

"Excellent. Sounds like something you two can work together on," I add. Kian smiles, eating his food with poise and grace. Mother sneers but turns her attention back to me.

"We shall see." Her ominous words hang as we finish our dinner. No one speaks any further. While many questions exist, now is not the time to ask. I scratch Finn's head as my plate is removed from the table. He has stayed perched between Clem and me all night, unwilling to leave us alone with my mother. He didn't even lie down to sleep. I trust his reaction over my own instinct any time, but seeing his disapproval of my mother only solidifies everything I already knew. She is dangerous.

Once all the food has been cleared, we adjourn for the evening. Mother informs me she is exhausted from her travels and would like time to recover in peace, meaning she doesn't want to be bothered. Got it. As long as my people watch her movements, I do not intend to interact with her. We walk to the door, with everyone exiting, including Clem and Kian. Mother stops me in the doorway, stepping in front to exit first, as a guest would do.

"I see these games you are playing, little girl," her voice is sheer ice, causing me to freeze. She leans near my ear, so close her cheek grazes mine, brushing against the scars she created. "You will not win this game. I will overthrow you, and it will finally be your end." She kisses my scarred cheek and turns to exit the room. As she turns, I can see the shift from the ice I just experienced to a warmer, more queenly manner. Seeing her shift gears so quickly makes me realize I may be unable to contend with her. This is beyond my experience.

Chapter 37

Dahlia

I have been pacing the room for hours now. Clem stopped by the room, briefly described what was happening, and then left. Emmeline has been with me since, but she has no new information. My mind is racing. Jasmin is with her mother. She is concerned about me being around Oleander, but I'm worried about her being around Oleander. She has done more damage to us than we would have done on our own.

The door opens after what feels like an eternity, and Finn walks in first. He doesn't even acknowledge Emmeline or me. Instead, he collapses in front of the hearth with a deep sigh. He'll be snoring in minutes. Clem and Jasmin finally enter the room. I rush over to her as he shuts the door behind them. I wrap my arms around her tightly, needing to hold her to know she is safe. She squeezes me back tightly, needing the same thing I do.

Clem walks over to chat quietly with Emmeline before she leaves the room through the secret passageways. He walks back to us, pulling both of us against his chest. His arms are warm, and feel safe. His lips press a kiss to Jasmin's forehead, then my own. I never would have thought being in a triad would suit me, but here, in this hug, I can't imagine being anywhere else. There is a genuine threat to us walking just a few halls over. Fear fills my body, and while I feel safer in Clem's arms, that fear doesn't subside.

Jasmin must think the same thing as me because her breathing picks up, coming faster. Clem and I adjust to look down at her. Tears are sliding down her flushed cheeks. She pulls back from us to wipe her face, but Clem pulls out a handkerchief, always prepared for tears. This curse has not been kind to any of us. Can I still blame the curse at this point? It is officially over, but the ramifications aren't.

"Why is she back?" Jasmin sniffles, not looking up at either of us. Her eyes stay down, wiping tears away with Clem's well-used handkerchief. "What if she tries to hurt you?" Her eyes finally meet mine. "Or Clem?" Her voice breaks as she looks at him. Jasmin seems so tiny. The couple of inches I have on her are even more noticeable as she hunches her shoulders in sorrow. "I can't do that again," she sobs. "It took me eight years to recover from losing you and my parents. I can't survive without you and Clem now. I can't..."

Her words turn to full-body sobs, sending Clem and me to pull her between us again. We offer kisses, caressing hands, tight squeezes but no promises of safety. Oleander has had a dire effect on all of us. The reality is we can't protect each other at this point. I hope Jasmin has curated enough favor that we can find people who can protect us.

"Jas," Clem speaks softly into her ear. "Let me help." She steps away, looking up at him with tearful, heartbroken eyes. The sight makes my own heart crack. I can't stand seeing her upset for any reason.

"Let me distract you and help you sleep for a little bit." His eyes have a mischievous glint, but his body language still portrays caution, letting her decide on her own. She sniffles but glances at me. I offer a soft smile, unsure of what Clem has in mind. I'm willing to do anything for her, though. She nods to him, wiping her nose with the cloth again.

"Good." He grabs her chin roughly, turning her face toward his. Her breath hitches as she meets his eyes. This girl, I swear. She is more deviant than she should be. He slams his lips against hers in a brutal but fast kiss. With his hands still on her face, Jasmin's eyes glued to him, his eyes scan over me, and I fight the urge to whimper under his gaze. I completely understand why she is so submissive to him. The ache growing in my core is proof of that. His eyes meet hers as his hand drops from her chin. "Strip."

He glances down at her clothes. Before I can react, his hand is around the back of my neck, pulling me into a similar brutal but fast kiss. Then he walks toward the closet, leaving me stunned. Jasmin, more familiar with his style, is already removing her clothes. My mind tries to focus on her task as she pulls her shirt over her head. He didn't give me any instructions, but I am not passing up any chance to get my hands on her. She still looks tired and consumed by her emotions. I help her remove her pants, then cup her breast as she stands up.

"You sure you want to do this?" My fingers drift slowly up her chest to her neck, grazing lightly across her jaw. Every inch of her skin feels soft, inviting, and exquisite. Her skin pebbles under my fingers, a slight shiver runs through her. Her eyes find mine as a playful smile spreads across her face.

"Yes." Her single answer is soft but so confident. I kiss her gently, completely opposite of the way Clem just kissed both of us. My hands are on her chest, skimming across her collarbone, neck, arms, anywhere my fingers can touch. She rests her hands on my elbows, her lips soft and tender against my own. Clem has something brutal and euphoric planned, but I'm still going to take a moment to offer peace and warmth. Because I plan to help him with whatever savagery will help Jasmin relax.

Our lips are still pressed against each other when he returns. He doesn't pull us apart, just steps behind Jasmin. He tugs her arms behind her, forcing her to let go of my elbows. I finally break the kiss, looking over her shoulder to see what he is doing. He has one of his favorite sashes, tying her forearms together behind her back. Her breasts arch out toward me, on perfect display. Sucking her nipple into my mouth; it buds beneath my swirling tongue. She moans softly as I move to the other breast, repeating the process. Clem is done with her binding and grabs her hair, pulling her head back as he catches her lips in a passionate kiss. I'm surprised that I don't feel jealous seeing them kissing. While I would love for it to be me with either of them, I'm excited to see them together, too.

He pulls away from her, leaving her breathless. Her chest rises and falls quickly. He yanks his shirt over his head, then tugs Jasmin back to the bed. He sits and scoots back, bringing Jasmin with him. Even doing something as awkward as sliding back across the bed, these two still make it look sexy. I follow them over, sitting on my knees near the edge. Clem looks at me, then tips his head to the space in front of Jasmin. I crawl over, settling between his legs. He positions Jasmin in his lap, her back to his chest. He pulls her legs, bringing her knees toward her chest, placing her feet on the outside of either of his thighs.

In her new position, she is on full display for me. She is absolutely gorgeous. Her wet, pink cunt is perfectly exposed for me. I want to nibble on her stomach, scrunched in these lovely little rolls. Her breasts shoved up into peaks begging for my mouth. Her face watching me as I devour her body with my eyes. Clem has that mischievous glint in his eyes, but it has taken over his whole face now. His lips form into a devilish grin.

Clem circles his hands around her waist, her eyes still focused on me. One hand cups her breast, squeezing her nipple between his fingers. His other hand slides down to cover her cunt. He rubs his fingers on either side of her slit, stroking up and down.

"Does our Queen look exquisite?" Clem's voice is deep and husky but not as domineering as usual. I glance at him, nod, and lick my lips but turn my eyes back to her cunt. That's where I want to be. Clem's fingers slide toward her stomach, and I start leaning in. His middle finger circles her clit several times, causing her to tip her head back onto his shoulder. Her breasts lift higher, and I groan, needing to kiss them, too. My lips find her breast, nibbling her skin, then latching onto her nipple. She moans under me while Clem pushes her breasts into my mouth. Clem's thumb flicks out, brushing against my clit. I jolt in surprise, leaning back from him. His grin is downright wicked. I can't help the smile that spreads across my face in response.

I lean down, wanting to taste her cunt now. His hand is over her breast, squeezing and pinching in ways she loves. His lips are on her neck as she stretches to give him full access. Soft moans escape from her while his finger lazily circles her clit. I press my tongue against her slit, tasting the entire length of her opening. She moans loudly, and I let my tongue dip inside her. I lick up and down her slowly, sliding my tongue through her. Clem's finger is still against her clit, but moving a little faster now.

"Look at Dahlia," Clem growls. "Watch her worship you." His hand is wrapped around Jasmin's neck as she looks down at me, biting her lip. I tease my tongue quickly between her lips. She groans loudly, undulating beneath my ministrations. I grab her ass to hold her in place while I tongue her. I massage her ass and thighs, plunging my tongue deep inside. Clem increases the speed of his finger on her clit, circling quickly. Her chest rises quickly, her pussy clenching around my tongue with her impending orgasm.

"There's my beautiful Queen. A tongue deep in her cunt." He slides his nose over her neck, then whispers against her skin. "So ready to come for us." His teeth press into her neck, and she shudders through her orgasm. Her pussy is clenching around my tongue. We work her in perfect unison through her orgasm. When her breathing slows, I pull back, sitting on my knees. She groans, but Clem keeps his hand against her clit, circling slowly.

"That was a good start, but I want more." Jasmin's eyes shoot wide open, then instantly droop as he slides one of his fingers into her wet pussy.

"Wha...more?" We both look at Clem, unsure of what he means.

"Yes. More orgasms." Before we can respond, he moves his hand, pressing his palm against her clit and plunging two fingers deep inside her. He begins to pound her with his hand. She arches back into him, moaning loudly as she closes her eyes tightly. After a moment, another orgasm crashes through her, sending her body twisting and jerking against him.

"So perfect," he whispers against her neck. She shudders in his arms, clearly enjoying his words. His eyes find mine. "You want more of our queen?" I don't need to be asked twice. I dive in as Clem pulls his hand back, giving me complete control. I lick her full length, then circle her small nub, causing her to shout and arch back against Clem. I can't help the devious grin spreading across my own face now. This is precisely why he always has this look on his face. I get it now.

He whispers more affirmations in her ear while I feast on her pussy. Within minutes, another orgasm tears through her, her body jerking harder this time. She still wiggles under my tongue when her breathing slows, though I move more languidly now. Her hips gyrate against Clem's.

"I can feel you under me. I want you inside me." Jasmin whines to him, rubbing her body over his the whole time.

"Did you just tell me how to pleasure you?"

"Please?" She begs, but we all know it is fruitless. Clem is either in charge or following instructions. He doesn't mix the two positions, unlike both Jasmin and me. He laughs beneath her so profoundly that I swear I can feel the vibrations.

"Okay, I'll be inside you." He shifts his thighs, his arms, his chest. He forces her to raise her legs as he wraps both arms around her thighs. Then he slams his hands against her. One goes to her clit, circling roughly. With the other hand, he slams three fingers deep inside her then begins to fuck her. She tries to buck under his grip, but he's stronger than she is. He holds her tightly as he continues to fuck her hard with his hands. Her face twists in both pleasure and pain. He simply looks crazed with lust, scraping his teeth against her neck. Her moans grow louder as his hands maintain the pace he sets. She shouts as her orgasm rips through her body again. She shivers and trembles longer as he continues working her dripping cunt. Her body shakes as she huffs a couple of laughs, leaning her face against Clem's. He finally pulls his hands back, and she sighs, relaxing through the last shivers of her orgasm.

"Take one more, Dahl." Jasmin gasps, but I start to lean in.

"No!" She shouts, and I hesitate before I lick her pussy, looking up at Jasmin and Clem.

"No? You can't give her one more?"

"It's too sensitive," Jas moans, pressing her face against Clem's, not looking down at me.

"That'll make it better. You can give Dahl one more." His hands are slowly rubbing her thighs, soothing but still arousing. I blow gently over her cunt. I won't do more until she says she wants it. I won't force another one out of her if she doesn't want us to. She shudders but nods her head. I lean in, pressing kisses to her lips, feeling her clench at my touch. My finger teases her entrance as I swirl her clit with my tongue. She groans, wiggling under me. Clem's grasp on her thighs tightens, holding her in place for me. She squirms under my increasing ministrations. I swap my finger and tongue.

I lick deep between her lips, savoring the feel of her smooth walls against my tongue. I pinch her clit between my finger and thumb, and her body jerks violently under Clem's grasp. I pinch her several more times, feeling her lips squeeze over my tongue. Her body tenses when her orgasm finally crashes into her. I briefly notice her exquisite shape before a massive gush of liquid bursts into my face. I'm startled and lean back suddenly. As if on impulse, I plunge two fingers inside her while thumbing her clit, drawing her orgasm out. I wipe my face with my free hand.

Clem grins at me, seeing my reaction to her orgasm. My fingers start to slow down inside her, but Clem shakes his head, telling me to keep it up. Jasmin shouts again as another crest of pleasure passes over her. I continue to stroke my fingers against her while her pussy squirts more fluids. I marvel at her body's reaction.

Clem instructs me to pull away slowly since she is so tender now. I do as he says, but she still jerks when I take my hand off. He slides over until she is on her side and unties her arms. He stretches her arms out, causing her to groan loudly. Clem kisses her shoulders, and I slide in front of her. I rub Jasmin's arms and shoulders soothingly. Her eyes stay closed as we caress, clean, and position her on the bed. We pull the blanket over, and she snores softly, unable to fight off the exhaustion any longer. I chuckle at her as Clem motions me toward the bath.

I follow him into the room, and he drops his pants. His erect cock stands straight out from his body. Jasmin wasn't kidding about being able to feel him beneath her. He steps into the bath as I continue staring at his nakedness. I don't know if it's fate or because he is just that beautiful, but I have never been as impressed with a man as I am with Clem. Once he sinks below the water, hiding most of his body from me, I undress and grab one of my silk scarves. Pinning my braids up before I get in the water is essential to caring for them, especially since Mama is gone. I'll have to find someone else to help braid my hair until she returns. Clem watches with curious eyes but doesn't say anything.

I sit near him but don't touch him. His head drops back against the edge, and he closes his eyes, relaxing in the warm water in this tub. I am eternally grateful for whatever spell was used to keep this tub warm all the time. I realize how uncomfortable I feel with Clem right now. I'm not as familiar with him as I am with Jasmin, and that keeps me from doing what I want, which is wrapping my hands around his cock. Then I remember I can do that with him. There is no reason I shouldn't. I'm also positive he would enjoy it more than I would.

I slide closer, pressing my body against his side. He wraps his arm around me, caressing my bicep with his fingers, but doesn't open his eyes or tilt his head. I settle on being bold. My fingers wrap around his cock as I plant my lips against his neck. I stroke up and down slowly, eliciting a low moan from him. The edge of my mouth curves against his neck, appreciating his response. I make a trail of kisses along his neck, slowly working his cock with my hand. I kiss a spot on his neck, and he sucks in a quick breath, tightening his grip on my arm. His penis jerks in my hand. That is a sensitive spot for him. I suck and lick against that spot as he writhes beside me.

Suddenly, he spins in front of me, pressing me back against the tub's edge. His hands are braced on either side of me, his face inches from mine. His eyes are dark and coated with lust. His chest rises and falls with quick breaths while his eyes bore into mine.

"I want to fuck you." His voice is soft but firm, almost like he struggles to hold back. He does seem to be restraining himself.

"Do it," I challenge. My core aches, remembering what he felt like inside of me. It's hard to believe it has only been a few days since I fucked him. With everything that has happened since then, I haven't had the chance to fuck him again, eager to take him completely. His eyes continue to bore into me, warring internally with accepting my challenge or denying himself.

His lips land against mine, gently but passionately. His mouth explores my own, searching for every taste and feel. I wrap my arms around his shoulders, brushing my fingers against his back. His shoulders are broad and strong, offering security even when unnecessary. His hands hold my waist as his body slides through the water until it is flush with mine. His rigid member is pressed against my stomach, rubbing between us, but not in the way I want. I wrap my feet around his waist, digging my heels into his ass to encourage him to put his dick inside me.

One of his hands raises to my cheek, caressing it softly. Tiny drops of water fall from his hand, splashing into the tub below. It's the only sound in the room now. Everything is quiet and still, waiting for him to make the next move. I am pressed between him and the tub's edge, silently begging him to move. His other hand slides down my side, over my thigh, and stops over my cunt. I hold my breath, waiting to see what he will do. I moan when he drags his fingers along my slit, teasing me. My hips undulate against him, but there isn't much room for me to move.

"Is someone getting all worked up?" His voice is playful and husky. The smile on his face is apparent even without seeing him.

"Yes. I want you to fuck me already."

"Okay," he says as he pulls back and lines his member up with my opening. I expected him to slam into me the way I've seen him do with Jasmin many times. I'm thankful he doesn't, but I hope he will one day. He presses in slowly, giving me time to adjust to the stretch. I close my eyes, pressing my head against his shoulder. His cock is thick, but the stretch feels divine. It's not something I'm familiar with. Fingers don't fit the same way his solid dick does. Once he reaches the hilt, he pauses, kissing me deeply. I adjust my position as my body wraps around him.

Without breaking the kiss, he pulls out then presses back in slowly. At first, it feels nice, but after a moment or two, I want more. I tug on his back, digging my nails into his skin. He doesn't change his pace, and it's still agonizingly slow and steady. My heels press against his ass and release, trying to change the speed. Again, he doesn't. My head falls back against the tub. I no longer care if my braids get wet. He's teasing me in the worst possible way, which has consumed my thoughts.

"I need you to fuck me harder," I finally demand. I don't particularly feel as vocal as Clem is during sex, but I need more from him now.

"I thought you'd never ask." His grin spreads across his face as he pulls out and slams back in. My arms tighten around his back, holding his chest close to me while his hips slam into my core. It feels like a pleasure I have never known before. It's different than being with Jasmin or even both Jasmin and Clem. He fills me with his member, then pulls out and fills me again.

The pounding against my clit is teasing me. It's frequent and hard enough to send me soaring, but it's over before it starts with his set pace. I debate grabbing my clit myself, but I don't really want to let him go. As if he were reading my mind, Clem's hand settles between us, his thumb rubbing against my clit. With the pounding from his cock and now the constant touch on my clit, my orgasm builds quicker than I am used to. Within minutes of his finger settling on my clit, my orgasm crashes through me. My mind begins to soar as my body clenches with pleasure. I cry out in ecstasy, clinging to Clem tightly, worried I might fall away from him. He grunts as he slams into me, moaning through his orgasm as his movements become erratic with release.

Our bodies slowly return to normal, and our breathing calms down. He sits back against the tub, pulling me into his lap. I'm not as comfortable with all this touching as he and Jas are, but I can't deny how good it feels.

"Why do you wrap your hair?" He asks while he stares at the silk scarf wrapped around it.

"To protect it and keep it from getting wet. Maintaining the braids is harder if they get wet too much." He nods in understanding, staring for another minute. He grabs the soap and a cloth and begins to wash my body. Nothing has ever been as intimate as having another person wash me like this. At first, I feel awkward and uncomfortable. This is a private thing; another person shouldn't be cleaning me.

But I remember Jasmin talking about how much she enjoys these moments with Clem. I try to relax and enjoy it for what it is. Clem chuckles at me.

"I can stop if you want. I don't have to wash you." I turn and meet his eyes, staring at him. My brain isn't fully processing his words when he adds, "I just like to help you clean up." His words are soft and genuine, making me realize there is no ill-intent, no awkwardness from him. I take the small cloth from him, and for a moment, he looks sad. I add a bit more soap to him before I begin washing him. His smile is soft and sweet this time, nothing like the devious grin he gave earlier.

Chapter 38

Clem

"I am not staying in this fucking room today!"

"You're not leaving here!"

Dahlia and Jasmin have been fighting for nearly half an hour now. Jasmin wants her to stay in the room. Dahlia wants to leave and not be trapped in here again. Both are wrong, and both are right. Neither has asked for my opinion, though. I'm just lounging on the couch, waiting until they figure this out or ask for my help. Both women are angry and upset, both with valid reasons, but neither really listening to what the other is saying.

"You are not going to wander around the castle while my mother is here doing gods only know what!" Jasmin plops down at her vanity, angry and trying to get the last word in. Dahlia won't give up her pursuit, though.

"I'm not staying in this room with nothing to do again! I did this yesterday, and I'll be damned if I do it today!" She stomps to the bed, collapsing on the edge with her arms crossed across her chest. Finn sits at my feet, watching the two women with caution. Jasmin gets angry like this but usually has enough decorum to listen to the other side. This is the first time I have seen her make up her mind and not accept further information on the topic. That is behavior Dahlia typically displays, which she absolutely is. They are back to yelling about who is doing what and who will stop them. Emmeline has taken to hiding in the bathroom and closet to avoid this argument. I simply watch, wondering how often they fought like this before the curse.

"Clem! Tell her she has to stay," Jasmin demands from her chair. She glares at me, assuming I will take her side. I glance over at Dahlia. Her shoulders slump, defeat visible in her dropping expression now that I have been dragged into the argument. She also assumes I will take Jasmin's side. I don't particularly like that either believes I will automatically take a side.

"No."

Jasmin gasps at me, her glare turning icy. Dahlia sits up straighter, looking more triumphant now. "First of all," I continue, "I'm not taking sides. Don't put me between you two. Second, you're both wrong." Now both women look angry at me. I'd probably chuckle at their behavior if the room wasn't so tense. Jasmin stands, facing me with her arms over her chest. She slings them around as she speaks.

"I am not wrong! She is not safe in the castle with my mother here!"

"I am not wrong about being forced to stay here all day again!"

I hold my hands up, hoping to silence them. They both look away from me, too angry to maintain eye contact. "Yes, you are both right."

"Then what the fuck, Clem?" Jasmin shouts. This time I do unwittingly chuckle. I'm pretty sure Jasmin is going to kill me now. I stand up and walk over to her. I brush a strand of hair behind her ear, but she jerks away from me quickly. I rub my hand over her arm, hoping to soothe her a bit.

"You can't keep her locked in here." I keep my words soft, worried about their impact on her. She hasn't realized how her actions appear, only focusing on keeping Dahlia safe. Her eyes meet mine as she realizes the implications of her argument. Tears build in her eyes as she turns to look at Dahlia. I stroke her back lightly, wanting to offer her any comfort. I speak up before she starts talking, though.

"But we also can't give you free reign of the castle, Dahl. We don't know what Oleander wants, and we can't risk your safety." Dahlia's gaze softens at my words, realizing the piece she has also been missing in this argument. Relief washes through me because both women are listening to me without putting up much fight. I was worried I would need to explain more thoroughly why they were wrong.

"What do we do?" Jasmin asks, tears falling down her face. I give her a clean handkerchief from my pocket, making a note to grab more. My father used to tell me when I was young to always carry one with me. I always thought he was crazy until I came to the castle last year. Now I can't imagine going anywhere without at least one, preferably two.

"I have an idea." They look at me with sad but hopeful eyes. I'm thankful they trust me enough to listen to my thoughts and ideas, especially in situations like this. Our relationship will only work out if we listen and communicate. "Let Dahlia go to the library today. You mentioned wanting to research some spell, right?" She nods enthusiastically at me while Jas just looks between us, unconvinced. "We can send a couple of the witches with her to help her and offer protection. There is only one way into the library. We'll post a couple of guards, deliver her food, and check on her throughout the day." Dahlia stands, face bright and shining with hope at my suggestion. Jasmin still looks unconvinced. "We could send Finn with her, too." He perks his head up, letting out a big yawn. He plunders over to Jasmin and collapses at her feet, causing her to chuckle.

"Okay, but you have to stay in the library. Please?" She begs, drawing out her last word. I wrap my arm around her shoulders, pulling her against me. "We'll send extra people with you in case you need someone to fetch something for you. But I will lock you up if you leave the room." Based on the look on her face, I have no doubt she will follow through on that threat. Jasmin walks over to Dahlia, hugging her as she apologizes. Dahlia also apologizes for being so brazen in her demands. I wrap my arms around them, kissing their foreheads and squeezing them tightly.

"Great. Now that we have it sorted, can we please leave and get some food? I am fucking starving." We all chuckle as we leave the room together, dropping Dahlia by the library and helping Emmeline arrange guards and witches to work with her.

After breakfast, Jasmin and I check in with Dahlia. She requests that we don't return until dinner so she can focus on her spell. She has found a protection spell she wants to work on and doesn't want any distractions from us while she does it. We leave her and find Kian. He tells us Oleander has stayed in her room all morning. She sent out some of her chambermaids with various tasks but has yet to leave herself. She hasn't requested anything other than food. He doesn't know what she's up to and isn't thrilled about it. He promises to watch her and let us know if anything changes. Jasmin thanks him for all of his hard work. She is always the first to show appreciation to anyone she interacts with. We decide to visit Bea; she's been in her suite for a few days because of the pregnancy. She has had more sickness than expected.

Ma and Claire are also in Bea's room when we show up. I'm relieved to know they are staying out of the way today. The uncertainty of Oleander's return has everyone on edge, but knowing our loved ones are out of the way is at least a small comfort. Claire lounges on the couch with a book while Ma and Bea are in their private bathroom. Jas goes to help Ma. Pride and love swim through me as I watch her walk into the room to help my mother and sister. When I was younger, I always wanted a wife that would be close to my family. I love that Jasmin wants that, too.

I call Claire over to sit with me on the couch. She brings her book and leans against my side. I wrap my arm around her and tell her to read to me. She gives me a dubious look but starts reading anyway. After Pa died, Ma took on extra work to make ends meet before Bea and I started working regularly. We helped her a lot with Claire when she was a baby. One of my favorite things to do with her was sit and read. I read whatever book I could get, which wasn't many, but we never cared. I held her in my arms and read the book I had at the time. When she was a little older, she would turn the pages for me. These are some of my favorite memories with her. She won't sit in my lap anymore, but I can still read with her. I listen to her read the story now, feeling her warmth against my side.

"That word is 'chose,' not 'choose,'" I correct at one point as Jasmin emerges from Bea's room.

"I always get those two mixed up," Claire explains. I nod, having struggled with those many times, too.

"Me too. Language is difficult sometimes.'" Claire considers my statement as Jasmin walks up to me. A slight sheen of sweat coats her forehead. I take her hand, kiss the back, and ask how Bea is doing.

"She's asleep now. Your mother is just finishing up; then she will be out."

She pours a glass of water and collapses on the chair across from us. Claire closes her book but stays against my side. Jasmin relaxes in her chair, letting out a heavy sigh. I can't help but wonder what they were doing that was so exhausting. I don't doubt the work was tiring, but she wasn't in there very long. Is Jasmin just exhausted from helping Ma, or is there more? Is the stress of Oleander's return weighing on her more heavily than I realized? As I consider this thought, Claire speaks up.

"The woman that showed up recently, that's your mother, right? The last Queen?" Jasmin looks at her and nods softly. Claire lets that information sink in before asking her next question.

"Was she a nice mother?"

"Claire," I interject, but Jasmin holds her hand up to stop me.

"No, she wasn't particularly nice."

"But, you're her only child, right? Why isn't she nicer to you?"

"Claire! That isn't appropriate." Again, Jasmin just waves away my concern.

"Clem does have a point. It's not a question you can ask just anyone. But I will answer it because I like you." Jasmin smiles and gives a playful wink at Claire, who beams in response. At least Jasmin explained why Claire can't just ask a question like that. "I think Mother had a different vision of how I would grow up, what I would do for the kingdom. When I made different choices than she wanted, she became angry. My father was very kind and loving. Mother just wanted more power and more control of the kingdom. Father gave her some power, but she also garnered her own through the Lords and other people. Even from a young age, I could see how cunning Mother was. I spent more time with Father when I had the choice. Mother mostly left me to other people, probably where I developed different ideas than she wanted. I think she always assumed I would be just like her instead of my own person."

Ma walks out of Bea's room while Jasmin is speaking. With her back to the room, Jasmin never even noticed. Once she stops talking, Ma steps up, placing a hand on her shoulder. Jasmin looks up at her, taking Ma's hand in her own. A silent conversation passes through them, Ma offering the love and acceptance Jas never got from her own mother. Tears well in Jas's eyes as Ma removes her hand to stroke her cheek. Ma would have kissed her head, a favorite move of hers, but Jas is wearing her smaller crown today, a subtle claim on her rank. Ma also fills a mug with water but doesn't look nearly as exhausted as Jas. This whole situation is definitely having an impact on her. As I formulate a plan to help her, Erik enters the suite, a little startled to see so many people in his sitting room. He tries to hide his confusion by nodding, but he isn't successful. I chuckle at him.

"Hey, Erik. Bea just got to sleep. Jas and I are going to get out of your way." I stand up, and Jasmin looks confused but follows along. Jasmin and I pat him on the back quickly as we exit their suite. Ma says she is finishing the laundry, and they will also leave. Ma was reluctant to come to the castle for fear of not having enough work. She always manages to find work to do. Before we go, I ask them all to lay low for now, stay with groups, or in their own rooms, at least for a few days. Ma nods, but Claire's expression says she will pester Ma with questions later. I don't think anyone has explained to them what Oleander has done. I'm not even positive Erik knows. We want to keep it quiet for now, at least until Maud and the other witches arrive. Kian sent a rider out the night Oleander arrived to request several of the witches come help with the situation.

"Where are we going now?" Jasmin asks as she wraps her hand around my arm. I rub her hand gently, smiling down at her.

"We're going to check in with Kian, then back to our room." She scrunches her nose in an adorably confused way, making me smile.

"Why?" She waggles her eyebrows at me, but I give her an exasperated look.

"You are exhausted, but you won't rest until you have an update. So, we'll get that, then you can rest." She gives me a sideways glance, clearly unimpressed with my decision, but she doesn't argue. She won't be able to face any situation if she doesn't get proper rest. We manage to hunt down Kian, but there is no actual update. Oleander is still in her room, and her servants have stayed there since they returned.

We grab lunch and make our way back to our room. We eat our food in the bed, then clear the trays. I have her remove her leggings, knowing she'll be more comfortable without them. I draw the curtains, making the room as dark as possible, before sliding into bed beside her. I don't need sleep or rest, but I don't want her to feel alone. Even after all this time together, I still love feeling her warm, soft body against my own. She fits into my side perfectly, like we were made for each other.

"Will you read to me?" Her voice is soft and timid, despite knowing I will always read to her. I kiss her head, now absent of her crown. I light a small candle and grab a book, crawling back into the bed beside her. She rests her head against my chest, insisting she loves the vibrations, and I begin reading. I have a child's fairy tale book about a princess who falls in love with a knight and lives happily ever after. It's fun and playful and not very dark, perfect for a bedtime story, even for grown adults. She sighs contentedly, eventually drifting off to sleep. Once she's asleep, I switch to the book I have been reading and finish it silently.

Eventually, dinner time arrives. I wake Jasmin gently, and she stretches her arms wide. Unable to help myself, I cup her breasts, burying my face between them and inhaling deeply. Her scent fills me with love and desire, but I tamp that down until later. I help her into her pants and crown before we leave for the library.

As we enter the library, it looks calm and unassuming. Near the back, where we last saw Dahlia, it looks like pure chaos. Dahlia and two other women huddle over the table, but pages, books, and pens are strewn all over the area. I try to fight the outrage at the state of my beloved library. I can't help picking up some pages to tidy the room. Jasmin swats my arm to stop me, but I refuse. I will not accept the state of this library. I love Dahlia, but she will not leave my library in complete disarray. This is an atrocity against humankind.

The two other women notice us first and stand up, looking nervous as they take in the destruction they created. They have the decency to realize what a travesty this is. The women scurry away and begin collecting books and papers strewn about. I sigh a breath of relief, glad they won't leave this mess. I am ready to instate a limit on who can be in this library! Dahlia finally looks up at us, and a huge, proud grin spreads across her face. I can't be entirely angry when she looks so content. I can be happy for her if I don't look at the rest of this area.

"I did it, Jas." She grabs a necklace off the table and walks around to us. She holds it to Jasmin, showing a silver necklace with a glistening opal. "I only had time to make one," she looks at me with a bit of sorrow but holds the chain out further toward Jasmin. "It's an amulet. It will protect you from anything Oleander may try against you." Jasmin breath hitches as she stares at the amulet. Dahlia grows tired of waiting and places the necklace around Jasmin's neck. The thin chain settles against her skin as Jasmin gasps with the contact. Dahlia tucks the gem beneath her shirt, hiding it away.

"I can feel the magic. I can feel you." Jasmin looks up at Dahlia with wonder and tears in her eyes. Dahlia kisses her cheek, grabbing her hands to hold.

"You should keep it hidden. Oleander will likely recognize it immediately. We couldn't find any spells that will overpower it, but we can't put it past her either." Jasmin takes a deep breath, then wraps her arms tightly around Dahlia. I kick myself for not thinking of something similar, but I am less familiar with magic than Dahlia is. A sense of calm washes over me, knowing Jasmin has this to protect her. She pulls away from the hug and grabs the chain to pull it over her head.

"I love it, Dahl, but you should wear this. You will be in greater danger from her than me." Dahlia grabs her hands, stopping her. Dahlia shakes her head and explains, "I can't take it. The spell only works for someone I love." Jasmin nods at first, but her expression changes to outrage.

"You don't love yourself?" Dahlia chuckles at her.

"Of course I love myself. I'm amazing." We all laugh at her confidence, but secretly, I'm glad she does. "The language of this spell is specific to a different person. I didn't have enough time to research a more versatile protection spell." She looks at me with sorrow in her eyes. "I plan to make one for you, but it will take me a few days. They take a lot of skill and effort." I kiss her cheek, assuring her I will be fine without one.

"But you will need one for yourself if you don't clean my library now." Jasmin and Dahlia laugh at my statement, but I don't. Because I am not joking. When they realize I'm not laughing, they laugh harder. They finally start cleaning the area. With the five of us working together, it only takes a few minutes to return the site to the state it should be. I finally sigh in relief when it's clean. Jasmin comments that no one has ever cared as deeply about this room as I do. Then she jokes that maybe I only love her for this room.

"Not just the library," I tease as I grab her ass, squeezing hard enough to make her yelp. She smacks my arm as we make our way to the dining room. We sit with our friends like we always do. There is no update on Oleander. She is still staying in her room, not coming out for anything. Dinner is subdued from our regular evenings. While I understand the caution, I'll be glad when things return to normal.

Chapter 39

JASMIN

The amount of stress I have been under lately is nearly unbearable. Despite that, the ache in my core is intense at this moment. I am sandwiched between Dahl and Clem on the bed, both still sleeping. The first streams of daylight are creeping in beneath the curtains. Emmeline has yet to come into the room, but she will be in soon to get us ready for the day. I am not looking forward to another day of anxiously walking around my castle, not knowing what will happen. Instead of thinking about that, I slide my arm around Dahl's waist, letting my finger trace the bare skin of her stomach.

She groans and rolls away from me. "Make Clem do it. I'm exhausted," she mumbles, dragging the blanket over her head. Confusion races through my body, eyebrows knit together, as my fingers drop to the bed beside Dahlia. I'm not familiar with being turned down by either of them. I understand she is tired; creating the amulet yesterday took a lot out of her, and she is still upset over her parents. I didn't realize it was enough to turn me down, though. I struggle with the uncomfortable feeling, turning to Clem.

My fingers wrap around his cock, stroking once, twice, as it hardens in my hands. He moans, turning his head toward me. I catch his lips with mine, his member completely hard in my hand now. I break the kiss to climb over him, sinking down around his dick without hesitation. I sigh deeply at the stretch, grinding briefly. The patch of hair above his cock excites my already throbbing clit. His hands grab my breast, squeezing tightly, twisting roughly in the way I like. I moan loudly as I begin to ride him. His eyes are half open, still shrouded in sleep but also lust. He drops his hands to my ass cheeks, squeezing so tight it feels like he might rip them off my body. I tip my head back, moaning again, not worried that Dahlia is trying to sleep next to me. She could have joined in and still could if she wants.

Suddenly the door bursts open.

"Jasmin! You need....shit."

Kian rushed into the room and quickly turned his back when he realized what was happening. I groan, stilling on Clem's dick. He shuffles beneath me to grab the blanket to cover us up, but if Kian didn't want to see it, he shouldn't have burst into my room like that.

"I'm a little busy, Kian." I drop my hands on Clem's chest, lifting my hips and sinking back down, his cock rubbing that spot inside me that sends my eyes rolling back in my head. Clem groans beneath me. He's angry at being interrupted and that I haven't stopped moving. As much as he likes watching Dahl and me, he doesn't typically want other people involved. I don't honestly care at this point. My body is too desperate to stop. I need this release. My body is thrumming with desire, and it's not going away until I get an orgasm.

"I see. I'm sorry, but it's urgent." His voice is strained, clearly uncomfortable, but also stressed. The only thing I can think about is how Clem's body is rubbing against my clit smashed against his pelvis.

"Five minutes," I speak loudly, not quite a yell, but not in my normal voice. "I need five fucking minutes to get off before I start with that bullshit!" I am yelling at the end, but I can't help it. Clem's hands are on my sides, his eyes staring at me with concern. I just glare at him, stressed and angry over being interrupted.

"Yes, of course. I'll gather some clothes for you." Kian responds formally. Great, now I owe him an apology. Well, better make this orgasm worth it. Dahlia slinks out of bed, sneaking into the bathroom. I sigh but begin riding Clem with urgency and vigor. He moans, thrusting up to meet me. His hands twist my nipples, sending pleasure and pain throughout my body. I tip my head back, looking at the sky as my body tightens with the approaching orgasm. Clem's nails rake down my back, sending my eyes rolling as lust burns through me. My core heats, tightening, ready to explode.

Right as I near the climax of my own orgasm, Clem sits up, putting more pressure on my throbbing nerve. His hand wraps around my neck, pulling me in to kiss him. I bounce on his cock again, letting it stroke over that sensitive spot inside me. Suddenly, I cry out as my entire body tenses. My pussy clenches around him as my shoulders collapse onto him. He slides his hand from my neck down my body to violently thumb my clit. Another wave of pleasure crashes through me as he wraps his free arm around my shoulder, keeping me in place against him. His hips jerk beneath me, filling me with his warm seed. He twists slowly, lowering me onto the bed as my body twists and jerks with the final waves of my orgasm. His lips are on mine as soon as my back hits the bed. He keeps me in a warm embrace for several minutes, gently rubbing my body.

I finally sigh in relief, pressing a kiss to his shoulder. He looks at me, clearly implying I need to apologize to Kian. I roll my eyes, mumbling, "I know." I push him off me, ready to find Kian but feel the wetness dripping down my leg. I think I can take another minute to clean up and get dressed before apologizing for yelling at my advisor while fucking my...What is Clem? He's not technically my husband, but we're pretty well beyond courting at this point. Are we still betrothed? We haven't discussed that much since Dahlia came back. Which is another point of concern. What is she to me? I just passed the non-traditional relationship proclamation, but we haven't discussed what that means for us.

Clem smacks my butt, interrupting my thoughts. I glance at him, my mind slowly processing what I am supposed to be doing. Once my thoughts catch up to reality, I clean up, slip on some undergarments, and find Kian in my closet with Emmeline and my clothes.

"Kian, I apologize for the way I spoke to you. It was uncalled for and rude on my part, and I won't be doing that again." He gives a solemn, single nod before he speaks.

"I am sorry for bursting in like that. I should have known better." We all chuckle at that.

"Yes, you should have," I tease. Kian helps me into one of my split-bottom dresses and places the smaller crown on my head. It's similar to the one Clem had made for my coronation. I love the larger piece, but it's impractical for everyday wear. This smaller one is far more comfortable but still as breathtaking. As I dress, Kian explains why he bursts in the way he did.

"Oleander has called a meeting with all of the Lords. I don't know what it's about, but Lucia and Dominick weren't invited. It's possible she doesn't know about those changes." I eye him suspiciously as I slip on my shoes. Clem walks in, and we also urge him to get dressed quickly.

"Does that mean Alwyn is here?"

"Yes," Kian responds with a wince.

"Fuck." I breathe, rushing through the rest of styling my hair. Dahlia is lounging in the tub. I give her a quick update and a kiss before leaving. Kian leaves to gather Lucia and Dominick, who are thankfully at the castle for other reasons unrelated to Oleander. Clem and I move quickly through the castle to the meeting room. My mind stays surprisingly blank as we walk. I can't fathom what Oleander is planning this time.

When we finally reach the meeting room, I disregard all decorum and walk in before Clem. Oleander is sitting in my chair; the other that Clem typically uses has been removed. Around the table, the four Lords and Alwyn rise and bow haphazardly, startled by my sudden entrance. Oleander just glares at me.

"What is this?" I ask calmly as possible. Clem stands by my side, anger and anxiety rolling off him. My gaze remains fixed on Oleander, but she makes no motion to answer my question. She is in one of her old dresses, the black one Emmeline brought for me to try on before the sparring contest. She is wearing a crown larger than the one I wear. It's gold, adorned with jewels of her liking.

"My Lady," Lord David starts when no one else does, "we received word yesterday that you had urgent matters and needed us to arrive quickly and quietly for a meeting this morning."

"I sent no such word." I briefly glance at the Lords. David and Gustavo appear stunned by my statement. Lord Erland from Obele looks indifferent about the whole situation. Lord Thurston and Alwyn are squaring their shoulders, a smug look covering their faces. It's evident in their pompousness they knew I wasn't the one that called this meeting. They were always closer to my mother than my father when he was still alive. I never knew how deep the divide was, though. I am about to find out.

"We were summoned by the Queen. That's what our messengers said," Lord Erland drawls in a bored, uninterested voice. I turn my attention back to the cold-hearted bitch sitting in my chair. She finally rises, ready to join this conversation. Clem stiffens next to me, moving closer by a hair.

"Yes, I summoned them." Her voice is too casual for my liking, but two can play that game.

"You are no longer the Queen. You have not been Queen in this kingdom for over nine years." She picks a piece of lint off her sleeve, dropping it on the floor. Nothing actually falls from her hand. This is a power play to show how bored she is, and I hate her for it. "Impersonating the crowned monarch is an act of treason." I keep my voice casual, walking toward the table, toward my seat she is still standing beside.

Her eyes jerk to mine, realizing the statement for what it is, an actual threat. Her gaze is a mixture of hatred, shock, and, somewhere behind her mask, a hint of pride. Alwyn speaks up behind her, all the Lords still standing at their spots.

"We don't need to jump to any conclusions. I'm sure this is just a misunderstanding." Disgust simmers through my veins over having him in my presence, defending my mother's actions.

"Alwyn, you..." I start but am quickly interrupted by Oleander.

"Do you always address your lords so informally?" I breathe, settling myself as I decide how to respond to her.

"I do not address my Lords informally, no. However, Alwyn is no lord in this kingdom." I turn back to glance at the door. "In fact, Lord Dominick and Lady Lucia should be here any moment now."

My mother was always good at hiding her emotions but is not quick enough to shield the surprise that appears on her face. Her eyebrows arch, and her lips part momentarily before she remembers herself. I take a small win at shocking her enough to warrant an expression. With her face back to a neutral expression, I speak before she can.

"There have been many changes in the last nine years, Queen Mother. Since Alwyn is leaving, why don't you take his seat, and I will fill you in quickly before my other Lord, Lady, and advisor arrive." Alwyn hesitates, glancing between my mother and me, but finally bows his head and walks toward the door. Mother doesn't make any effort to move, but I call over one of my staff and ask them to bring in Clem's chair along with three more. My mother only having five seats at the table isn't unexpected. She remained locked in her room since she arrived. We haven't had time to discuss any changes. The other Lords not having any concerns is astounding.

As the chairs are shifted around, the Lords take their seats. Mother finally occupies the chair Alwyn just left. I take my seat back from her, with Clem by my side. Three other chairs are brought over, ready for my friends. The stark contrast of Mother on one side with the remaining Lords from her era and my side with the currently empty seats. I take a deep breath, pushing down the doubt and fears rising inside me. Clem rubs the back of my hand, bringing a calm awareness to my body. Even if we are currently divided, many people are still on my side out of this room.

"When was Alwyn removed as a Lord?" Mother's tone is icy and sharp.

"Just a couple of months ago, actually," I start, adjusting my position to sit straight, presenting more confidence than I feel. "Though, the issues stem back many, many years. He was relieved because of his treatment of the witches, his unwillingness to help with the curse and his general disdain for more than half of his territory." With that, Kian, Dominick, and Lucia walk in. Mother gasps as they take their seats on the other side of Clem.

Once they are settled, I continue speaking. "When Alwyn was relieved, the witches and I met. I wanted their opinion on the new Lord. It was decided at that time the witches would create their own territory. Govern themselves as they have been under Alwyn's reign but with approval from the crown. " I point to her, "Lady Lucia is now my Lady of Covens and reports to me on behalf of the witches. Lord Dominick," I motion to him, and he nods, "has replaced Alwyn as Lord of Greynon."

Mother glares at the three new arrivals in the meeting with palpable disdain. Any more of a reaction, and she would be growling and baring her teeth. Her response is almost laughable. I have had years of training to school my emotions and only show what I want people to see. Nothing prepared me for what Oleander says next, though.

"Who is this other witch?" The words aren't so shocking, as is her tone. Pure hatred oozes from her like fog over a lake. There is not a soul alive who wouldn't recognize the emotions she is showing. I want to believe it is an act, something to throw us off and disguise her true feelings. But there is no way to fake this much anger or hostility.

"He is my advisor." My voice is soft, not quite weak, but not holding the vitality it did earlier. Memories of a childhood of belittling, demands of more than I can give, crash into my mind. For a single, brief moment, I let discomfort wash through me. I remember the times she called me worthless, useless, weak. Every insult and indignation rolls through my mind. A soft light shines through the wave of slurs as I realize Clem is holding my hand, squeezing tightly. I turn to look at him, letting my focus shift to him instead of my mother. He glares at her with as much hostility as she gives off. Beyond him, Lucia, Dominick, and Kian all show varying degrees of being insulted.

"What do you have against the witches?" I slowly, somewhat unwillingly, turn my attention back to my mother, sitting opposite me at the round table. Without missing a beat, she responds to me.

"Witches are not to be trusted." She doesn't realize we know what she is. Now it's my turn to break character. Shock spreads across my face before I quickly pool my face back to a neutral position. This explains why Alwyn refused to work with them. He was in Mother's pocket for as long as I can remember. Was he always like that, so hateful? Or did she turn him? It doesn't matter either way. Both are hateful now, and that will not be tolerated in my kingdom, especially not of leaders.

"I see." I start, pausing to take a deep breath.

"This kingdom, *my* kingdom," I emphasize, " is a safe, welcoming place for all people. Everyone will be treated with dignity and respect. If you cannot abide by this, I suggest you return to Hollyhock and remain there. Oppression of any person will be punished accordingly." I pause for a moment, gathering my next thought. "You are entitled to your own opinion. You are not entitled to treat people poorly." We are back to her glaring at me. In her silence, I decide to continue with this meeting. I have no plans for a formal meeting, but I may take the opportunity for updates.

"Kian, have we had any contact with Hollyhock in a formal capacity?" The statement is intended to poke at my mother, as she has not claimed to be here with any information. Before he can answer, she speaks up.

"I do have information for you." She snaps her fingers, holding her hand out to accept something. I watch in disdain as a small woman rushes from the corner in a cowering manner, places a scroll in Mother's hand, then returns to her position again. "As you recall, the King of Hollyhock has a son a few years older than you, and he is still unwed." She mentioned all of this a few nights ago when she first arrived. Why is she bringing it up now?

"It has come to my attention that you are also currently unwed." Fuck. I gaze away from her, noticing fear coat Lord Thurston's face. He informed Oleander I have not married Clem.

I cannot fathom a world without Clem. The courts may approve of taking someone from outside to marry the monarch, but fate has already decided he is mine, and nothing will change that. He finally turns to meet my gaze. I let the corners of my mouth turn up slightly, squeezing his hand to let him know I am his and wouldn't consider any other option.

"A union between you and the Prince would benefit both kingdoms. Hollyhock could offer power, and Sweet Briar could offer our navy and trade routes across the sea. With this union, you would still be Queen one day and expand our kingdom tenfold. Plus, we wouldn't need to worry about this whole witch debacle. Hollyhock has an area where all the witches are located, providing magic for the kingdom as needed."

Something in the way she says this last sentence makes me believe this isn't a beneficial relationship for the witches. Something in her voice implies they are all slaves in their own kingdom. That is absolutely not something I want for any of my people. She tosses the scroll she was holding, and it lands before me. I open it and read. It is a letter from the King proclaiming marriage, a trade agreement, consolidation of our military forces and land, and consolidation of slave witches. They had the audacity to include the term slave in this document.

"No."

I pass the scroll to Clem, letting him read it and pass it on. Typically, these agreements are not shared beyond one or two advisors. I will let everyone in this room read and understand why I will not accept this deal.

"But, Milady," Lord Gustavo starts, "think of how beneficial this could be for our people."

"I am. My answer is still no." Kian has the document now. I watch as his eyes go wide at the last piece of information. He gives me a slight nod to me before passing it to Dominick. Lucia leans in, and they read together.

"This is a wonderful opportunity for my kingdom!" Mother bellows from her seat, outraged at my answer.

"For you or your people?" I question as Lucia audibly gasps, bringing her hand to her mouth. Dominick passes the bill to Lord Thurston, consoling Lucia by rubbing her back. "You may not know this, but one of the first proclamations I made in this kingdom was to free all the enslaved people. No one in this kingdom is used to benefit another person without proper recompense. I will not allow anyone to fall into slavery again." Mother's face flashes between shock and outrage, but I remain calm as the scroll is passed between the rest of the Lords. They lower their heads one by one, realizing this is not a treaty we can agree on. When I first announced the proclamation, several Lords fought with me over the enslaved people. However, they have grown to understand how much better it is when they treat their people fairly, at least our workers.

"You can accept this agreement now and fight for the rights of slaves when you are Queen. This treaty will ensure you have more power than you could ever want." Mother is still pushing this issue with me, and I cannot understand why. There is some reason, some deal she has worked out with the King to benefit her. I just know that is what is happening.

"I do not want power, especially not at the expense of my people. If you honestly believe a treaty between Sweet Briar and Hollyhock would be beneficial, I am willing to discuss this further. I will consider a treaty that does not entail marriage, slavery, or combining lands and forces. We will remain our own kingdom. If you have input, you are free to give it, but I will speak directly with the King before any deal is made." I pause, glancing around the table to be sure everyone is listening. "Need I remind you, your position is Queen Mother. You hold no power in this court. Based on your proclaimed biases and hatred, understand that no power will be given to you." She slams her hands on the table, rising quickly while glaring at me. I breathe deeply, not cowering to her like I used to.

"With that being said, I wish to adjourn this meeting. I have other matters to attend to." I rise, everyone else following. "Lords and Lady, you are not to discuss official court business with Oleander. Any discussion will be seen as treason. Her position has been made clear. I would like to reconvene tomorrow morning to discuss this issue further after we have had time to calm down. Queen Mother, you are welcome to attend if you can hold your temper." Her jaw clenches so tightly that I worry her teeth may break under pressure. With that, everyone bows, including my mother, finally showing me some of the respect I deserve. I don't believe for a second it is out of respect or that she isn't planning something nefarious. I need time to unwind after that meeting. My whole body aches like

I just ran from here to Arkaley. Shock, anger, hurt, and confusion are rolling through my body, and I need to be away from this for a time to recollect myself.

Chapter 40

JASMIN

After leaving the meeting, my feet take me back to my room. My mind is painfully empty but also very loud. It sounds like a river rushing through my mind. No thoughts are complete. No questions are answered. Why is Mother here? Roaring silence. How do I protect Clem and Dahlia? A crashing wave of nothing. What do I do next? Thick emptiness.

Kian and Clem are walking behind me. I can sense their presence but can't hear their words. Their lips move, and concern fills their eyes, but I keep walking. I don't know where I'm going, but my body has an idea. So I let my feet lead me through the hallways. Kian and Clem turn back toward the dining hall, but my feet shuffle along the padded hallways. The worn carpet is soft beneath my feet, padding the noise of my steps from my ears. At this moment, I am thankful for the silence in my head. It will break soon, and everything will hurt then.

I arrive in my room, where Dahlia is lounging. Her body is stretched out, hanging softly on the chaise lounger. Her eyes are closed with small bags under them. Her face is relaxed but worn. She opens her eyes a crack, watching me as I continue my path to my vanity. My body crumbles onto the bench, landing awkwardly. I pull the crown off, going through the motions of combing my hair.

Dahlia watches me through the mirror but doesn't speak. She looks as exhausted as I feel right now.

"Why is it so hard, Dahl?" My voice breaks at her name, but no tears come. Too many have been shed already, and none are left in my body. Dahlia walks over to me, pulling my shoulders to face her.

"It won't always be this hard, Jas. I'm here now." Her hands stroke my cheek as she leans in. Her presence is so calming. This is why I fell in love with her all those years ago. She is my peace, my anchor in the storm, my everything. My body relaxes as her lips settle against mine, plump, full, and soft. Her kiss is gentle, reminding me of everything she is. Just as I touch her side, the door opens. Kian and Clem are chatting as they walk in. Dahlia doesn't break the kiss, and neither do I. We both need this touch to reconnect at this moment.

Kian and Clem stop talking, placing food trays on the table near us. Dahlia finally pulls back, kissing my forehead quickly before turning to the table. Clem gives her a quick kiss on the cheek. A soft smile spreads at their interaction. As difficult as things are with my mother, I still get excited at the reality that Clem and Dahlia are mine and each other's. Things were so tenuous with them for so long. I'm so glad it's behind us, and we have each other.

Clem kneels in front of me, taking my hands in his. His approach is different than Dahlia's. She would burn the world down for me, removing any threat, any danger. Clem would stay with me and protect me while the world burns. Dahlia is wild and untamed. Clem is steady and hard.

I hold his hands in mine, mulling over the difference between the two. My mind focuses on his fingers. It's customary for married couples to wear rings, showing their relationships. We never quite got to that part. We tried a couple of times. It was continually interrupted. My eyes lift to Dahlia, picking food off the trays, then back to Clem. He is oblivious to the thoughts in my head. A smirk spreads across my face. He's oblivious to everything when it comes to our emotions. He kisses the back of my hand, squeezing it tightly.

"Are you okay?" His words are soft, only meant for me. A calm has settled over me in the last few moments. I don't want to harbor the way my mother makes me feel. I want to spend time with those I love and love me in return. Emmeline enters the room, heading straight for the table with food. She's brought several bottles of wine with her and is working on getting them open, despite Clem's attempted ban on it. I nod at Clem, taking a deep breath and letting it settle over my shaken body. Oleander has already stolen so much from me; I won't give her anymore.

I kiss Clem as gently and lovingly as Dahlia just kissed me. He pulls away with a smirk, never able to stay worried when kisses are involved. Dahlia is already in the single chair. Clem and I grab food and wine, sitting on the larger couch. Emmeline gets her food, then sits with Kian on the smaller sofa. They sit closer but make no other attempts at intimacy. I haven't been able to spend much time with her alone and miss time with my best platonic friend. Being with Clem and Dahlia is always fun because I get to kiss them, but I also miss Emmeline and gossiping and chatting and not kissing. We all speak lightly as we eat, sharing funny stories, keeping things light, and avoiding the giant cloud looming over our heads.

Kian announces he will track down more information on my mother when we finish eating. I ask him to check back in with us before dinner. I walk with Emmeline to return the food trays to the kitchen. The thought of questioning her relationship with Kian swims in my brain, but she is gleefully telling me about one of the kitchen maids spending a lot of time with one of the new witches training with Dahlia. I can't help but bask in my friend's excitement over this bit of gossip. So I listen, express the proper emotions, and ask the right questions, thoroughly enjoying the brief moments with my best friend.

She leaves me to tend to other matters after we drop the trays off in the kitchen. When I turn around, Zander is standing behind me. I startle at his seemingly sudden appearance, and he apologizes. We both laugh over my reaction. I hug him, then position myself beside him as we walk away.

"How are you doing, Zander?"

He shrugs, not looking directly at me. "Fine. Tomas has been a great help to me in the stables and..." his words slow, cheeks darkening with a blush, "in private."

His words are nearly a whisper, but he still says them out loud. I grin at him, knowing the nervous but emboldened feeling of wanting to discuss a relationship.

"How did you know Clem was the one for you?" He eyes me cautiously, so I offer a soft smile.

"Kian told me," I chuckle over the absurdity of the answer. It's the truth, but it does sound odd to say it like that. Zander matches my laugh, nodding along, remembering how everything came to be so many months ago.

"What about D? How did you know you wanted to be with her? You knew that before any of the curses happened." Thoughts of our youth flash through my mind. I knew for a long time she was mine. I always knew I would keep her by my side, regardless of capacity.

"She..."I pause, searching for the right words to tell her younger brother. "Dahlia completed me in a way I had never experienced and still haven't. My relationship with her is different than Clem's. She gave me something I didn't know was missing. She's..." What is the right word here? My true love? My soul mate? My fated lover? What is she?

"Everything." Zander fills in softly. I start to nod but notice his far-off look. He understands my words more than I realize. My heart squeezes; he's thinking about Tomas. I wrap my arms around him, leaning my head against his shoulder, celebrating this little joy with him. We walk for a few minutes until we stop by the door leading to the stables. I have a feeling Tomas is on the other side, but Zander doesn't make an effort to move through. He turns, facing me, with nervousness written on his face.

"The non-traditional relationship proclamation, does that cover marriage?" He doesn't look at me, chewing on his bottom lip. This is something I've seen Tomas do before, but never Zander. They say you pick up little habits from your partners.

"Yes."

"So I can marry him?" I nod, finally making eye contact with him. Hope blooms on his face, then nervousness. His face begins to cycle through a wide range of emotions as excitement courses through my body. I squeeze him in a hug as tightly as I can.

"Let us know when the wedding is." We laugh together, me excitedly, him nervously. I leave him, returning to my room with thoughts of marriage and forever in my mind. I envision a wedding between Zander and Tomas. A winter wedding with both men in deep green suits. White snow covers the ground with fat red berries decorating evergreen twigs. Or a spring wedding, with soft colors and flowers everywhere.

Then I imagine a ceremony for me. An autumn wedding, with deep reds, oranges, and bright yellows to contrast everything. Clem and Dahlia on my side as we announce to everyone that we are together, that our love is forever. With Ada in the front row, my dream crashes when I think of the rest of our parents. All three fathers are gone. Would we wait for Sunette to return? Would my mother be invited? Would I want her involved? Not really, but can I prevent her from being at a ceremony like that? Not a public one, for sure.

Just as my thoughts run away from me, I enter our bedroom. Clem is on the couch with a book. This man can pull off many looks, but some of my favorites always involve a book in his hand. Dahlia is lying on the couch with her head in his lap. Her long braids Sunette styled before she left are sprawled across Clem's legs. His free hand is on her shoulder, stroking her slowly.

This is where I am meant to be, with them. Thoughts of marriage and forever dance through my mind. I kneel on the floor in front of Clem's legs. Dahlia's eyes crack open but close as she smiles at me. I press a kiss against her forehead, soaking up the warmth of her skin. I rub Clem's leg, sending gratitude to all the gods I can remember for giving me both of these people. The curse was absolutely terrible, and I wouldn't want to live through it again, but I can't deny the gratefulness that it brought them to me. I never would have ended up with Clem without it. Even my relationship with Dahlia would have been tenuous without the curse. These thoughts drive the words out of my mouth more than anything else.

"I want to marry you both." Dahlia's eyes open fully, but her expression stays the same. I'm sure Clem stops breathing at my words, but I continue speaking, needing them to know everything I want. "And I want you to be Queen and King with me."

At that, Dahlia sits up straight, staring at me. Clem timidly looks between both of us. He struggled with the thought of being King before but had mostly come to terms with it. We haven't discussed it in a while, though, not since we started pursuing the triad. Clem is breathing normally now but not speaking. I know Dahlia heard me, but she is frozen in her place. She looks like she has seen a ghost or a grim reaper. The pause is growing awkward, so I keep speaking. That always helps things when I just say more random ass words.

"We could have a ceremony similar to a wedding. It would be different for the three of us. We could adjust the legal documents to make it official. And probably just add the coronation into the ceremony, if you don't mind. That would make it easier for the kingdom and everyone that wants to attend. Plus, it would be cheaper to have one ceremony, especially since we have already started one wedding and had my coronation this year. I mean, I guess there isn't a rush..." The words keep tumbling out of my mouth. At this point, I haven't even looked at Clem or Dahlia. I am picking at some imaginary lint on Clem's legs. As the words keep falling from my lips, Dahlia wraps her arms around me, jerking my body up to the couch between her and Clem. They crush me between them in a tight, full-body hug. I squeal at first but quickly wrap my arms around her as Clem squeezes us together.

"Yes!" She presses quick kisses to my cheek, hugging me tighter.

"Really?" My voice is cautious, uncertain. "I wasn't sure you would want something like that." Disbelief covers her face as she tips her head down, purses her lips, and raises her eyebrows at me. I laugh at her expression, burying my face in her neck as relief pours through my body.

"I want to share everything with you. Even your stupid title." We chuckle over her words. I wipe tears of disbelief and joy from my eyes. I thought I would have to do more to convince her. Then I realize Clem hasn't actually answered. I twist in Dahlia's arms, meeting Clem's eyes. His expression is unreadable, and I hate how stoic he is becoming. I want to read him like a book, like normal.

"I've already tried to do that. Several times, in fact. You won't stop me from doing that eventually." He shrugs casually as if this is the most obvious thing in the world. He was always going to marry me and be my King. Obviously, I didn't need to ask. I roll my eyes, giggling as I shove his shoulder playfully.

"She thought we would say no, Clem." Dahlia's face turns hungry, demanding. "We need to show our queen what she means to us." Her eyes are trained on mine, glazed in lust and desire. Wetness pools in my core almost instantly. I fight the moan, unable to deny my body's reaction to her. She will always elicit this reaction from me. My breathing becomes shallow as she leans closer to me. Even with my morning tryst with Clem, I still want more. I will always want more with them. Clem jumps up from behind me, startling us both. "I have something for this!" He rushes toward the closet, where he stores all the fun items he brings out during our playtime. "Get naked!" He shouts to both of us as he closes the door to rummage around the room. Dahlia stands, pulling me to my feet.

"You heard the man." She snaps her fingers, and the sound reverberates through my clit. My thighs press together, trying to get some friction there. Four minutes ago, I was worried about what they would say to my question. Now my core is dripping, and I'm on fire. I begin to remove my clothes, watching Dahlia. She removes hers but doesn't take her dark, hungry eyes off me. I lift my tunic over my head, and her eyes land on my breast, tongue licking across her lips. That's not where I want her tongue. I turn around, sliding my pants off my hips, letting her see my ass and thighs as I bend over to pull my feet out. Her dress is on the floor with my clothes, but her hands are on my ass now, squeezing tightly. She drags one finger from my clit, across my opening, teasing my ass. I groan, pressing into her hand as she moves across me.

Clem walks out, handing a bundle to Dahlia. She pulls the strings as Clem assumes his position behind me. He does the same thing, dragging his fingers across my opening, then pressing against my ass.

"Godsdamn, Jas. You are so fucking wet." He pulls me to standing, my back to his chest. One hand grabs my breast while the other works its way to my clit.

He makes soft circles around the nub, and I lean back into it, his clothes rubbing roughly against my skin.

"What is this?" Dahlia holds up a leather strap and what looks like a small glass bottle, but smoother and without an opening. The end has a flat edge with a deep lip around the outside. It's several inches long and has a definitively phallic shape. Clem takes his hand off my clit, and a small whimper escapes at his absence. He takes the glass tube in his hand, instructing Dahlia to put some oil on the tip. She does as told, obscenely rubbing the tube with oil. The sight of her stroking this phallic shape sends pulses through my pussy. He slides his hand down my thigh, not letting the object touch me.

"Leg up, dirty girl." I place my foot on the table, spreading my core open for him. He slides the tube between my legs, pressing it against my opening. He slips it inside me smoothly, and I moan at the pressure building. He slides the device in and out several times, my eyes rolling back in my head. The tube isn't nearly as large as Clem's cock, but it still feels fantastic. Agonizingly slow, he presses it in, then lets it slide back out. My cunt is clenching tightly around it already, needing more. His hand circles my neck, his fingers stroking the bottom of my jaw.

"Open your mouth, my little slut." His fingers stay around my throat as I follow his instruction. He pulls the tube from my vagina and slides it straight into my mouth. The taste of my arousal mixed with the oil has me groaning, wanting more. I don't gag by the size of this item. Instead of thrusting it, he just leaves it sitting on my tongue. My mouth waters around it, spit leaking out the sides of my mouth.

"This part," Clem's voice is deep and laced with arousal as he points to the deep lip just outside my mouth, "fits in that belt." Dahlia's eyes grow big and bright as he speaks. I don't fully understand the implications; my mind is clouded with arousal and need. I just want to see what else they can do with this tube. "You can wear it as a belt, or it should fit as a gag." Dahl's grin is pure salacious enthusiasm. Her face borders on evil as she stares at me, listening to Clem explain the item. My core throbs at her gaze. I don't know what she is thinking, but my body is ready to find out.

"So I can fuck her like you?" She almost giggles with excitement as her words sink into my brain. She's going to put this item in the belt, then fuck me with it. I try to nod in consent, but Clem's hand tightens around my neck, not letting me move. I try to look at him, but his grip is too tight for me to move. The tension on my neck sends a pulse of pleasure through my body, sending my eyes to the back of my head. Clem is primarily supporting my weight at this point, as my muscles are just lust-filled mush.

"We can both fuck her." I can hear the words, but the vibrations in his chest keep me from processing what he is saying. "Look how fucking needy she is." His hand trails my inner thigh, caressing the skin around my cunt, leaving me whimpering and dripping for them. Dahlia fastens the belt around her body, low over her hips. She steps to me, slipping the item out of my mouth nearly all the way. Then she slides it back down my throat. My pussy clenches with her actions. Clem moves away from me, but my focus is on Dahlia and her devious stare. She slowly slides the tube in and out of my mouth, watching me the whole time. Clem is rustling behind us, but he could be a million miles away for all I know.

"You like when I fuck your throat? It's not just Clem that's going to use you anymore." I do hear him growl from behind us. Dahlia smirks at him, breaking her gaze with me but not halting the item sliding into my mouth. She keeps her body away from mine, not touching or letting me touch her. The lack of contact charges my arousal. I need her body on mine. I love the feel of her thrusting this tube down my throat, but my body aches for her warm touch.

"Bring her back here." Clem is sitting on the bed, motioning us over. Dahlia pulls the tube from my throat and latches her lips on mine. Her tongue is in my mouth, blending her taste with mine and the oil. The taste of everything is nearly overwhelming. My knees go weak as she finally grabs me. Her arms wrap around my back and waist, guiding me backward without breaking the kiss. Once we get to the bed, she pulls back from the kiss.

"Be a good girl and do what you're told. Then we'll reward you." Reward, yes. I want that. "Crawl to him." Her voice is just above a whisper, husky, and sex-laden. My cunt is dripping down my thighs, going from the desire to marry them to the desire to have them inside me in mere minutes. I need them in so many ways. I turn onto my hands and knees, crawling toward Clem, when Dahl smacks my ass hard. I groan, stopping in my tracks, pressing my ass back toward her hand. She rubs the cheek she slapped, then quickly hits the other side. Fuck, the pain and pleasure are almost too much. I'm going to orgasm if a soft breeze blows over my clit at this point.

Clem is staring with hooded eyes and a rock-hard cock. Unable to help myself, I wrap my lips around the head, eliciting a groan from him. My lips are still wet from having the tube in my mouth. As I swirl my tongue over the head of his dick, Dahlia crawls behind me, sliding her hand up my slit. She swats my thighs, spreading my legs further apart. I raise my ass, taking more of Clem into my throat. Then Dahlia slides the tube inside me. Her thighs are flush with mine, her stomach pressed against my ass. She is inside me. Dahlia is fucking me now. I slide off of Clem's cock, turning to look at Dahlia, where our bodies meet. She slips in and out of me as I watch. The reality of what is happening here grows with my orgasm. Clem has found a way to give us something we never thought we would have. This will open a new level of sex for all of us. Just as that idea sets in, my orgasm almost reaches its peak.

"Stop. You'll make her come, and we don't want that yet." Dahlia slides the tube out of me, and I yell anger and frustration at them. They laugh at me, rubbing my body. At least they are still touching me. I would literally explode without that. Literally, I can feel it. Every inch of my body is tense and aching, and I want and need so much more.

"I've got a special idea for our needy slut. Turn around, and I'll show you." I spin around, and Clem guides me so my back is against his chest. He positions both of my feet on either side of his legs, a position we've been using more lately. I settle into the familiar position, his hands sliding under my ass. But instead of fingers in my pussy, or instructions for Dahlia to lick me, he spreads my cheeks, pressing at my other hole. I gasp as his oiled finger breaks through, pushing inside me in a delicious stretch.

Dahlia rubs light circles around my clit, not to let me orgasm but to increase my pleasure. I moan, tipping my head back against Clem's shoulder. He presses several kisses to my forehead as another finger enters my ass. Dahlia strokes my breasts as her finger continues its lazy circles on my nub. My hips begin to jerk under their ministrations, needing more from both.

"One more, dirty girl," Clem whispers as a third finger slides inside my tight hole. I cry out at the intrusion. Clem's fingers work masterfully, stretching me, building my pleasure. Dahlia's lips crash into mine, swallowing my moans as Clem fucks me with his fingers. My hips grind between them, undulating of their own will. My brain is clouded with pleasure and touch and smells. The oil, my arousal, Clem and Dahlia's scents. It's nearly overwhelming. I keep my eyes closed as my tongue dances with Dahlia's.

Both pull back from me all at once, leaving me gasping and whimpering. Clem adjusts me with both hands, spreading me for him as he slides into my stretched hole. My ass lands against his hips, stilling momentarily as I adjust to his girth. My breathing is labored, from the stretch, from the pleasure, from the idea of what's to come. A sheen of sweat covers my body as it quivers beneath Clem and Dahlia's fingers, working my breasts and ass. Clem's hands tighten, drawing me up along his length, then letting me sink back down. My head rolls in pleasure, burying my forehead against his neck for support.

"You ready, my little whore?" I nod, but I have no idea what I'm ready for. It doesn't matter. I'm prepared for whatever he gives me at this point. I'll take it all. His finger circles my clit, and my brain turns to slush. He's talking to Dahlia, giving her instructions, but I can't hear his words. I'm already living in another plane of existence. My soul floats in the room as fingers flick against my clit. I moan, my hips undulating, driving Clem deeper inside my ass. I groan loudly, rolling my head on his shoulder.

Clem's hands grasp onto my hips, holding me still. I will my head to look down to see what they are doing, what they are planning, but my body is no longer responding to my commands. My body is only driven by desire at this point. Dahlia slides between my thighs, the warmth of our contact spreading through my core, causing me to clench my pussy around nothing. Clem groans low obscenities, urging Dahlia to move faster. Something is nudging my empty hole, and I finally look down. Dahlia has the tube strapped to her waist and is pressing inside me. Suddenly, I realize what their intentions are. Fear fills me that I won't be able to fit them both like this. I've had Dahlia's finger and the other vibrating cylinder, but this tube is much larger than both. As if sensing my concern, Clem begins to whisper in my ear.

"You can take us both, little slut. You're so good at taking us. Just imagine how good it will feel to have Dahlia and me inside you." My body tenses at his words. I want that. I can take it. I will take it all. "Fuck, Jas." He rarely uses my name during sex, so it's startling that he does. "If you keep clenching, I'm gonna come inside you before we can even enjoy it." I laugh, and Dahlia uses that distraction to press inside me. I moan as she fills me more than I ever have. I suck in a deep breath, trying to force air into my body as it adjusts to the stretch. She shifts slowly but eventually sinks until her hips are pressed flush between my legs. Both of them are still for a moment, letting me adjust, but I need them to move. I whine, my noise growing louder as my hips begin to wiggle.

Dahlia slides out slowly, my eyes rolling back in my head in pleasure. I turn my head, finally lifting it to look at Dahlia. I glance down where her hips are slowly thrusting into me. "Kiss me, please," I beg, needing her mouth to cover mine. Her lips find mine, throwing a slight hitch in her thrusting, but she finds her rhythm again quickly. Her hips roll, thrusting the tube inside me. Her fingers push the soaking hair off my forehead when she pulls back to watch my face. Clem palms my ass, then starts thrusting in tandem with Dahlia.

The sensation of the two of them moving inside me is overwhelming. My body tenses, and I cry out. Just before I orgasm, Dahlia flicks the bundle of nerves between the dams holding my orgasm break. I scream as pleasure crashes through my body. I jerk and shake between them as they chase their own satisfaction. I am outside of my body now, watching as I twist between Clem and Dahlia, overwhelmed with the never-ending orgasm.

Clem clamps his teeth on my shoulder, releasing deep inside me. Dahlia shudders, her own orgasm tearing through her. A brief question of how she got off flashes in my mind but is quickly replaced with another wave of pleasure, another jerk of my muscles, another flash of lightning behind my eyes. For a moment, I believe the magic is back. It's not the curse, though. Being with these two is a different kind of magic. A fulfilling, everlasting magic.

Dahlia pulls out of me first, leaving my pussy clenching as my body levels out. She climbs off the bed as Clem lifts me off him, placing me on my side next to him. Dahlia returns with a wet cloth, wiping my face, chest, then core, sending more pulses of pleasure through my body. My eyes close softly, letting her and Clem be responsible for cleaning up.

Soon they return, wrapping their warm bodies around my own chilled one. Between my heart rate returning to normal and being covered in sweat from the activities, I nearly started shivering before they arrived. Clem wraps his arms around me as Dahlia strokes my sides, leaving me cooing between them. I am already a puddle of mush, and they are maintaining my liquified state.

"How did you get off, Dahl?" My words are soft and light, eyes still closed, enjoying the post-orgasmic bliss.

"I used the magic fun ball." Ah, I nod my head lazily, enjoying the space between my two favorite people. We're all quiet for several minutes, breathing, relaxing, and enjoying our comfort. I decide to speak, wanting to say my idea now while everyone is calm, worried they may freak out on me. They didn't before, but that doesn't mean they will like this idea.

"I want to announce our plans at the meeting tomorrow. And I want you there, Dahl." She tenses beside me, but Clem is the one to speak.

"What if your mother is there?"

"Then she will finally know the truth, and we won't have to hide Dahlia anymore. We'll keep extra guards around us if she reacts poorly, but I'm tired of hiding. I created the non-traditional relationship proclamation for us, and it's time to use it." In front of me, I watch Dahlia process my words. I rub her sides lightly, offering her whatever comfort I can without using words. I don't want to interrupt her thoughts right now. She finally speaks.

"Okay."

Chapter 41

DAHLIA

S he wants to marry me.

She asked me to be Queen.

My heart doesn't know how to handle this information. I love her so much. She is my world, and I would give anything for her. Obviously, I want to marry her. There was never a day in my life since I met her that I didn't want to spend with her. It was easy to answer her question when she asked.

But...

Baba is gone. Mama may or may not return. Oleander is back and being her usual fucking bitch self. I swear, we just got over the drama between Clem and me. Will we ever get a break from the drama? Unfortunately, Oleander presents a real threat to our safety. She cursed the kingdom once; what's to stop her from doing that again? She could be working on totally new spells and curses for all of us. I am honestly terrified of going to the meeting with her shortly.

Jasmin, Clem, Kian, and I are waiting in a small room for everyone to arrive for the meeting. Jasmin and Kian are speaking softly about this particular topic, a challenging one for all of us. Clem is pressing me into his chest, supporting more of my weight than I want to admit. He has been our rock for the past couple of weeks.

Jasmin is really struggling with her own state of mind. She also lost Mama and Baba, who supported her during the curse. She hasn't implied that she saw their departure coming, but it hasn't hit her as hard as it did me. I still haven't entirely accepted that they are gone. Mama said she would return, but why would she? Her family is there, in her home. The one she loved. She is a free woman; why wouldn't she stay and live with her people in her culture. Sure, she has Zander and me, but is that enough to bring her back? Assuming, of course, she survives the journey.

I shake my head against Clem's shoulder, trying to clear my mind of these thoughts. His arms tighten around my back, pressing me tighter against his smooth chest. I breathe deeply, burying my face against his neck. He tilts his head against mine, kissing my ear softly. He doesn't whisper promises of safety or security to me. We both know it wouldn't be real. We can't be sure what kind of power Oleander has. His love and presence are comforting but not enough to erase the genuine threat sitting in the next room.

Jasmin rubs my back, informing us it's time. I kiss her deeply, needing the reassurance she is safe. We line up to walk into the meeting room. Kian in front and Clem behind him. I walk in between Clem and Jasmin. I suck in a deep breath as we start moving. I haven't seen Oleander since she returned. I wish more than anything that Mama was here. She would know what to do, how to keep us safe, what to say. Instead, I channel her energy. I let her spirit guide me, her words of the past leading my actions. I may still be young and irresponsible, but Mama isn't. She would know what to do.

As we near our seats, my heart rate spikes. No one has seen me yet. I could still turn and run. I could whip around Jasmin and head back to the room. It doesn't sound so foolish now. I can stand another day in her bedroom. Who am I kidding? I couldn't stand another hour in that room alone. I need to be strong and face this bitch threatening our way of life. I will not spend more time locked away. This back-and-forth between fear and confidence is making my own head spin. I'm not used to being this frightened. I'm also not used to dealing with a ...massive...donkey...dick. Okay, I need a better insult, but she's a huge bitch.

I straighten my shoulders, shaking my head again. The loc jewelry Jasmin found for me clinks together. After dinner last night, Emmeline, Jas, and I spent time together, putting them in and drinking wine, making plans for the ceremony Jas wants. It was a nice distraction from reality. Several court members look toward Clem, trying to find the source of that sound. It's me. He steps to the side, standing behind his chair on Jasmin's left.

I am now fully exposed to everyone in the room. There are audible gasps as I step behind a matching chair on Jasmin's right. Then she steps up to hers. All eyes are on me. The Lords show varying degrees of interest and boredom. The newest members of the court hold curiosity in their eyes. They all know me but haven't seen me in a meeting before. I finally connect with Oleander's gaze. Pure, unfiltered hatred oozes out of her stare. She wanted me dead ten years ago and still feels the same way. I smile sweetly, focusing on Jasmin, who is watching me. I fill my chest with as much love as I can, trying to force it onto her. Anything to replace the evil in the room.

After a quick bow, Jasmin motions for everyone to take a seat, but she remains standing. She gazes around the room, taking in all of the guests. It's an impressive display of the people in her kingdom. She has garnered a diverse group representing her true kingdom, not just the rich and powerful.

"Thank you all for being here. This is the first court of a new era. We are here to represent the entire kingdom and its best interests." Several people nod around the table, and some look more hesitant. Those are the ones in Oleander's pocket. I try to remember who they are. "Typically, I don't do introductions. We all know each other, but I want to address everyone with their title before we begin the meeting." She motions to Kian on my other side.

"Kian of Greynon, my personal Court Advisor. Lady Lucia, Lady of the Covens. Matron Maud, head of her coven and first appearance in court. Thank you." Maud nods, keeping a wary eye on Oleander. I can't help but wonder what her thoughts are on this situation. "Lord Dominick of Greynon." He chose to sit with the other witches instead of the other Lords. He is taking a stand against the discrimination the witches faced under his predecessor. I love his determination to right that wrong. I haven't spent much time with Dominick, but he's easily my favorite Lord. The others are just old wash buckets, as far as I am concerned. Damn, I have got to work on my insults. This is embarrassing.

"Henry, Head of the Guards." Erik isn't at the table for the first time in a really long time. He is standing behind Jasmin, ready to defend her if needed. She went back and forth on whether she wanted him there, but ultimately, he is her most trusted guard, proving himself repeatedly. Given his relationship with Bea and Clem, she didn't want to bring him danger. He argued that she wouldn't hesitate to have him there if it weren't for them. He eventually won the argument, and Jasmin let him stand behind her. I understand her reluctance, but I'm thankful for his change of position. He is an astounding guard, and she deserves that.

"Lord Thurston of Vadried, Lord Gustavo of Tilrade, Lord David of Arkaley, and Lord Erland of Obele." Each man offers a slight nod. The wash bucket insult is actually an insult to wash buckets. At least some buckets have interesting rust stains.

"Queen Mother Oleander has returned from Hollyhock." She makes no attempt to show respect. No head nod, wave, bow, nothing. Just glaring at Jasmin. I don't understand how this woman can be her mother. It doesn't make sense.

"Clem, who is Master of Gardens." He nods to everyone else but then turns toward Jasmin, with love shining through his expression. No one could ever deny his feelings for her. It is so apparent. "And Dahlia, who is filling in as Royal Gardener while her mother is away." I haven't been given or asked for an official title. I'm entirely comfortable just being Dahlia, here to fuck the Queen when she wants it.

Interestingly, both of her love interests currently hold titles related to the earth. Jasmin's efforts to change the kingdom affect every aspect of life here; people, magic, and earth. She wants a better kingdom, and she will get it.

"For the first order of this meeting, I have an announcement." She takes a deep breath, the nervousness visible in her shaking hands. I wouldn't be upset if she backed out. We can move on to the second topic, and I won't be mad. We can deal with this later. Everyone knows I'm alive now. We're good. But she opens her mouth and starts talking like I knew she would. She is tired of hiding. Tired of hiding me, parts of who she is, our triad. She wants to be who she is all the time, not part of the time. I don't blame her; I'm just terrified.

"Dahlia, Clem, and I are in a triad. This is what broke the curse." The difference in reactions on either side of the room is laughable. The people on Jasmin's side, the witches, Henry, and Dominick, all have smiles on their faces. They are excited about this announcement. Meanwhile, the other Lords and Oleander, all leftover dish rags from the previous court, are outraged. They gasp, then start yelling. Why do they always begin with yelling? Jasmin holds her hands out, effectively silencing them.

"The non-traditional relationship proclamation was written for my people, but it would be hypocritical of me to hide my own relationships while allowing this for the rest of my people." She takes a deep breath, looking to Clem, who grabs her hand. I follow suit, and she squeezes mine. "We are planning a wedding and coronation. We will marry and crown both Clem and Dahlia as King and Queen with me." Her hand tightens, ready for the fallout. Quiet settles across the room. The stunned silence would be laughable if I weren't scared of the repercussions.

"Ha," Oleander yells, a humorless laugh. "You are no daughter of mine. I always knew you would do something this terrible. A farmer? And a half-baked witch? Is she the one that gave you that weak amulet? Yes, don't look so surprised. I recognized it for what it was the first time I saw you wearing it." She looks directly at me, humor and hatred piercing her icy eyes. "Do you honestly think that will protect her?" Oh no, this dirty cum stain didn't.

"Why would she need protection, Oleander?" I keep my voice as sweet as possible. Jasmin takes her seat next to me, still holding my hand tightly. Oleander purses her lips, not breaking her stare from mine.

"You assume she is under some threat. You always did have a wild imagination."

"It's hardly a threat when our kingdom has been cursed for nine years," I drawl casually.

"It's not your kingdom! We brought you here with that damned horse because the owner was desperate to get rid of your family. A bunch of dirty, lazy heathens he didn't want around any longer. Refused to sell the damn horse without you." I take a deep breath, trying to settle the rising anger in my body. Mama and Baba spoke a few times about the man they had worked for before. He wouldn't have forced our family into this situation. He genuinely believed it would be a better opportunity for us. He wasn't perfect, but he treated us decently. Her lies still sting, though. Even if they aren't his words, it is still a common opinion of enslaved people.

"That is enough. You can leave if you cannot remain in this meeting without insulting my wife." I can't fight the smile rising on my face. She hasn't referred to me as her wife yet, and I fucking love it. Before it can really sink in, Oleander responds, ruining my sweet moment.

"Your father would be disgusted."

"Where is he?" Jasmin snaps, jumping up from her chair, slamming her hand on the tabling, yelling louder than I have ever heard. The entire room flinches, leaning back from the table. This is Jasmin unhinged. The stress, fear, depression, all of it has finally taken its toll on her. Clem and I glance at each other, unsure of what to do. Her mother answered that question when she arrived, but no one completely believed her. It was just too convenient. Everyone, including Oleander, sits quietly as Jasmin breathes heavily.

Clem finally rises, putting his body between Jasmin and Oleander. She looks at him, a calm settling over her body. I wave over a butler with wine, filling a glass for Jasmin. She and Clem whisper quietly for a moment before she settles back in her seat. Without addressing her outburst, she takes my hand and continues.

"We believe one ceremony for the wedding and coronation will be sufficient. We will change some of the language to adapt to our situation. Kian will lead this ceremony, also." She takes several large gulps, staring across the room without seeing anything, daring anyone to disagree again.

"This is unprecedented, Queen." Lord David starts, probably the only Lord, aside from Dominick, Jasmin trusts. She is throwing daggers at him with her stare, but Kian intervenes.

"It's not, actually. This is how the kingdom was started." He rummages in a bag I didn't notice he had. Now that I think about it, he always has a bag with everything we could need. How have I not paid attention to that before? Between my insults and lack of attention to detail today, I feel slightly disappointed in myself. Not a real disappointment because I'm amazing. But a weak, undue disappointment.

Kian continues, telling the same story he gave us, explaining the difference between our triad and the original and why he believes ours will be more successful. The vote of confidence gives me a boost. I lean over, kissing Jasmin's cheek softly, drawing her attention. She offers a weak smile, still raging from earlier.

"No!" Oleander shouts, jumping up from her seat. "No! I will not sit by and watch you ruin my kingdom." Jasmin opens her mouth to speak, but Oleander continues. "This is not right. You are giving this kingdom over to the trash, and I will not stand idly by. Oh, no. Certainly not." She is clearly rambling now. Jasmin lets her speak, but Thurston and Gustavo look more concerned as she continues her tirade.

"I did everything in my power to keep this dirty slut away from you. Everything! I spent months researching those curses. I sacrificed your father to push you in the right direction, and you still ended up here with that harlot in your ear. I can overlook the farmer, but not her! Thurston, Henry, do something!" Everyone sits in stunned silence. She admitted to casting the curse and using Jasmin's father as the sacrifice. Henry stands slowly, moving behind her, several other guards following him. Thurston looks downright terrified, as he should, especially if Jasmin decides to question his involvement.

"Would you repeat that again?" Jasmin says calmly. I don't know where her calmness comes from. I'm nearly shaking out of my seat, bouncing my leg. Oleander looks confused. She opens her mouth to repeat her words but realizes what she said and closes her lips quickly. Jasmin stands slowly, surely.

"Oleander, you are under arrest..." Jasmin starts with her accusations, but Oleander screams, reaching into her pocket. Everything happens so quickly that I can't quite process what happens. Oleander flings something from her pocket. Clem dives in front of Jasmin. A cloud of black smoke fills the air. Henry and the guards surround Oleander. Kian, Maud, and Lucia rush over to help subdue Oleander. The Lords jump from their seats, moving out of the way. A body lands hard on the floor, and someone starts screaming.

It's me.

I'm the one screaming. Clem is on the floor, eyes closed, not moving, but still breathing. The dark smoke moves over him briefly, then dissipates. My hands are on his shoulders, shaking him. Why isn't he waking up? Is this a game? In my heart, I know what has happened. It happened to me, but I can't admit that. I don't want to. Not Clem. I didn't have time to make the amulet for him. I've been too exhausted from the last one. I should have pushed through. My hands are on his face, his hair. He just needs to open his eyes. He should sit up. Water drops on his forehead. No, not water. That's tears. I'm crying; no, sobbing. I'm still screaming his name. He needs to wake up.

Kian arrives at my side, but I wrap my body around Clem's head. He just needs to know how much I love him. How much Jasmin loves him. Then he can wake up. It will be fine. We can do that. We broke the last curse. We can wake him up.

Jasmin pulls my shoulders, trying to pull me away from his body, but I won't go. I'm not leaving him. I just need to love him harder. A kiss! True love's kiss! That's what works in all the fairy tales. That's what he needs. I press my lips to him, willing him to wake. Pushing all my love into him through our kiss. He doesn't kiss me back, doesn't wrap his arms around me. Doesn't move at all. Jasmin! She needs to kiss him, too. The words tumble out of my mouth loudly. Everything is so loud. She just needs to kiss him, and this will be over. There is so much commotion around us, but my vision is a blur. All I can see is Clem. She kneels beside me, between Kian and me.

"Kiss him!" I yell at her. "Kiss him! He needs true love to wake him up." She gives me a heartbroken look but glances at Kian. He shrugs softly, and Jasmin leans in slowly to kiss him. Her eyes are filled with doubt. She doesn't believe this will work. She has to believe. She has to love. That will wake him up! She kisses him gently, but it does nothing. A sob breaks from her lips. This is real. Clem is cursed. Oleander cursed him this time.

I throw my arms around Jasmin, wailing in pain. We can't lose Clem. We have lost so much already. Parents, years, our whole lives, our futures are gone now. Will he be cursed for nine years now? How will we break his if it isn't true love? Where is the curse? I didn't hear Oleander yelling the curse when she threw the item at Jasmin. Fuck, she was trying to do this to Jasmin. Her own daughter. Jasmin and I are still tangled together when Erik pulls us up.

A handkerchief is placed in my hand. I dab my eyes with it and instantly realize this isn't one of Clem's. His always have a distinct smell of soap and dirt. No matter how much time he spends away from the farms, he will always have some dirt with him. This realization hits me hard, and I crumble with a wail. Someone guides me into a chair. Jasmin sits on the arm of the chair, pulling me into her side. I bury my head in her lap, trying to calm the tears I can't stop.

"Maud and Lucia are escorting the guards to the dungeons to secure Oleander. They will put an effective barrier in place and strip her of any power she may have." Jasmin sniffles, nodding as Erik explains. How much time has passed since Oleander threw the curse at Clem? Are Jasmin's people that effective, or has it been longer than I realized? I open my eyes, looking down at where he is. He lays still, eyes closed, arms by his side. He looks peaceful. If his curse is anything like mine, he is unaware of anything happening. Another sob breaks through as Jasmin strokes my back. She doesn't shush me or tell me to calm down. She is putting on a better act than I am, being the strong one in Clem's absence. A flash of real disappointment crashes through, upset that I can't be the strong one for her. But I will be soon. I'll be strong for her tonight, so she can fall apart like this in private. She'll need me later.

"We have a stretcher to move Clem. Where would you like us to take him?" I lift my head now, looking up at Jasmin, and she seems to hesitate. I sniffle, not sure if my voice will work now.

"Take him to our room." My voice is broken and hoarse from the screaming, but the words come out well enough. Erik nods at me but waves his arms to the side, indicating Jasmin and I need to step aside. I pull her with me, dragging the chair along, too. A couple of guards come up, placing a stretcher down beside Clem. Erik and Kian help shift him onto the stretcher. Jasmin chokes back a sob, and I wrap my arms around her. I notice she also has a handkerchief that does not belong to Clem. I wonder who they belong to, briefly debating digging in Clem's pockets to find his. However, I ultimately decide now is not the time. Once he is on the stretcher, Erik asks if we want to lead or follow. Jasmin is panicked now, unable to hold the tight control she usually has on her emotions.

"We'll lead," I say, still hoarse but stronger now. I pull her with me as we leave the meeting room, heading toward our own.

"Ada." Jasmin blurts out the name, turning back to the men carrying Clem behind us. "We need to tell Ada, and Bea, and Claire." Dominick places his hands on the stretcher, telling Erik to find them and bring them to Jasmin's room. Erik hesitates but does eventually walk away. Another guard steps in, lightening the load for Kian and Dominick. They follow us through the castle in the most morose and melancholic parade.

In the room, we place Clem on the bed, removing his formal jacket and shoes. He won't need those anytime soon. The guards leave the room with Dominick, leaving us along with Kian. I'm glad for his presence, unsure we should be alone. Jasmin is fretting over Clem, his clothes, his hair, the blankets, and the pillows. I tell her not to worry over it when she spins around, the glass tube and belt in one hand and a bottle of oil in the other.

"Guess we should put these away before Ada arrives." Her laugh starts small but quickly grows louder. Just before I join her laughter, she devolves into a fit of tears. I grab the items from her as Kian pulls her into a hug. I hide the items haphazardly in the closet, planning to deal with them later. As I walk back into the room, Ada and her girls enter. I didn't think my heart could shatter any more than it already had, but the look on Ada's face when she sees Clem nearly crushes me. She chokes on her sob, covering her face with her hands.

Ada walks with poise and grace to the side of the bed, where Kian and Jasmin are just standing. Claire screams, sending a fresh wave of tears throughout the room. She crawls onto the bed, stumbling over the blankets to get to her brother. She shakes his chest, screaming at him to wake up. I bite my lip, watching Clem's mother and sister struggle with heartbreak. Ada manages to get a grip on Claire. She pulls her into her arms, soothing her, assuring her things will be fine. She reminds Claire of all the witches at the castle that will bring Clem back to us. They settle next to him on the bed. Bea leans on Erik as they walk over. She holds onto him tightly, not letting go. I can't help but think how much this looks like a funeral. But he's not dead. He's not. We'll get him back. We will. We will...

Chapter 42

JASMIN

Kian, Maud, and Lucia have spent hours hovering over Clem, trying to understand what happened and how to undo it. They haven't been successful, and all three are frustrated and tired. When they aren't around, Ada frets between Clem and Bea. Bea spent an hour or two in the room with us when we brought Clem back, but she was too ill to stay. Erik took her back, and I dismissed him for the day with some arguments. In the few times when all of them are away, Claire crawls into the bed and begins to read to Clem. She's fallen asleep crying on his chest more often than not.

I stayed in the room at first, but it's overwhelming. Seeing the pain my mother has caused again, in addition to my own pain over Clem's condition, is too much. I've taken solace in Dahlia's old room, my old nursery. The very room that holds all of my most painful moments and my attempts to heal from them. How does one heal from these situations? There are so many of them.

Kian finds me eventually; I am not particularly well hidden. I am sitting on Dahlia's bed, staring at the mantel that contains the flower she gave me so long ago. It is beginning to whither, the curse no longer holding it intact. The small spell Dahlia cast over it eventually wore off. Several petals lie on the ledge. My life is crumbling just like this flower. I gaze at Kian for a moment before rising from the bed. He seems like he will offer some support or encouragement but changes his mind. I'm thankful for his silence. Now isn't the time that I need encouragement. My world is bleak, and I just want Clem back.

We walk together to the dungeons. Kian does eventually speak but reserves the positivity for another time. "We have strong barriers around her cell; only certain people can give her food and water. The barrier has sound blocking, so we don't hear her, and she can't hear us. She has been stripped of her magical abilities, but we can't be certain it's safe, given her knowledge of the old magic. We will place a second barrier for you to communicate with her, but it will prevent her from attacking you. Matron Maud and I, along with the normal guards, will be close by."

I nod absently as he speaks. We have relocated many guards to the dungeons. There aren't as many hovering around my family and me. A little piece of my heart swells briefly, realizing I can call all these people my family. These are my people, and they have shown they will do anything for me. We can afford a bit more privacy right now.

Oscar heckles me as we walk by, making comments about my mother. He threatens that he won't be in here forever. He has forgotten the length of time he stays depends entirely on my perception of his behavior. I would laugh at his claim if I had any interest in engaging with him. Instead, I walk by without even acknowledging him. I'm not here for him and don't want to waste my delicate confidence on him.

I arrive at Mother's cell. We both stand, staring at each other, while the witches ensure their spells are ready. Once they are, I step into the barrier created for me. A silence falls over me, immediately met with a sense of dread over being this close to her. I remind myself I am safe, at least relatively.

We stare at each other for several minutes. I finally remove the small box from my pocket, open it, and place it on the requested stool. Mother eyes it but waits for me to speak. We are in a power struggle at the moment. I may have come here of my own volition, but I want her to admit to what she did without my probing.

I want her to give me that much. She won't. I know she won't. She knows, I know, we all know what this is. It's a stupid battle with limited benefits.

"Tell me about Father."

"Your father was weak. He refused to try to expand our kingdom. He didn't want a war with Hollyhock when we could have won. He was happy with the status quo and didn't want to change things. When I found the curse, I figured you would find someone within a year, and no real damage would be done. Then while you were still newly in love, I could come in and take what I wanted. You would be distracted with pregnancy and your new husband, and I could take over the kingdom." Her words fall so freely. I have never heard her speak so brazenly. Either she realizes this is the end, or, more likely, she doesn't see me as a threat. She doesn't know me anymore, though. I am more dangerous than she realizes, but I'm not showing my hand yet.

"Did he pass quickly?" Her laugh is cold and harsh. I can't stop the wince at the sound she makes.

"Oh, no." I have never heard such a malicious laugh. It's bone-chillingly awful. "I drew it out several days to ensure the curse held. And I must say, your father did better than I expected. Nine years! What a feat!" I square my shoulders, pretending she isn't talking about my father. Right now, I am not her daughter. I am Queen. I have to maintain my persona to get the information I need. I close my eyes briefly, focusing on the points my crown touches my head. Feeling the literal and figurative weight of the small crown Clem designed for me. When I open my eyes, Oleander picks her nails, boredom written across her face.

"What did you do to Clem?"

"Oh, that. Well, that was intended for you. Since he isn't the target, it's hard to say what will happen to him." Her shrug reeks of indifference, and it grows harder to maintain my facade. I want to climb into the cell and throttle her with my bare hands.

"What was it meant to do to me?" My words are chopped out through gritted teeth. Anger is simmering beneath my skin, heating my body, tensing every muscle.

"It was meant to kill you. Since you are unwed, the kingdom would have fallen to me. I have enough support from the families and Lords; I wouldn't have been charged with your death. Then I could reverse these stupid laws you have put into place, protecting witches, slaves, and whores. It's disgusting that you surround yourself with such vile people. I never should have left you alone all those years. I should have molded you more carefully. I always assumed you would see the correct way to do things." I open my mouth to refute her claim, but I am not here to argue with her. I am here to get answers. I take a deep breath, swallowing my urge to fight back. This isn't the time.

"So you can't tell me anything about Clem?" She shakes her head, staring at the corners of the cell as if they are more interesting than this conversation.

"They tell me he is still alive. I suppose you should be thankful for that. The curse was specific for you. I've never seen it hit an unintended. I don't know what will happen to him. Maybe he'll live. Maybe he'll die." I suck in a breath, biting the inside of my cheek at her harsh words. Kian will find a way to save him. I can always count on Kian. A tiny voice knows I shouldn't put that much faith or pressure on him, but at this moment, I can't consider anything else.

"Why did you curse me? And Dahlia? Why not find another way to get what you wanted?"

She shrugs far too casually for my care. She considers for a moment, eyeing me up and down. When she speaks, her voice is tired. "I was tired. I never wanted children. That's why it took so long to conceive you. For as many attempts as your father made, I made that many to undo it. At some point, I realized I couldn't keep fighting him." She literally rewrote her history to save her public image. All the stories of my parents include their deepest desire to have children and how difficult it was. It was never actually tricky for her.

"I cursed Dahlia when I realized what she had done to you. She was meant to stay that way until I deemed it fit for her to return. I don't know why she is back now. Damn whore must have figured out how to unlock my curse on her. As for you," she practically spits as she eyes me repeatedly. "I never assumed you would take so long to find your true love. Having your father out of the way made it easier for me to get what I wanted. I used my grief," she sniffles, faking a sob as she taps her eyes before continuing, "to get in with the King of Hollyhock. I have him under my thumb. He will give me anything I want." She intended to essentially give Sweet Briar to Hollyhock, expanding their kingdom. I have no doubts she would have eventually overthrown the King to rule the new, massive kingdom herself. That was her end goal. Father, Dahlia, me, we were all just in her way. With that, I take the small box from the stool, close it, and turn it over.

"Can I tell you a story before I leave?" Mother shrugs, uninterested but not turning me away either. "Last year, in an attempt to break the curse, all of the Lords brought in two men, with a plan to rotate through bachelors until we found my true love. Kian was one of the first that I connected with. I found him dancing to music in one of our empty formal dining rooms. But there were no musicians in the room. It was the strangest thing." Oleander's interest is piqued now, listening to my story with curiosity but not quite understanding. I tap the box, holding it up in front of me.

"When witches start training with magic, they create a sound box. It's a difficult enough spell, without major consequences, but thoroughly delightful when they succeed. Because of the time and effort needed to create one, they aren't given lightly. I received a few for solstice and my coronation, prefilled with music. A precious gift I always treasure." I hold this box between my fingers, on display for Oleander. Her eyes are wide with understanding now. She realizes what I have done, what a threat I actually am.

"Earlier this year, I visited the witches. I stayed in their buildings, toured their villages, and spoke with matrons and everyone I had time for. To show their gratitude, they gave many gifts. Spells, spices, books, fabrics. These are all things I would expect from witches. But one, in particular, heard about my love of the music boxes. They didn't have the means to gather a band and trap the music. So they gave me a blank box I could use for any moment I deemed important. I planned to record music, perhaps a ceremony, but I saved it. Never quite finding the perfect moment to bring it out. Until today."

She glares at me, hatred and fear colluding in her eyes. A smirk spreads across my face. I have outsmarted her, and she won't be able to talk her way out of this situation. She consistently underestimates me, and this will finally be her demise.

"Tomorrow, we will travel to Vadried. You will be tried and sentenced in front of all who can attend. It will be a public trial." I turn to walk away but stop. She is grief-stricken now. Her mind races as she tries to figure out what all this means. I decide to give her one more story before I walk away.

"I have overseen one trial since the curse began. Oscar, over there." I point to where he is, but Oleander doesn't look. "He decided to attack and cause bodily harm to one of the younger bachelors last year. Tomas is from the stables, but you probably don't know him. Oscar was sentenced to several years in the cell, then several in the fields, only to be released when I and several others deem him changed and ready to rejoin society." A hesitant hope fills her face. She stands a bit taller, thinking she can outsmart me again. She really has such a small opinion of me. I would be insulted if I could still care about her.

"However, since the curse began, there has been a trial for treason. Lord David oversaw those proceedings. I have a feeling you may remember Jackson." It takes her a moment to place the name, but she finally meets my gaze when she remembers all that happened. I nod, accepting her understanding. "Yes, he attacked me in Arkaley. His attempt was futile, wildly unsuccessful. He only managed to give Clem a black eye."

I pause, remembering all the bruises Clem has been covered with over the past year. The black eye, in particular, was frustrating because it took so long to heal it was still visible at our wedding. I shake the thoughts from my head, straightening my posture. "He was executed the next day." She lunges at the cell, forgetting about the witches' barrier. She screams as her arms reach out to snatch the box from my hand. I jump back as hands grab my shoulders and pull me further from the cell. Oleander cries out in pain as she comes in contact with the barrier, a shock running through her body. Her screams fall silent as I am pulled from the barrier around me.

"Hope you got everything you needed." Kian looks down at me as he drops his hands from my shoulders. The guards and witches are in a position to fight, but the barrier seems to be holding. I give a small smile for the first time in nearly two days.

Oleander is frantic in her cell, screaming, banging against the bars. We can't hear her, though. I update everyone on what she said and what needs to happen. Lucia and Maud work with the guards to ensure they can transport Oleander safely. Kian walks me back to my room, not speaking. I appreciate his company. His presence is helping me hold everything together and not wander around my castle in a wave of tears. While everyone would understand, it's still not an image I want to present.

Ada and Claire are sitting on the bed beside Clem, both doing separate quiet activities. They have been around constantly, and my gratitude for their presence will never end. We don't know if he knows what is happening around him. Dahlia couldn't offer much insight on that since she was alone for the entirety of her curse. Knowing that this curse was meant to kill me makes me more nervous than I will admit. I will not share that information with his family until we know more.

I ask them to leave us alone for the night, letting them know of our travel plans tomorrow. I request that they stay with him while we are gone, and both agree before leaving with hugs. I sit in front of my vanity as Kian asks a few questions about the trial. He will leave to make the preparations necessary. During a lull in his questions, Dahlia speaks up.

"I'm staying here with Clem." My broken heart shatters again. Obviously, she should stay here so he isn't without one of us if he wakes. I would love to have her by my side, but I don't want to ask that of her. I try to fight the tears in my eyes but can't stop them.

"It would be better if you were at the trial by her side," Kian speaks softly. Dahlia glares at him, but I just watch through my mirror. I don't want to express my mind on this topic. They can decide what is best for everyone, and I'll proceed. Very little will make any of this situation better anyway.

"You can stay by her side," Dahlia retorts.

"I will stay here with Clem and tell him what happens if he wakes. He may not wake up, though. We haven't seen any signs that might indicate he will. I will have time to research this type of spell. The kingdom will see you by her side, see the full impact of what Oleander has done. They will also get a chance to see you in a more official capacity." Dahlia opens her mouth to argue but hesitates, meeting my gaze instead. Tears streak down my face while I watch Dahlia's resolve burst. She pads to my side, wrapping her arms around me.

"I'm sorry. I'll go with you," she whispers, peppering me with kisses. Kian quietly leaves the room. I embrace Dahlia, holding to her everything left in my body. It's not much at this point, though. Clem has been my rock for the past year. I didn't realize until now how much I have leaned on him for support. Now would probably be the best time to find better coping mechanisms, but I want him back. I don't want to learn new shit without him.

Dahlia and I eventually snuggle in bed next to him. Sleeping next to him in his state is bizarre, but I also can't imagine not having him next to me unless he is dead. I no longer know right or wrong or weird or normal. My entire world has been turned upside down yet again. I was not raised to deal with these issues. Just give me some asshole stealing bread or something. That I can handle. Not this, though.

The journey to Vadried is slow. Dahlia and I will be staying for a few days. The trial is this afternoon, before sunset. I plan to stay a few extra days to connect with my people. Clem and I intended to spend the summer visiting the villages, but so far have only spent a few weeks in Greynon. Even that ended in life-altering changes made within the community. Thankfully, those were positive, beneficial changes, but it was still stressful. Vadried is only a couple of hours by horse away from the castle. Should things change with Clem, we will find out quickly.

People line the streets again, watching as we pass by. A few are waving, and a couple jeering. Most of the people are solemn. Dahlia and I pass by first with our guards, followed by the other Lords. Matron Maud and Lady Lucia lead a combination of guards and witches surrounding the carriage with Oleander. We agreed on a closed carriage to make it easier to contain her. We are taking no chances with her. Her reign of terror is over.

We are greeted by Lord Thurston when we arrive at the courthouse. He argued for a long while about the specifics of this trial. He wanted a closed-door, private trial. I want the people to see and hear everything. I don't want any doubt about why the Queen Mother is on trial. This is not a situation that will soon be forgotten, and I will not risk discord within my community by not being transparent.

We have a brief meeting over the proceedings, then some time to rest while the crowd outside grows. I watch from a window on the courthouse's second floor as people from across the village, even other villages within the kingdom, begin to file in, finding places to stand and wait. We didn't have much time to alert everyone, but we spread the word as quickly and widely as possible. This isn't a trial I want to put off because of the safety concerns and the energy the witches and guards are expending to contain Oleander.

Soon it is time for the trial. I am wearing one of the split-bottom dresses I purchased. This one is closed more tightly than others, looking more like a dress than a wrap. I want to be more presentable to the kingdom on this occasion. The tall crown Clem had made for my coronation sits upon my head. It is heavy, and I have to hold my head still to keep it on, but gods, it's so beautiful. Dahlia is wearing a dress that matches mine but is thinner. She is wearing the smaller crown I typically wear. We haven't officially announced the ceremony or our relationship, but this will be the first time we are seen together in an official capacity.

"Thank you all for coming," I address the crowd, which is teeming with curiosity and anticipation. Dahlia and I sit on a platform in the courtyard with the Lords,

Lady, and Matron Maud. Guards surround us, both on and off the platform. It feels excessive, but we didn't want to risk anything with this trial. Maud gave me a spell to amplify my voice so everyone in the crowd could hear, and I didn't need to yell.

"Before we begin, this trial will be difficult. Terrible things have been done by a person we all loved and respected." I can no longer refer to feelings toward my mother in the present tense. She isn't a person I am willing to expend any energy on. "If you need to leave or prepare yourself for what you will hear, please do so now while we bring the accused out." No one in the crowd moves. I didn't expect them to, but I couldn't, in good conscience, continue without the warning.

Oleander is escorted in chains and a clean dress onto the stand. The shimmering bubble from the witches is still around her. We debated dropping it but ultimately decided against it. The sound barrier is being released now, but everything else holds firm, glistening around her in the late afternoon sun. This was always Clem's favorite time of day. The sun's golden hue on everything made it more magical for him. I wish I could agree, but at least he isn't here to watch this travesty. This trial won't taint his lovely views of the afternoon sun.

"Oleander Reis, Queen Mother of Sweet Briar, you are hereby accused of treason, murder, endangerment of royalty and the kingdom, and conspiracy. How do you plead?" She is more subdued than I have ever seen her in my life. She once fell sick when I was a child. Even then, she continued stomping around the castle, demanding updates between coughing fits. It took my father and several guards to contain her in her room for two days. That was all they could manage. Seeing her crumpled, looking defeated is surprising. I would be remorseful if I had any feelings left for her, but I'm not. There is too much bad blood between us now.

"Innocent." She cries out, and the crowd is divided between cheers and boos. I didn't know what to expect from the people. Many people loved her, but I think many could see through her and see her for what she was.

I begin with the trial, starting with the Lords recounting the meeting from yesterday. Lord Thurston and Gustavo try to downplay some of her words and actions, but at the end of their time, they cannot mask the atrocities she admitted to. I asked Dahlia if she wanted to speak against her, but she chose not to. I respect her decision. Dahlia had less first-hand experience with Mother and couldn't accurately name those that worked for her. Her testimony isn't necessary for the trial. Matron Maud explains many aspects of the trial, what they knew about the curse, how they knew Oleander cast it, what it entailed, and the severity of the case. She speaks to the necessary death required to cast the spell, only mentioning that Oleander briefly claimed to have killed my father for it.

Many more people could testify against her, but I don't want this trial to take all night. It has already lasted more than an hour. The crowd is growing anxious and discouraged. It's devastating to hear all this information about a Queen that has served for so long. After Matron Maud finishes her speech, I ask Oleander if she wants to speak on her behalf. She says she does. I knew she would. She is a sweet talker and could convince a man to buy air from her. I will let her speak her piece only after I say mine.

"I have one more testimony I want everyone to hear before you speak." I hold out the sound box I used during my meeting with her. Her eyes go wide with terror. The crowd notices and begins to wiggle with anticipation and excitement. Matron Maud explains the box, assuring the public there is no way the sound has been tampered with. When she finishes, I adjust the baton Maud used for the amplifying spell to cast the sound from the box. I open the box, letting my words flow out. Oleander's voice fills the courtyard. The crowd listens, gasping and shuddering throughout the brief conversation. Some people begin to weep. Anger simmers through the public, outraged over her crude words. This is the reason why we agreed to so many guards. The crowd is angry, and rightly so. They are likely to riot, but I hope to avoid that. Once the conversation ends, I close the box, passing the baton to a guard to hold in front of Oleander.

Oleander stands, facing the crowd. She is already defeated. There is nothing she can say at this point that will change the minds of her people. They are all angry and no longer on her side. Even Lords Gustavo and Thurston are showing disgust and anger.

"I only did what I thought was best for my kingdom. You are my people. I am..." Her words are drowned out by angry shouts. Items begin flying through the air: pebbles, handkerchiefs, bread, even a tomato or two. The corner of my lips jerks upward briefly at the tomato that splats at Oleander's feet. I take the baton back from the guard, having them assume a defensive position. Their movement placates the crowd temporarily. It won't last, though.

"Quiet, Quiet!" The crowd simmers, turning their attention to me. "Due to my relationship with the accused and the severity of this case, I alone will not be deciding her innocence." I turn to the Lords and Lucia, addressing each one and asking for their verdict. All vote guilty. I ask Matron Maud and Dahlia, also guilty. I finally address the crowd again.

"She was your Queen for many years. If you find her guilty, please raise your hand high." One by one, hands shoot into the sky. There are too many to count. I can't say for certain it is a unanimous decision, but it is certainly a majority. Oleander stares at the crowd with a blank expression. She knows the verdict but is staring at some point in the distance. There is a tug of sorrow in my chest. I feel it for a moment, breathing through the ache. She was my mother, after all. The hands slowly fall from the sky, returning to their sides in the crowd.

"The people have spoken. Oleander Reis, Queen Mother, you are hereby found guilty of treason, murder, endangerment of royalty and the kingdom, and conspiracy." I take a breath, needing to recenter before speaking the next words. I didn't issue the punishment for Jackson, and don't take it lightly. However, these specific charges have penalties set by kings long before I was born. "You are hereby sentenced to death by hanging. You will be hung at the next sunrise." A roar spreads through the crowd, drowning out my words, even with the amplifying spell. I stop speaking, returning to my seat. Dahlia takes my hand, offering me the small comfort I have grown accustomed to with Clem.

Oleander is carted away with the witches, ensuring her barriers hold for the night. Guards escort the rest of us into the courthouse. A dinner has been prepared for us and is ready when we arrive. While I am sure the food is delicious, it is dry and tasteless in my mouth. I eat as much as I can tolerate, knowing I will need the strength. The dinner is primarily silent; only a few words are spoken about the execution tomorrow. We already knew where it would end, and everything has been arranged. There is nothing to do now but wait for the sun to rise again.

Dahlia and I retire to our room. The bed is far smaller than ours at the castle, but without Clem, we still have plenty of room. We don't need it, though. We sleep wrapped tightly in each other's arms. Or, rather, we lie in bed through most of the night, neither really sleeping nor resting. We don't talk, though; we just hold each other tightly.

Finally, a lady in waiting enters the room to help us get dressed. Emmeline stayed behind with Kian, helping him do research and keep an eye on Clem. The thought crashes through my mind that we likely don't need to keep an eye on him. He can't do anything. I shove that from my head as the lady styles my hair. She pulls the brush through the long strands.

"Cut it."

"What?" Dahlia chirps in harmony with the lady. The lady looks more nervous, while Dahlia looks outraged. I love her passion for everything.

"My hair, let's cut it. It was short for so long. It's hot now, and I rather liked it shorter. Not as short as it was, but shorter." I glance around, spotting a pair of scissors, and chop several inches off one chunk of my hair. The lady gasps while Dahlia starts laughing hysterically. I cut another chunk of hair before the lady finally takes over, cutting away bits and pieces nervously to make my hair even and smooth. When she is done, my hair falls just beneath my chin. I love the look, feeling more confident with my style instead of the one given to me. Oleander tried to cut my hair as punishment all those years ago. I was ecstatic when it started growing back last year. But now, at this moment, no one will tell me how my hair should be worn or how it should look. It is mine.

Dahlia places my crown on my head, then bends down so I can put the smaller one on hers. I kiss her deeply, keeping one hand on my crown. Today will start terribly, but I will not let that bring me down. Today is the end of a reign of terror. It isn't going to be a sad day. It will be a new beginning.

I take Dahlia's hand as we walk through dark, quiet hallways. The crowd's murmur grows louder as we get closer to the courtyard. I'm surprised to see so many people, nearly as many as yesterday. The chairs have been removed from the stage, switching a platform to the gallows. I force air into my lungs at the sight. I've never been fond of public executions, but I feel the people deserve to see the end of this. They have been trapped for nearly a decade. They deserve this last bit of finality I can give them.

Torches burn softly in the dark sky. People hold candles or lanterns as more trickle in. Sunlight will start peaking over the mountains in a few moments, with the sun rising above the horizon in half an hour. That is all the time my mother has left on this earth. Not a single ounce of my soul mourns her loss anymore. Today, I grieve for my father, the hundreds lost due to the curse, the years squandered, and for Clem.

I was instructed to wait on my dais until the execution began, but seeing my people in the crowd, I cannot sit above them. I rise, dropping Dahlia's hand, and walk toward the steps. She quickly catches me, taking my hand as we descend the stairs together. I glide between my people, shaking hands, giving hugs, and offering kind words. Many offer condolences to me. At first, I remind them of how long this has been coming, how I have already grieved the loss of who I thought my mother was. After a few, I stop speaking, simply nod, and return the sentiment to them. This is an unprecedented situation, and no one knows what to say.

Henry's voice booms out over the crowd, calling me back to the dais. The crowd parts and bows as Dahlia and I walk by. It takes considerable effort not to cry at the show of respect and camaraderie from my people. When we reach the dais, Matron Maud gives me the baton, spelled to amplify my voice again. A hush falls over the crowd. I debate whether I want to use it, feeling like it takes away from the moment's intimacy. Ultimately, I decide to use it. Whatever intimacy I perceive in this situation would be negated if people cannot hear me. Oleander is finally escorted out. She is wearing a clean, simple dress and appears to have been bathed. Her hair is tied up on the back of her head. She has been stripped of all makeup and jewelry. It's an unusual look for her. She looks old and weathered.

"Oleander Reis. You are sentenced to death by hanging. Do you have any final words?" Her eyes don't meet mine. She stares at whatever spot she has chosen. This is not how she thought things would go. She never anticipated this ending for herself.

"You will regret this." Her words are filled with abhorrence. The crowd hisses and boos at her, but she remains focused on her spot. I nod to the executioner, letting him do what he needs to do. I take my seat next to Dahlia. Her hand instantly wraps around mine. I offer her a small smile, a momentary distraction, as the rope surrounds Oleander's neck.

Breathe in and out. In and out. I repeat this mantra in my head, watching the executioner. It has been a long time since I attended a public hanging. I am prepared as I possibly can be for what happens next. A hush falls over the crowd as anticipation builds. A loud snap sounds through the silence, causing gasps around the courtyard. I flinch at the sudden noise. I knew it was coming, but it sounded so much louder than I was ready for. I watch as Oleander kicks, her life slowly fading before my eyes. It's a surreal moment for me. In my heart, she died many years ago when the curse first fell. The woman that has been in my castle, back in my kingdom, she wasn't my mother. She was the evil witch that tried to ruin me. She is the person I have to thank for where I am today. She is the person that has caused so much unnecessary pain to my family, my friends, and my people. She is the hag that cursed me.

Chapter 43

Clem

It's so dark. My body hurts, and I can't open my eyes. Panic swells inside of me. This isn't right. Where am I? I can't see anything. Am I restrained? I can hear someone talking. Who is that? Where am I? I am not safe here. I need to move. I need to get out of here. Something is wrong.

My breathing increases as the voice moves closer. I can't make out the words. I don't know who that is. Fear takes over my body. I still can't see, but I can feel my arms and legs. They feel heavy, like I'm buried under bags of grain. It's hard to move, but I manage to swing my arms. My legs flail over the edge of the surface I am on. A woman screams; a fist connects with my face, and I land flat on the ground. My consciousness fades.

A wet cloth is on my face. I can open my eyes but can only see lights and shadows. I close my eyes for now. Memories flash through my eyes as I try to figure out where I am, what happened. I remember being in the meeting room with Oleander and Jasmin and Dahlia. Oleander threw something at Jasmin. That's the last thing I remember. Panic rises again as the soothing voice turns into words.

"Clem, stay calm. It's me, Kian."

Kian. I slowly become more aware of my surroundings. My entire body aches as if I have been running for days. The wet cloth feels cool on my cheeks. When it grazes under my eye, I wince. Pain radiates from my cheek where I was hit.

"Sorry about that." Kian is the one apologizing. Did he hit me?

The room around me comes into my vision slowly. I am sitting on the floor in my room, propped against the bed. Finn's giant head is in my lap, holding steady against me. Kian is kneeling before me, dabbing my face with the cloth. My head is pounding, more potent than the dull ache throughout the rest of my body. I can't turn my head to see the whole room, but I can tell it is just Kian and I in here. Where are my girls? My heart rate spikes with fear for their safety.

"Clem," his voice is soft but laced with concern. "Let me check your face for broken bones, then I'll explain what happened." I nod, almost indiscernibly, because of pain and stiffness. His fingers poke my cheek, causing me to wince again. A slight tingle travels through my face under his touch. When content, he sits back on the other side of Finn, holding the wet cloth for me. My arms move slowly, laboriously, but I place the cool rag on my cheek, soothing some of the aches.

"I don't think anything is broken, but you will have a nasty bruise." He pauses, eyeing me curiously. "Again," he adds playfully. I chuckle weakly, remembering all my bruises in the past year. Jasmin won't be happy about this one. I raise my eyes to him, ready to speak. He holds his hand up, silencing me as he explains.

"You were hit with a curse intended to kill Jasmin. It was specific to her, which is why it didn't kill you, but you've been unconscious for several days now." My breath hitches at his words. I remember diving in front of her. I'm glad that I did. Even with her amulet, there's no telling what the spell would have done to her. "Oleander was arrested. Jasmin and Dahlia traveled to Vadried for her trial. The trial was yesterday, and she was executed this morning. That must be what lifted the curse from you."

My head bobs up and down, processing what he said. I rub Finn's head, scratching between his ears like he prefers. He adjusts in my lap as if trying to get closer to me. I've been cursed for several days now. No wonder he is trying to get closer. He wants to be sure I am fine. I'm not, but I'm getting there. I look down at him, planning to offer some comfort to the overgrown ball of fluff. I flinch at the pain in my cheek, keeping my head level. Kian grimaces, somewhat apologetic, but his eyes still show anger.

"You started moving when Emmeline was adjusting the curtains. She came to help you, but you attacked her. Or tried to. You were moving slowly but still enough of a threat to her. She was screaming, but you didn't stop. I intervened. I was crass in my methods and should have made a different choice. I apologize for that. I...it's just when you were moving after her, I...I couldn't think. I had to stop you because..." His words trail off like he can't voice the rest of them. He won't meet my eyes, and I realize what he is trying to say.

"Because you love her?" My voice is hoarse from lack of use. Kian finally meets my gaze, and he nods.

"I do." I smile at him, glad they have each other and that he admitted it. We've long suspected they were together, but neither has acknowledged it.

"How long has it been going on?" He sighs, laughing softly at the question.

"Honestly, I wanted her when I first met her but stayed focused on Jasmin. When I knew you were her true love, I left immediately and found Emmeline." I can't stop the laugh that erupts from my chest. Jasmin will be thrilled.

"Why didn't you tell us? Jasmin will be ecstatic." He shrugs, rubbing Finn's back as a distraction.

"At first, we didn't want her to worry about divided attention or anything. Then it was more fun to just not tell. And, well, that never really went away." I can understand that thrill of keeping a secret. I wish he would have told us sooner, but I get it.

"Can I at least tell Jas? She's been asking for months." Kian chuckles but nods.

"Let's keep it secret from everyone else, though. It's more fun to leave people guessing." We laugh together as the door opens, and Emmeline pokes her head through. I try to stand, putting my arm on the bed. All I can manage is a groan and lift my ass precisely two inches in the air. I plop back heavily with Kian pressing on my shoulder.

"Stay here for a bit longer. Emme," he calls over to her, "bring some wine and snacks. Clem's back now." Her eyebrows rise in shock at his shortened name for her. I've never even heard Jas refer to her as Emme. It must be a name only he is allowed to call her. She walks over warily, carrying a small plate and jug of wine. Erik steps into the room behind her but stays near the door. Emmeline tries to place the plate of food in my lap, but Finn starts to sniff, looking for handouts. She admonishes him, insisting this food is just for me. She places the plate on the bed, the glass of wine on my other side. I grab some of the berries while she and Kian chat with Erik. I still slip some of the berries to Finn, slowly eating a couple myself. They sit heavy in my stomach, but my body is starting to feel less sluggish.

Once the food is gone from the plate, Finn only eating half of it, I rise slowly from the floor and move over to the sitting area in the middle of the room. Everything still hurts, but it feels nice to change positions. The others join me in the sitting area. Erik eyes me wearily, clearly being told about my actions toward Emmeline.

"Mrs. Byrne and your sisters would like to see you if you're up for it." Erik is always so formal.

"When are you going to start calling her Ada? You could also call her Ma; she would like that." He shakes his head, looking offended at my suggestion. We laugh at him, but I tell him I'm ready to see them. He leaves the room, and Emmeline hops up, tidying the room a bit. It looks clean, but I've never been fussy over tidiness.

"By the way, Clem," Emmeline starts as she adjusts items on the mantle above the fireplace. "You should really be more careful when you leave your," she clears her throat, "items," she emphasizes this word with a glare in my direction. "Jasmin and Dahlia had you brought in here and placed on the bed. Thankfully, your mother and sister were several minutes away, and we found the belt and glass phallus under the covers. Your poor younger sister would have sat directly on top of it!" I can't suppress the laughter at her words and the potential situation. Emmeline can be such a prude but always looks in the other direction when we leave our "items" out. We've never been good at putting them away.

I can't even imagine trying to explain those to Claire. She would have so many questions I do not want to answer for my younger sister. Not only is it inappropriate because of her age, but who wants to explain that to their sister? I shudder at the thought as Ma and my sisters walk through the door. I turn to look at them, but Claire is already leaping over the couch, crashing into my side. I try to hide the wince from the pain, but she doesn't notice. Ma does, though, and she admonishes Claire for being too rough. She doesn't let up, though. I return her hug, holding her tightly. She sniffles, and I reach for my handkerchief, realizing I'm not in my regular day clothes. I still have trousers on, but this is a shirt I typically sleep in.

"I thought you were going to die," Claire cries into my chest, breaking my thoughts from my clothes. Ma also has tears in her eyes but has her own hand-kerchief. Sorrow flows through that she has come to the castle and now needs to carry one around. She never needed one before I came here.

"Nah," I coo, "you can't get rid of me that easily." She laughs, finally looking up at me. She gasps, covering her mouth. I feign offense at her reaction, but Bea beats me to the commentary.

"Oh, Claire, are you just realizing he is ugly?" Ma groans at Bea's insult but can't hide her chuckle. Ma wraps her arms around my shoulders, kissing my uninjured cheek. I wrap one arm around her back, the other staying around Claire.

"I'm so glad you're awake, Clem," she whispers.

"I love you, Ma." She squeezes me tighter before sitting in a chair across from the couch I am on.

"What happened to your face, Clem?"

"I reacted poorly when I first woke up, and Kian dealt with me quickly." Bea rolls her eyes.

"Clem? Doing something poorly and getting punched? No! That's absurd!" She leans in, giving a quick hug. "Glad your back." I offer a smile as she sits in the chair next to Ma. Finn waltzes over, taking the last spot on the couch beside

Claire. She squeals as the ginormous dog climbs on her. She slips a biscuit out of her pocket, feeding it to him.

"When will Jasmin and Dahlia return?" I look to Emmeline and Kian, wondering when they will.

"We sent a rider to let them know you are awake. Jasmin planned to stay several days in Vadried and visit with the villagers."

"I'll go to them. I can pack quickly and leave now and be there before dark." I try to stand, but aches in my body slow me. Everyone can see my pain through the flinches and jerks of my body.

"That's not a good idea. You need time to heal and recover." Ma responds, staring at me in a way only she can when she gives her child a new rule.

"She's right. We still don't know if there will be any lingering effects from the spell," Kian adds.

I concede unwillingly. They may be correct, but that doesn't mean I will be happy about it. I try to push the thoughts of my girls from my mind. It may be the first time I've spent a few days away from them, but it likely won't be the last. Instead, I try to enjoy time with my family, savoring the precious moments I have with them, even if they are teasing me. It's nice to have some ordinary moments after so many crazy, cursed moments.

Spending the day with my family has been refreshing. It's been nice to just relax and not deal with stress or curses or evil mothers. We all head to the dining hall for dinner. Cheers erupt as I enter the room. Dozens of people offer hugs, regards for a healthy return, and hope for the end of these curses. I return their sentiments, glad to be around so many people who are thankful for my return. Jasmin has commented on how different the castle is now, full of life and love. I didn't understand, but I do now. These people, they are our people. We don't stand above them, and they know that. A calm sense of belonging settles over me as I sit in my regular spot, Ma and Claire taking Jasmin and Dahlia's regular spots. Before I have time to miss their presence, a loud shout breaks through the dining hall.

"Clem?!"

I jump from my seat, searching for the voice I know so intimately. I finally spot her in the doorway at the exact moment she spots me. She rushes through the tables, people jumping out of her way quickly. I have enough time to stand and take two steps before Dahlia crashes into me. My awkward position and sore muscles cause us to topple to the ground, but I keep her on top of me. My muscles already ache; what are a few more bruises at this point?

I squeeze Dahlia tightly. Her hands are on my face, neck, and chest when she finally kisses me. Love and happiness spread through my body, soothing the deep aches in my muscles. I return her kiss passionately, needing contact with her. I hold the back of her head, stroking my thumb over her cheek. Her cheek is damp, but she refuses to break the kiss. Despite my hesitance, my need to see her face, to know she's okay, I understand why she is crying and give her the intimacy she is also craving. Her legs drop to my sides, straddling my waist. For a moment, I forget where we are, sliding my hand down her back.

"Okay, we need to stop," Kian's voice interrupts us, pulling Dahlia away from me. "You are still in the dining hall with half the castle present." I laugh, sitting up now that Dahlia has been pulled from me. But her arms wrap around my shoulder, her face pressed against my chest.

"I didn't think you'd come back so soon." Her words are whispered and sad, tearing through the happiness with despair. I squeeze her tightly, pressing a kiss to her head.

"I'm still here," I whisper softly so only she can hear, repeating the words she uttered when she interrupted my wedding. She laughs in my arms, still choked with sobs. "Sit and have dinner with us?"

She nods but doesn't move to get up from my lap. "Dahl, I can't lift you right now. I need you to get up." She leans back quickly, staring at me with a startled, concerned look. "I've been in bed for three days; I'm a little sore." She nods, accepting that response. For the first time, she really sees my face. The shocked look spreads quickly as her fingers near my cheek. She doesn't touch but looks like she might cry again. I see the humor in this situation. She was so angry at me when she first returned and now wants to cry over a black eye. Love swells in my heart, basking in her concern. I place both hands on her cheeks, kissing her lips quickly.

"I love you. And I will explain that later, but can we please get up and eat? I'm hungry, and my ass hurts." She laughs, dropping her forehead against mine but still not moving off me. I hold her face, stroking her cheeks lovingly, offering her the connection she desperately needs now.

"I don't want to let you go, Clem." I pull her into a hug, inhaling deeply, consuming her smell, her body fitting perfectly against mine. After a moment, I lean back.

"Okay, don't let me go. You can help me up, though." She gives a weak laugh, standing to take my hand. Ma slides over, letting Dahlia take her seat. Emmeline brings over a plate with food for her. Claire leans against my side again, and I realize Jas isn't here.

"Where is Jasmin?" I ask Dahlia, shoving a piece of sausage in my mouth.

"She wanted to stay in Vadried and finish her visit." I nod, a small hurt piercing my chest that she didn't rush back. I understand her desire to stay with her people, but I want her with me, too.

"Maybe we could go to her? If we leave after dinner, we can make it just before sunset." Kian shakes his head at me.

"I still want more time to be sure the curse has no lingering effects." I roll my eyes at him, something I have picked up from Jasmin. She still rolls her eyes far more than I do.

"What about after breakfast?" Kian eyes me wearily but finally agrees. Excitement grows within me at seeing my other girl tomorrow. We can spend extra time in Vadried like we had planned to earlier in the summer.

"If you're leaving for a few days, can I stay with you tonight?" Claire asks in a sad voice, trying to sway me with big, sad eyes. Before I can say anything else, Kian and Emmeline nearly shout a response.

"No!" Everyone looks shocked, but Dahlia and I slowly start grinning. Ma seems to understand their response and fills in Claire, who looks bewildered.

"Claire, you can't stay with him tonight. Maybe when he gets back."

"But he's my big brother and has been cursed for several days!" She whines, peppering me with her big sad eyes again.

"Dahlia is his future wife and hasn't spent any time with him in several days." Ma's voice is firm, causing Claire to cross her arms over her chest in anger.

"Claire," I start softly, willing to compromise to make her look less sad. "What if I tuck you in and read you a story tonight, then I'll come find you first thing in the morning, and we'll have breakfast together before I leave?"

"Will you bring breakfast to my room?" I can't stifle the chuckle. She will definitely be a good courtier one day.

"Yes. I will bring breakfast to your room, and you and I can eat together." She perks up in her seat, smiling sweetly.

"Okay then."

Dinner continues in a lighthearted manner. Everyone is in good spirits. We don't speak about Oleander or any faction of any curse. We briefly mention plans for the ceremony but mostly stick to plans for autumn and the approaching winter. Finn sits under the table, placing his head in laps for food, getting scratches, and wagging his tail, bruising toes and ankles. It's a pleasant dinner, but I am eager to return to my room. My body may be somewhat sore, but not every part is.

After dinner, Dahlia returns to our room while I walk with Claire. She holds my arm similarly to how Jasmin does. She's almost the same height as Jasmin, just an inch or two shorter than my shoulders. I long to see Jas, but I am also glad for this time alone with my younger sister. She readies for bed in her room, and we chat idly, not saying anything substantial but keeping a constant conversation. Once in bed, I pull the covers around her, tucking her in snuggly. I kiss her forehead, then settle beside her as I begin reading. My mind inches toward my bedroom, but I continue reading the words in the book. Soon, she begins to drift off, and I close the book and kiss her again before sneaking to the door.

"I love you, Clem," she mumbles in her half-asleep state.

"I love you, too, Claire. See you in the morning."

Once in the hallway, I rush to my room, not even concerned about who sees me moving quickly. It's no secret what will happen and doesn't need to be. I find

Dahlia in the bed, not wearing any clothes. I strip my shirt off, tossing it on the floor. I walk out of the pants, managing to not fall on my face. My cock is already half erect, ready for Dahlia. I crawl across the bed, planning to plant my face between her legs. Before I get there, she grabs my face, pulling me toward hers.

"Fuck me, Clem."

She doesn't need to tell me twice. I grab her ass, sliding her lower and pressing into her slowly. She inhales deeply as I sink inside her. I rest my forehead against her, savoring the tight warmth wrapped around my cock. I bite my tongue, wanting to say all the dirty things racing through my mind. I hold them back, knowing Dahlia doesn't like my perverted words. I'll save them for tomorrow. Instead, I press my lips against hers as I begin thrusting inside her. Her hands drift into my hair, then tug tightly. I break the kiss, groaning at the pressure. She presses me down, and I suck a nipple into my mouth, and I pound her welcoming pussy. She moans under my ministrations.

She grasps my shoulders, shoving me to the side. My back hits the pillows then she hops on top of me in a fluid motion. Her cunt sinks over my cock, drawing a string of obscenities from me. Her hips swirl and bounce over me. I grab her hips but hold lightly. She sets a brutal but desperate pace. Her tits bounce playfully in my face. My fingers drag up her side, cupping her breasts. I lean forward, sucking her brown nipple in my mouth. Her hand circles my head, keeping my mouth firmly planted against her breast. I lick, suck, and nibble on her tit, eliciting moans from her. The telltale tingling in my balls indicates I won't last much longer. I pull back from her, leaning back to watch her ride me.

I prop my arm behind my head, watching her beautiful body move over mine. My eyes roll back in my head as pleasure courses through my body. My teeth sink into my lips, trying to keep my eyes on her. "I'm going to come, Dahl," I whisper, barely able to hold back.

"I'm not there yet." She sounds desperate, riding harder. That has the opposite effect of what she wants. I get one hand to her clit as I erupt deep inside her. I groan as she keeps bouncing, drawing out my orgasm. As my body finally winds down, dick going soft, her movements become erratic, anguished.

"No, no, no," she whines, rubbing against my lower abdomen. I guide her off me, lying her beside me on the bed.

"Dahl, I'm not done with you." I consider licking her but don't particularly want to taste my own seed inside of her. Instead, I move to the closet, where we store all the best items. She writhes on the bed, moaning with discontent. I don't know why she thinks I wouldn't finish her off, even if I already came. Typically, I can hold off and be the last to finish. But, typically, I'm not exhausted and am in more control. I grab the magic fun ball and walk back to the bed. She's nearly in tears, her own fingers on her cunt now.

"Lie back, Dahl. I'll take care of you." Her hands grab my face, planting a searing kiss on my lips. For a moment, I am stunned. Her wet fingers tangle in my hair, bringing me back to the task at hand. I slip my fingers between her legs, tapping the device as it nears her pussy. She groans, sucking in a breath. My tongue tangles with hers. I press the vibrating item against her clit, letting my fingers slip into her pussy, still coated with my cum.

I lean on my side, partially covering her. My fingers work her cunt over, inside and out. I break the kiss, placing my lips against her neck. She whines under me as if something is holding her back. This is more emotional for her than usual. Her inability to finish isn't just physical. Just as this realization hits, so does an idea to rectify this problem. She may not like dirty talk, but that doesn't mean she won't like other words.

"You are mine, Dahlia." She groans as I speak, goosebumps spreading across her chin. "I will always come back to you." She arches under my chest; she breathes quickly now. "I'm gonna take care of you, my love. You are safe with me now." I press kisses to her neck and ear. Her hips jerk erratically under my hand, but I hold steady. I keep the magic fun ball pressed against her clit, and my fingers thrust steadily inside her. She has always done better with consistency. Her pussy clenches around my fingers, and I whisper, "I love you, Dahlia." She screams, twisting and jerking through her orgasm. I don't stop my fingers, keeping up my pace. Her body tightens and presses against me, but I keep working her. Her scream fades to gasps, and she finally pushes my hand away. The fun ball drops between her legs, but I grab her hip, pulling her against me. I kiss her deeply, holding her tightly to my body. She is soft and pliant, allowing me to reassure her with kisses. When her hands finally move to stroke my sides, I pull back from the kiss, giving her a soft smile.

"I'll always take care of you, my sweet girl." She chuckles, settling down comfortably in the bed. I reach between her legs, and she gasps. She's not a big fan of multiple forced orgasms. She loves doing it to Jasmin, but she doesn't like receiving them. I grab the cylinder, tap it off, and hold it up for her. She chuckles while I clean it off and put it away. I return to the bed with a cloth to clean her, then my cock. I toss the rag aside, climbing in bed with her. I hold her tightly to my chest, realizing I want intimacy as desperately as she does. I whisper words of affection and adoration to her as we settle into a relaxed state.

"What happened to your face?" Her words are soft, eyes fixed on my cheek.

"I was apparently aggressive when I came out of the curse and tried to attack Emmeline. Kian punched me to snap me out of it." Her eyes dance with confusion, anger, and concern.

"He punched you?"

"This is a secret, so don't repeat it. He's in love with Emmeline and wasn't thinking when he saw me." She nods in understanding, having attacked people for less on Jasmin's behalf. I don't know how good Dahlia is at keeping secrets, but I can't keep this one from her. She doesn't press the issue any further, though. Her fingers trail over my sides.

"When I woke up, I was drawn to the throne room. It was like a rope had been tied around me, dragging me there. I hesitated in here but couldn't resist the pull." I tighten my grip around her body, holding her as close as possible. It's hard to believe we were at each other's throats only a few months ago. Fate and magic definitely work in strange ways. We soon drift off into a restful sleep, as content as we can be without Jasmin.

We wake to light breaking through the windows. Emmeline didn't come with us last night, and she normally closes the curtains. Neither Dahlia nor I thought to do that. Dahlia is still sound asleep, wrapped up in the blankets. Remembering my promise to Claire, I slip out of bed, closing the curtains so Dahlia can sleep longer. As I get dressed, Finn climbs into the bed, snuggling beside Dahlia. He has been forced onto his actual bed Jasmin has for him. It went unused for years until we brought Dahlia in here. Now our bed isn't big enough for him too. He still gets in the bed any chance he gets. Dahlia sighs, wrapping an arm around Finn carelessly. A smile spreads across my face, seeing the two in the bed.

I sneak out of the room and head for the kitchen. The sheer joy I feel over having breakfast with my younger sister is overwhelming. Before I left Arkaley, we would wake up early and make breakfast for everyone else. Spending time with my little sister was fun and delightful, making a mess and creating something delicious. I always knew in my mind that it would eventually end. I would marry and move out, or she would. I never wanted to admit it, though. Even though we don't cook now, enjoying breakfast with her in her room is still lovely. I can't express how delighted I am that she and Ma moved into the castle with us. I couldn't have asked for a better situation.

We chat about her studies and what she is learning about court protocol. She knows more than I do, finding it more interesting than I ever did. She speaks casually about the ceremony we're planning, having good ideas from books she has read. I tell her she needs to relay this information to Emmeline or Jasmin. I gather the trays when we finish breakfast, promising to return in a few days. I return the tray and seek out Dahlia, who is now dressed and ready. She packed a bag for me, saving time so we could leave faster. After a few quick goodbyes, we mount our horses and take off to Vadried.

We pass the fields that are producing better than they have in years. A soft longing passes through me. Maybe I'll spend some time helping during the harvest. I miss the feeling of dirt and collecting food straight from the earth. We pass the orchards, where the fruits are just starting to turn colors to ripen, indicating the upcoming change of seasons. There are only a few weeks until the autumnal equinox. It's hard to believe I have only been here for a year. So much has changed in that time.

The rest of the trip passes uneventfully. We finally arrive at the courthouse where Jasmin is staying. I can't contain my excitement as we enter the courtyard. Dahlia tells me to go find her, and she'll deal with our horses and bags. I don't argue, hopping down and nearly falling over. I really need more practice on horseback. It's definitely not a strong suit. I rush inside, not spotting Jasmin right away. One of the younger servants shows me to her room, but she isn't there. I'm growing frantic over not finding her. Dahlia finds me, having secured the horses and luggage already.

"Where is she?" Dahlia senses my rising panic but takes my hand and guides me to the street that leads to the market district. Of course, she would be there. We didn't send word that we were coming, making plans too late to send a rider. We walk together, searching for her through the crowds of vendors and shoppers. Thankfully, few people recognize us or stop us. Some notice us but don't say anything. Eventually, I spot her standing at a stall with rolls of material. She holds one in her hand, nodding at the vendor as she speaks about the material. Unable to resist, I rush up behind her, wrapping my arms around her tightly. She squeals, shocked by being grabbed like that. She spins in my arms, recognizing me instantly.

"Oh, gods," she mumbles as tears fall down her cheeks. She buries her face in my neck as I lift her feet off the ground, squeezing her body as tightly as I can. I bury my face in her hair, realizing it's shorter than the last time I saw her.

"You need to maintain some decorum. You are Queen, you know," I whisper teasingly in her ear. She just chuckles as I gently lower her to the ground, leaning in to kiss her. She jerks back, seeing my darkened cheek. I keep forgetting about that.

"Fuck, Clem. What did you do?" I laugh at her reaction. She knows me so well. I relay the story to her, not sharing the secret now since so many people are around. She eyes me suspiciously, but I just give her a playful wink, pressing a kiss to her cheek. She sighs at the contact, turning to take my arm. She leans over to kiss Dahlia's cheek lightly.

We spend the rest of the day walking through the market, buying a few things, eating tasty food, and talking with the locals. The next day is spent wandering through the arts district, viewing paintings, sculptures, and listening to musicians. It's a different feeling than Obele has. It's more formal but still enjoyable. In the evening, we attend a play together, laughing and crying over the actors' portrayal.

On the final day, the three of us wander through the streets, enjoying the architecture and scenery of the wealthiest village in the kingdom. The residents like to showcase their wealth with exuberant plants and sculptures on their property. We talk with many of the villagers, listening as they express emotions about the curse and trial of Oleander. There is an overwhelming amount of support for Jasmin among the villagers. When we return to the castle, we are all exhausted but filled with joy and love.

Chapter 44

JASMIN

It's the day of our ceremony. Since we returned from Vadried, the past few weeks have been busy but wonderful. Everyone has been in good spirits. Clem spent time in the fields, returning late in the evening, covered in dirt, but grinning from ear to ear. Dahlia has spent time with the witches, working on various spells and improving her mastery of magic. I've been working with Emmeline and Kian to make plans, both of whom keep up the pretense that they aren't secretly in love. Despite my strong desire to do so, I don't push them for information.

Ingrid is at the castle now. I asked her to make new crowns for Dahlia, Clem, and me. She informed me Clem also requested this after I asked her to keep it a secret. She told him she was too busy with other projects but promised to make it up to him later. He was disappointed, but he'll be excited to see what we have created. With the addition of the new territory for the witches, we need a different design to encompass everything in our kingdom. Instead of the individual panels for each village like my current crown, we settle on one panel, with all villages on the same level and the castle emblem in the middle.

Our new crowns look identical; there is no difference between the three. This is to represent our equal power and devotion to the kingdom. They are set in silver bands, with flowers, leaves, and sparkling swirls around the gems for each kingdom. They are smaller than my previous crown, making them more comfortable for less formal events. Ingrid is a miracle worker and so skilled at the work she does. I am absolutely amazed by the crowns she created.

Our celebration will be held outside at the castle. We originally planned to hold the ceremony inside, like my previous coronation. Then we learned how many people wanted to attend. Thousands of people have requested to come to the ceremony. Suddenly, the throne room feels tiny and inadequate. Our builders have been working non-stop to fashion benches and stages for us to celebrate together. We requested the villages provide as much furniture as possible so we don't need to store an exorbitant amount of pieces that will only be used a few times a year. We still need more, though.

Emmeline has brought in a crew to help decorate. Without Sunette here to help, she needed far more assistance than before. The castle is stunning, though. Brightly colored leaves adorn the walls and railings, mixed with ribbons, evergreens, and branches. Emmeline has truly outdone herself this time. Gourds and pumpkins sit between stacks of hay and sunflowers, creating a gorgeous scene for people to enjoy. Late blooming flowers and the ever-blooming jasmine from the greenhouse have been scattered around the castle. It feels like a magical world of life and color.

Like before, Emmeline has forced the three of us to get ready separately. Dahlia has been taken to her brother's quarters, Clem, with his sister. We all fought, but ultimately, there was no arguing with Emmeline. I reminded her she could run the kingdom if she wanted, but she balked at me, brushing through my hair. Unlike the last time, we have a soft, off-white dress for me. It's my preferred fashion: long panels graze the floor, and a pleated piece over my breasts. It's not the extravagant dresses royalty usually wear, but I'm not standard royalty. I feel more beautiful, comfortable, and happier than I ever have. There is no nervousness, no anxiety about what is to come. I know, with all my heart, we can face any challenge that comes our way.

I walk through the halls, heading toward the door where I will meet Dahlia. We will join Clem on the platform, where Kian will officiate our ceremony. As I arrive at our meeting spot, I finally see her. The woman I have wanted to be with for so long. The woman I knew was meant to spend forever with me. My breath hitches. She is wearing a yellow gown, similar to mine, but with more details. She's always been a little extra. I fight the tears, not wanting to ruin the makeup Emmeline insisted on. Knowing I would cry today, I didn't want any, but it looks incredible.

"Jas." Her whispered word breaks my fragile hold on my tears. They stream down my face as I run into her arms. I hope this feeling never fades, this excitement every time I see her. She laughs as I crash into her chest, resting my ear against her, listening to her heartbeat. The steady thump calms me, reminding me we made it; we're alive and together. I turn my face up to hers.

"You can't kiss me yet."

I sniffle through my laughter, stepping back from her. She reaches inside the bust of her dress, removing a small handkerchief. She shrugs playfully as she dabs my eyes.

"I stole one from Clem, knowing I would see you first."

I laugh again, loving how thoughtful both of my partners are. Emmeline catches up to us, fretting over my makeup. She hands us a bouquet of bright, colorful roses that stand out against our gowns. I wrap my hand around Dahlia's arm, realizing how different this feels from holding Clem, but just as comforting. Unable to resist, I rise on my toes and kiss her cheek. Her smirk tells me everything I need to know about where her mind is. She's ready for this evening. She and Clem have been whispering and keeping secrets from me, and I am unabashedly excited about what they have planned.

The doors open, sunlight beaming through, casting a magical golden glow on the grounds. So many people are here. Even more showed up than expected. I offer smiles to many before my eyes finally catch on Clem. He is standing on the platform with Kian. He is wearing a deep red tunic with tan pants. His long hair is down, flat against his back. His eyes are beaming with love as he watches us stroll down the aisle. Behind him, Kian can't contain his happiness, grinning larger than any officiant I have ever seen. He is wearing a black tunic and pants, his dark hair slicked back to appear more professional.

We finally reach the stage, and Clem comes down to take our hands, helping us up the few steps. Once at the top, Kian speaks, addressing the crowd behind us. I stand between Clem and Dahlia. This is as much to honor my current position as it is to give Kian a better sight to address the audience. With me being the shortest, he can see over my head better than the others. He speaks of overcoming the curse, our future's brighter days, and our dedication to this kingdom. We decided to start with the coronation part of our ceremony. We want the kingdom to know they will come first for us and that we will stand united to serve them.

Like my coronation, the three of us pledge to each Lord and Lady in unison, vowing to serve our kingdom. They accept our vows, bowing before us, then return to their seats. Kian brings out our crowns, the three of us kneeling now. The crowds coo with admiration for the crowns on display. Clem eyes me curiously, suspicious of the maker. I wink at him, turning my attention back to Kian. He speaks our promises to protect the kingdom, to make wise choices, and always serve our people as he places the crowns on our heads. Once he puts the final crown on Clem's head, he speaks to us.

"Now rise as the crowned rulers of Sweet Briar and face each other."

I turn my back to Kian, facing the crowd. Clem and Dahlia stand by my sides. We all join hands, and tears begin to stream down my face. I cannot contain the sheer joy of this day. I told Emmeline I would spend the whole day crying. Clem squeezes my hand, offering a small comfort that only brings more tears to my eyes. I fight the laugh that rises over my inability to control my tears, and Kian finally starts speaking, distracting me from my own thoughts.

This time, Kian speaks of overcoming great trials and tribulations. He shares his first-hand experience with our ability and willingness to communicate, compromise, and work through problems many will never face in their lifetime. He mentions the loss and heartbreak we have suffered together and overcome. He finally speaks of the unique composition of our relationship and how we are distinctly prepared for a lifetime of love and happiness despite all the difficulties.

He has us repeat words of love, affirmation, and promises. Clem produces three rings from his pocket, each a silver band inlaid with identical gems to our crowns.

I immediately recognize Ingrid's work, realizing while she didn't make the crowns for him, she did create these rings for him. I glance at her in the crowd, and she shrugs. Clem slips the ring on my finger, then hands me the next two. I slip one over Dahlia's finger, placing the last one in her hand. She glides the final ring onto Clem's hand. I step up, kissing Dahlia's cheek, then Clem's. We decided to forgo the traditional kiss to avoid dealing with all three of us kissing while everyone watched. I'm not interested in putting on a show for the whole kingdom. We finally turn, facing the crowd with our hands linked together. From behind me, Kian makes the final announcement of our ceremony.

"Sweet Briar, I present your crowned royalty, Queen Jasmin, Queen Dahlia, and King Clematis."

The crowd roars as we descend the staircase. Given the sheer number of people present, we decided to skip a formal dinner, instead moving straight to an open area for dancing, mingling, and buffet-style food and wine provided. We lead the crowd from the ceremony area while people rush to remove the benches. We will still need the space for extra seating but want to create a more welcoming space for everyone. Three thrones have been brought out for us to sit in throughout the night, though we will not be forced to stay. We can eat and dance and mingle as we see fit. Before we sit, though, I kiss both of my newly joined partners.

The evening carries on joyously. The air cools off with the setting sun. We dance and chat with people from the kingdom. Unfortunately, little time is spent with our families, but we squeeze in some time with them. Clem dances with Ada and Claire while I dance with Kian and Dahlia. Dahlia enjoys a dance with Zander when Tomas takes a break. So many people wish us a lifetime of peace and happiness. I so desperately want that after everything that has happened so far.

Finally, Kian announces we are retiring for the evening, but everyone is invited to stay and mingle as long as they want. The musicians from Vadried change from an upbeat performance to more subdued music, encouraging people to leave but still providing entertainment for those that choose to stay. Clem grabs mine and Dahlia's hands and practically drags us through the castle to our room. Despite my exhaustion from the long day, excitement builds in my body, butterflies floating around my stomach. In the room, Clem actually locks our door before turning his gaze on me. Dahlia has disappeared into the closet, and my body tingles with anticipation.

"You are the most beautiful thing, but that dress has got to go." Before I can respond, Clem is on me, tossing the crown onto the chair, hands grasping at my dress, ripping it over my head. I wore nothing beneath my clothes and now stand fully exposed before my king. He growls, actually growls, when he sees my naked body. With desire rampant in his eyes, I don't hate that Emmeline made us spend the last night apart.

Dahlia emerges from the closet with ropes, multiple bottles of oil, and the box Clem found for all of our toys. Her clothes are gone, too, standing as naked as I am. My eyes widen, her supple breasts covered by all the items she carries. With my focus on her, I didn't notice Clem move. He grabs my throat, pulling my back against his now bare chest. His other hand holds my cunt, slipping a finger inside me.

"We are going to claim you and fuck you and use every inch of your body for our pleasure."

I groan, chest heaving under his arms. His teeth graze my ears. I watch Dahlia walk toward me, dropping all the items on the bed. She turns to face me, catching my lips with hers. Her lips are soft and firm, pressing mine open as her tongue searches my mouth. I moan as Clem's fingers slide out of my wet cunt, then back in agonizingly slow. I'm swept away by the pleasure of having these two pressed against my tingling body. Dahlia's fingers wrap around my budding nipples. Just as I am about to moan, she squeezes tightly, twists, and pulls them down violently. I jerk toward her, screaming in both pain and pleasure. My sudden movement causes Clem's hand to put more pressure against my throat, silencing my scream.

"That's right, slut. We're in charge now, and you will be the last to come tonight."

I whimper at his words, and he loosens his hand enough for me to make a slight noise. Dahlia breaks the kiss, releasing her hold on my breasts. My nipples tingle as the blood surges through them. She instructs Clem to remove his pants and get on the bed. He removes his hand from my cunt, but his fingers tighten slightly around my neck. He grabs Dahlia's cheeks and pulls her into a kiss just inches from my face, forcing me to watch without being able to join.

He ends the kiss with a wicked grin, knowing I want to be kissed, too. He releases me and does as Dahlia instructed. Before I can react, she spins me around, pulling my back against her chest. Her breasts squish between us. My hips press back against hers. She grabs my wrists, overlapping them over my stomach, rendering me unable to touch her. I groan, grinding my ass against her hips. She chuckles, holding one hand over my wrists; the other grabs my face, forcing it toward Clem, who is now removing his pants.

"Look at your king; already hard for you."

Sure enough, his cock sticks straight out from his body. He restrains from touching it as he slides into the middle of the bed, propping his arms behind his head in a cocky manner. My eyes bounce between his and his cock. Desire and lust burn through me from his gaze, his cock twitching as I lick my lips. Dahlia releases me, smacking my ass hard. I yelp at the sudden impact but am instantly met with a soothing rub.

"Go suck him," she whispers in my ear. I don't hesitate to climb on the bed, crawling toward him. I swirl my tongue around the tip of his cock, gazing up at him. His eyes roll back in his head, hands clenching to keep from forcing my head down. With my own budding cockiness, I spit on his cock, eliciting a groan from him. I swallow him whole, hollowing out my cheeks as the head of his cock hits the back of my throat. Unable to resist, his hand lands on the back of my head, tangling in my hair as he guides me up and down.

In my focus on Clem, I lost track of Dahlia. She makes her presence known when an oil-covered finger presses deep into my ass. I groan around Clem, him forcing my head down further over him as the vibrations in my throat hit his cock. Dahl's finger slides in and out smoothly as I tongue the underside of Clem's member. She slips another finger inside me, Clem's cock jerking in my mouth this time. She works my hole, spreading her fingers and thrusting them in and out.

She pulls them out suddenly, leaving me whimpering and slobbering around the hard dick in my mouth. The glass phallus, coated in lube, presses against my ass. Dahlia puts her hand on my hips, lowering them into a better position. She slowly slides the glass phallus into me. I suck in a deep breath around Clem's penis before running my tongue around the length. His hips jerk beneath me, grabbing a fistful of hair.

"Take Dahlia in the ass while I come down your throat." I swallow his whole length, sucking hard as I draw back. Dahlia sinks to the hilt inside me, pausing momentarily to be sure I don't have any objections. I don't. Not tonight.

"There's my dirty little slut." Clem's words are clipped out through gritted teeth, indicating how close he is. Dahlia begins pounding inside me, causing me to moan around Clem. With her rough impact, I struggle to move against Clem. He realizes this and grabs my hair tighter, holding me still. "Suck, slut," he mumbles as he thrusts inside me. I switch between sucking and tonguing his cock as he pounds the back of my throat relentlessly. The ache in my own pussy is growing unbearable. I need to touch my clit, my pussy, something more than what they are taking from me now. With one hand, I reached toward my own cunt, but Dahlia swats my hand away.

"Not your turn," she mumbles between thrusts. Her hands grab my hips as she thrusts deep into my ass brutally. I gag around Clem's cock, spit dripping down onto his balls. His warm release squirts down my throat as he roars through his orgasm. I increase sucking as his hips settle against the bed. Dahlia still pounds behind me, growing more erratic with her looming orgasm. I hope it comes quickly so they will focus on me.

I swirl my tongue over Clem's softening cock, keeping my lips firmly around it. His body twitches beneath me, his groans intermingled with laughter at the pleasure wreaking havoc on his body. When his dick is soft, I release it, letting it land against his stomach. He lifts my head, kissing me deeply as Dahlia continues pumping erratically in my ass. Her hands slide over my body, lips pressing against my shoulder now that I am more upright. Clem reaches past my body, this his fingers sink inside my dripping core. The magic fun ball is vibrating at the highest setting against my clit. I break the kiss, yelling as a wave of pleasure crashes through my body. While I'm not as full as when Clem and Dahlia are inside me, there are still a lot of sensations happening in an already worked-up area.

His fingers pound inside me in time with Dahlia's. She soon cries out with her own orgasm, her body pressing against mine for support. As her body shakes with pleasure, my own crashes with the most powerful orgasm I've had. My mouth opens in a silent scream as my body shakes against Clem. Dahlia thrusts a few more times before sliding and toppling onto the bed. Clem continues to work me through the most prolonged orgasm I have ever experienced, refusing to let me come down. Soon, my clit becomes overly sensitive. I cry out against him, my body convulsing and jerking away. He holds me firmly as my body tenses with another orgasm. Dahlia's hands caress my side, offering an anchor point for my soaring mind and body. Finally, Clem stops, pulling away from me, sending my body through a few more jerks as I settle on the bed beside Dahlia. Her hands caress my body softly in a soothing manner. Clem turns, grabbing items from the table beside the bed I didn't notice before.

"I'm going to clean you." His words are soft but hold an edge of warning. He spreads my legs, passing a cool, wet cloth over my overly sensitive core. I jerk, trying to pull away from him, but he holds steady. He cleans me gently but thoroughly, grabbing another cloth and doing the same for Dahl, who isn't as sensitive as me. He manages to clean up this time without leaving the bed. Finally, he settles against me, wrapping his arms around Dahlia and me. I sigh, deeply contented with how this day has gone. We whisper words of love and gratitude before drifting off to sleep together, officially married and ruling a kingdom.

Chapter 45

CLEM

TWO YEARS LATER

The sun is rising outside our window. I thrust my cock deep inside Dahlia, burying my face against her neck. Jasmin, wearing the glass phallus, is behind me, pounding ruthlessly into my ass. It started last year when a drunk Dahlia suggested fucking me in the ass. I didn't let her then because she was too drunk, too restless with my delicate ass at the time. But it didn't take long for that seed to sprout. Now, both women frequently request to fuck me. I'd be lying if I said I didn't love it. Jasmin shifts her hips, causing the phallus to rub against my prostate.

"There, Jas! There, fuck." I groan loudly, savoring the orgasmic rapture spreading through my body. I try to adjust my position, letting Jasmin hit that spot over and over. My balls tighten, indicating I won't last much longer here. I tap the device pressed against Dahlia's clit. We realized long ago she comes easier with multiple sensations.

"Fuck, Jasmin, finish him."

Jasmin chuckles behind me, smacking my ass as my orgasm finally hits, sending my seed deep inside Dahlia. She comes at the same time I do, crying out beneath me. I latch onto her neck, finding the spot that drives her wild. She twists beneath me, her orgasm winding down. Jasmin thrusts a few more times inside me, sending tortured spurts of semen from my body. She finally orgasms, leaning against me and biting my shoulder instead of yelling. Biting has become a favorite of hers, and I can no longer go anywhere without a shirt. My body is constantly covered in three to four bite marks in various states of healing. Pain sears through my shoulder, but Dahlia caresses my chest, mixing the pain with pleasure.

Jasmin slips away behind me, gathering all devices to clean and store away. Dahlia and I move to the bathroom, cleaning up before our guests arrive. I drop into the bath as Jasmin enters.

"I think I broke skin that time. Sorry, Clem." She shrugs nonchalantly, not sounding the least bit apologetic. I chuckle, kissing her gently as she climbs in with me. Dahlia steps in next, hair wrapped up in a scarf.

Sunette returned a couple of months ago, braided her hair the next day, and has kept it that way since. None of us complained about the hours it took her to do so. We all sat in Zander's living room, exchanging stories as time passed. Sabeko made it to his home and connected with his remaining family. He enjoyed a couple of months with them before he passed. Sunette details the beautiful ceremony they held to celebrate his life. She spent another year in her home, burying her parents when they passed and getting to know multiple nieces and nephews. She eventually began the perilous journey home.

Sunette was sad to realize both of her children had married while she was away, but she was thrilled with their chosen partners. We ultimately decided to find new lodging for her and allowed Tomas and Zander to keep the suite they had been in for the past two years. Sunette is settled now, taking over her duties in the royal garden. She works closely with Ada, and the two have a beautiful friendship.

Dahlia climbs out of the bath after washing her body. She slips on her thin dress and leaves the room. Jasmin and I enjoy the warmth, washing each other's body and hair before finally climbing out. She dries off, slipping into leggings and a thin shift. She has quit wearing dresses altogether, only donning a simple one for special occasions. Dahlia still prefers the ease of dresses over pants. Emmeline doesn't bicker with Jasmin over her attire as much anymore. After the ceremony, Jasmin changed Emmeline's title from Lady in Waiting to Lady of the Castle. She now has more control over the day-to-day tasks around the castle. She still occasionally helps with more personal tasks Jasmin or Dahlia may need, but she has a broader range of duties. Others say the castle runs smoother than it has in decades.

Emmeline and Kian share a suite now, but neither will admit to any official relationship. Both flirt shamelessly with other people around the castle but always return to the suite together. They are always happy around each other. Jasmin and I have both pried for more information on the workings of their relationship. Neither will give us any details, though. Emmeline gets a dreamy look and wanders away when we ask about Kian. Kian just shrugs and changes the subject. He is dangerously good at changing the subject. While we know what he is doing, we are often distracted by his chosen topic.

Jasmin and I leave the bathroom together. She settles at her vanity, tying her wet hair back. I nibble at the tray of food that was brought up for us. Today is a special day. We are watching over Bea and Erik's baby together. It's not really fair to call him a baby, though. He's nearly a year and a half old. He loves to walk and wreak havoc wherever he is. Bea's pregnancy was difficult the entire time. Her labor was thankfully uncomplicated. Baby Mikko was born the day before the spring equinox and has been happy and spoiled ever since. There was much debate over what to name him. I insisted Clem was a perfect name for a baby. Claire insisted he should be named after our father. Many namesakes were mentioned, but Bea ultimately wanted him to have his own name to live up to, to set his own path, and not live in someone's shadow. Mikko suits him perfectly.

A knock at the door lets us know Bea is here to drop him off. Jasmin, Dahlia and I usually have meetings or other obligations to attend to, but we didn't today. Bea and Erik have support but still don't get much alone time. I am beyond thrilled to offer to keep Mikko for them. Dahlia learned how to change the limits on the barrier around the pond. She changed the spell to allow Bea and Erik to go there today and have privacy. Claire is well known for bursting into space unannounced. More than once, she caught my girls and me in a compromising position.

I answer the door with Dahlia by my side. Mikko squeals when he sees us, throwing himself away from Bea. I catch him just in time, planting a giant kiss on his cheek. He hugs my neck tightly but quickly lunges for Dahlia. I pass him over, and he settles in her arms. I roll my eyes at him but don't blame him a bit. I'd spend all my time against Dahlia's chest if I could, which seems to be growing lately.

"Everything is set up for you two," Dahlia tells Bea. Bea looks tired but grateful.

"Thank you for everything. It means a lot to us." She turns to me, giving me a serious look. She has always had that parental stare down, but it's become more impactful since she gave birth to Mikko. I hide the shiver my body wants to release. "Keep it in your fucking pants today, Clem." I laugh, remembering the last time we kept Mikko. It was several months ago. He fell asleep, and I took advantage of the quiet to fuck Jas. It just so happened that Claire walked in then. She immediately ran to tell Bea, and I haven't lived it down since. I roll my eyes at her.

"Fine, but you don't keep it in yours." She rears back, punching me in the arm. I wince, grabbing my arm as Dahlia walks away with Mikko, telling him how ridiculous we are. I had once thought becoming a mother would lessen Bea's violence toward me. I was desperately wrong.

"Fuck, Bea."

Jasmin walks up to my side, laughing and assuring Bea we won't be doing anything like that. "Yeah, because I already did that today. So I'll be fine until you get back." She groans and turns to walk away. We move back into the suite, settling on the rug with Mikko. I plop down on the floor, lying on my side while I hand him blocks to stack together. We all sit quietly for a few minutes before Dahlia gets up and rushes to the bathroom. We can hear her getting sick, which has been ailing her frequently. Jasmin rises, concerned about our wife.

"Leave her be. She'll be okay in a few minutes." I hand Mikko a block, but he throws it at my head and laughs hysterically. I purse my lips together but hand it back to him anyway.

"What do you mean?" She walks over to me with a mix of confusion and anger. I glance up at her as I'm hit in the cheek with another block.

"She's been sick like that for a week or so now. Every day. She gets sick for a little while, then is mostly fine for the rest of the day." Jasmin is deep in thought when Dahlia finally emerges, dropping heavily into the chair.

"You've been sick for a while now?" Dahlia shrugs, closing her eyes as she leans back.

"She has been more exhausted lately, too. Maybe we should call the healer?"

"No shit, Clem!" Another block flies past my head, and another bout of laughter breaks through the room.

"No, Jas. It's not a big deal. It always passes by the afternoon. I'll be fine."

"You're only sick in the morning?" A wave of understanding passes over Jasmin's face as she stares at Dahlia. Dahl seems to have the same knowledge, jumping from her seat. The two women rush into the closet, coming out a moment later with white cloths in Dahlia's hands. She looks ill again as she runs into the bathroom.

"Oh, gods." Jasmin's laugh is clouded with disbelief as she plops into the chair Dahlia was just sitting in. I absently hand another block to Mikko as I try, without success, to figure out what they know. Dahlia walks out of the bathroom, eyes wide with shock, the cloths still in her hand. She steps to Jasmin, who tugs her down into her lap. Jasmin holds her tightly, laughing as tears start streaming down her face.

"Wait, what? Why are you crying? What is going on?" Both women look at me but burst out laughing instead of answering me. I sit up, looking at Mikko, who is staring at them now. Finn saunters over from his bed, moving a bit slower than he did a couple of years ago. He nuzzles his head in Dahlia's lap, pressing against her belly.

"What's happening?" I demand again. Dahlia rises with a grunt from Finn. She sits on the floor next to me, resting her head on my shoulder. My anger grows over being left out of whatever is happening. She hands me the cloths, but I have no idea what they are. "What is this?" Jasmin laughs, drawing my attention to her.

"It's clean cloths, Clem."

"I can see that, Jas. What does that have to do with Dahlia being sick?" Dahlia chuckles, wrapping her arms around my waist. I don't understand what her clean cloths would have to do with her nausea. People get vomiting diseases all the time without needing cloths. Do they need me to clean her? Will these make her feel better? I look at the cloths in my hand as if they hold the answer.

After a minute and a block to the stomach, I recognize these as the cloths Dahlia uses during her monthly bleed. But what would...the answer crashes into me like a falling boulder. I jump from the floor, stepping on the corner of a block but not registering the pain.

"These...you..." My brain has stopped working. The thoughts aren't processing the way they should be.

"There it is." Jasmin teases, but I don't look at her. My eyes stayed glued to Dahlia, still on the floor.

"I forgot to take the tea when I started having breakfast with Mama." A shocked laugh escapes as tears fill my eyes.

"You...you're really..." She nods, standing up gently, pressing her fingertips low on her abdomen. I choke on a few more laughs, grabbing my pregnant wife in a tight hug. Jasmin scoops Mikko off the floor, away from my careless feet. I squeeze her body against mine as we cry happy tears. We knew Dahlia could get pregnant, but we never talked about having kids. We have been happy with the way things are. Before Dahlia, Jasmin and I accepted we wouldn't have kids. Having spent most of her life believing she would only be with women, Dahlia never considered having any of her own. Fate has decided it is time for us to have our own child. The three of us get to embark on a new journey together.

Epilogue

Nine months later, Dahlia gave birth to a baby girl. She was named Rose. She was surrounded by love and more family than any child could wish for. She was a perfect blend of Dahlia and Clem. Rose grew up in the castle, learning to love reading, magic, and traveling. She thrived having three parents that loved her deeply. Someone was always available to help, entertain, and teach her. Finn protected her for the first few years of her life until his life ended peacefully, asleep in the big bed. He was buried in the royal cemetery with a marker listing him as the best Royal Guard dog. They were never able to find a pet to replace him. Nothing could top their love and affection for the giant, furry beast.

Dahlia, Clem, and Jasmin lived long lives, all passing within months of each other. They were unable to survive without the other. They reigned over their kingdom for four full decades, leading Sweet Briar into the most prosperous era it has ever seen. The villages thrived under their rule; people were happy and content. The witches, over time, left the Crescent Mountains, settling throughout the kingdom, bringing their magic to benefit the other villages. Before Jasmin's death, the witch's territory was dissolved. The land was given back to Greynon and Vadried. Since the witches were integrated into every village in the kingdom, they no longer needed or wanted their own. While the older witches were grateful for the separation period, they were ecstatic to no longer need their own village. The Crescent Mountains are still sacred to the witches but no longer exclusive.

Trade expanded through other kingdoms, bringing new spices, plants, arts, and people. Many people immigrated to Sweet Briar to seek refuge from less kind kingdoms and find their own happiness. When Rose became Queen, she was older, unwed, and childless. She implemented a nomination system for people who wanted to rule the kingdom. She gave people time to learn the job and all the nuances of the position. She gave more power to the Lords and Ladies her parents had appointed, ensuring the crown royalty could not destroy the kingdom as her grandmother had tried to.

Bea gave birth to one more child, a strong girl who took after her father. Both children, Mikko and Sylvvi, joined the guard like their father's family. Sylvvi thrived, becoming the first female to be named captain under Jasmin's reign. Mikko took over his father's training, applying the lessons to the villages and expanding to include the navy. Erik and Bea lived full lives at the castle, proud of their children and niece.

Claire stayed at the castle, finishing her court training. When she was old enough, to Ada's dismay, she began to travel to other kingdoms, garnering trade and relations for Sweet Briar. She had many lovers but spent most of her time with a woman named Simone, whom she met on her travels. Simone traveled with Claire, spending time learning the court's politics and benefitting from traveling with the sister of a king.

Ada eventually married Mikhail, Emmeline's father. The two spent their years together, watching their children grow and live robust lives. Ada's children led lives far better than she had ever envisioned. When William, Clem's father, was still alive, he and Ada had many conversations about their children's potential. They had never come close to envisioning their reality. Even with the heartbreak and trials they faced, all three of her children led long, happy lives.

Emmeline and Kian kept their relationship hidden, never telling anyone what their personal lives held. Jasmin and Clem pestered for years before finally growing weary of the topic. At the end of their lives, Kian and Emmeline were found together in their suite. They were in separate beds, holding hands over the space in between. Many rumors spread about the secrets of their relationship, but no one ever knew the truth about what happened between them.

Zander and Tomas shared the suite after Sunette moved out. Sunette never remarried content with the life she had with her true love. Zander and Tomas eventually asked to take in a parentless child from the villages. This was met with enthusiastic approval from Jasmin. They took in a small, dark-skinned boy whose parents had passed from sickness. Marick was raised, much like the other children now in his life, surrounded by love and joy. He had multiple cousins to play with and attend classes with. He grew up to be an artist, creating paintings commissioned from villages far away and sold by his Aunt Claire.

Just like every good fairy tale Jasmin scoured during her curse, despite the many difficult days throughout their lives, they all live happily ever after.

Check out this link

aprilgaisford.com

to read more queer spicy books

Bonus Chapter

ERIK

Author's note: this was originally chapter 14 in the book. I decided to cut it because it is from a different perspective, and I wanted to stay true to Jasmin's story. This is written from Erik's POV after Jasmin insisted he travel to Arkaley to marry Bea. It is not vital to the story but simply a fun inclusion. Enjoy Erik's attempt to marry Bea.

I can't believe Jasmin ordered me to go to Beatrice. Not only to go to her but to marry her also. That has been my intention since I first met her when she came to save Finn. Beatrice is a fantastic woman. When I first went to the castle for the True Love Edict, I hoped to find love. I didn't know if it would be Jasmin. I watched her as a young boy but never felt a pull toward her. I didn't feel like she was mine. I wanted to protect her for the kingdom, maybe as a friend, but nothing romantic. The day of the snowball fight confirmed all of that for me.

Jasmin is amazing. She is and will be a wonderful queen. I will do everything I can to protect her, but she isn't my love.

Beatrice is.

Shena and I race into Arkaley. I need to get to Beatrice as quickly as I can. She has been gone for too many days. I need her in my life. I love her with everything I have. She hurt me when she refused to stay with me. She didn't say no. It was more of a 'not right now' response, but it is bullshit. She belongs with me. She brings out the best in me. I can relax around her. I can let my own guard down when she's near me. I want her with me all the time.

Once I arrive in Arkaley, I debate what I should do next. I could show up at the farm she works at, except I don't know where it is. Asking around would likely raise suspicions, and I don't want to scare her off before I even find her. I doubt she will be at home while there is still sunlight. Her mother may be there. It seems like Mrs. Byrne likes me; she's probably a safe bet. Plus, that would allow me to talk to her instead of springing it all on her.

I settle on going to Beatrice's home. I amble with Shena, having a pretend conversation with Mrs. Byrne. I don't know how she will react, so I try sounding out the conversation to be more prepared. She could yell at me and send me away. If that were the case, I would return to the castle and count my losses. Maybe she'll be accepting. I could cook dinner for them. In fact, showing up bearing gifts may be a better idea. Just before the road to her house, I head toward the market. I can get flowers, meat, vegetables, and a nice pastry for dessert. Maybe a toy for Claire. She would appreciate a bribe. What would Mrs. Byrne like, though? I need to woo her as much as Beatrice.

I find all the food I want in the market to make a nice meal. I'm no cook but can handle my own in a kitchen. I can prepare a meal for four people. That isn't terrible, not something I frequently do, though. I find a doll for Claire, but I second guess myself since she is 11. What do 11 year old's like? I settle on a leather-bound journal instead. Surely that will suffice. I stumble across a clay vase with white flowers painted on the side and purchase that for Mrs. Byrne. It's a lovely pot, and I imagine she will appreciate it. There are still a few hours until the sun goes down. I don't know how long Beatrice works at the farm, but I should still have enough time.

I check into a room at the local inn. I'll need a place to stay if they turn me away. If things go well, maybe I can bring Beatrice back with me. Not that I expect anything to happen. We haven't actually had sex. We've messed around, but Beatrice has been more reserved since Clem caught us before the wedding. She's been worried about being seen again.

I finally arrive at Beatrice's house. Claire is outside, feeding the animals. She squeals when she sees me. She greets me with an enormous hug. I'm almost caught off guard by her friendliness, but I quickly embrace her hug. I inquire about Beatrice, but she tells me she'll stay at the farm until near sundown. This is actually good news for me now. I fill Claire in on my plan, and she gets this adorably excited grin. She insists she will help me make everything perfect.

I give her the journal as I unload the rest of the items I purchased. She begins to tell me about her desire to write stories. I forgot how chatty she can be since I last saw her. This isn't a problem for me. I'm content listening. Inside, Claire explains my entire plan to her mother. I barely need to add any additional information. Claire even adds a few things I haven't considered, like candles and a nice cloth on the table. Her mother looks happy at our ideas, and we get to work. Claire and her mother work on sprucing up the area while I begin cooking. A couple of hours pass, and the sun finally sets. Claire announces Beatrice will be here at any moment.

"Erik, you said you have a room at the inn?" Mrs. Byrne asks.

"Yes, ma'am. I'll stay there so as not to intrude."

"Nonsense." She huffs, wiping her hands off her apron and removing it. "Claire, quickly grab some clothes. We'll stay there tonight, Erik. You and Bea can have the house. I don't know what she'll say to you, but we'll sneak out the back and leave you alone." My heart swells at her consideration. It will be easier to remain here than to travel back to the inn. I offer to prepare food for them to take, and they let me do that. I tell them to take Shena, but they don't want to take her.

They are gone soon, and I wait in the living room. I sit. Then stand. Then pace. Then sit again. Finally, Beatrice walks in.

"Erik?" She looks around, taking in the candles and decorations Claire and Mrs. Byrne placed. The flowers are in the vase, on the table, next to the food I prepared. A roasted hen with vegetables soaked in butter and herbs, a loaf of bread from the market, and pastries. "What's going on? Is Clem okay?" Of course, she would be worried about him. I didn't even consider how my being here would appear. Claire didn't question it and filled in Mrs. Byrne quickly, so she didn't worry either.

"He's fine, Beatrice. I'm here for you." She looks confused, unsure of what to say. "I can't live without you. I need you in my life. I want you to reconsider my proposal." She looks ready to respond, but I can't take a 'no' right now. "Wait, before you answer, come have dinner with me. Let's just talk." I stand, motioning to the table. She nods and walks over, sitting down at the table. I sit across from her, serving her food.

We chat about her work at the farm and what it's like without Clem there. She compliments my cooking. I avoid bringing up the topic of marriage again. I tell her about everything that has been happening since she left, about Dahlia and Kian's discoveries. We finish the dinner slowly, enjoying the pastries after.

"Where are Ma and Claire?"

"They insisted on staying in my room at the inn. I assured them I didn't need to stay here, but they wanted to. Claire is very persistent and wanted to stay at the inn." We both chuckle over the thought of Claire arguing to get her way. It didn't take much convincing for me to allow them to stay in my place, but Claire wouldn't have stopped until I did.

"Beatrice, I can't go on without you." I reach across the table, place the ring box before her, and take her hand in mine. "I will do anything for you. I will give up my job with the guard to be with you." She gasps and covers her mouth. "I don't care about any of that. I will stay here, or we can find our own house. I just need you, Beatrice. I love you and want to make you my wife." I pop open the box, showing her the ring again.

I don't want to give up my job with the guard. It is my dream job, and Jasmin is amazing to work for. Clem and Henry, too. But I will give it all up for Beatrice. I will stay home, cook, clean, and raise children if she wants. I will do anything at all for her. I tell her all of this. Her eyes stay focused on the ring.

"I don't care what we do, Beatrice. I just need to be with you."

"But what if..." She pulls her hand back from me. I try to stop her, but she tucks it under her thighs, keeping her eyes focused on the ring. I get up and move next to her, wanting to be closer.

"I only care about you. Nothing else matters."

I tug her hand out from under her thigh. I kiss her hand softly before grabbing the ring to slide it on her finger. It fits perfectly and looks beautiful against her calloused skin. She stares at the ring, holding it out in front of her. Her eyes finally meet mine. I can see the fear and doubt in her mind. I won't let that ruin what we have, though.

"Beatrice Byrne, I want you to be my wife. No matter what that means."

"What if I'm too old to have kids?" She drops her hands to her lap, looking down and depressed over her confession. I don't care about that at all.

"It would be sad, but it won't be the end of the world. But you," I pull her hand into mine, rubbing the back with my large fingers, "not marrying me would be the end of my world." I add the last bit softly. She sits quietly for what feels like an eternity. Is she going to say no again? I don't know what I will do if she does. I don't want to live without her. There has never been anyone like her. If Clem and Jasmin are true loves, I genuinely believe Beatrice is mine. She finally looks up at me, meeting my eyes. She gives a soft, quick nod, so small I almost miss it, but it's there.

"Yes?" I ask, needing to be sure. A wide grin spreads across her face as a matching one spreads across mine.

"Yes."

I jerk her body to mine, crashing my lips against hers desperately. It's been so long since we last kissed, but it doesn't feel like any time has passed. Her hands wrap around my neck as I circle her waist, tugging her closer. She grunts, trying to stop me from pulling her into my lap. Beatrice is a large woman, built for working in the fields. But I am a large man who can handle all of her.

I stand up and bend at the waist so our lips remain connected. I grab her waist, lifting her off the bench and pulling her against my body. She grunts but wraps her legs around my waist.

"Erik! You can't carry me!"

"Like hell I can't." She gasps at my language, not being one to use such obscenities, but I won't allow my woman to think less of herself on my account.

I carry her to her room and kick the door open, go to the bed, and drop her on her back. I lean over her again, kissing her deeply. My hands caress her sides, loving every curve and roll of her body. My tongue presses against her lips, wanting to deepen the kiss. Her hands are on my back, holding me tightly against her. She doesn't part her lips for me, so I pull away, kissing her cheek and neck.

"We don't have to do anything right now, but I'm not leaving your side." I crawl over her so I am lying next to her. We are nearly the same size; her breasts are more prominent, but we match in other regards. I press my body along her side, kissing her cheek and neck. She lets me for several minutes. She finally turns on her side, facing me.

"I think I wanna do more with you, Erik," she whispers.

"Good, because I wanna do more with you too."

I climb on top of her, kneeling between her legs, forcing them open for me. I return my lips to hers, pressing my tongue against her lips right away. She opens her mouth for me this time, and I swirl my tongue in her mouth, tasting her, exploring her, savoring her. I grind my hips against hers, my member already springing to life. I want to be inside her but don't want to push her too far. We haven't done more than some light teasing. I place my hand over her breast, caressing her nipple under her shirt. It's been a long time since I've been with a woman. Thankfully, practically everyone at the castle is sex-crazed and always discussing their latest endeavors.

"Can I take off your shirt?"

She nods at me, biting her lip anxiously. I sit back, pulling mine off first and tossing it to the floor. I loosen the collar on her shirt. I could probably remove the shirt without undoing it, but I want to enjoy things. I tug the sweater out of her trousers, slowly guiding the fabric over her body until she lifts up so I can remove it entirely. Her breasts settle to the side when she lays back, her stomach wide and soft, so inviting. I place my hands over her stomach, tracing over the skin, then over her breasts with large nipples.

I lean down, wrapping my lips over one. I tongue the pebbled bud, enjoying the moans she emits. My free hand caresses her other breast. Her fingers wrap around my head, massaging the short hair on my head. I drag my mouth to the other breast as her hands slide down my neck, over my shoulders. Her calloused hands are rough against my skin, but it feels so nice to finally be in her arms. I work her breasts and nipples for several more moments until I feel her wiggling under me. I lift my head to see her face flushed, pupils blown with arousal.

"Can I take your pants off now?"

She nods again, but more enthusiastically this time. I stand from the bed, removing my own pants first. My member juts out from my waist, ready to please my woman. She shifts her hips as I untie her pants and pull them down. I toss them into a pile with the rest of our clothes. I stare at her body. She's the most beautiful woman I have ever seen, with her wide hips, thick thighs, breasts, and full stomach. She's so sweet and perfect, no matter what she believes. My member is aching to touch it, but I don't want to release too early. I climb over her again, letting my erection settle between her legs. She gasps at the sensation. She says my name softly.

"I've never done this." She whispers softly. I'm not surprised she hasn't; I've only done it a few times. I kiss her gently, pressing my body against hers. I don't want her to feel rushed or uncomfortable, but at this point, I won't last much longer. My body longs for her, not just to be inside her, but to be with her entirely, mind, body, and soul. I shift, intending to deepen the kiss, but my erection notches in her entrance, and I groan at the sensation. She moans my name, the most beautiful sound I have ever heard. I take several deep breaths, feeling the telltale signs of a release.

"Beatrice, I want to be inside you," I whisper against her chest, trying to breathe through my erection. "I want that, too," she mutters, and my self-control breaks. I press inside her slowly, but I have to move. She gasps as I bottom out against her. I wait for a moment, letting her adjust. She wiggles her hips, causing me to grunt at the sensation. I finally manage to pull back, pressing back in slowly. Her fingers scratch down my back, driving me to increase my speed. My breathing increases as my pace does inside her. Within minutes, I release a yell, burying myself deep inside her warm entrance. She grunts as her core tightens around me, and I settle against her, supporting my weight with my arms. I take deep breaths, trying to return to normal. My fingers find her head, massaging the short hair on her scalp.

I seem to recall someone mentioning cleaning up each other after intercourse. I slip out of her, a gasp escaping her as I remove myself. I find a cloth and clean my member before awkwardly wiping her entrance. I glance at her to see her cheeks flushed with embarrassment. Mine are, too, and we both fall into a fit of giggles. I finally crawl into bed next to her, kissing her cheek.

Tomorrow, we will get married at the village chapel with her mother and sister. Then we will do as Jasmin asked. I'll check in with the borders before escorting Beatrice, my wife, back to the castle, where we will spend several days locked in our bedroom, doing this and only this. I am so utterly thrilled, I almost think I won't sleep, but it finds me faster than expected. Just before I doze off, I whisper to her.

"Good night, my wife."

"I love you, Erik," is the last thing I hear before falling asleep.

Also by

HIDDEN GODS SERIES

A series of dark romance ranging from sapphic mafia, FFM motorcycle club, MMF mafia, and more.

Corrupt Goddess

Hidden God

Secret God (coming 2025)

SWEET BRIAR SERIES

A completed why choose fairy tale series about a cursed princess who must find her true love. Spicy, queer, and magical.

Curses and Thunder

Fate and Lightning

ROOMMATES

A queer why choose romance about a guy down on his luck taken in by three roommates.

About the author

APRIL GAISFORD

April is a non-binary parent living in Minnesota. They are an avid reader, with a special interest in smut. They love collecting random things, such as coffee mugs, posters, graphic tees, scrunchies, and more. They love long romantic trips around Target and buying new books to add to their emotional support pile.

Acknowledgements

Thank you to all of my readers. Without you, all of the effort wouldn't feel worth it. Your kind words, reviews and posts mean everything to me! Even if I don't respond personally, I appreciate everything you've given me along my writing journey.

From the bottom of my heart, thank you!